To Mammy, Maureen O Connell
and to my Daddy John Goldsmith
A rainbow round my shoulder.

Chapter One

Brighton, 1930

I wasn't sure how long I'd been sitting in the tree – I think it was a long time cos my leg was going numb from trying to balance on the branch. I wriggled about a bit and peered through the leaves; the boy was still there. He was concentrating very hard on lining up the tin soldiers. A line of green and a line of blue, opposite each other, ready for battle. His hair was yellow like margarine. Every now and again he would brush it out of his eyes and the sun would catch it, making it dazzle. I didn't think much of boys, most of them were scruffy and smelly and they laughed too loud and called you mean names when you walked down the street. I knew this boy wouldn't be smelly or loud, this boy would smell of strawberry jam and lemons and nice things. I wanted to stay there forever watching the boy. He was wearing a blue jumper and grey shorts. I just knew that if he turned around, his eyes would be as blue as his jumper. He looked older than me but it was hard to tell as I couldn't see his face. Just then my younger sister Brenda came running down the garden.

'Maureen,' she shouted. 'Daddy says for you to come indoors.'

I put my finger to my lips and beckoned her over. Brenda was six, two years younger than me. 'Tuck your dress into your knickers,' I whispered. She did as she was told and I reached down and helped her up into the tree.

'What are you doing?' she asked, settling herself on a branch.

'Shush,' I said. 'I'm looking at him.' I parted the leaves so she could see into next door's garden.

'Why?'

'I like him.'

'Daddy's made a stew,' she whispered.

Just then, a woman came out of the house next door. 'Jack,' she shouted down the garden. 'Nelson's here.'

I tried the name out. 'Jack,' I said.

'Jack,' said Brenda softly.

I watched the boy run down the garden towards Jack and kneel on the grass beside him. Nelson's hair was brown, in fact everything about him was brown, including his jumper. Nelson was an ordinary boy. He wasn't a bit like Jack. He wouldn't smell of strawberry jam and lemons, Nelson would smell of boy. Anyway, who calls their kid Nelson?

'And we've got bread for dipping,' said Brenda. 'Dada told me to fetch you in.'

I ignored her and carried on watching the two boys. They were making noises like guns going off. 'Bang, bang, bang,' they went.

'Surrender or die!' cried Jack.

'Surrender yourself!' shouted Nelson.

I watched as Jack jumped on him and they started rolling around on the grass.

'The stew smells lovely,' said Brenda.

'Go and eat it then,' I snapped. 'No one's stopping you.'

Brenda didn't move.

Just at that minute Jack's mum shouted from the back door. 'Lunch is ready, boys.'

I watched as they left the soldiers and ran into the house, jostling each other and throwing punches. It felt as if the sun had gone out. I felt as abandoned as the toy soldiers lying in the mud.

'Now, where are my girls?' It was Daddy come looking for us. We giggled.

'Is that two little birds up in that tree or is it my angels?'

Brenda started climbing down. 'It's not birds, Dada, it's me and Maureen.'

'Well, so it is,' he said, scooping her up into his arms.

I jumped down and ran to him.

'Daddy,' I whispered.

He crouched down so that he was on my level. 'What is it, darlin'?'

I cupped my hands around his ear. His cheek felt warm and bristly and he smelled of Senior Service and the margarine he smoothed on his hair to make it shine.

'He's wonderful,' I whispered into his ear.

'And who would that be?'

'It's the boy,' said Brenda, very seriously. 'Maureen likes watching the boy.'

'A boy, eh? Aren't you going to be your daddy's sweet face any more?'

'His name's Jack, Daddy.'

Daddy nodded. 'Well, I hope he's got good prospects.'

'What's prospects?'

'Well, I hope he's got a good job and he can support you properly.'

'He's just a boy, Daddy. I don't think he's got a job,' I said.

'He'll have to get one at once then, won't he? Perhaps we should send him down the mines.'

I started giggling. 'You're a silly-billy.'

'My name's not Billy. Is my name Billy, Brenda?'

'No, Dada, your name's Dada.'

'Go to the top of the class, Brenda O'Connell. Or you can jump on my back.'

Brenda jumped up onto his back and I held his hand as we walked towards the house.

I could smell the stew as he opened the back door and my mouth watered.

'There's bread for dipping, Maureen. Isn't there, Dada? There's bread for dipping!'

'Big doorsteps of it. I made it this morning, just for my girls.'

I giggled. 'No you didn't, Daddy, you got it from the baker's shop.'

'Whoops, you caught me out! You should be a detective.'

Brenda was looking at him, wide-eyed. 'Can *I* be a detective too, Dada?'

'Of course you can, my love.'

'What's a detective?' she asked.

He ruffled her hair. 'A bit like a policeman.'

'I don't want to be a policeman.'

'Then you won't be. Now, let's eat our stew on the back step, eh?'

I didn't want to eat my stew on the back step – I didn't want the boy to see me dipping my bread.

I crossed my fingers behind my back. 'I'm cold, Daddy, can I eat my stew in the kitchen?'

Daddy put his hand on my head. 'Are you sick, love?'

'No, just a bit cold.'

'Then we'll *all* eat our stew in the kitchen.'

Actually I was quite hot. The late morning sun streaming through the kitchen window and the stew were making me feel even hotter.

'You've got a red face,' said Brenda, dribbling gravy down her chin.

Daddy felt my head again. 'I think that you should stay indoors for the afternoon.'

'Oh no, Daddy, I'm not sick, really I'm not.'

'Are you sure?'

I jumped around the kitchen a bit to prove I was OK. 'See, Daddy, I'm not sick at all.'

'Well, as long as you're sure but I think your mum would have kept you in.'

'But *you* won't, Daddy, will you? *You* won't keep me in.'

'You have me wrapped around your little finger.'

I sat back down at the table and spooned the stew into my mouth. I loved my daddy's stew, it was thick and tasty and lovely. It had bits of meat in it that got stuck between your teeth and big chunks of carrot; blobs of white fat floated on the top. I took a big piece of bread and dipped it into the gravy. Then I watched as the bread turned soft and brown.

'I like this house, Daddy. Do you like this house?'

'It's a fine house, Maureen, and tonight you and Brenda can have a lovely bath in a proper bathroom. Isn't that just the best thing?'

'Oh yes, Daddy, it's the best thing.'

'Now, why don't you two eat up your stew and go and explore your new surroundings?'

Me and Brenda scraped our bowls clean with the bread and ran outside. I climbed the tree and looked into the garden next door but the boy wasn't there. Maybe he was playing in the street.

I jumped down. 'Come on, Brenda, let's explore.'

Chapter Two

All the houses on the estate looked exactly the same except for the colour of the doors. Some were green and some were blue, ours was blue. We'd only moved here yesterday. Uncle Fred had loaded all our stuff onto a barrow, then Daddy had lifted me and Brenda up on top of the furniture. We'd clung on for dear life as the barrow rumbled through the streets. Our old house was in Carlton Hill and the street was made of cobbles; it was a wonder me and Brenda had any teeth left by the time we got to See Saw Lane. If I'd known about the boy next door, I would have walked and not turned up sitting on top of a chest of drawers.

As we'd turned into See Saw Lane I'd felt a bubble of excitement in my tummy.

'This is See Saw Lane, Brenda,' I'd said. 'This is where we are going to live.'

'This is a very special day, isn't it, Maureen?'

I'd put my arm around her shoulder. '*Very* special,' I'd said, smiling down at her.

There were some kids playing in the street. One of them stuck their tongue out at us as we passed.

'Charming,' I'd said.

'Charming,' said Brenda.

We'd eventually stopped outside number fifteen. Daddy had helped me and Brenda down off the chest of drawers. We'd stood on the pavement and stared up at the house.

'It's very beautiful,' whispered Brenda. 'Are we *really* going to live here, Maureen?'

'This is our new home,' I'd said. 'It belongs to us and we are going to live here forever.'

'Don't you want to go inside and explore?' Daddy had said, lifting bits of furniture down onto the pavement.

'I'm just putting it into my heart,' Brenda had said very seriously.

My little sister came out with the strangest things but it was just the way she was and we all loved her for it. 'Is it in your heart now?' I'd said gently. 'Shall we go inside?'

Brenda had nodded and I'd taken her hand in mine. 'Come on then.'

We'd walked up the path; the blue front door was open and we went inside.

We stood in the little hallway. There were doors leading off it and a staircase in front of us. Brenda's eyes were like two saucers as she'd gazed around her. 'It is perfectly beautiful, Maureen,' she'd said.

'Yes, it is,' I'd answered. 'Perfectly beautiful.'

Daddy and Uncle Fred were struggling through the door with our old brown couch.

'Is this as far as you've got?' said Daddy, smiling at us.

Brenda had looked up at him. 'I want to remember everything, Dada,' she'd said.

'And you will, my love,' he'd said. 'We will all remember this day.'

'Because it's special?' said Brenda.

'Because it's special,' said Daddy.

Uncle Fred had put the couch down with a thump. Sweat was running down his big fat face and he was glaring at us. 'We'll be all bloody day at this rate,' he'd said.

Daddy winked at us. 'Best get on.'

'Best had,' I'd said, grinning at him.

Mum had come into the hallway. 'Come and see my beautiful kitchen, girls.'

We'd followed her through a door at the end of the hallway. The room we entered was twice the size of the kitchen we'd had in Carlton Hill.

Mum was running her hand lovingly over a shiny new cooker and smiling at us. She looked so happy I thought my heart would burst. My mum deserved a nice big kitchen and a lovely new cooker. I'd suddenly felt like crying and I didn't know why. Brenda noticed that my eyes were full of tears.

'It's the beautifulness of it all, Maureen,' she'd said very wisely. 'Beautifulness can make you cry sometimes, don't you think?'

'I think you're right, Brenda,' I'd said, wiping my eyes.

'This isn't a day for crying,' said Mum. 'This is a happy day.'

'Yes, but happiness can take you like that, can't it?' said Brenda.

Mum and I had looked at each other and shaken our heads.

She had walked across to Brenda, knelt down in front of her and took her face in her hands. 'Promise me you'll never change, my baby girl,' she'd said.

'I'll try not to,' said Brenda.

Mum had taken her coat from a hook on the wall. 'Now I have to go to work.'

But I didn't want her to go to work. I wanted her to stay here in her beautiful kitchen. 'Do you have to?'

'I do indeed, otherwise my ladies would have to clean their own houses and that wouldn't do, would it now?'

'Why wouldn't it?' said Brenda.

'Because they haven't got the hands for it.'

'Do rich ladies have different hands then?' said Brenda.

Mum had spread her hands out in front of her. 'I think that they probably do, love.'

'Imagine that,' said Brenda.

'But I'll be back in time for tea. Now, why don't you both explore upstairs? Me and your daddy will have the front bedroom and you can fight over the other two.'

We'd kissed Mum goodbye and raced up the stairs two at a time. Mum and Daddy's room looked out over the street, another room looked out at the side of next door's house. The third bedroom looked out over the back garden and this was the one that I wanted.

'Bagsy this one,' I'd said.

'OK,' said Brenda. 'I don't mind which room I have, because they are all very lovely.'

'Thanks, Bren.'

I looked down at the long back garden. It had a proper lawn and a little path leading down to a wooden shed. In Carlton Hill we'd only ever had a yard and the only shed we'd had was a dirty old coal-hole. There was a beautiful big tree with thick branches that hung over the fence into the garden next door. I'd stood at the window, looking out over all the gardens of all the houses in See Saw Lane and I'd felt something wonderful was about to happen. I'd felt suddenly as if my life was about to change.

Chapter Three

I didn't like my Uncle Fred. I didn't like the way he talked to my daddy; it made me feel bad inside. He was always telling him to get a job. He gave me and Brenda pennies for sweets but I knew it wasn't because he liked us, it was because he knew that Daddy didn't have any spare pennies to give us himself. I gave my pennies to Daddy for his Senior Service.

Aunty Vera was my mum's sister and she was married to Uncle Fred. I didn't like her much either. She was always moaning and gossiping about the neighbours, saying this one or that one were no better than they should be.

She said my mum was a saint for putting up with my dad. Sometimes I'd overhear them talking in the kitchen.

'You should leave him behind, Kate,' she was telling my mum. 'You should move into that new house on your own with the kids. That man of yours is neither use nor ornament.'

'He's the children's father,' Mum had said.

'Pity he doesn't provide for them then.'

'He's not able to, Vera.'

'According to *him*.'

'He's tried, he *has* tried.'

'Well, my Fred says he's a disgrace.'

'Sorry, Vera, but according to your Fred, half the people in Brighton are a disgrace, so give it a rest, eh?'

I went to bed that night with a bad feeling in my tummy. I didn't want to leave my daddy behind. If my daddy didn't move to the new house then I wouldn't bloody move either.

I loved my daddy. He was the best daddy in the whole world but sometimes being around him made me feel sad and I didn't know why. It was just a feeling in my tummy, like I needed to run to the lavvy. Sometimes it felt like I was grown-up and he was the child, especially when Uncle Fred and Aunty Vera came round. Uncle Fred would get all puffed up with self-importance and tell Aunty Vera to show Mum the new necklace he'd bought her or the new coat, or the new shoes or the new bloody country, and Mum would smile and say, 'Very nice, Fred.'

Then Daddy would walk out of the room and I would be sad again because my daddy was sad, because he couldn't buy nice things for my mum. I knew that if he *had* money he'd buy her beautiful things and she'd look better in them than Aunty Vera, because even though Aunty Vera was my mum's sister she was lumpy-looking with horrible thin hair and thin lips. But my mum was pretty, everyone said she was pretty and that she could have picked any man she wanted, and she wanted my dad. So stick that where the sun don't shine. 'Bugger Uncle Fred, bloody, bloody bugger! Sorry, dear Lord Jesus and the Blessed Virgin Mary, but bugger Uncle Fred.'

I thought my Uncle Fred looked like an under-ripe tomato, sort of yellow and red and patchy. I decided that even when Uncle Fred died, hopefully of something awful and painful and lingering, I would never light a candle for him in the church and I made Brenda promise she wouldn't either. Even though I always lit a candle for two-doors down's dog who got stood on by the milkman's horse. I always lit a candle for that poor dog even though we weren't that well acquainted, because I'd laughed when I was told he'd got stood on by the milkman's horse and I'd been filled with guilt ever since. I mean, whichever way you look at it, it's not a great way to end your days, is it?

Aunty Marge was Mum's other sister. She was married to Uncle John and I loved them both very much. They didn't have any children of their own so they spoiled me and Brenda something rotten. Aunty Vera said that Aunty Marge was barren, whatever that meant. Mum said better to be barren than to produce the fat lump of humanity that Vera had managed to push out. I guessed she was talking about my cousin Malcolm, who was a horrible boy and best avoided at all costs. Mum said it amazed her that Malcolm had been the best swimmer, which amazed *me* because I knew for a fact that he couldn't swim. Someone pushed him into the canal at Shoreham once and a passing boat had to fish him out and Aunty Vera had kept him in bed for a week.

Aunty Marge and Uncle John ran a fruit stall near Brighton station and sometimes when they were busy, like Easter and Christmas, Daddy would help out and Uncle John would give him some money and a pouch of baccy. Every Sunday evening they would bring round a wooden crate filled with the fruit and veg that was about to go off. Mum said we would likely all starve to death if it wasn't for Marge and John. Dad had said, 'I would never let that happen, Maureen,' and Mum had slammed the larder door.

One day, when Mum was crashing and banging round the kitchen she said, 'You've got three fathers, Maureen, and none of 'em bloody work.'

I didn't ask her to explain because when my mum was crashing and banging around the kitchen it was better to keep your trap shut. But if I had three fathers, where were the other two? I didn't know anyone who had three fathers.

I used to think about it when I was in bed and try to figure out who they might be. I liked the coalman who always pinched my cheek and left a black smudge on my face. Sometimes he gave me a Fisherman's Friend that tasted rotten, but it was kind of him to give it to me. He said it helped to get the phlegm off his chest. I didn't fancy having a father with phlegm on his chest. The other possibility was Mr Chu the tallyman but I think my skin would have a more Oriental sheen to it. I discounted the rag and bone man who smelled something awful and the milkman who had sticky-out ears.

I worried about it a lot but I didn't share my worries with anyone, not even Brenda, because if I had three fathers, God only knew how many Brenda might have had and I didn't want her to have to worry about it. And then I realised that my mum had been telling me the truth: I really did have three fathers.

There was the one who was gentle and kind and wise and took me and Brenda to the park. Who held our hands at the water's edge and showed us how to skim stones over the water, who made up stories at bedtime, who played silly games with us and let us ride on his back. Then there was the daddy who shut himself in the bedroom and wouldn't come out. The one we heard screaming out in the night, making me and Brenda cling to each other under the covers. Then there was the one who scared me. The one who laughed too loud and walked too fast so that we couldn't keep up with him. The one who threw Brenda up in the air and caught her but didn't realise how frightened she was and wouldn't stop throwing her even though I was yelling at him. The one whose laughter turned to tears and who hugged us too tight and cried like a baby and kept saying, 'Sorry, I'm sorry.'

I had three fathers and none of 'em bloody worked.

Chapter Four

My dad pretty much brought me and Brenda up, on account of the fact that he couldn't work and Mum had to go cleaning for the rich ladies. The three of us did everything together. When Brenda was very little we'd push her all the way along the sea-front to the lagoon. Uncle John had found a pushchair up the council tip and cleaned it up. It worked pretty well except for the squeak but we got used to that. Sometimes, if I was tired on the way home, I would sit in the pushchair with Brenda on my lap. We spent a lot of time down the lagoon because it had a sandpit and some swings and a slide. If Daddy had any money he would let us ride on the little railway and ring the bell. There were two lakes, a big one and a little one, and running between them was a path. Me and Brenda and Daddy would lie flat on our stomachs and stare into the water at the crabs. Some boys caught the crabs by dangling string with bits of bacon on the end. We preferred watching them swimming about. Brenda used to whisper into the water, 'Don't touch the bacon.'

Behind the lagoon was our favourite beach. To get to it you had to slide down a stone wall then jump onto the pebbles. I loved it best when the tide was out – I loved the way the sun shone on the shiny sand and the way the water trickled its way back to the sea. We would take off our shoes and socks and giggle as the wet sand squelched between our toes.

Daddy would often tell us stories about his childhood in Ireland. He came from a small town called Youghal, which he pronounced as Yawl. He had nine brothers and sisters but only two of his sisters remained in Ireland. His elder sister, Mary, would write to Daddy and Daddy would read the letters out to us.

'The rest of them are scattered to the four corners of the earth,' he said. 'But I stayed as long as I could because, to me, there was no finer place in the world.'

'I wish me and Brenda could go there,' I said.

'I wish you could too. We would climb the hill together.'

'What hill?'

'There's a grand big hill beyond the town that I used to climb when I was a boy. I'd stand on the top as if I was the King of the Castle and look down over the River Blackwater below me. I never tired of climbing that hill and looking down on that river.'

'Couldn't you go back?' I asked.

'Now where would your daddy get the money to be going across the Irish Sea? And why would I want to leave you and your sister and your mammy?'

I remembered wishing that I could get some money so that Daddy could climb the hill again and look down on the river.

Those were the long summer days by the sea when the sun warmed our skin and the blue sky went on forever.

Come autumn, we would play in the park. Daddy would gather the fallen leaves into piles and we'd jump into them, making them fly all over the place. Then Daddy would jump in and throw great handfuls of leaves up in the air so that they tumbled round our heads. Reds and oranges and browns, clinging to our clothes and tangling our hair. We'd walk home through the park and listen to the crinkly leaves crunching beneath the wheels of the pushchair.

In the winter we'd wait for the bad weather, the wind and the rain. Then we'd put on our raincoats and head for the seafront. This was the best game. The three of us would stand by the railings holding hands and we'd wait for the tide to bash against the sea wall, then run backwards, screaming, as the foamy white water sprayed onto the promenade.

In the springtime we would walk for miles across the Downs, picking the wild flowers and chasing the dirty sheep. The pushchair was useless on the grass so Daddy would carry Brenda on his back. We would walk to the top of the Devil's Dyke and look down over the valley to the little villages below us. Daddy would lie down on the grass, smoking his Senior Service fags and then he would go to sleep while Brenda and me made daisy chains that we put on our heads. When Daddy woke up, he would say, 'What has happened to my two little girls? Someone has replaced them with two princesses.' Then we'd jump on him and roll around on the grass.

Those were the seasons of our life, just me and Daddy and Brenda. Most of the time it was lovely and we were happy together. Brenda was a good little girl. She rarely cried or got upset, she didn't get a pain in her stomach at some of the things that Daddy did; she loved him and trusted him. Brenda was nicer than me, she was better for Daddy than I was. My little sister just accepted him. She was too young to judge him or to be embarrassed by him but sometimes I think he saw himself through my eyes and that wasn't any good for either of us. Like the time we were on the top deck of a tram going along the seafront. Sometimes when Daddy had worked for Uncle John he would take us on the open-top tram for a treat. We always ran up the stairs to the top deck, we didn't care a bit what the weather was like. We'd hang over the side and let our hair blow around our faces. There were lots of posh houses along the seafront and Daddy would make up stories about the people that lived there.

'See that little girl playing in the garden, girls?'

We both stared at the little girl.

'Yes, Dada?'

'Well, she's a poor little orphan girl sent to live with her rich aunt and uncle.'

'Are they kind to her, Daddy?' I asked.

'Oh yes, for they had no children of their own. They cherished her.'

'Cherished,' said Brenda softly. Brenda liked new words and once she heard one she would use it for weeks, even when it didn't make sense.

As the tram pulled away, I twisted round in my seat to look back at the little girl.

We were looking down into the posh people's gardens when Daddy rang the bell to make the tram stop. We had never got off at that stop before, but I helped Brenda down the stairs while Daddy got the pushchair.

'Where are we going?' I said.

'Wait and see,' said Daddy, winking at me.

We walked back along the road until we came to a large white house. Daddy opened the gate and started to push Brenda and the pushchair up to the front door. I hung back.

'What are you doing, Daddy?' I hissed. 'Come back.' I felt sick to my stomach because I hadn't noticed anything odd about my daddy that day. I thought he was my normal daddy but there he was, pushing Brenda up the path of the posh white house.

Oh my God, he was ringing the bloody doorbell.

Nobody answered. 'Come on, Daddy,' I said. 'Let's go.'

Then the door opened and a man stood there, glaring at us. He had a big fat belly that flopped over the top of his trousers and he kept licking his lips as if he still had some dinner left on them.

Daddy tipped his forehead as if he was wearing a hat, which he wasn't, and said, 'I'm sorry to trouble you, sir, but I was wondering if—'

The man looked at my daddy as if he'd just crawled out from under a stone.

'What?' he said. 'What?'

'It's about the dolls' pram, sir,' said Daddy.

'Who are you?' asked the man. 'What are you doing in my garden?'

Just then a woman called from inside the house. 'Who is it, Peter?'

'Some tinker feller,' said the man. 'Going on about a dolls' pram.'

'Tinker,' whispered Brenda.

I felt so angry I wanted to punch the man in his big fat belly. My daddy wasn't a tinker, my daddy was a person just like he was – no, he was better. I pulled at my daddy's coat. 'Let's go, Daddy. Let's just go.'

A lady came to the door and the horrible man went back inside. She smiled at us, she looked nice. 'What can I do for you?' she asked kindly.

Daddy touched his forehead again and I wished he wouldn't, she wasn't royalty.

'I noticed that you have a dolls' pram in the bushes, missus.'

Why did he have to call her 'missus'? 'And I wondered if you wanted it because, if you don't, my girls would love a dolls' pram.'

I wanted the ground to open up and swallow me. I didn't want a dolls' pram. Brenda's eyes were like two saucers. 'Dolls' pram?' she said, grinning.

The lady knelt down beside the pushchair. 'What's *your* name?' she said, touching Brenda's cheek.

'Dolls' pram?' said Brenda softly.

The lady stood up and smiled at my daddy. 'Well, if you don't mind pulling it out of the hedge you are very welcome to it. I was going to get rid of it anyway.'

'Thank you, missus.'

'I hope your girls enjoy it as much as my nieces did. It's nice to know that it will be played with again.'

Me and daddy hauled the pram out of the brambles. It was covered in weeds and twigs and one of the wheels was wonky.

'There now, isn't that lovely?' said Daddy.

'Lovely,' said Brenda.

Bloody wonderful, I thought.

We had no more money for the tram. We started the long walk back home, with Daddy squeaking along with the pushchair and me pushing the pram with the wonky wheel.

Chapter Five

We thought that those days would go on forever, until the day Mum said, 'Pat, you need to buy shoes for Maureen, she starts school next week.'

Daddy was heartbroken and spent most of the next week shut in the bedroom. Aunty Marge had to take me to get the new shoes. But on the following Monday morning Daddy came out of the bedroom washed and dressed and announced that he would be taking me to school.

The school was called St Mary Magdalene and it wasn't far from where we lived in Carlton Hill. Daddy was very quiet as we wheeled Brenda along the seafront. I was quiet too, but it wasn't because I was nervous, it was because I was excited. My new shoes were very shiny; I kept looking down at them. I was happy to go to school, I wanted to learn new things and meet new friends. I loved my daddy and my sister but I wanted to stop feeling sad and worried and I wanted to stop feeling guilty about feeling that way.

There were lots of children and mothers and fathers in the playground. Some of the children were crying and clinging to their parents. Get a life, kids, you're not about to be hung!

I wanted to go to school, I really did, but I was worried about Brenda. What was going to happen if Daddy had a sad day and shut himself in the bedroom? Who would look after my little sister? Even worse were those other days when Daddy was laughing one minute and crying the next. Maybe Mum would have to take Brenda with her when she cleaned for the rich ladies. I got the feeling that they wouldn't be that thrilled to have Brenda and the pushchair in their front garden. I knelt down beside her. 'I'm going to school today, Brenda,' I said. 'But I will be home later and we'll have our tea together, OK?'

'School,' said Brenda.

Just then a lady came into the playground and started ringing a bell. 'Line up,' she shouted. 'Boys one side, girls the other.'

I kissed Brenda and put my arms around my daddy.

'You don't have to go, love,' he said.

'I do, Daddy. I have to go to school.'

'School,' said Brenda again.

He was hugging me so tightly that I could hardly breathe. All the other children were lining up now and I wanted to join them – I didn't want to be different. I pulled away from him; he had a desperate look on his face that made me want to run for the lavvy.

'You have to look after Brenda, Daddy. Take her down the lagoon.'

The children had started to file into the school. I wanted to scream at him, 'Let me go, please let me go.'

The lady with the bell was shouting again. 'Will all parents please leave the playground. You can pick your children up at four o'clock.'

'Take Brenda to the park,' I hissed. 'Go on.'

Daddy hugged me again and I watched as he wheeled Brenda away. I could hardly see for the tears in my eyes.

All the children had gone into the building and the playground was empty except for the bell lady, who strode across to me like a sergeant major.

'Come on now, child,' she said. 'There's nothing to be afraid of.'

I wanted to yell at her, *It's not me that's afraid, it's my dad!*

Now she would think that I was one of the snivelling kids and I didn't want her to think that. She took hold of my hand and we walked together into the school. She showed me where to hang my coat up and then took me into my classroom. I was feeling cross and my tummy didn't feel right. Why couldn't my daddy just say, 'Have a lovely time, Maureen.' Why couldn't he have said that?

'We have a little reluctant one here,' said the bell lady and left me standing at the front of the class. As I fixed my eyes on the floor, I could feel the eyes of all the kids gawping at me. *Thanks a lot, Dad, just how I wanted to start the day.*

Then a voice said, 'I'm your teacher.'

I looked up. The lady standing in front of me was lovely. She had golden hair and blue eyes. 'I'm Miss Phillips, dear,' she said, smiling. 'What's *your* name?'

'Maureen O'Connell,' I said shyly.

'Well, Maureen O'Connell, you have nothing to worry about here.'

She pointed to an empty desk. 'Would you like to sit there?'

I nodded.

My classroom was lovely. The walls were painted yellow and sunlight was streaming in through the long windows. There were pictures of the saints all over the walls and a wooden Noah's Ark on a shelf with all the animals lined up, two by two. On my desk was a brand-new pencil and a book for writing in. The girl I was to sit next to had bright red hair in two long plaits. She grinned at me and said, 'I'm Monica Maltby.'

'Maureen O'Connell,' I said and grinned back.

'Shall we be friends?'

Monica had lots of orange freckles on her face that matched her hair. I liked her face.

'Yes,' I said.

'Best friends?' said Monica.

'Best friends,' I said.

Miss Phillips was standing in front of the blackboard, smiling at us.

'Now,' she said, 'I am going to go round the class and ask everyone to say their name out loud and then I shall write your name on the blackboard. That way we can all get to know each other. I am Miss Phillips and I will write my name on the board first.'

Some of the kids shouted out their names as if the rest of us were stone deaf and some were so quiet you could hardly hear them. Me and Monica said our names just right.

As I sat there listening to Mabel and Janet and Cyril and Stanley calling out their names, I began to relax.

My shoes felt tight because the new socks that my Aunty Marge had bought me were a bit too big, so Daddy had folded them over my toes.

The Blessed Virgin Mary smiled down at me from the wall. I slipped off my shoes and I was happy. That was until I heard Brenda's pushchair squeaking along the bloody corridor.

Chapter Six

Daddy stayed outside the school gates for three whole days. I knew he was there because I could see the smoke from his Senior Service fags drifting up over the wall. Every break time and lunchtime he would push Brenda into the playground and drink out of the water fountain. He would go up to one of the teachers, tip his non-existent hat and say, 'Just getting a drink for the child, missus.' You could see the teacher didn't like it. Then him and Brenda would squeak across to me while I was in the middle of a game with Monica. Brenda looked miserable and cold.

'Take her home, Daddy, or take her to the beach. Just take her *somewhere*. She looks frozen and have you fed her?'

'We want you to come with us, Maureen, don't we, Brenda? We could all go down the lagoon, you like the lagoon.'

'Lagoon,' said Brenda.

'I can't go down the lagoon, I have to be here. I like it here, Daddy. This is where I have to be. And you have to look after Brenda, that's what *you* have to do.'

Daddy looked sad. 'We miss you, girl.'

I looked at my daddy's lovely face and I wanted to cry. I could smell the warm margarine on his hair. 'I miss you too, Daddy,' I said gently. 'But I'm happy here and I've made a new friend. Her name's Monica and she's got red hair and she's lovely.'

'Monica,' said Brenda.

'Promise you will take Brenda somewhere so that she can run around and get her something to eat.'

Daddy touched my cheek, 'I promise,' he said.

'I promise,' said Brenda solemnly.

I watched as they squeaked out of the playground. Brenda turned around and waved.

I watched till they were out of sight then I walked across to the steps that led up to the school field and sat down. How can loving someone make you feel so bad? It should make you feel happy and safe and all sorts of nice things. It shouldn't give you a belly ache and it shouldn't make you want to cry, should it? Monica came across and sat next to me. She slipped her arm through mine.

'Your dad looks nice,' she said.

'He's lovely,' I said. 'But he's not very well.'

I had never said that before. I had never even thought it before but I knew I was right: my daddy wasn't very well. Nobody had ever told me what was wrong with him, nobody had ever told me why he couldn't go to work like all the other daddies. I mean, he was never sick, he never got colds or tummy aches like the rest of us and his legs were OK. Not like the man down the road who only had one leg because he lost the other one fighting for King and Country. I mean, you could see why he couldn't go to work. I thought if Daddy could just get a job then everything would be alright and Aunty Vera and Uncle Fred would have nothing to yap on about. I loved him so fiercely it hurt and yet there was part of me that was angry with him. I wanted to punch anyone who was mean to him. I wanted Mum to stop yelling at him. I wanted someone to tell me what the hell was wrong with him but most of all, I wanted him to be happy and my heart told me that he wasn't.

He kept his promise though and I told him that from then on I would walk to school with Monica, who only lived a couple of streets away.

I loved school. I loved the way it smelled; a mixture of chalk and books and kids. I loved my teacher; she said that I was a very clever girl because I was the best reader in the whole class and I could make up really great stories. Even Monica's stories weren't as good as mine and her stories were pretty good. Daddy had taught me to say my alphabet on those long days we'd spent down the lagoon and on the beach.

Me and Monica became monitors. She gave out the milk and I sharpened the pencils. I tried not to think about Daddy and Brenda.

Then I found out that instead of waiting outside the playground all day, he had taken to sitting on the wall opposite the rich lady's house, waiting for Mum. I heard them arguing about it.

'For God's sake, Pat, do you want me to lose my job? Is that what you want?'

My dad didn't answer her.

'Because that's what's going to happen. The neighbours have complained. I was ashamed, Pat. I was ashamed.'

'I'm sorry, Kate. I won't sit there again.'

'That would be good.'

'I miss Maureen.'

'I know you do, love, but you have to let her go. She needs to be with other children. Sometimes I think we put too much on those little shoulders. Let her go, Pat, let her enjoy her childhood.'

I didn't always think about my mum, about how hard she had to work cleaning for the rich ladies. If only my dad could get a job, then Mum could stay at home like Aunty Vera and she could look after Brenda. I knew that my daddy wouldn't let any harm come to Brenda but sometimes he did silly things and he'd forget that Brenda was only three years old. I spent so much time with my dad that I didn't always think about my mum and how hard it was for her.

I decided to help Mum more. I made mine and Brenda's bed before I went to school and if Brenda had wet herself in the night, I swilled out her wet knickers and brought the sheets downstairs. Mum noticed and she smiled a lot more and that made me happy.

Me and Monica became the best of friends. Even when we moved up to the next class we still sat together. On the weekends we took bread and marge and a bottle of water down the beach. Most of the time we had to take Brenda with us in the pushchair, squeaking our way through the streets then lugging the push-chair onto the pebbles. Sometimes we had to bring Monica's little brother Archie as well but we didn't mind. Brenda and Archie would sit on the pebbles playing. Monica had to wear a hat on her head on account of her freckly skin; her mum said that if she didn't wear it she'd crisp up like a rasher of bacon.

Brenda loved the water. The three of us would tuck our dresses into our navy knickers and paddle in up to our knees. We both held one of Brenda's little hands and jumped her over the waves, screaming when the water splashed onto our knickers. Then we'd sit with our backs against the old wooden groyne and eat our bread and marge and take turns drinking water out of the bottle. There were bathing machines where the rich people got changed into their swimming costumes. The machines had big wheels on them and a horse would pull them down to the sea so that the rich people could step into the water and not have to walk on the pebbles. We would giggle when they came out of the huts in their funny outfits. The ladies wore pantaloons under little cotton dresses. The men looked the funniest in stripy costumes and straw boaters. Some-times the hats would fly off their heads in the wind and bob about in the water and me and Monica would wade in and get them. If we were lucky we'd get an orange each for our trouble.

As Brenda got older we abandoned the bloody pushchair and she trotted along happily beside us. I knew that Daddy wanted to come too, I could tell by his face but I was seven years old now, almost grown-up, and I didn't want my daddy with me all the time. Monica's dad never wanted to come with us. I was always quiet when we left the house and a part of me wanted to run back and say, 'Come with us, Daddy. Come with us.' I never did though and Monica never asked why I was quiet.

I think she knew.

Chapter Seven

Brenda started school when she was five years old. She was a bit nervous but I told her: 'You will have the nicest, kindest teacher in the world, Brenda. Her name's Miss Phillips. The walls in your classroom are yellow and there's a Noah's Ark and little wooden animals and you get to learn to read and write and become a clever girl. And at playtime you can play with me and Monica, so there is nothing to be frightened of.'

Mum wouldn't let Daddy take us to school on Brenda's first day; she didn't want a repeat performance of my first day at school.

Then Daddy got sad again. Daddy got so sad that they took him away in an ambulance. As they took him away, a bunch of kids from the street were standing outside our front door, trying to see what was happening. Bloody nosey lot. I stuck my tongue out at them and the ambulance men told them to clear off. I cried all night and my mum lifted me out of my bed and into hers. She held me close to her and stroked my hair; she made me feel safe.

'Don't be sad, love,' she said. 'Your daddy will be taken care of now and once he is well again, he will come home to us.'

'Can I go and see him?'

'I'm afraid not, love, they won't let children in but you and Brenda can come with me and wait outside so you can feel close to him.'

'OK,' I said and I fell asleep in her arms.

Aunty Vera had a lot to say about it but then Aunty Vera had a lot to say about everything.

Me and Brenda were eating our tea one day when she swanned in the back door, looking pleased with herself.

'Well, I won't say I told you so, Kate, but I told you so. I always knew that man of yours would end up in the loony bin.'

'The children,' hissed Mum.

'Well, isn't it time they knew about their wonderful daddy?'

Me and Brenda stopped eating and stared at her.

'You may be my sister, Vera, but if you say one more word about my husband so help me God, I will pour this pan of soup over that nasty little head of yours.'

Aunty Vera went red in the face and slammed the back door shut as she strode out. Her parting shot was: 'Well, don't expect any more help from me and Fred, Kate O'Connell. You've made your bed, now you can bloody well lie in it!'

Mum opened the back door and shouted up the street after her, 'Well, I'd rather lie in my bed with Pat than next to your fat, boring, opinionated excuse for a man!'

When Mum came back into the kitchen she was grinning all over her face.

'I've wanted to say that for a long time.'

Me and Brenda just smiled at each other and got back to our dinner.

The hospital was in Haywards Heath and it was twelve miles away. Mum said she couldn't afford for all of us to go on the tram after all. I said that was OK, because I didn't want to make her feel bad, but I had liked the idea of being close to my dad even if we couldn't go in.

'You're a great girl, Maureen,' she said.

Then Uncle John came round. He put his hand in his pocket and handed Mum a ten-shilling note.

'I can't, John,' she said.

'You can and you will, Kate, because it's given with love and we are family and family stick together. You would do the same for me and Marge if you were able to.'

'I would of course, John.'

'Well, there you are then, you can all go on the tram together. Marge said that if you would like her to come with you, she would be more than happy to.'

'Please, Mum?' I said.

'Tell her I'd be glad of her company, John, and thank you both. I won't forget this.'

Uncle John put his hand in his pocket again and pulled out two gobstoppers. He pretended to be surprised.

'Now where did they come from? Did they jump into my pocket as I passed the sweetie shop?'

'*Did* they?' said Brenda, wide-eyed.

'Don't be daft,' I said. 'Uncle John bought them. You bought them, didn't you, Uncle John?'

Uncle John smiled and ruffled our hair.

'Thank you, John,' said Mum quietly.

It felt like an adventure, going on the tram to somewhere we had never been before. Me and Brenda ran up the stairs to the top deck, while Mum and Aunty Marge sat downstairs. I let Brenda sit by the window so that she could see all the new places that we passed. There were villages and streams and cows and horses on the hillside. Children made faces at us as we passed and we made faces back at them. It was a long journey and the sun streaming through the window made me sleepy.

At last we arrived in Haywards Heath. As we got off the tram, Aunty Marge asked the conductor where the hospital was.

'What, the loony bin?' he said.

Aunty Marge gave him one of her looks and pulled us away.

'What's a loony bin?' asked Brenda.

'It's nothing for you to worry about,' said Mum, grabbing Brenda's hand and hurrying us along the street.

Mum stopped and asked directions from a lady who was pushing a pram. Me and Brenda peered into the pram and made funny faces at the baby, who smiled back at us. It was sucking on a dummy and its little face was going up and down like a hamster. Mum looked into the pram and said, 'He's lovely.'

'It's a girl,' said the woman, glaring at Mum.

As the woman walked away, Aunty Marge whispered, 'Why dress it in bloody blue then?'

The lady with the baby had said, 'It's just up the hill, you can't miss it.'

She was right, the hospital was enormous. I had never seen a prison but I thought that that was what a prison would have looked like. It gave me a bad feeling. I felt Brenda's hand slip into mine.

I looked down at her and smiled.

'Loony bin?' she whispered.

'Course it's not,' I said. 'It's a proper hospital and the doctors are going to make Daddy better.'

The four of us walked up the drive towards a huge front door. There were lots of steps leading up to it and next to the door was a tall tower with a clock on it. Everything about the place scared me. There were rows and rows of little windows that seemed to be staring down at us. I was glad that me and Brenda weren't allowed inside. Judging by the looks on Mum's and Aunty Marge's faces, I didn't think they wanted to go in either.

'We won't be long,' said Aunty Marge, smiling at us.

'I'll give Daddy your love,' said Mum.

'Tell him to get better soon,' I said.

'Better soon,' said Brenda.

We watched as Mum and Aunty Marge went through the big door then we ran down the grassy bank to a lawn. We sat down under a big tree.

Brenda was yawning. I leaned back against the tree. 'Put your head on my lap and have a kip,' I said.

The building looked even bigger from down here and it was really quiet. It was so quiet that you could hear the leaves rustling in the tree and the sound of birds in the branches. Where was everyone? Was my daddy behind one of those windows? Maybe they'd let Mum bring him home today. We had enough money for his tram ticket. I didn't like to think of my daddy in that place. If me or Brenda had to go in there, Daddy would stay outside until we were well enough to come home. That's what my daddy would do. I wasn't brave enough to do that though. It was scary enough in the day, it would be terrifying at night.

Brenda's head was heavy on my lap. She had fallen asleep almost at once. I looked up through the branches at the sky and I prayed for my daddy to get better.

By the time Mum and Aunty Marge came sliding down the grassy bank, my legs were numb and if I'd tried to stand up straightaway, I would have fallen over. I gently shook Brenda awake.

'Is it time for school?' she said.

'We're not at home, love. Don't you remember? We're at the hospital.'

She sat up, rubbing the sleep out of her eyes. 'I don't like it here,' she said.

'Me either. It's bloody awful.'

'Bloody awful,' said Brenda.

Mum and Aunty Marge sat down next to us and they were both smiling, which I thought was a good sign.

'Is Daddy better?' said Brenda.

'Nearly,' said Mum.

'Did you ask them if he could come home? Did you tell them that you've got enough money for his tram fare?'

'He's not ready to come home yet, love.'

I looked up at the rows of windows, rubbing my legs to get the blood back into them.

'Is he alright though? Is he happy, Mum? Did you give him my love?'

'Yes to all those questions, Maureen. He's happy and, yes, I did give him your love and he sends his love to both of you.'

'This place makes me feel sad, Mum.'

Aunty Marge put her arm around my shoulder.

'It makes me feel sad too,' she said.

'Bloody loony bin,' said Brenda.

Chapter Eight

Me and Brenda didn't go to the hospital again and even though I wanted to be near to Daddy I didn't mind, because the place had given me bad dreams. I kept dreaming about the rows of windows staring down at me and running through long dark corridors looking for my daddy. I would wake up crying and Mum would bring me downstairs to the kitchen and give me hot cocoa. On the weekends when Mum visited him on her own me and Brenda helped Aunty Marge and Uncle John on the fruit and veg stall.

We had to get up really early while it was still dark and Mum would dress me and Brenda up in our coats and scarves and gloves. Mum would wave at us from the front door and we'd walk through the dark streets holding onto Aunty Marge's hands. Then we'd help Aunty Marge put up the stall while Uncle John went to the market to get the fruit and vegetables. It was like an adventure but all the time I was putting apples and pears and tomatoes into paper bags I was thinking of my daddy in the hospital behind one of those windows.

Daddy was in the hospital for a long time and I missed him. Me and Brenda would go down to the church and light a candle for him. The candles were next to a statue of the Blessed Virgin Mary. Me and Brenda loved the Blessed Virgin Mary. She wore a beautiful blue dress that came down to her feet, a long white veil and she was holding her hands out to us and smiling. It beat looking up at Jesus hanging on a cross with blood dripping down his head. I preferred Jesus when he was all tucked up in the manger. Not that I didn't love Him and I really did feel sorry for Him hanging there, but if it was a toss-up between Him and his mum, me and Brenda always opted for his mum.

You were supposed to put money in the slot before you took a candle but I thought that God would understand and not mind. Holy God knew everything and he would know that we didn't have any pennies, because we were bloody skint. I prayed to St Jude to make my daddy better because he was the patron saint of lost causes and I thought if anyone could help, he could. I knew that Daddy was a lost cause because Aunty Vera said he was. I asked St Jude to please make my daddy better so that he could be like other daddies and go to work and buy a fur coat for Mum. I wanted my daddy to come home but I wanted a different daddy. Not like Monica's daddy though, because Monica's daddy was really grumpy and he shouted a lot. He had red hair like Monica's and he had a red beard too. He smoked roll-ups and Monica said that one day he caught his beard on fire and her mum had to throw a teapot full of tea over him to put it out. That made us giggle.

Me and Monica giggled about her dad a lot but I think that Monica's dad was a bit of a bully. I think that Monica was afraid of her dad but I never asked her about it, just like she never asked me about my dad.

I loved Monica. She was the kindest girl that I had ever met and she never minded that we had to take Brenda everywhere with us. She was lovely to Brenda and she looked out for her the same way that I did. I couldn't have asked for a better friend.

Apparently we lived in a slum, at least that's what the letter from the council said. Mum read the letter out to us. It said that as part of the slum-clearance programme they would be demolishing Carlton Hill and we would be moving to the new council estate on the edge of Brighton. In other words, they were going to flatten our house. Mum was all for it but Dad wasn't happy.

'I like it where I am,' he said. 'I like being close to the sea.'

'Well, you'll be close to the Downs instead,' snapped Mum.

'It won't be the same.'

'And thank God it won't, Pat! The walls won't be running with damp. The girls' bedroom ceiling won't be covered in mould. Thank God it *won't* be the same!'

Ever since Brenda had started school Daddy had spent a lot of time walking along the seafront on his own. He missed us both, I know he did, but the sea seemed to make him happy.

'The Downs are nice, Daddy,' I said. 'We can go up there every day after school and look at the dirty old sheep.'

'Of course we can, my love,' he said.

Mum folded the letter and put it in the kitchen drawer. 'Unless of course you want to wait until they pull the house down around your head.'

'You have a sharp tongue, Kate.'

'Is it any wonder? We are being given a chance, Pat. The girls are being given a chance and I, for one, am going to grab it with both hands. I want my girls to have a better life than the one they've got here. I will stand and cheer the day they knock this rat-infested street down.'

'There haven't been any rats around here for ages,' said Dad.

'That's because they've got better taste in houses than we have. They probably packed their cases weeks ago.'

That made Daddy laugh and soon all four of us were laughing. It was lovely.

'OK, Kate, you win. We'll all move to the posh new house and we'll have a wonderful life up there on the Downs.'

Mum smiled at him. 'Thank you, love.'

'Where is our new house, Mum?' asked Brenda.

Mum took the letter out of the drawer and read it again. 'They have allocated a house for us at 15, See Saw Lane.'

Me and Brenda jumped around the kitchen shouting, 'See Saw Lane, See Saw Lane, we're going to live in See Saw Lane!'

Then Mum and Dad joined in and I thought my heart would burst with happiness.

Chapter Nine

When I first learned that we were moving away I felt sad. I mean, I was excited about moving to the new house and I wouldn't miss the old one but I would miss Monica, who lived up the road. Then Monica's mum and dad got the same letter that we did, telling them that they too lived in a slum and they were going to move to the same estate as us.

School started again a week after we moved to See Saw Lane. We weren't going to the local one just up the road, we were going to the Catholic school and that meant we had to go on the tram. Daddy wanted to come with us but Mum said no because he got too emotional and showed us all up. Besides which, she only had enough tram fare for the two of us. Mum wasn't happy about us having to go to the Catholic school when there was a perfectly good school just round the corner that we could walk to. The reason we had to go there was because when Mum had married Dad, she had to promise the priest that she would bring us up in the Roman Catholic faith and, as my dad pointed out, a promise to a priest is like a promise to God. Aunty Marge said that it was a mixed marriage and Aunty Vera said it was doomed.

I think that, given half a chance, Mum wouldn't have thought twice about breaking her promise to the priest and I have to say I didn't blame her. According to the Catholic Church, when my dad died he would go straight to Heaven and get his own wings and a harp, while my mum would be left hanging around outside the gates without a hope in hell of getting in and not a harp in sight. I didn't think that was very fair. Both Monica's parents were Roman Catholic so her mum wouldn't have to hang around outside the Pearly Gates. Not only that, but it meant that we would both be going to the same school. We were highly delighted.

Our new school was called The Sacred Heart Convent and we didn't have normal teachers, we had nuns. They were dressed all in black and they walked along the school corridors looking down at the floor, with their veils floating behind them. Some of the nuns were nice and smiley but some of them were cross and grumpy. Monica said that she didn't know what they had to be grumpy about, seeing as how they were actually married to God. She said given what God had gone through, getting nailed to the cross and everything, the last thing he needed to come home to was a miserable wife.

Unluckily for us our teacher was one of the grumpy ones. Her name was Sister Concepta Aquinas, which was a hell of a name to be lumbered with but as she was so mean, we thought it served her right. She used to call us Little Barbarians. 'What Little Barbarian has dropped paper on the floor?' she would yell across the classroom. She had a long ruler that she would use to whack kids across their knuckles if they didn't know their catechism. Me and Monica always made sure we knew it off by heart. The whole class would have to chant it every morning.

'Who made you?'

'God made me.'

'Why did God make you?'

'God made me to know Him, love Him and serve Him in this world and to be happy with Him forever in the next.'

Half the time we didn't know what the hell we were going on about but it kept us in Aquinas's good books.

Brenda's teacher was lovely. Her name was Sister Mary Benedict and she looked just like a film star. Brenda loved her and that made me happy. Monica said that at least God would have one decent wife to come home to, which might make up for being saddled with old Aquinas.

There were lots of things in the Catholic religion that were hard to understand. For instance, if a baby died before it was baptised it went to a place called Limbo. I couldn't understand that because it wasn't the baby's fault it wasn't baptised. It would have been too young to pour water over its own head, wouldn't it? So it didn't seem very fair. There were lots of things we couldn't get our heads round but Daddy said we must just have faith and not question anything. Mum said it was a load of old cobblers and we should question everything. Life became very confusing.

Me and Monica joined the choir, which was even more of a mystery because all the hymns were in Latin. We didn't have a clue what we were singing about but we didn't mind because it all sounded so lovely. We sang in church every Sunday morning. When it was time to receive Holy Communion, we all trooped down the centre aisle together and everyone was looking at us and me and Monica felt very important. Brenda was too little to join the choir, so after Mass we would meet her and Daddy in the park. We'd play on the swings and the slide then we'd go home and eat a lovely dinner that Mummy had made for us. I loved Sundays.

I always hoped that Jack would be in the park, but he never was. I told Monica about him.

'You like a boy?'

'He's not any old boy, Monica. He's special.'

'What sort of special?'

I rubbed the bridge of my nose and thought. 'It's hard to explain,' I said. 'It's just a feeling I get when I look at him. A bubbly kind of feeling in my tummy.'

'Like a bilious attack?'

'Not like a bilious attack, Monica. Why would it feel like a bilious attack?'

'That's what a bilious attack feels like, sort of bubbly and then you throw up.'

'Jack doesn't make me want to throw up.'

'What does he make you feel like then?'

I closed my eyes and tried to remember. 'It's a bit like the Holy Trinity, hard to understand.'

'The Holy Trinity's not hard to understand,' said Monica, mimicking old Aquinas. 'It's three people rolled into one. What's hard about that? You Little Barbarian!'

Monica made me laugh.

'Well, I'm going to marry him when I grow up, so there.'

'Then I wish you well and hope you both have a fine life together.'

'Thank you for your kind wishes, Monica Maltby.'

'You are very welcome, Maureen O'Connell,' said Monica, crossing her eyes and making me giggle.

'I am though,' I said.

'You are what?'

'I *am* going to marry Jack.'

'And who is going to have the pleasure of breaking this happy news to the lucky boy?'

'I shall tell him myself when I'm sixteen.'

'Well, that should come as a pleasant surprise to him. Let's hope he hasn't met someone else while you're waiting to grow up.'

'He won't.'

'Won't he?'

'No, because we are destined to be together.'

'Imagine that,' said Monica.

The first thing I did when I came home from school every day was to climb the tree to see if Jack was in the garden. I loved watching him. I loved the way his hair curled over the back of his collar and the way he scratched the soft place behind his ear. I liked listening to his voice when he was pretending to be one of the tin soldiers. I could happily stay in the tree all day and never get bored or hungry or want to go for a pee, I just liked watching Jack. I would settle down on a branch and peep through the leaves. Daddy said that soon the leaves would be gone and my secret place would be discovered. I hadn't thought of that.

'What on earth will I do then, Daddy?'

'What on earth will she do then?' said Brenda.

'I shall make a spy hole in the fence,' said Daddy, smiling.

'You are the best daddy in the whole wide world,' I said, hugging him.

'And you are the best little girl,' he said, ruffling my hair.

'What about me?' said Brenda.

'And you are my best little girl too.'

'You can't have *two* best little girls.'

'Of course I can, for I have enough love for the pair of you.'

'And Mummy?' said Brenda.

'And Mummy,' he said.

I liked it best when Jack was on his own – I didn't like sharing him. I didn't like it when Nelson was there, with his brown hair and his brown jumper. One day my foot slipped on a branch and I nearly fell out of the tree. I must have made a noise because Nelson looked up and saw me. He dug Jack in the ribs and whispered something in his ear.

Jack looked up at the tree. 'You, girl,' he shouted, 'show yourself!'

'Yes, show yourself!' yelled Nelson.

Bloody hell! I started pulling my dress out of my navy drawers. I didn't want Jack to see my knickers. It wouldn't be so bad if they were my Sunday best but they were my everyday ones and they had holes in them. I decided to show myself. I parted the branches and peered down at them.

'Are you spying on us, girl?' demanded Jack.

'No!' My stupid voice came out like a squeak.

'Speak up,' said Jack. 'Can't hear you.'

'Can't hear you,' echoed Nelson.

Jack whispered something in Nelson's ear. 'You know what happens to spies when they're caught?' he yelled up at me.

I cleared my throat. 'I'm not a spy!' I shouted.

'What are you then,' said Jack. 'A nosy parker?'

'A nosy parker?' echoed Nelson.

Bloody cheek, what right did he have to call me a nosy parker? 'It's a free country!' I yelled. 'And this is *my* tree so I can do what I like in it.'

'Brave words,' said Jack, grinning.

I grinned back at him. He was beautiful. I could look at him all day and I was right about his eyes, they were as blue as his jumper. I wished his stupid friend would go home.

'So how come I haven't seen you at school?' asked Jack.

'I go to the Sacred Heart Convent.'

'Taught by the penguins, eh?'

'Penguins?'

'Well, that's what they look like.'

'Oh, the nuns. I suppose they do look a bit like penguins.'

'What's your name?'

'Maureen O'Connell, what's yours?' I said, even though I already knew.

'That's for me to know and for you to find out,' he said, grinning.

'But I just told you mine.'

'How do I know you're not a spy?'

'How do I know you're not an idiot?'

'He's not an idiot,' said Nelson.

'Who's asking you?'

Nelson didn't answer.

'Well, I know your first name's Jack,' I said.

'Ah, so you *are* a spy.'

'No, I've just got good hearing.'

Jack was laughing. 'My name's Jack Forrest.'

'Pleased to meet you, Jack Forrest.'

'Likewise, Maureen O'Connell.'

'What about him?' I nodded towards Nelson.

'Ask him yourself.'

'Well, I know he's named after a famous admiral. What's the next bit?'

I could tell that Nelson wasn't sure whether to tell me or not, then Jack said, 'Go on, tell her.'

Nelson muttered something I couldn't hear.

'I can't hear you.'

'Perks!' he shouted.

'Pleased to meet you, Nelson Perks.'

Nelson glared at me.

'Got any brothers?' said Jack.

'Just a younger sister.'

'Pity,' said Jack.

'Yes, pity,' said Nelson.

I stared hard at Nelson. 'Do you copy everything he says?'

Even from up in the tree I could see that Nelson looked embarrassed. He stared down at the ground and started scuffing his shoes in the mud.

'No,' he said quietly.

'Well, you give a good impression of it.'

Jack started laughing. It made me feel brave.

'Haven't you got a mind of your own?'

Nelson glared at me. 'You're just a stupid girl.'

'I'd rather be a stupid girl than a parrot.'

'I'm going home,' said Nelson and stomped off up the garden.

'You've upset my friend,' said Jack, making a poor-me face. 'I've got no one to play with now.'

'I expect you'll survive,' I said and I jumped down out of the tree and ran up the garden.

I was grinning when I came in the back door.

Daddy was stirring something on the cooker. 'You look like the cat that's just had the cream,' he said.

'He spoke to me, Daddy!'

'Now who would that be?'

Brenda was sitting at the table. 'Was it the boy?'

'Yes.'

'Is he your boyfriend now?'

'Not yet, but he will be one day. And we will get married and live happily ever after.'

'Just like Cinderella?'

'Exactly like Cinderella.'

'Can I be your bridesmaid, Maureen?'

'Course you can.'

'And what will I be?' said Daddy.

'You can be my bridesmaid as well,' I said, grinning.

'No, I will walk you down the aisle, my darling girl, and it will be the proudest day of my life.'

'Promise?'

'I promise,' said my dad.

All of a sudden I didn't feel happy any more.

Daddy sat down beside me. 'What's wrong, my love?'

'I was mean to Nelson.'

'Who's Nelson?'

'Jack's friend. I was mean to him.'

'Did you make him cry?' said Brenda.

'I don't think so.'

'That's good then,' said Brenda.

'Why were you mean to him?' said Daddy.

I shrugged my shoulders. 'Don't know.'

I did know though. I'd wanted Jack to think that I was clever and funny and not some silly girl. I'd embarrassed Nelson in front of his best friend and now I felt really bad about it and not funny or clever at all. That night, in bed, I snuggled down under the blankets and tried to think about Jack. About how lovely he was to look at and the sound of his voice and the way he smiled. I concentrated really hard on keeping the memory in my head but just as I was drifting off to sleep I remembered the look on Nelson's face and how I had tried to make a fool of him and then I couldn't remember Jack's face at all.

Chapter Ten

I tried to be nicer to Nelson after that, because I realised that he loved Jack as much as I did, just in a different way. Sometimes, when they were playing marbles in the gutter, they let me and Brenda join in. Nelson taught me how to play the game and he let us borrow some of his best marbles. The more I got to know Nelson, the more I liked him. Of course he wasn't Jack, no one could be like Jack, but he was kind and he wasn't mean, even though I'd been mean to him. I even lit a candle for him next to the dead dog's candle. We were both happy to follow where Jack led. Monica liked Nelson too, in fact I got the feeling she liked him better than Jack, although she never actually said so. Maybe Monica could marry Nelson when she grew up, then we could all be friends and live together in the same house. I'd like that.

It turned out that Jack and Nelson were only a year older than me and Monica, but Jack seemed way older than that. Neither of them had any brothers or sisters, so I guess that's why they were such close friends. Nelson said that Jack was like his brother. That would have made me jealous once, but now I'd got to know Nelson I didn't mind so much.

I wondered how many babies me and Jack were going to have. Monica said she would like to have two, a boy first and then a girl. I decided that if I had a girl I would call her Margaret Rose after the new princess. Monica said she would call hers after Princess Elizabeth Alexandra Mary, which I thought was a bit of a handle to saddle a baby with. A name like that was OK if you were royalty like the Princess and you lived in a palace and you had servants and stuff, but a bit of a mouthful if you lived round here. I was beginning to think that Monica had aspirations above her station. I liked the word 'aspirations'. I'd learned it from the tallyman who was talking about the woman down the road who'd gone to the Isle of Wight for her holidays.

Me and Monica didn't have a clue where babies came from. Shirley Green at school said that a stork brought them. Well, me and Monica had never seen a bloody stork flying over the pier with a baby in its mouth and if we had, we would have told a policeman. Ruth Watkins said the nurse delivered it in a black bag. Which makes you wonder why the poor thing didn't suffocate on the way. Christine Ward said that you got pregnant if you kissed a boy. Me and Monica didn't believe that for one second, because if it was true then Julie Baxter would have had a tribe of kids by now. We knew it had something to do with boys though, we just didn't know exactly what and there was no one that we could ask. The nuns didn't know anything about having babies so it was no good asking them, not even Sister Mary Benedict who looked like a film star. So we had to keep guessing.

'I bet your dad would tell you if you asked him,' said Monica one day.

She was probably right. My dad always told me the truth when I asked him a question.

One day, me and Brenda and Daddy were walking on the Downs. I took a deep breath and said, 'Daddy, where do babies come from?'

Daddy was smoking one of his Senior Service fags and he started coughing and nearly choked.

'Where do *what* come from?' he said, when he'd caught his breath.

'Babies.'

Daddy scratched at his head, which made his hair stand up on end on account of the margarine. 'Well...' he started.

'*I* know where they come from,' said Brenda.

'No you don't.'

'Yes I do.'

'Where then?'

'Sister Mary Benedict says that babies are a blessing from God and she should know, she's married to him.'

'And that's perfectly right, Brenda,' said Daddy, looking relieved.

But I wasn't satisfied with that. I knew that there had to be more to it and I was determined to find out what it was.

'How does God put them in the mummies' tummies, then?'

'Through a straw,' said Brenda.

'Don't be daft,' I said.

'It's true, isn't it, Dadda? It's true!'

'Now where did you hear that, my love?' said Daddy.

Brenda chewed at her lip. 'I dunno.'

'That's because it's not true,' I said.

'How do they get in there then?' demanded Brenda.

'That's what I'm trying to find out if you'd shut up for a minute.'

We both stared at Daddy. 'Well?' we both said.

Daddy looked uncomfortable and concentrated on undoing and doing up his shoelace. He cleared his throat. 'I think that's something you need to ask your mum.'

'Mum's not going to tell us, is she?'

'Remind me how old you are?'

'I'm nearly nine,' I said.

'And I'm almost seven,' said Brenda.

'Ask me again when you're sixteen.'

'SIXTEEN!'

'At least,' said Daddy.

'Is it a tricky subject?' said Brenda very seriously and that made us both laugh.

'*Very* tricky,' said Daddy.

'I thought so,' said Brenda solemnly.

Daddy started running ahead of us. 'Let's roll down the hill!' he shouted.

So instead of finding out where babies came from, we all rolled down the hill instead.

Monica and me were sitting, side by side, on the swings.

'I asked my dad how babies were made and he said he wouldn't tell me until I was at least sixteen. I don't think it's got anything to do with storks and black bags though,' I said.

Monica stopped swinging, tossed her plaits over her shoulder and said, 'I think it's got something to do with boys' willies.'

I screwed up my face in disgust. 'Boys' willies?'

'That's what I think.'

'Why?'

Monica leaned back on the swing so that her plaits touched the ground. 'I just think it has.'

'I've never even seen a boy's willy.'

'I have.'

'When?'

'I saw my brother's willy when he was a baby.'

'What did it look like?'

'Well…' began Monica.

'I'll tell you what, I haven't had my tea yet, so don't bother.'

'OK.'

'I think we need to rethink the whole baby thing, Monica.'

'I'm with you on that.'

From that moment on, I couldn't look at Jack without thinking of his willy and then there was Nelson, he would have one as well. Then there was my dad and Uncle Fred and Uncle John and the milkman and the coalman and the tallyman. The whole world was full of willies. I decided not to tell Brenda; she was too young to know about stuff like that. Bloody hell, I'm glad we never asked the nuns.

Chapter Eleven

When Brenda was seven, she had to make her first Confession. I'd already made mine at my old school. You had to be in a state of grace before you could receive Holy Communion, which was the body of Christ. You had to go to Confession every Saturday, so that you could stick out your tongue for the wafer on a Sunday morning. It was a mortal sin to eat the wafer if you hadn't been to Confession the day before. You couldn't have any breakfast, so your tummy rumbled all through Mass. In fact, the whole congregation's tummies rumbled all through Mass.

So every Saturday you had to go into a cupboard that looked a bit like a wardrobe and tell the priest all the bad things you'd done. I explained all this to Brenda.

'What bad things have I done, Maureen?' she asked, with a worried look on her face.

'I dunno.'

'What shall I say, then?'

'I just make it up,' I replied, grinning.

'Isn't that a sin?'

'Probably, but I haven't been struck down by lightning yet, so I'm not too worried.'

'So what do you say, then?' asked Brenda.

'I tell him I told a lie, I pinched stuff from the sweet shop, I was rude to my mum and dad. You know, the usual stuff.'

'But I haven't done any of those things, Maureen.'

'Well, you have to say something, you can't just sit there with your gob shut. Just tell him a load of sins, then say you're very sorry and mean it. The upside is that when you go back next time, you can say you've told lies and you'll be telling him the truth.'

'What happens *then*?'

'The priest forgives you of your sins and hands out a penance.'

'What's a penance?'

'Blimey, Brenda, don't you know anything?'

'How am I supposed to know anything when I've never done it before?'

'Fair comment. OK, a penance is a kind of punishment.'

'He won't hit me, will he?'

'Course he won't bloody hit you, he'll just give you some prayers to say.'

'Can you come in the wardrobe with me, Maureen?'

'Don't be daft, you have to go in on your own. It's really small, we wouldn't both fit in there.'

'Is it dark?'

'For heavens sake, Brenda, you're in and out in five minutes! Except Danny Denny, of course, who's got loads of sins to tell him. He's in there ages but *you* won't be.'

'What prayers will I have to say for me penance?'

'Now that's another thing you've got to be careful of.'

'Why?'

'Well, if say he gives you five Hail Marys, it's best to do just the one at the altar and the rest on the way home, otherwise people will think you're a terrible sinner who is destined to languish in the fires of Hell for all eternity. You don't want that, do you?'

'No, I bloody don't.'

'Do you know what, Brenda? Your language is getting really bad.'

'I can't imagine where I get that from,' she said, grinning.

'Cheeky monkey,' I said, giving her a hug.

That spring I turned nine and Mum said that I could have a birthday party. I had never had a party before. She said that I could invite a few friends, so of course I invited Jack, Nelson and Monica. I was beside myself with excitement and counted the days leading up to it. Aunty Marge had made me a new dress: it was dark blue taffeta with little white dots all over it. I had never owned a dress like it before, it was the most beautiful thing that I had ever seen.

As I stood looking at myself in the mirror, Mum came into the bedroom. She stood behind me and put her hands on my shoulders so that I could see both of us in the mirror. She was smiling at me.

'My little girl is growing up,' she said.

'Do I look pretty, Mum?'

'You are beautiful, my darling, inside and out. I am so proud of you.'

I turned around and put my arms around her waist. She smelled of home. Then I sat on the stool in front of the dressing table, while Mum did my hair. First, she brushed the knots out of it, brushed it until the silky, flyaway ends floated around my face. Then she smoothed it with the palms of her hands. That was the bit I liked best – the feel of her hands on my head, stroking my head as they smoothed the hair back away from my face and out of my eyes. Often, when she was doing this, she would lean forward, over the top of me, and plant a kiss on my forehead. My mum's hands were strong. They weren't soft hands; the skin was rough and red and chapped because of all the work she did; all the washing up, all the laundry, all the scrubbing and cleaning and polishing. They were strong, rough hands, but when my mum gathered my hair together, she was gentle as anything. When she tied the blue velvet ribbon around my ponytail, she was so careful not to hurt me, or pull my hair. And when she had finished, she always ran her fingers around the back of my neck, tidying up the loose wisps, and when she did that, those rough fingers touched me so softly, she could have been wearing gloves made of silk.

'Now I must get on,' she said. 'I have a birthday party to see to.'

After she'd gone, I looked in the mirror again. Was I really pretty? Daddy said I was. Daddy said that I was the prettiest girl in See Saw Lane, but then he would, wouldn't he? He was my dad. I wanted to look pretty; I wanted Jack to think that I was pretty.

I ran downstairs and was immediately shooed out into the garden by Aunty Marge. I leaned against the wall watching Brenda play hopscotch down the path.

She hopped towards me and said, 'Shall we climb the tree?'

'Don't be daft,' I said. 'I'll dirty my new dress.'

'I wish I had a new dress,' she said.

'It's not your birthday, is it? It's mine.'

'When's my birthday then?'

'Don't hold your breath, Brenda. It's not for bloody months!'

'And I'll be seven?'

'That's right.'

'And I'll get a new dress?'

'How should I know?'

I looked at Brenda's little face and put my arm around her. 'I'm sure you'll get a new dress. I expect Aunty Marge will make you the nicest dress in the whole world when you're seven.'

Brenda reached out and gently stroked the soft taffeta. 'Will it be as pretty as yours?'

'Prettier, I should think.'

Brenda grinned at me. 'You look very beautiful indeed,' she said solemnly.

I ruffled the top of her head. 'You're a funny old bunny, do you know that?'

'I don't mind being a bunny,' she said.

Daddy came into the garden. 'I've been thrown out of my own house, girls. Now why do you think that is?'

'It's because Maureen is going to have a party, Dada. Did you know that it's Maureen's birthday?'

'Really?' he said, pretending to be surprised.

'She's, um… How old are you?'

'Nine,' I said.

'Dada, Maureen is nine today and she is going to have a birthday party and when I'm seven, I'm going to have one as well and Aunty Marge is going to make me a new dress and it's going to be yellow.'

'And when is this momentous birthday of yours going to happen?'

'Don't hold your breath, Dada. It's not for bloody months!'

When Daddy looked at me, he wasn't smiling. 'You look lovely, my darlin',' he said. 'As pretty as a picture.'

'Thank you, Daddy.'

It was the best birthday party ever. Jack looked very handsome. He was wearing a white shirt and a tie and a navy jumper with no sleeves and long trousers. Nelson was still wearing his brown jumper but he had slicked his hair back. Sometimes when I looked at Nelson I got the same feeling in my tummy as I did when I looked at Daddy and I didn't know why. Jack gave me a little brooch in the shape of a bird. I knew that I would treasure it forever. Monica gave me a hanky with an 'M' embroidered in the corner. Brenda didn't have a present for me so she sneaked a jam sandwich off the kitchen table and wrapped it in a bit of old newspaper. I hugged her as if she had given me the Crown Jewels. I ate the sandwich even though most of the jam had stuck to the paper and I told her that it was the nicest sandwich that I had ever eaten.

Nelson handed me a paper bag. Inside were two Black Jacks and two Bullseyes. I knew it must have been hard for him to buy me a present so I told him that they were my very favourite sweets and he went red and scratched behind his ear but he looked happy. 'I think your dress is very nice,' he said.

I could feel my face going red. 'Thank you, Nelson.'

I wished it had been Jack that had said my dress was very nice and not Nelson. Then I felt bad because Nelson had bought me Black Jacks and Bullseyes, even though he was skint, so I said, 'I think your jumper is very nice.'

Nelson looked down at his old brown jumper and grinned. 'I like brown,' he said and we both laughed.

We played statues and in and out the dusty bluebells and hide and seek and hunt the fag packet, even though we didn't have a thimble.

My birthday present from Mum was a birthday cake with nine candles on the top. I looked at Jack through the glow of the candles and I thought again that he was very beautiful. Daddy had his arm around Mum's shoulder and I was happier than I had ever been.

'You have to make a wish,' said Jack, smiling at me.

I closed my eyes and made my wish, then I took a deep breath and blew the candles out. Everyone sang happy birthday to me. It was the best birthday party ever and even if I never had another party in my whole life it wouldn't matter, because this one was perfect.

When everyone had gone home and Mum and Aunty Marge were tidying up, me and Daddy sat side by side on the back doorstep. Daddy handed me a parcel. I opened it and inside was some dolls' house furniture. He had made the furniture out of fag packets and matchboxes. There was a little couch and a table and some chairs and two little beds. I threw my arms around his neck. 'This has been the happiest day of my life,' I said.

'Then it's the happiest day of mine,' he said, kissing my cheek.

That night when I went to bed I put the little brooch under my pillow, then just as I was going off to sleep, I added the bag of Black Jacks and Bullseyes. Then I thanked Jesus and the Blessed Virgin Mary and all the angels and saints for letting my daddy be my normal daddy for my birthday party.

* * *

Jack loved everything to do with the movies. Me and Monica never had the money to go to the pictures but I loved listening to Jack talk about the big stars in Hollywood that lived in mansions with swimming pools and servants. It sounded like a million miles away from See Saw Lane. He told me about Greta Garbo, who was a screen goddess, and Mary Pickford, who was beautiful, and Clark Gable, who was the dashing hero. Jack always seemed to have money to go to the cinema but he had to go on his own, because Nelson was just as skint as we were. Jack's dad worked in a bank and went to work wearing a proper suit and his shoes were always shiny and clean, so Jack got pocket money. I liked Jack's dad, he always had a smile for me and Brenda and he talked about important things with Daddy, like the state of the world and pigeons, as if he thought Daddy was a regular person and worth talking to. Jack's mum was a different kettle of cod though. She looked down her nose at us, as if we weren't as good as her. Mum said she had ideas above her station and Daddy said it looked as if she was sucking on a lemon.

Me and Nelson and Monica would hang around outside the cinema until Jack came out, then the four of us would go down to the beach. We'd sit with our backs to the wall and wait for him to tell us all about the film he'd just seen. Jack was good at telling stories. I'd close my eyes and listen to the sea tumbling the pebbles, as he brought the film to life. Nelson liked it best when Jack was describing Western films starring John Wayne or Gary Cooper. Afterwards they would run around the beach shooting each other, diving behind rocks and pretending to be cowboys. I didn't mind what film he had seen, I just liked listening to Jack's voice – I could have listened to his voice all day.

Once, Jack gave me and Monica the money to go and see *John Sawyer* at the Duke of York cinema. The cinema was beautiful inside. The walls were orange and pink and grey and the seats were red velvet. Me and Monica had never been anywhere like it in the whole of our lives. Daddy said that the Duke of York cinema was like sitting in the middle of a giant womb. I didn't ask to him explain because I had a horrible feeling it had something to do with the willy thing and I was confused enough as it was. Most of the men lit up fags and the smoke drifted in swirls and loops through the beam of light coming from the film projector way above us. Me and Monica held hands as we watched John and his friends witness a murder late at night in a dark creepy graveyard, then run away to an island on the Mississippi River. We laughed when they came home and attended their own funeral because everyone thought they had drowned. When we came out of the cinema the boys were waiting for us: it was our turn to tell the story.

The four of us were the best of friends; we went everywhere together. We swam in the icy sea, we balanced on the wooden groyne and we shared chips out of newspaper. One day I asked Monica if she would marry Nelson when she was older.

'I'm not going to marry anyone,' she said.

'Of course you are.'

'No, I'm not.'

'What then? Don't you want kids?'

'Why would I want kids?'

'Well, most people do.'

'Yeah, well, I'm not most people.'

Well, that blew my cosy vision of all of us living together out of the water.

'I don't mind going out with boys though,' she added, grinning.

'Thank gawd for that,' I said. 'I thought for a minute you were thinking of becoming a nun.'

Monica looked at me as if I had three heads.

Chapter Twelve

When Jack was eleven he passed an exam to go to the boys' grammar school. His mother acted as if she'd just been told that he was next in line to the throne. One morning she knocked on our front door. She had never come round to our house before and she'd lived next door to us for two years. Me and Brenda ran to open the door. She was standing there with this strange look on her face; she was smiling but it looked like the effort was killing her. Jack had stayed at the gate; he was wearing his new grammar school uniform. I grinned at him and he raised his eyes up to the heavens.

'Who is it?' called Mum.

'It's Mrs Forrest,' I called back.

Mum came to the door, wiping her hands on a tea towel. 'Do come in, Mrs Forrest,' she said.

She came into the hall then turned round. 'Come on, Jack,' she called.

Mum brought her into the front room and she sat on the edge of our chair as if it was contaminated. Jack stood behind her, looking as if he wanted the ground to swallow him up.

'Now, what can I do for you?' said Mum, smiling.

'I'm so sorry to bother you, Mrs O'Connell,' she said, 'but I wondered if you had change for sixpence.'

Of course we all knew why she had come round, it was to show off Jack in his new uniform. Poor Jack didn't know what to do with himself. I smiled at him to let him know that I knew how he was feeling and he grinned back at me. He was wearing a maroon blazer edged in grey and a maroon cap with grey stripes. I thought that he looked very handsome but I could tell by the look on his face that he felt like a right lemon.

Mum went into the kitchen and came back with her purse. 'Change for sixpence, you say?'

'What?' said Jack's mum.

'You said you wanted change for sixpence.'

'Oh… Oh yes,' stuttered Jack's mum.

'For the tram, is it?' said Mum.

'The tram?'

'Do you want change for the tram?'

'That's right. Change for the tram.'

Jack was making faces behind his mum's back and I was trying not to laugh because I was facing her.

We sat there in silence. No one had mentioned the new uniform, so eventually Jack's mum got up and said, 'Well, we had better get going, we don't want Jack to be late on his first day at the grammar school, do we?'

Me and mum smiled politely as if she'd said, 'We don't want Jack to be late for his first day down the mines.'

After she'd gone we all burst out laughing. Mum put on a posh voice and said, 'We don't want Jack to be late on his first day at the grammar school, do we?'

We had tears rolling down our faces.

'It's not Jack's fault though, is it, Mum?' I said, drying my eyes on my sleeve.

'No, love, it's not Jack's fault and I thought that he looked very handsome in his new uniform.'

'So did I.'

'I wasn't going to tell *her* that though,' said Mum.

The only thing that worried me about Jack going to the grammar school was that he might make new friends and not want to play with us any more. That didn't happen though, even though I'm sure his mum would have liked him to. The only thing that changed was that he had loads of homework and he wasn't allowed out until he'd finished it. Me and Monica and Nelson used to sit in the tree and Jack would wave to us out of his bedroom window. I felt sorry for him, especially on those long summer evenings when everyone was outside playing and he was stuck inside doing bloody homework.

I liked it when the four of us were together but I liked it best when it was just me and Jack. We would sit on my back step and talk – well, mostly Jack talked and I listened. One day he said, 'When I grow up, I'm going to fly a plane just like Amy Johnson.'

'Who's Amy Johnson?'

'She's the woman who flew to Australia all on her own. Don't tell me you haven't heard of her?'

I shook my head.

'She flew from England to Australia single-handed and if a woman can do it, then so can I.'

'What do you mean, if a woman can do it, so can you?'

'Well, women aren't as strong as men, are they? So if a woman can do it, so can a man.'

'Well, that's where you're wrong, clever dick.'

'What do you mean?'

'Men can't have babies, can they?'

'OK, you've got me there.'

'So when you grow up, you're going to fly planes?'

'Just as a hobby. I'm going to be a doctor.'

'I thought only posh people could be doctors.'

'Anyone can be a doctor if they study hard enough.'

I'd seen a Panel doctor once; you had to pay to see a proper one and we didn't have the money. Brenda had to go into a charity hospital when they thought she had the scarlet fever; as it turned out, it was the measles. Daddy didn't want her to go there because he said once you went in there you never came out. Mum said that was rubbish but he stayed outside the building for days until they let her out. Mum had said that Daddy was bonkers but I thought he was a hero. I always knew that my daddy would watch over us wherever we were. While Brenda was in the hospital the people in Carlton Hill did a collection for her, even though they were all skint. They bought her a mother-of-pearl rosary which she still has. I never knew any doctors and I never knew a kid that wanted to be one, but if Jack was going to be a doctor, that meant that I was going to be a doctor's wife. Bloody hell!

'What do you want to be when you grow up?' said Jack.

Golly, I'd never given it any thought and now that I knew that Jack was going to be a doctor I didn't know what to say to him. I didn't think that I was clever enough to work in a shop and I didn't want to clean for the rich ladies, but I didn't want to say that maybe I could work in a factory.

'You're clever, Maureen,' he said.

'I'm not clever like you.'

'I think you are.'

'Really?'

Jack nodded. 'You're cleverer than most girls I know.'

I didn't believe him but I was glad he thought I was clever. 'Thanks, Jack,' I said.

I told Daddy that Jack was going to be a doctor and that I was going to be a doctor's wife.

'Being a doctor is a fine thing to be,' he said. 'It takes a very special kind of person to be a doctor. They have a calling, just like a nun or a priest. Their hands are guided by God.'

'Do you have to have a calling to be a doctor's wife?'

'I don't think so, love.'

'Well, that's a bloody relief!'

'You might have to stop swearing though.'

'I can't do that, Daddy.'

'Why not?'

'I love the word bloody,' I said, grinning.

Chapter Thirteen

We hadn't seen Nelson for almost a week and we were getting worried about him. At least, me and Monica were getting worried about him, it didn't seem to be bothering Jack.

'Perhaps we should go and see him,' I said to Jack.

'No, he's probably just got a cold or something.'

'He's had plenty of colds before,' said Monica, 'but he still comes out to play.'

Jack was looking everywhere except at us. 'He'll come round when he's ready.'

'Why can't we just check on him?' I demanded.

Jack went red in the face. 'Because you can't, alright?'

'Why not?' said Monica. 'What's the big secret?'

'Why don't you both mind your own business?' snapped Jack and he stomped off down the road.

We caught up with him. 'You don't have to shout,' I said. 'We're just worried about him. There's nothing wrong with that, is there?'

Jack stopped walking and faced us. 'Nelson wouldn't want you to go round to his house, alright?'

'Why not?' I said.

I could see that Jack was struggling, that he didn't know what to say to us. I got the feeling that he was somehow protecting Nelson.

'Look,' I said, quickly, 'it doesn't matter.'

'Doesn't it?' said Monica.

'No, it doesn't,' I said, glaring at her.

'Oh right, OK. It doesn't matter, Jack.'

We walked onto the green that was at the end of our street. There were loads of kids playing on the field. The boys were kicking a ball around and the girls were sitting on the grass. We walked to the far end, away from everyone else, and sat down.

Me and Monica exchanged looks; we didn't know what to make of it. Jack was pulling up bits of grass. After what seemed like forever he said, 'I've already been to see him.'

'Why didn't you tell us that in the first place?' said Monica.

'What's wrong with him?' I said.

'I can't tell you.'

I was even more worried now. 'He'll be alright though, won't he?'

'He'll be alright in a few days.'

I felt like crying. Nelson was my friend but then I realised that I knew very little about him. I didn't even know where he lived. Nelson didn't say much, he was a quiet boy, but somehow you missed him. *I* missed him and I was scared. I could feel my eyes filling with tears. 'Has someone hurt him?'

'He won't thank me if I tell you. He'll tell you himself if he wants to.'

'You'll look after him though, won't you, Jack?'

'Of course I will.'

And I knew that whatever had happened to Nelson, Jack would be there for him.

Another week passed before we saw our friend again. We didn't say anything about the bruises on his face and his legs, we acted as if they weren't there but we all tried to be extra kind to him.

That night in bed I cried into my pillow.

'What's wrong, Maureen?' whispered Brenda.

In See Saw Lane we had a bedroom each but we were so used to being together that Brenda climbed into my bed every night. I liked her being next to me; I liked to feel her warm little body next to mine.

'Why are you crying?'

'Someone hurt Nelson.'

'Who hurt Nelson?'

'His bloody dad.'

'Are you going to tell Daddy?'

'I don't think so.'

'You should tell Daddy, Maureen. That's what you should do.'

'Go to sleep, love,' I said.

Brenda put her arms around me. 'I like Nelson,' she said.

I kissed the top of her head. 'So do I, now go to sleep.'

Brenda yawned. 'I think we should light a candle for him next to the dead dog. We could ask the Blessed Virgin Mary if she would be so kind as to kill his bloody dad.'

'I think that's a great idea, Brenda. We'll go down the church first thing after school tomorrow.'

I lay there thinking about Nelson in his brown jumper that had holes in the elbows. I hoped his mum loved him, even if his dad didn't, that's what I hoped and I hoped that the Blessed Virgin Mary could see her way clear to causing his dad some grievous bodily harm.

The next day after school me and Brenda headed straight to the church. I loved our little church, I thought it was beautiful. The altar was blue and gold and there was always a candle lit beside the statue of the Virgin Mary and it always smelled of incense, even when the Blessed Sacrament wasn't there. We dipped our fingers in the holy water that was just inside the door and we made the sign of the cross.

'I don't think that we should light a candle for two doors down's dog today, I want the Blessed Virgin Mary to concentrate on Nelson.'

'Are you going to ask her to kill his dad, Maureen?'

'I'm just going to tell her what he did to Nelson and leave her to make up her own mind.'

Brenda looked worried. 'She couldn't help Jesus though, could she? What makes you think she can help Nelson?'

'I don't think she was supposed to help Jesus, Brenda, because he had to die on the cross to save the sins of the world. Jesus probably told her not to get involved.'

'I'd forgotten that.'

'We just have to send up a silent prayer and appeal for her to intercede.'

'What's intercede?'

'I'm not sure but Aquinas is always banging on about it.'

'Perhaps she'd take us more seriously if we put a penny in the slot.'

'We haven't got a penny.'

'Do you think she answers the rich people's prayers first?'

'No, I don't. Now close your eyes and appeal.'

We both knelt down in front of the statue. *Dear Blessed Virgin Mary*, I said in my head. *I know that your son Jesus is all-seeing and all-knowing and if you are as well, then you'll know that Nelson is a good, kind boy and he doesn't deserve to be beaten up by his dad…*

'I don't know what to say,' whispered Brenda.

'Ask her to intercede.'

'Intercede,' whispered Brenda.

'You have to say more than that, she won't know what the hell you're going on about.'

'What shall I say then?'

'Ask the Blessed Virgin Mary to intercede on your behalf. We're going to be here all day at this rate.'

I closed my eyes again. *'Sorry about that, Mary, now, where was I? Oh yes. As you know, Nelson is a good, kind boy and—'*

'What's that word again, Maureen?'

'Inter-bloody-cede,' I hissed.

'It's not an easy word, is it?'

'This is not an easy situation, Brenda, but we have to appeal to her in the best way we can.'

Bear with me, Mary, I'm doing my best here but Brenda keeps butting in. Now, I don't want you worrying about the dead dog today, this is all about my good friend Nelson. What I really want is for someone to bash his dad over the head with a hammer. Now I realise that maybe you don't go in for murder but I'm hoping you might know someone who does. Perhaps you could have a word with that sinner who was hanging on the cross next to Jesus. You must know each other pretty well by now. I looked up at the statue, she was smiling down at me like she always does. *Look, Mary, if you can't manage the murder bit perhaps you could just amputate his hands so that he can't punch Nelson any more. Amen.*

Satisfied that I'd done all I could, I sat down and thought about my friend. I thought about his smiley face and his hair that stuck up all over the place and I thought about how different he was to Jack and how the two of them had become friends and why Jack's mum had even allowed it, given that she was such a bloody snob.

'Shall we go now?' said Brenda.

I nodded and we started to walk out of the church. Halfway up the aisle, I stopped.

'What?' said Brenda.

'I just want to ask the virgin for one more favour.'

I walked quickly back down the aisle and knelt down again in front of the statue.

I hope you don't think I'm pushing it, Mary, but once you've sorted his dad out, could you see your way clear to getting Nelson a new jumper? Amen.

I got up, then knelt back down again.

He likes brown.

Chapter Fourteen

It was nearly Christmas and it was really cold in our house. Every night Daddy piled coats on our bed to try and keep us warm. One morning he came into the bedroom and said, 'Quick, girls, look out of the window!'

Me and Brenda scrambled out of bed and pulled back the curtains. Outside everything was white. While we had been sleeping a blanket of snow had covered the grass and the trees and the fences in all the gardens. It looked like a winter wonderland. 'Snow!' we screamed.

We got dressed quickly and ran downstairs. Mum made us both eat a big bowl of porridge before we were allowed outside. We wrapped up in coats and hats and gloves and opened the back door. Everything looked clean and beautiful. We stood on the back step, almost afraid to step out into the snow.

'Oh, Maureen,' whispered Brenda, holding my hand. 'It's very beautiful, isn't it?'

'Very,' I said.

'What are you waiting for, girls?' asked Daddy.

Brenda looked up at him. 'I'm not waiting for anything, Dada. I'm just looking. I could look at it forever.'

'Well, *I'm* not waiting!' said Daddy and jumped down the step and into the snow. 'Come on, you two!'

I took hold of Brenda's hand and together we raced down the garden, screaming with joy, our feet crunching into the crisp white snow and leaving footprints behind us as we ran. Just then a great big snowball came flying over the fence and landed on my head.

'Was that you, Jack Forrest?' I shouted.

'Certainly was!' he shouted back. 'I'm coming round, we're going up the Downs.'

'Is that OK, Daddy? Can we go up the Downs with Jack?'

'I think the Downs is the best place to be on a day like today. You go and enjoy yourselves.'

Me and Brenda ran round the side of the house. Jack was standing there with another snowball in his hand.

'Don't you dare, Jack Forrest.'

Jack grinned but dropped the snowball.

'I'll call for Monica and you get Nelson,' I said.

'No need,' said Jack.

I looked up the street to see Nelson and Monica running towards us. Nelson was wearing his old brown jumper but no coat. Jack didn't say anything; he just went into his house and brought out a coat, which he threw at Nelson. He also handed him a piece of bread and jam.

'I've had my breakfast,' mumbled Nelson.

'Of course you have,' said Jack. 'But I couldn't manage all of mine and Mum doesn't like wasting food. You'll be doing me a favour.'

'Thanks, mate,' said Nelson quietly.

Something wasn't right. I just knew something wasn't right but I also knew that I couldn't ask. I wondered why his mum had let him go out in the snow without a coat and I wondered why Jack had given him bread and jam. The whole thing was making me feel bad inside, just like worrying about my dad used to.

The only difference was that I was used to worrying about my dad. I caught Jack's eye; he was staring at me. I wanted to smile at him but I couldn't and it looked as if he couldn't manage a smile either.

'We need something to slide down the hills on,' said Monica. 'Has anyone got anything?'

I ran back into the house. Daddy was sitting at the kitchen table polishing the shoes.

'What are you doing back?' he said. 'I thought you'd be sliding down hills by now.'

'We've got nothing to slide down on, Daddy.'

'Now, let me see,' he said, scratching his head.

'Mind the margarine, Daddy.'

'Thank you, love.'

I stared at him, waiting. Then he smiled. 'What if I take the wheels off the old pushchair?' he said, getting up. 'That should work, what do you think?'

'I think that would work nicely, Daddy.'

I went outside and told the others.

'My old pushchair?' said Brenda, grinning. 'Do you think it will still squeak?'

'Not without the wheels,' I said.

'I remember that pushchair,' said Monica, laughing. 'It was a pain, you could hear it coming for miles.'

We all sat on the wall and waited for Daddy to take the wheels off the pushchair.

'I love the snow,' said Nelson. 'It's looks as if someone has dipped a brush into a tin of white paint and made everything clean and fresh and new.'

We stared at him with open mouths. Nelson wasn't in the habit of coming out with stuff like that.

'You sound like a poet, Nelson,' said Monica and he went red and scratched at his head and we all laughed.

Eventually Daddy came round the side of the house carrying the pushchair minus the wheels. 'What do you think, kids?' he said.

'I think you've done a great job, Mr O'Connell,' said Jack. 'We'll fly down the hills on that.'

Daddy looked pleased and I felt really proud of him. As we started off down the road, I turned around. Daddy was still at the gate. I waved to him and he waved back. I wondered, as I always wondered when leaving him, whether I should have asked him to come with us. I knew that he would have loved it. I looked at the others walking ahead of me. Monica was hanging on to Brenda in case Brenda slipped over and Jack and Nelson were carrying the old pushchair. These were my friends and this was the way it should be. Perhaps me and Brenda could go up the Downs with Daddy tomorrow. Yes, that's what we'd do, we'd go with Daddy tomorrow. That made me feel better and I ran to join the others.

The sun was shining on the hills and they sparkled like a million pieces of crystal. I stood for a moment and breathed in the cold air. It caught the back of my throat and made me cough. I was glad to be here in this magical place with my best friends. I watched as they tumbled in the snow. Brenda was scooping up handfuls of it and letting it fall around her like a white cloud. Then I thought of Daddy and I wished he was beside me. I wanted to feel his hand in mine and I wanted him to feel the stillness and wonder of this magical day in this magical place. I wanted him to feel the silence, to taste it on his tongue and let it slip down into his heart. I wanted him to breathe it in and be comforted and at peace.

I remembered other snowy days, when Daddy would take me and Brenda and the squeaky pushchair down to the beach. We would lean on the railings and watch the sea tumbling the white pebbles, washing away the snow and turning them back to greys and browns. I gazed out over the sparkling hills. I missed my daddy so much that the pain was colder than the air that I was breathing in. I missed my daddy when I wasn't with him and I missed him when I *was*. It was like the Holy Trinity, it made no bloody sense.

I ran to join my friends and we lay on the icy-cold ground and stared up at the grey sky and the trees bowed down under the weight of the snow piled on their branches.

We had the best time ever; we took turns sliding down the hill. Some people had proper sledges but we didn't care, we couldn't have been more delighted with Brenda's old pushchair. We sped down the hill, holding the handlebars tight and screaming as the snow sprayed around us, covering our coats and hats and scarves in a blanket of whiteness. Great thick flakes of it fell from the skies, sticking to our eyelashes and turning our hair snowy white. I caught Jack's eye and we smiled at each other, my happiness complete. We stayed out until it got dark – we didn't want the day to end, even though we were blue with the cold. We said goodbye to Nelson and Monica and the three of us walked home, pulling the old pushchair behind us.

Chapter Fifteen

It was two days before Christmas. Daddy took me and Brenda up onto the Downs and we collected armfuls of mistletoe and holly. The snow had gone, leaving the hills wet and slushy, but I had seen them in all their snowy loveliness and I remembered.

Mum draped the green holly and bright red berries across the mantelpiece and stuck the mistletoe over the doors. Everywhere looked lovely. We had a roaring fire in the grate. Daddy had put the wheels back on the old pushchair and me and Brenda had squeaked along behind the coalman's cart as fast as we could, waiting for the coal to tumble into the road. Some kids put bits of wood down so that more coal bounced out off the cart. Then there was a scramble as all the kids nudged and elbowed their way to the precious black lumps. The coalman shouted at us but I don't think he really minded because he knew that we were all bloody skint. We always saved the last mince pie for him as a thank you.

Me and Brenda didn't have any money to buy presents but Uncle John and Aunty Marge came to the rescue and let us help on the stall. Everyone at the market was in a Christmassy mood. People were dragging trees along the street and wearing tinsel around their heads. A choir started up and we packed oranges and apples and bananas to the sounds of 'Silent Night'. It was lovely and I wished it could be Christmas every day. We stayed until it was too dark to see anything, then helped Uncle John to clear up. Aunty Marge gave us two whole shillings each: we were rich.

We walked along Western Road staring into all the shops, dazzled by the brightness of the windows. Each one was decked out for Christmas and they sparkled with gold and silver tinsel and fairy lights that shone out across the wet pavements. Wade's was the best shop in town. We couldn't afford to buy anything there but we pressed our noses against the big window and stared at the beautiful dolls, dressed in pink satin coats and bonnets, and the dolls' houses with all the little pieces of furniture and the shiny new bikes and the beautiful Teddy bears with their button eyes. We knew that we would never get presents like that but we didn't mind, it was just lovely to look at it all. While we were standing there a man and a woman walked into the shop, holding the hands of a little girl. The girl looked about Brenda's age and was wearing a dark blue velvet coat and a little blue felt hat. She stuck her tongue out at us as she passed.

The beautiful dolly with the pink satin coat would probably be under her tree on Christmas morning. I wished I had enough money to buy that dolly for Brenda. I pulled her away from the window and half dragged her down the road.

'Why are you cross, Maureen?'

'Oh, I don't bloody know! I just am.'

'I don't want a silly old doll.'

I stopped and put my arm around her thin shoulders. 'You deserve that dolly more than that stuck-up little madam.'

Brenda smiled up at me. 'She doesn't have *you* though, does she? And I'd rather have you.'

'What would I do without you, Brenda O'Connell?'

'You don't have to do without me, I'll always be here.'

We left Wade's and walked down the road until we came to Woolworths.

'I like Woolworths best,' said Brenda.

'Me too,' I replied, grinning.

The two shillings were burning a hole in my pocket but I knew that I had to spend them wisely.

Just inside the door was a beautiful Christmas tree covered in lovely decorations. Me and Brenda stood looking up at the fairy sitting on the top.

Brenda gave a big sigh. 'How perfectly beautiful,' she whispered.

I smiled down at her.

'Are we going to have a tree?' she said.

'I don't expect so, but we've got the lovely holly and the mistletoe so we don't need a tree, do we?'

'I suppose not. It would be nice though, wouldn't it?'

'Yeah, it would be nice but I don't think we've got the money to buy one.'

'I don't need a tree.'

'Course you don't. It's only a lump of wood with a few needles on it. Anyway, we've got nothing to decorate it with.'

'No bloody point then, is there?'

'You shouldn't swear, Brenda.'

'*You* do.'

'That's different.'

'Why is it different?'

'Cos I've got a bad mouth on me and you haven't.'

'I'd like to have a bad mouth on me, Maureen.'

'Well, you can't. It takes practice, you can listen to mine.'

'Thanks.'

The counters were piled high with baubles and tinsel and paper lanterns and red crêpe paper and plastic Father Christmases and little wooden soldiers in green and red uniforms.

We used some of our money to buy a packet of hairgrips for Mum and a pouch of baccy for Dad.

'Now I'm going to do a bit of shopping on my own. I'll meet you back here by the tree, don't talk to anyone and don't leave the shop,' I said.

'Can I look at the toys?'

'Yeah, you go and look at the toys.'

I wanted to get something for Brenda and Jack and Nelson. The store was packed, kids were running around, mums were screaming at them and dads were smoking their heads off and looking grumpy. There were so many people in there that there was hardly room to breathe as they pushed and shoved their way towards the counters. It was perfect, it was the way Christmas was supposed to be, and I loved it. I squeezed under armpits and through peoples' legs to get to the front of the queue.

The bloke behind the counter was dressed up as Father Christmas and he smiled at me. 'What yer looking for, love?'

'I want something for my sister Brenda and something for my friend Jack.'

'What did you have in mind?'

'I don't exactly know.'

He rummaged around under the counter and said, 'Do you think your sister would like this?'

He was holding up a wooden monkey that climbed up a stick, did a somersault at the top and then climbed back down again. 'I think Brenda would love that,' I said. 'How much is it, please?'

'It's a shilling,' said the man.

I shook my head. 'That won't leave me enough to get something for Jack and Nelson.'

'Oops, I've made a mistake! It's sixpence. Will that suit you?'

'That will suit me perfectly,' I said, smiling at him.

The man winked at me and put the monkey in a paper bag. 'Have a nice Christmas, love.'

'And you have a nice Christmas.'

Now, what should I get for Jack?

I walked over to the toy section where I could see Brenda gazing longingly at the dolls peeping out of their boxes. I put my arm around her. 'When I start work, I'm gonna get you one of them.'

'Really?'

'I said so, didn't I?'

'Thanks, Maureen.'

'I'm looking for something to give to Jack.'

'How about a tin soldier? He likes tin soldiers.'

'He's got loads of them already. It won't be special. I want to get him something special.'

'What about a hankie?'

'Nah.'

And then I saw it, the perfect present. It was a little wooden box and on the lid was a picture of John Wayne on a horse. I still had some pennies left and I knew exactly what I was going to get with them. I wandered around until I found the wool counter.

There was a young girl standing behind the counter. She looked bored out of her skull.

'I'll have this, please. It's for a Christmas present,' I said, picking up a ball of brown wool.

'Funny sort of present,' she said.

'No, it's not,' said Brenda, jumping to my defence.

'Well, I wouldn't be thrilled if you gave *me* a ball of brown wool for Christmas.'

'Well, that's alright them,' I said. 'Cos I'm not giving it to you, am I? I'm giving it to someone I like.'

'Well, I hate to think what you're giving to someone you *don't* like.'

She put the wool in a bag and I passed over the last of my pennies.

'Silly mare,' I said, walking away.

'Silly mare,' said Brenda.

Chapter Sixteen

I was woken by Brenda shouting, 'Wake up, he's been!'

'Who's been?' I said, sitting up and rubbing my eyes.

'The fat bloke with the stuff, there were two socks at the end of the bed. Shall we take them into Mummy and Dadda's room, Maureen?'

I jumped out of bed and pulled back the curtains. I had to scrape the ice off the window to see outside and everywhere was white and frosty. It was bloody freezing, so I jumped back into bed and snuggled down under the covers.

'I think it's too early to get up.'

Brenda snuggled into me. 'It's Christmas Day, Maureen. Isn't that just perfectly wonderful?'

'Perfectly wonderful,' I said, giving her a squeeze.

'Can I have a feel of my sock?'

'Course you can.'

'Do you want to have a feel of yours?'

'OK.'

Brenda reached to the bottom of the bed and got the socks. They were knobbly and squishy and exciting.

'I think I can feel an orange,' said Brenda.

'I think I can as well.'

'And something hard.'

'A pencil?'

'Maybe it's a pencil. Can we get up now?'

Daddy put his head around the bedroom door. 'I thought you two would be downstairs by now.'

'We didn't want to wake you,' I said.

'I've been up for ages. Hasn't anyone told you that it's Christmas Day?'

'We know it's Christmas Day, Dadda, because the fat bloke's been.'

'Has he now? Well, you must have been very good girls.'

'Do *you* think we've been very good girls, Dadda?' said Brenda.

'I think you've been the best girls in See Saw Lane. Now, come on, I've lit a lovely big fire.'

We jumped out of bed, grabbed the socks and raced downstairs.

'Now close your eyes,' said Daddy.

The first thing I noticed was the smell. It was like being in the middle of a wood, in a land that I'd never been in before. It made my heart swell with happiness.

'OK, you can open them now.'

There in front of us, taking up nearly all the room, was the biggest Christmas tree that I had ever seen in my life. It was nearly as big as the one in Woolworths. There were Senior Service fag packets covered in silver paper hanging from the branches. It was perfect.

Brenda burst into tears. Daddy gathered her up into his arms. 'This isn't a time for crying, my darling girl.'

Brenda gulped. 'But it's so… It's so…'

'Big?' said Mum, coming into the room.

'Beautiful,' said Brenda.

'Where did you get it, Daddy?' I said.

'Your Uncle John brought it round last night. They were giving it away down the market, nobody wanted it.'

'I wonder why?' said Mum, making a face.

'Are you cross because it takes up most of the bloody room?' I said.

'Mouth, Maureen.'

'Sorry, Mum, but I do love that word.'

'I know you do, love.'

'It is bloody lovely though, isn't it?' said Brenda.

We all fell about laughing.

Brenda held up the sock. 'Look what the fat bloke brought, Mummy.'

'Are you going to look at it all day? Or are you going to open it?'

We sat in front of the big roaring fire and we plunged our hands into the socks. We had an apple and an orange and five marbles each and a colouring-in book and a yo-yo and a bag of Pontefract sweets.

Brenda's eyes were shining and her cheeks were pink from the fire. 'I am too happy for my body,' she said.

'Where does she get it from?' said Mum, shaking her head.

'She gets it from you, my beautiful Kate,' said Dad.

'Get on with you,' said Mum, going all red.

Daddy went out of the room and came back with a big parcel covered in newspaper.

'This is for both of you,' he said. 'Happy Christmas, my angels.'

We tore off the paper. Inside was a dolls' house. It had windows and a little door and it smelled of apples.

'Oh, Daddy,' I said. 'It's beautiful.'

'It's spectacular,' said Brenda.

'Your daddy made it himself,' said Mummy, sitting down on the floor beside us.

'I made it out of one of your Uncle John's fruit boxes.'

'It's the best dolls' house in the world,' said Brenda, hugging him.

'Upstairs now,' said Daddy. 'It's time you got ready for church.'

I ran upstairs and put on some warm clothes.

'I need to see Jack, I want to give him his present,' I said when I came down.

'Can't you see him when we get back?'

'No, Daddy, he's going to his granny's house today. He'll be gone by the time we come back.'

'Don't be long then.'

I knocked on Jack's door and his dad answered.

'Happy Christmas, Maureen. Do you want to see Jack?'

'Yes please, Mr Forrest.'

'Come in out of the cold then.'

I stood in the hallway. I'd never been inside Jack's house before – it was the same as ours only the other way round.

'Jack!' shouted his dad. 'You have a visitor.'

Jack came running down the stairs. He smiled at me. 'I'm going to my gran's today.'

'I know.' I held the present out to him. 'Happy Christmas, Jack.'

'For me?' he said.

I nodded.

Jack ran back up the stairs and came down again with a parcel wrapped in red paper. He held it out towards me.

'I was going to give it to you before we went to Gran's.'

'We're going to church now.'

'Oh, I'd forgotten.'

'Jack?' I said.

'Mmm?'

'Will Nelson have a lovely Christmas?'

Jack looked sad. 'I don't know, Maureen.'

'His dad wouldn't hurt him on Christmas Day, would he?'

Jack chewed at his nail.

'Jack?'

'He hasn't got a dad, Maureen,' he said quietly.

'What?'

'Nelson hasn't got a dad.'

'Well then, who?'

Jack's mum came out of the kitchen. 'Happy Christmas, Maureen,' she said. I could see her mouth moving but I was so shocked at what Jack had just told me that I couldn't take in what she was saying.

'I said, "Happy Christmas, Maureen".'

'Sorry, Mrs, Forrest. Happy Christmas.'

'Right, Jack, say goodbye to your little friend. We have to get going.'

Jack walked outside with me.

'I don't understand,' I said.

'I know you don't. Look, I promise that we will talk about it after Christmas, OK?'

I could feel my eyes filling with tears. 'He's not going to have a nice Christmas is he, Jack?'

We stood staring at each other, both of us worried for our good friend Nelson.

'Light a candle for him this morning.'

'I always do.'

'He knows he's got us.'

'Always.'

Then Jack did the most surprising thing. He leaned across and kissed my cheek.

'Happy Christmas, Maureen,' he said.

I walked back home in a dream. Jack had said that Nelson didn't have a dad and he had kissed my cheek. How could you be confused and worried and happy all at the same time? But I was.

People were calling out 'Happy Christmas' as we walked through the estate.

I wanted to call out 'Happy Christmas' as well but I just couldn't. Daddy stopped walking and looked down at me. 'What's wrong, my love?'

'I've got a lot on my mind.'

'Can you tell your daddy what is worrying you?'

'Not right now.'

'When you're ready.'

Brenda slipped her hand into mine and squeezed it. 'I'd give the dead dog a miss this morning and have a word with the baby Jesus about your worries.'

'Good idea, Brenda,' said Daddy.

'Ask him to do that inter… inter… What's that word again?'

'Intercede,' I said.

'Yeah, well, ask him to do that. It's his birthday so he'll be in a good mood.'

'Great thinking!'

I loved going to church on Christmas morning. As we walked down the centre aisle I could feel the warmth from a million candles. The Blessed Sacrament was on show. We genuflected in front of it and made the sign of the cross, then we went over to the side altar where the stable was. The Blessed Virgin Mary was gazing down at the baby Jesus, all swaddled in the manger. Joseph was standing behind her and the Wise Men and shepherds were grouped around. It was lovely. I lit a candle and prayed for Nelson and then, as it was Christmas, I prayed for the dead dog, too. I wandered if he was still squashed flat or whether one of the saints plumped him up once he got to Heaven. Were dogs allowed in Heaven?

We sang 'Once in Royal David's City' and 'Away in a Manger'. Then we knelt at the altar and stuck out our tongues so that the priest could put the wafer in our mouths. My tummy was rumbling as usual. 'Corpus Christi,' said the priest, which means 'Body of Christ'. We had to let the wafer melt because Sister Aquinas said that if we chewed it, it would be like putting a knife in God's heart. Personally I thought that was a bit over the top. I mean, as long as you got it down your throat, I shouldn't think it mattered how it got there.

When we came out of church it was raining. Not ordinary rain but the icy stuff that stings your face and makes your nose run.

'Have you got a hankie?' said Brenda.

'Wipe it on your sleeve,' I said.

We hurried up the road. All we wanted was to be at home in front of the fire and I wanted to see what Jack had bought me.

Then I saw him; he was sitting on Jack's front door step. He had his arms wrapped around his body and his head was down. I ran over and knelt in front of him. He was shaking with the cold and he was soaking wet. 'Nelson?' I said softly. He looked up at me with such sadness that I wanted to bawl my eyes out. Suddenly Daddy was beside us. 'Come on, old chap,' he said and he gently lifted Nelson into his arms as if he was a baby.

'Kate!' he yelled urgently as we came in the front door.

Mum ran towards us. 'Oh dear God!' she said. 'Maureen, get blankets off the bed. Brenda, get a towel.'

I ran upstairs, shaking and crying. Then I pulled the blanket from the bed. I nearly died when I went into the front room: Nelson was stark naked and Mum was rubbing his body, trying to get some warmth into it. She was gently murmuring, 'There's a good boy, soon get you warm. There now, there now. Brenda, hand me the towel.' Mum dried Nelson's poor thin little body so tenderly, tears running down her face as she saw the bruises that covered his back. She wrapped him in the blanket and Daddy picked him up and laid him on the couch.

'Maureen,' said Mum. 'I want you to run round to Aunty Vera and ask her to let us borrow some of Malcolm's clothes.'

The last thing that I wanted was to see Aunty Vera on Christmas Day but I did as I was told and went back out into the freezing rain. I was drenched by the time I got to the house.

Malcolm opened the door and smirked.

'What are you after?' he said, blocking the hallway.

'Let me in, you idiot, I'm bloody soaked!'

'Who is it, darling?' called Aunty Vera.

'It's Maureen.'

Aunty Vera came to the door but she didn't ask me in. 'What do you want, Maureen? We're just about to sit down for our dinner.'

'Some of Malcolm's clothes.'

'What are you talking about, child?'

'They're for Nelson. His clothes are soaking wet.'

'Oh for heaven's sake, you'd better come in and stand on the mat! I don't want you dripping water all over the place.'

I stepped into the hall as Uncle Fred came out of the front room.

'What's all this about, Maureen? We're just about to have our dinner.'

Well, you're just going to have to bloody wait, aren't you? I thought.

'She wants some of Malcolm's clothes.'

'Is this one of your jokes?' said Uncle Fred, glaring at me.

'It's not a joke, Uncle Fred. My friend Nelson has been hurt and he needs some dry clothes.'

'You want me to give my Malcolm's clothes to some strange child?'

'Nelson's not strange. Anyway, Mum says it's just for a borrow.'

Malcolm was making faces at me. 'I don't want you to give my clothes to this boy, Mummy,' he simpered.

'I know you don't, darling,' said Aunty Vera, putting her arms around him. 'We'll just give him some of your old stuff.'

I felt like telling her where she could stick Malcolm's bloody clothes. I'd rather give Nelson one of my dresses.

Aunty Vera went upstairs and Uncle Fred and the horrible Malcolm left me in the hallway on my own but not before Malcolm stuck his tongue out.

'Grow up,' I mouthed at him.

Eventually Aunty Vera came back downstairs. 'Tell your mother that I don't want them back,' she said glaring at me.

I nearly had to prise the bundle of clothes out of her arms. I stuffed them under my coat so that they wouldn't get wet and ran home.

When I got in, Nelson was fast asleep on the couch. It was the quietest Christmas that we had ever had but that was OK, because Nelson was OK. He shared our Christmas dinner, dressed in horrible Malcolm's clothes but he didn't seem to mind that they were miles too big for him on account of the fact that Malcolm stuffed his face for a living.

'Don't let your mum chuck my jumper out, will you?' he said when we were on our own.

'Of course I won't.'

Nelson's jumper reminded me of something. I ran upstairs and came down with his present. He opened the bag and took out a pair of brown gloves. I'd given Aunty Marge the wool and she'd knitted them for me.

'This is the best present I've ever had,' he said, smiling.

'Happy Christmas, Nelson.'

'Happy Christmas, Maureen.'

He hadn't told us what had happened and no one asked. Mum said that he would tell us when he was ready but for now he was safe and that was all that mattered.

'You won't send him back home, will you, Daddy?' I said.

'No, my love, he won't be going home.'

'Will he live here, then?'

'I don't know what will happen but I'm going to see to it that from now on that little boy will be properly looked after.'

'You promise, Daddy?'

'I promise.'

That night Nelson slept in Brenda's room.

'Is he going to live here forever?' said Brenda, snuggling into me.

'I don't think so.'

'Jesus didn't put himself out much, did he?' she whispered.

'Yes he did,' I said. 'He brought Nelson home to us on Christmas Day so that he would be safe and no one would hurt him.'

Chapter Seventeen

Jack, Brenda and me were sitting on the wall watching Nelson get into a black police car. He was wearing his brown jumper again. He looked across at us and gave a sad little smile. Daddy got into the car and sat beside him. I was glad that Nelson wasn't on his own – I knew my daddy would look after him.

'Where are they taking him, Maureen?' said Brenda.

I put my arm around her shoulder. 'I don't know, love.'

'Do *you* know where they're taking him, Jack?' she asked.

Jack looked angry and fierce. 'I don't know, but I'm jolly well going to find out.'

Jack wasn't like a kid. You just knew that he'd find out where Nelson was and that we'd see him again soon. I believed in Jack; I loved Jack.

We watched as the car disappeared down the road, a crowd of kids running after it. Bloody idiots.

'Perhaps they just want to talk to him, then they'll bring him back,' I said hopefully.

'Shouldn't think so,' said Jack. 'I reckon he's for the children's home.'

'What's that?' asked Brenda.

'It's where they take the orphans,' I said.

'Is Nelson an orphan, then?'

'He might as well be,' said Jack.

'What about his mum?' I said.

'Nelson's mum lives in the bottom of a bottle, Maureen.'

Just at that moment Mrs Forrest came out of her front door. Her hair was still in rags and she looked cross. 'Come in, Jack!' she shouted.

'Blimey, what's her problem?' I said.

'Who knows,' said Jack, rolling his eyes. 'Look, I'll see you later, OK? We might know a bit more by then.'

'Jack?'

He turned around. 'Yes?'

'We *will* find him, won't we?'

He stared at me for a moment then said, 'Of course we will.'

'See you later then.'

'See ya, Maureen.'

Me and Brenda sat on the wall, waiting for Daddy to come back.

'I'm cold,' said Brenda.

I was cold as well but my eyes were fixed on the road, waiting to see Daddy coming round the corner.

'Shall we go indoors, then?' said Brenda.

I didn't want to get off the wall but I didn't want Brenda to be cold. 'OK then, we can watch for Daddy out the window.'

We jumped down off the wall and went indoors. There was a lovely fire burning in the grate and it was warm in the room. I looked at the tree that I had once thought so wonderful and I didn't much like it any more. The fag packets looked silly, the silver paper had started to peel off, and you could see the words 'Senior Service' underneath. I thought about the rich little girl who had gone into Wade's and I was pretty sure that she wouldn't have empty fag packets hanging off *her* tree. Rich children got dolls dressed in pink satin and bikes, not bloody fag packets. Then I felt bad inside because I loved my life and I wouldn't swap it for hers, not for anything, and certainly not for a load of glass baubles and candles.

'We've got a lovely tree, haven't we, Maureen?' said Brenda, gazing up at it.

'We've got the best tree in See Saw Lane,' I said, smiling at her.

We waited by the window for a long time and then we saw Daddy walking down the road. He looked upset and worried as he came through the gate. The stubble on his chin looked very dark against his pale face and he didn't have any margarine on his hair so it was sticking up all over the place. I was worried that he'd shut himself in the bedroom but he didn't. 'Would you let me and your mammy have a little chat on our own, girls?' he said, coming into the hall.

Me and Brenda nodded and went and sat on the stairs.

'Is Nelson dead, Maureen?'

'Of course he's not bloody dead, why would you think he's dead?'

'Our old tallyman went in a car like that and then he was dead and they had a funeral.'

'Our old tallyman was in a box! Nelson wasn't in a box, was he?'

Brenda didn't look convinced. 'No,' she said.

'So he's not dead then, is he?'

'Well, our old tallyman was.'

'For heaven's sake, Brenda! Daddy was in that car as well and he's back and he's not dead.'

'I never thought of that.'

'Nelson's not dead,' I said gently. 'Jack is going to find him and then you'll see for yourself. OK?'

We were sat on the stairs for ages. I tried hard to hear what they were saying but I couldn't. Eventually Daddy opened the door and came out. 'You can come in now, girls.'

We went into the front room and sat side by side on the couch. Daddy looked very serious and Mum looked like she'd been crying. I felt Brenda edge closer to me until we were touching. 'Is Nelson dead, Dadda?' she said.

'I keep telling her he's *not* but I don't think she believes me. You don't believe me, do you, Brenda?'

'It's because of the tallyman, Dadda.'

'Brenda saw the tallyman put in a black car and he was dead,' I said.

'That poor man was *old*, Brenda. Nelson is just a child,' said Daddy.

With that, Brenda burst into tears, so Daddy sat between us and put his arms around our shoulders.

I started gabbling. 'Jack says they're going to put Nelson in a children's home because he's an orphan but he's not an orphan, Daddy, he's got a mum who lives in the bottom of a bottle. How can you live in the bottom of a bottle, Daddy?' I said, then I started blubbing, just like Brenda.

Daddy kissed the tops of our heads. 'I think what we all need is a nice hot cup of cocoa, Mummy.'

'I'll do that, Pat,' said Mummy, going into the kitchen.

Daddy took hold of our hands. 'Now, dry those tears and I'll tell you what's happened.'

We dried our eyes and listened.

'Now, the most important thing is that Nelson is safe and being looked after properly. Isn't that what we want for him?'

We both nodded.

'Well, that's what is going to happen. He is going to live somewhere where he will be safe and where no one will ever hurt him again.'

'Did you know that his mum hits him, Daddy? I thought it was his dad but Jack says he hasn't got a dad so it must be his mum.'

'I think Nelson's mum was ill, Maureen. That's what I think.'

'When I had the chicken pox I didn't hit anyone,' said Brenda.

'Is Nelson's mum dead, Daddy?' I said.

'Yes, my love, she is.'

'I thought so,' I said, sadly. 'Does Nelson know?'

'Yes, he does.'

'Did he cry?' I said.

'Yes.'

'Even though she was mean to him?'

'Yes, Maureen, even though she was mean to him. You see, she was still his mum.'

'Did she die in the bottom of that bottle, Daddy?' said Brenda softly.

'I suppose she did, my love. I suppose that's exactly what she did.'

Then Mummy came in with the cocoa and we sat in front of the fire and we thought about Nelson.

That night, in bed, me and Brenda cuddled up together under the blankets.

'Maureen?' said Brenda.

'What?'

'Must have been a bloody big bottle.'

Chapter Eighteen

Me, Jack and Monica were peering through the wrought-iron gates towards the long drive that led up to the house. There was a sign next to the gate that read: 'Home for destitute boys'.

'What exactly does destitute mean?' asked Monica.

'It means kids who have nowhere else to go,' said Jack.

'That would be Nelson then,' I said sadly.

'I'm afraid so,' said Jack.

Jack's dad had gone down to the welfare people and he had no trouble finding out where they'd taken Nelson, probably because he wore a suit and polished his shoes.

The orphanage was in Portslade, just along the coast from Brighton. Me and Monica didn't have the money for the tram, so we'd all walked. We spent Jack's tram fare on a bag of gobstoppers for Nelson. I'd been worried all the way there. I was trying to imagine what an orphanage would look like. All I could think of were two books that Aquinas had read to us. One was called *Oliver Twist* and the other one was *Jane Eyre*; both books had given me nightmares for weeks. Daddy had gone down to the school and told her she should be reading decent Catholic books to us, not filling our heads with horror stories and giving us nightmares. That went down well. Thanks, Daddy!

Anyway, that's what I was imagining but this place didn't look scary at all. The sun shining on the red brick made the building look warm and welcoming and it was surrounded by tall trees and lush green lawns. I was pleased to see that it didn't have rows and rows of windows like the hospital where Daddy had been.

'It doesn't look so bad, does it, Jack?'

'Well, it looks better than the place he came from, that's for sure.'

'But he's not free, is he?' said Monica. 'I'd rather be free and live in a slum.'

Jack looked surprised. 'You're right, Monica,' he said, smiling at her.

I wished I'd said that and not Monica, then Jack would have smiled at *me* and not her.

Jack pushed the gate and it opened easily, so we started to walk up the drive.

'Do you think they'll let us see him?' I said.

'They might not,' said Jack. 'Most people treat kids like they're a load of morons.'

'Which most of them are,' said Monica and Jack smiled at her again.

I was beginning to feel like a spare part. Jack was mine, not bloody Monica's.

'What do *you* think?' said Monica.

I hadn't even heard the question. 'About what?'

'Wake up, sleepy head,' said Jack.

'I *am* awake,' I snapped.

'We were wondering whether to knock on the front door or go round the back. Is something wrong, Maureen?' he asked.

'No, sorry I snapped. I'm just worried, I suppose.'

'I think we all are but we're here now so let's do it.'

'Fighting talk,' I said. I got one of Jack's beautiful smiles and I was happy.

We decided to try the front of the house. Jack rang the bell and we could hear it echoing inside the building. Eventually a man opened the door. He didn't look a bit like Mr Bumble or the headmaster of Lowood School where poor Jane Eyre went.

'And what can I do for you?' he said, smiling down at us.

'We've come to see our friend, sir,' said Jack.

'And what is your friend's name, young man?'

'Nelson Perks.'

'Ah yes, Nelson. I'm sure he'll be delighted to see you. Now, why don't you go down into the grounds and wait for him there and I will send him out to you?'

We thanked him and ran down the slope into the gardens.

'That was easier than I thought it would be,' said Jack.

'He seemed like a nice man,' I said.

'Well, I wish he'd invited us in, I'm freezing,' said Monica.

So was I. The sun was shining but it was only January and there was a cold wind that whipped around my bare legs.

The boy running down the bank towards us didn't look like Nelson at all. He was wearing long grey trousers and a nice navy coat.

'I can't believe you found me,' he said, running up to us.

Me and Monica threw ourselves at him and Jack gave him a playful punch on the arm.

Everything about Nelson was shiny, from his hair down to his boots.

'Look at you, all posh,' said Jack.

'And so clean!' said Monica. Which made us all laugh.

'They've got a thing about cleanliness here,' said Nelson, grinning.

Monica was staring at him.

'What?' he said.

'How did you get so fat? You've only been here a couple of weeks.'

He didn't answer her question but said, 'Let's go for a walk. Away from the house.'

We followed Nelson as he led us across the lawns, through a stone archway and into a rose garden. I could just imagine how beautiful it would be when the roses were in bloom. We all sat down on a wooden bench.

'This is my favourite place,' said Nelson. 'You can be on your own here.'

'You *are* OK though, aren't you?' I said. 'No one's mean to you?'

'I can stick up for myself. Everyone keeps telling me how lucky I am to have ended up here. Some of the boys have been in places that weren't so good.'

I'd never thought of Nelson as being particularly good-looking but seeing him today, with his new clothes, shiny hair and scrubbed face, I thought he looked nice, not as handsome as Jack, but nice. Monica was right though; he had got very fat. The buttons on his coat were straining against the navy material.

'I guess the food's good then?' I said, looking at his tummy.

Nelson laughed, put his hands inside his coat and pulled out his old brown jumper.

'Will you look after this for me, Maureen? They threw away all the clothes I arrived in. I managed to rescue this out of the bin.'

He handed it to me. There were more holes in it than wool; I could see why they threw it away. 'Of course I'll look after it,' I said.

'Thanks, Maureen.'

We sat quietly on the bench, just happy to all be together again.

'I'm sorry about your mum,' said Jack, breaking the silence.

'She wasn't well,' said Nelson.

'I know she wasn't,' replied Jack, softly.

'She'll be better now.'

'Course she will,' said Jack. 'And you've still got us, mate.'

Nelson smiled around at us. 'I can't believe you came.'

'You didn't think we'd leave you here on your own, did you?' I said, linking my arm through his.

'I didn't know what to think. I just had to do what they said I should do and go where they said I should go. No one asked for my opinion, I just had to do what they said.

'I was sent here and I didn't know anyone and I missed you lot and my house and my mum.'

Tears were now running down his face and he wiped them away with the sleeve of his new coat.

'Haven't you got any relatives at all? Someone who would take you in?' said Jack.

'That's what they kept asking me but I don't think I have. It's always been just me and Mum.'

'Well, you'll always have us and we'll come and see you every week. Do you think they'd let you come out with us on Saturday?'

'Not without an adult, it's one of the rules.'

'My dad'll come here with us,' I said. 'Then we can spend the day together.'

Nelson grinned. 'That'd be great.'

We could hear a bell ringing in the distance.

'I've got to go in for my tea.'

We walked back to the house and said our goodbyes.

'Don't let anyone wash my jumper, Maureen. It's likely to fall apart.'

'I won't, but I'm sure my Aunty Marge can patch up the holes.'

'Thanks, Maureen, but I'd rather have it the way it is.'

'Fair enough.'

'We'll see you next Saturday then,' said Jack. 'And Maureen will bring her dad along.'

'That'll be great,' he said, smiling at us. 'By the way, Maureen, where's Brenda?'

'Daddy said that it would be too far for her to walk.'

'Say hello to her for me.'

'I will.'

We watched him go back into the house and then we started walking back down the drive. I held his brown jumper close to my heart.

Chapter Nineteen

One of Mum's rich ladies said she wasn't needed any more so she was crashing and banging around the kitchen.

'And not so much as a thank for all those bloody years I cleaned up after her ungrateful children and smarmy husband!' she yelled, nearly taking the hinges off one of the doors. 'Never a birthday card or a Christmas card in all that time, miserable cow! She made me feel as if she was doing me a favour, letting me clean for her.'

'Who's going to clean for her now, Mummy?' I asked.

'Some fourteen-year-old strip of a girl straight out of school that will only cost her pennies.'

'I could leave school, Mum. I could. I could leave school and get a job.'

'You're not even twelve yet, Maureen. Me and your dad want you stay on till you're fourteen.'

She stopped crashing around and smiled at me. 'Look,' she said softly. 'I don't want you worrying, we'll manage. Brighton is full of rich ladies, I was just letting off a bit of steam. I want you to learn all you can at school, I don't want you out working until you have to. Childhood is short enough as it is.'

'Maybe Uncle John and Aunty Marge would let me help out on the stall.'

'I think your daddy likes to do that when he can.'

'Is Daddy alright?'

'He's not great, love.'

Daddy had been my normal daddy for so long now that I'd almost forgotten that I had two other daddies. Now he was acting funny again and it was making me feel bad inside. The house had a feeling about it when Daddy was ill. You could sense it as soon as you walked through the door, you just knew that your normal daddy was gone and there was a different one in his place. When me and Brenda came home from school we didn't know which one would be there.

I'd asked Daddy if he would come to the orphanage with us to take Nelson out for the day and he'd said, 'Of course I will, it will be like a rescue mission. We'll rescue Nelson and run away with him.'

'He has to be back in time for his tea, Daddy.'

'Then we'll rescue him until teatime. How about that?'

'That would be great,' I'd said.

And now it was nearly Saturday and Daddy had been shut in the bedroom since Sunday and we wouldn't be able to rescue Nelson at all.

Me and Monica and Brenda were sitting on the field at the end of the road. It was chilly and the three of us were wrapped up in warm coats, scarves and gloves. There was a group of boys kicking a ball around. They were wearing short trousers and thin shirts; their little bony knees were all scratched and muddy.

'I don't think boys feel the cold like girls do,' I said.

'That's cos they're thick,' said Monica, grinning. 'The cold can't get through.'

'Jack's not thick,' I said.

'You wouldn't notice if he was,' said Monica.

'Wouldn't I?'

'It's because she loves him,' said Brenda. 'You do, don't you, Maureen? You love Jack.'

All of a sudden Monica pointed across the field. 'That's your dad, isn't it?' she said.

My heart gave a lurch as I looked over at the boys playing football. There was my dad in the middle of them, wrestling the

ball away from them and dashing down the field with them all
running after him. They were laughing and pointing and making
fun of him. I wanted the ground to open up and swallow me.

'Do you want to go home?' asked Monica, softly.

I was staring at Daddy as he continued to make a fool of himself, running round and round the field with the boys running
after him. Mum was at work so it was up to me to do something.

Brenda had gone very quiet. I took her hand. 'It's OK,' I said,
'Daddy's just having fun with the boys.'

She looked up at me. 'Is he?' she said doubtfully.

'Yes. Look how fast he can run.'

Brenda smiled. 'He can run faster than any of them, can't he,
Maureen?'

'He can. Now I want you to go home with Monica and I'll
wait for Daddy.'

But Brenda was looking worried again. 'Why must I go home?'

'Because it's bloody cold, that's why.'

'You won't be long, will you?' she said.

'Nope. I'll just wait until Daddy's finished playing football
and I'll be home.'

I mouthed 'Thanks' to Monica and I watched them both walk
across the field. Brenda looked back at me and I gave her the biggest grin I could manage.

I had never seen Daddy do this before – he usually stayed in
the house when he was bonkers. But then I didn't know what he
was doing when I was at school and Mammy didn't know what
he was doing either because she was at work.

I didn't know what to do; I was a child, I wasn't a grown-up.
Mum could always calm him down but I'd never managed to.
Usually I took Brenda out of the way and hoped that he'd be
calmer when we got back. But Mummy wasn't here.

I started to walk towards the boys. One minute I was walking
towards them all and the next minute I was flat on the ground

and I could hardly breathe. I'd got in Daddy's way as he tore after the ball. Daddy was down on his knees beside me, stroking my face and crying, 'Sorry, I'm sorry, I'm sorry.' It was as if something had switched in his brain and made him normal again. He helped me to my feet and brushed the grass off my coat. Then he put his arms around me and held me tightly against him. I loved him and I hated him and I clung to him and I wanted to run away from him. The boys weren't laughing any more and they drifted away from us.

'It's alright, Daddy,' I said. 'It's alright.'

He shook his head from side to side as if he was trying to clear it. 'Oh, Maureen,' he said sadly, 'my little Maureen.'

'It was my fault, Daddy, I got in the way.'

He took my face gently in his hands. 'It will *never* be your fault. Don't ever think that it is your fault.'

Suddenly I felt at peace and all the worry and sadness seemed to leave me. The boys must still have been on the field but all I could hear was the soft rustling of the wind as it blew gently through the trees. I leaned into him and I felt his heart beating beneath his coat. It felt as if we were alone in the world and I wanted to stay in his arms forever and never let him go. I wasn't afraid any more. I knew in that moment that I only had one daddy and the other two were just another part of him. I wished that I could hold him forever and keep him safe forever. I wished that I could wrap this moment up and keep it in my pocket. I loved my daddy; I always would.

Chapter Twenty

As it turned out, I ended up going to see Nelson on my own. Daddy was getting better but he was very quiet and had taken to going for long walks on the Downs. Mummy preferred it if one of us went with him and today Brenda was going. Monica had to look after her little brother Archie and Jack had to stay indoors and study for some stupid school exam. I knew that Nelson would be looking forward to going out for the day, so someone had to go and see him and explain, besides which I missed Nelson a lot.

The walk to the orphanage seemed even longer than the last time because I had no one to talk to. I thought that I'd never bloody get there. By the time I arrived at the gates I was exhausted. I pushed them open and they moved easily just like the last time. It had been threatening to rain all morning so I hoped they'd still let Nelson out into the gardens.

I rang the doorbell and waited. It was opened by a miserable-looking woman and not the friendly man that had come to the door the last time.

'What?' she barked.

'I've come to see Nelson Perks,' I said.

'Well, you can't,' she said abruptly and started to close the door. I stuck my foot out so she couldn't close it.

'Yes I can,' I said. 'It's all arranged. He was supposed to coming out with me and my dad today.'

'Well, I can't see no dad,' she said, smirking.

'He wasn't well enough to come.'

'He can't go out without an adult, it's the rules.'

'Well, there's no rule about spending time with him in the garden.'

'You've got too much lip,' she said.

And you've got too much belly, I thought.

Just then Nelson appeared behind her. 'Hi, Maureen.'

'This woman says you can't come out.'

Nelson pushed past her, caught hold of my hand and together we ran down into the grounds, laughing. We could hear her yelling behind us. 'Come back here at once, Nelson Perks!' Once we were clear of the house we slowed down and began walking towards the rose garden. We went through the stone arch and sat on the bench.

'Blimey, who's she? She's awful,' I said.

'Nobody takes any notice of her. Mr Farley, the head, is out for the day and she thinks she's in charge.'

'Won't you get into trouble?'

'I'm already locked up, what else can she do?'

'My dad couldn't come,' I said. 'So we can't go out for the day. I'm really sorry.'

'You came and that's all that matters. How are the others?' said Nelson.

'Monica had to look after Archie, Jack has to study for an exam and Brenda's gone for a walk with Daddy.'

'Thanks for coming all that way on your own.'

'No problem, it's nice to see you.'

It was very peaceful in the garden and we were happy to just sit quietly on the bench. Nelson looked very clean and tidy again. I had always thought that his hair was dark brown but it was actually quite fair. I suppose it had never been washed before. It made me wonder again why Jack's mum allowed him to be Jack's friend. I found that really odd, given how stuck-up she was.

'I never thanked you properly for looking after me at Christmas, Maureen,' said Nelson suddenly. 'I never thanked your mum either.'

'You didn't have to. Mum was just happy to take care of you. We were all happy to take care of you. She knew that you were grateful.'

'That's OK then. It's been worrying me.'

I touched his arm. 'I'm sorry your mum died, Nelson.'

He got up from the bench and knelt down beside the dying roses. He was quiet for a while, pulling up weeds, patting the ground around the plants and smoothing it down with his hands. 'I don't think she loved me,' he said, almost to himself.

He had his back to me. I noticed how thin his little shoulders were and I had this sudden urge to hold him and take care of him. I couldn't imagine what it must be like not to be loved. Me and Brenda had always been loved.

'I'm sure she loved you, Nelson. Daddy said she wasn't well.'

He stood up and faced me. 'Well, I don't think she loved me, Maureen. I don't even think she liked me very much. If she'd liked me she wouldn't have kept on hurting me, would she? You don't keep hurting someone you like. I think that people keep telling me she did it because she was ill because they don't know what else to say to me. Your dad's not well, is he? But he doesn't use you as a punchbag. Because that's what she did to me, Maureen. She used me like a bloody punchbag and I'm supposed to forgive her because she wasn't well.'

I walked towards him and took his two hands in mine. 'You don't have to forgive her, Nelson, you can hate her as much as you like. She was a rotten mother and she didn't deserve you. So go ahead, Nelson, you hate her as much as you bloody well like.'

Me and Nelson held hands as he yelled, 'I hate you, Mum!'

'Tell her why,' I said.

He took a deep breath and shouted: 'I hate you for hitting me.'

Then I joined in: 'And I hate you for not feeding him properly.'

'And I hate you for selling my books to buy booze!' yelled Nelson.

'And I hate you for sending him out in the snow without warm clothes on.'

'And I hate you, I hate you, I hate you!'

There were tears rolling down his face. I put my arm around his shoulder. 'Did that make you feel any better?'

He sniffed and wiped his nose on the sleeve of his good coat. 'A bit,' he said sadly.

We both sat down on the grass. It was damp and cold but we didn't care.

'I should have bought you a hankie for Christmas. You're going to ruin that coat, always wiping your nose on it.'

Nelson smiled at me and that was good.

'Was she *ever* kind to you?' I said.

He was quiet for a while, then he said, 'She bought me a comic once.'

'Did you hate her the day she bought you the comic?'

'I think I loved her that day, because she bought me a comic when she could have bought booze.'

'Tell her,' I said gently.

'Thanks for the comic, Mum!' he shouted up to the sky.

'Thank you for buying Nelson a comic,' I said, 'when you could have bought booze.'

'Can you think of any other time that she was kind to you?'

'She brought home a little kitten once. We called it Rabbit.'

'You called a kitten Rabbit? Why would you do that?'

'Someone gave it to her when she was drunk. He told her it was a rabbit and she believed him. So that's what we called it.'

'What happened to it?'

'It got squashed.'

'I'll light a candle for Rabbit next time I'm in church.'

'Thanks, Maureen, you're a good friend.'

'How do you feel now, Nelson?'

'Better. I'd forgotten the times that she was nice to me.'

'I bet there were lots of times that she was nice to you. Maybe try remembering those things instead of just the bad things.'

'I will,' said Nelson, smiling.

'My mum says that she believes there is good in everyone – you just have to look for it. Now, how about we thank her for Rabbit?'

We held hands and yelled: 'Thanks for Rabbit!'

We were laughing as we sat back down on the bench.

'I've got something for you, Maureen,' he said, putting his hand into his pocket. 'I made it in Woodwork.'

He handed me a piece of wood. 'It's a ruler. Look,' he said, 'I've marked in all the inches and then I varnished it.'

I ran my hand across the smooth wood. 'It's perfect, Nelson,' I said. 'I don't have a ruler, I can take it to school.' And then I kissed his cheek and he went red and scratched behind his ear.

'I'm glad you like it, Maureen,' he said and shyly kissed me back.

As I was walking home, I thought about my friend Nelson and I thought about how I had kissed him on the cheek and how he'd kissed me back. And I remembered how he smelled. My good friend Nelson smelled of strawberry jam and lemons.

Chapter Twenty-One

The next Saturday Daddy was well enough to come to the orphanage with us and rescue Nelson for the day. As we walked towards the big house we could see him sitting on the steps leading up to the front door, the nice man sitting next to him.

Nelson ran to us, grinning, and Daddy went over to the man and shook his hand.

'Have a great day, Nelson,' said the man.

'Thanks, Mr Farley,' said Nelson. 'Get me out of here,' he whispered to us.

We hurried down the drive and made our way down Boundary Road towards the sea.

When we got the beach Daddy said, 'Now I'm going to leave you and I'll meet you back at the lagoon at five o'clock, will that do?'

'Where are you going, Dadda?' asked Brenda, looking anxious.

It bothered me that Brenda was becoming as worried about Daddy as I was. I suppose she was getting older and realising that there was something not quite right with her Dadda. I didn't want her to feel like that. She was just a little girl, she shouldn't be carrying that fear on her shoulders.

'Daddy will be fine,' I said to her. 'Won't you, Daddy, you'll be fine?'

'Of course I will,' he said, smiling.

We'd started to walk away when Daddy called me back. He knelt down on the ground so that he was on my level and he put his arms around me. 'You know how much I love you, don't you?'

'Yes, Daddy, I know,' I said.

He touched my face. 'You're such a good girl,' he said. 'Take care of your sister, won't you?'

'I always take care of her, Daddy,' I said.

I looked into his face; he looked sad. Was he my normal daddy today? I thought he was, I hoped he was, but I started to feel bad in my tummy and then he smiled, a big smile that made me happy again.

'Now go and have a lovely time with your friends,' he said.

'See you later,' I said.

I started to walk away, then I looked back at him. He was still smiling.

'Bye-bye, sweet face,' he said.

'Bye-bye, Daddy,' I said and I ran to join the others.

We all climbed the stone wall and slid down onto the pebbles.

'Can I paddle, Maureen?' said Brenda.

'Course you can. Tuck your skirt in your knickers. It's going to be freezing though.'

'I don't mind.'

Brenda took off her shoes and socks and placed them neatly side by side on the pebbles. It really hurt to walk on them when you didn't have any shoes or socks on.

'Get on my back, Brenda,' said Jack. 'I'll carry you.'

'Thanks, Jack,' she said and jumped up onto his back.

Nelson followed them down to the water's edge and me and Monica sat on the old wooden groyne, swinging our legs.

'Nelson looks good, doesn't he?' said Monica. 'Do you think he's happy there, Maureen?'

'I think he's as happy as he can be,' I said. 'At least he's being looked after properly and he's getting proper food. I hate to think of all the times he must have been hungry and none of us knew.'

'I expect Jack knew.'

'Yes.'

The wooden groyne felt damp and slimy beneath us and I hoped it wasn't going to ruin my dress. I watched Jack and Nelson skimming stones into the sea. They were having a good time and Nelson looked happy to be with his friend.

'Why do you think Jack's mum allows him be friends with Nelson?' I said.

'I've often wondered that. Why don't you ask Jack?' said Monica.

'I might one of these days.'

There was a cold wind blowing off the sea, chopping at the grey water and tipping the waves with white foam. I hoped it wasn't too cold for Brenda. I didn't want her going down with anything.

How long do you think they'll keep him there?' said Monica.

'I don't know. He's thirteen now, I don't suppose they'll keep him much after fourteen when he leaves school.'

'And then where will he go?'

'God knows,' I said. 'It's all pretty worrying, cos he hasn't *got* anywhere to go.'

'Has he got a dad?'

'Well, if he has, he's never mentioned him.'

'Because if he had a dad he could live with *him*, couldn't he?'

'His dad might be worse than his mum.'

'I never thought of that,' said Monica.

I could see Brenda waving to us.

'Fancy a paddle?' I said to Monica.

'It looks bloody freezing in there,' she said.

'Come on, Miss Wimp,' I said, grinning.

We jumped down onto the pebbles and joined the others at the edge of the sea. Both the boys had rolled their trousers up and waded into the water. Looking at Nelson, so small and thin next to Jack, it was hard to believe that he would be going out to work in a year. Me and Monica had always tucked our dresses into our knickers but suddenly we didn't want to. We were too big to do that any more, especially in front of the boys.

We stepped gingerly into the sea and Monica immediately jumped out again.

'Bloody hell, it's like stepping into a load of ice!' she said, shivering.

Brenda was happily splashing about and didn't seem at all bothered about the cold.

'Brenda, I think you should come out of the water, I don't want you getting a chill,' I said.

'Two more minutes?' she said, smiling.

'Just two then. Me and Monica are going to sit up by the wall.'

'I'm hungry,' said Monica as we walked up the beach.

'Me too,' I said.

'I don't suppose you've got any money, have you?'

'Not a bean,' I said.

'We'll just have to starve then.'

'I suppose so,' I said.

We sat against the wall and watched the others messing about in the sea. It was a bit more sheltered by the wall but it was still really cold. The sky and the water looked grey and uninviting.

'Now I'm starving hungry *and* freezing cold,' said Monica. 'I think we should start walking, it might warm us up a bit.'

Just then Jack came walking towards us up the beach with Brenda on his back and Nelson following behind.

'We're cold and hungry,' said Monica.

'I can't do anything about the cold,' said Jack, bending down to let Brenda slide off his back. 'But I can treat us all to chips.'

'Yeah, chips!' cried Brenda.

'Let me dry you first.'

I dried Brenda's feet and legs with my petticoat and then she put on her shoes and socks.

'Chips it is then,' said Jack.

We climbed back onto the promenade and started walking. It was warmer up there and it helped that we were on the move.

'There's a chip shop just past the beach huts,' said Jack.

We hurried along the prom, looking forward to eating the chips. As we got closer to the shop we could smell the vinegar. Brenda, Monica and I sat on the steps leading down to the pebbles and waited for Jack and Nelson to get the chips. Thank God for Jack, he was the only one of us that ever had any money and he always shared whatever he had with the rest of us. When me and Jack got married, we would never be poor because Jack was going to be doctor, then we could make sure that all our friends and family would never be skint again and we could eat fish and chips every day if we wanted to.

Jack and Nelson came back with a bag of chips for each of us and we dived into them. They tasted lovely and vinegary and salty.

'I could eat this forever,' said Brenda, her mouth full of chips. 'I could, Maureen. I could eat this forever.'

I smiled at her. 'Me too,' I said. 'Thanks, Jack.'

'Yes, thanks, Jack,' said the others.

We all felt warmer now our tummies were full of chips.

We walked all the way along the seafront to the West Pier. There weren't many people on the beach but there were quite a few walking along the seafront, taking in the sea air. It was starting to get dark, so we turned around and headed back to the lagoon where we were to meet Daddy.

Five o clock came and went but there was no sign of him and we didn't know what to do. Nelson had to get back to the home for his tea, they might not let him out again if he was late. We waited until six o clock but Daddy didn't come.

Chapter Twenty-Two

We didn't know what to do. I didn't want to leave the lagoon in case Daddy came but it was dark and it was cold; we couldn't stay there all night.

Then Jack took charge. 'Can you get back on your own, Nelson?' he said.

Nelson shook his head. 'I'm not going anywhere until I find out what's happened to Maureen's dad.'

I was worried sick. Did we get the time wrong? 'He *did* say five, didn't he?' I said to the others.

They all nodded.

'I think we should get home,' said Jack.

Brenda started to cry. 'Where's Dada?'

'I don't know, love,' I said.

'Let's go,' said Jack.

Monica put her arm around Brenda's shoulder. 'He'll be OK,' she said gently. 'He must have just forgotten.'

But I knew he hadn't forgotten. Daddy wouldn't forget us. Even if he was sad, he wouldn't forget us. Even if he was bouncing off the ceiling, he wouldn't forget us.

It was miles to See Saw Lane and it was going to take ages to get home. I had to get home, I had to find Daddy.

'I've got an idea,' I said.

We ran along the seafront until we got to the big white house. I pushed open the gate and started to walk up the drive with the others following behind me.

'What are you doing?' said Jack.

I rang the doorbell and, thank God, it was the nice lady who came to the door and not her horrible husband.

'Hello,' she said. 'Can I help you?'

Brenda was still crying.

'You're the little girls who had the dolls' pram, aren't you?' she said.

'Yes, we are,' I said. 'And now we need help.'

She opened the door wider. 'Come in,' she said, looking concerned.

We hesitated at the door, then stepped into the hallway. It was full of light and mirrors and soft cream carpets.

'Can you tell me what's wrong?' she asked gently.

I tried to speak. 'My daddy…' I started.

'Take your time, darling,' she said.

I took a deep breath and tried again. I could feel my eyes filling with tears. 'He didn't come, he said he'd come, but he didn't come.'

The lady put her arm around my shoulder and gently guided me into a room just off the hallway. I'd never seen anything like it in the whole of my life. A beautiful chandelier hung from the ceiling, casting a golden glow across the pale sofas and glass tables. I looked at the others standing in a huddle just inside the doorway. It was like stepping into another world but this wasn't our world, this would never be our world.

This world was perfect and we were spoiling it. We were dirty and we were poor, and we didn't belong here; we would never belong here.

The lady eased me down onto one of the soft velvet sofas. I could feel my petticoat damp against my bare legs and I knew that my skirt was dirty from sitting on the groyne. I started to stand up. I felt embarrassed, I couldn't sit there.

'My skirt,' I began, 'it's dirty.'

'Sit down, darling,' she said, smiling kindly.

I sat down and stared at my dirty old shoes. I felt worthless and stupid and out of place; I should never have come here.

The lady was kneeling down in front of me now. 'You said you needed my help, please tell me what I can do to help you.'

Jack walked across to where I was sitting. 'We need to get home quickly,' he said. 'We think Maureen and Brenda's dad is in trouble. We don't have the tram fare to get home. We can pay you back,' he added quickly.

'Don't worry about that,' said the lady.

Just then the lady's horrible husband came into the room. 'What's all this?' he demanded.

I looked up at him. 'We're not tinkers,' I said, 'we're proper people.'

'Of course you are,' said the nice lady, glaring at her husband. 'These children need our help, Peter. I want you to get the car out and take them home.'

You could see he wasn't happy.

'Right now, Peter,' said the lady.

'I'll get my coat,' he said.

We waited for him to get his coat and then back the car out of the garage.

The lady put her arms around me. 'Come back and let me know that everything is alright, won't you?'

I hugged her. 'I will, and thank you.'

'My name's Mrs Bentley.'

'Maureen O'Connell,' I said.

'I'll see you again, Maureen, and try not to worry. I'm sure your daddy will be fine.'

We all climbed into the car. Jack sat in the front with Mr Bentley and the rest of us sat in the back. The car had soft leather seats and it smelled lovely. At any other time we would have been excited. Me and Brenda had never been in a car before and I was pretty sure that Monica hadn't either.

I stared out of the window into the darkness and I prayed. *Dear God and the Blessed Virgin Mary and all the angels, please let my daddy be alright. Please don't let anything bad happen to him. Please, please don't let anything bad happen to him.*

Chapter Twenty-Three

Mr Bentley took us as far as the alleyway. As soon as the car stopped, I jumped out and started running. I was halfway down the alley when a group of boys from the estate came running towards me.

'It's her!' one of them shouted.

I tried to pass them but they had formed a circle around me.

One of the boys came very close to me, almost touching my face, and then, very slowly, he said, 'Your dad's topped himself.'

'No he hasn't!' I screamed.

'Yes he has,' sneered the boy. 'He's topped himself. Slit his wrists he has, there's blood runnin' all down the walls.'

'You're a liar!' I screamed. 'You're a liar, you're a bloody liar!'

I pushed him to the ground and started hitting him. 'You take that back, you bloody take that back!' I wanted to kill him. He was trying to defend himself but I was strong; I was stronger than I had ever been. I could hear screaming but I wasn't going to stop, and then someone was pulling at my arms and dragging me off him: it was Jack.

The boy's nose was all bloody and he was crying. 'I'm gonna tell on you, Maureen O'Connell,' he snivelled.

Jack pulled him roughly off the ground. 'Clear off, you idiots, or you'll have me to deal with.'

I yanked myself away from Jack and started running again. I could hear the others running behind me. As soon as I turned the corner into See Saw Lane I saw the ambulance and the police car. Someone was screaming in my head: *Don't be dead, Daddy. Don't be dead, Daddy. Don't be dead, Daddy. Don't be dead, Daddy.*

There was a policeman standing at my gate. I tried to get past him but he was big and wide and I couldn't see anything. 'Where's my daddy?' I screamed. 'Where's my daddy?'

'You can't come in here, love,' said the policeman gently.

I was pulling at him. 'I *have* to see my daddy, please let me see my daddy.'

'Is someone with this child?' said the policeman, looking around.

'I am,' said Jack. 'I'll take her into my house.'

'I'm not going anywhere until I see Daddy!' I screamed.

Jack had his arms around me, my head was pressed against his chest and I could feel his heart beating beneath his coat. He held me away from him.

'Brenda needs you, Maureen,' he said gently.

'Brenda?' I said.

'Yes,' said Jack. 'She needs you.'

I looked around and saw Brenda and Monica sitting on the ground. I walked over to Brenda and gently lifted her up. There were tears pouring down her cheeks and she was shaking.

'It's alright, love,' I said, taking off my coat and wrapping it around her.

She looked up at me.

'Dadda?'

'We're going to go into Jack's house, Brenda. That's what we're going to do now.'

'Is Dadda going to the hospital, Maureen?' said Brenda.

I didn't know what to say to her because I knew that Daddy wasn't going to the hospital, I knew that my daddy was gone.

'We have to go into Jack's house now, Brenda.'

'OK,' she said.

Monica stood up. 'Oh, Maureen,' she said.

'You go home, Monica,' I said sadly.

'Will you be alright?'

I shook my head; I knew that I would never be alright.

'Your lovely daddy,' she said and kissed my cheek.

I held Brenda's hand and we all walked up the path and into Jack's house. Aunty Marge was sitting on a couch in Jack's front room with her arms around Mum, who was bent over with her head in her hands. Aunty Marge was sobbing. She came over to us, shaking her head.

'My poor babies,' she said, hugging us both.

Brenda went over to Mum, needing comfort, but Mum didn't touch her, she didn't even look at her. Aunty Marge gently guided her away and brought her back to me.

'Your mum's not very well, Brenda,' she said.

I hadn't sat down; I was still standing just inside the door to the front room.

I felt a hand slip into mine: it was Nelson.

Mrs Forrest came into the room carrying a tray of tea.

'Do you want some tea, Maureen?' said Nelson.

I looked at Nelson. I had so much pain inside me that I couldn't speak – I didn't think that I would ever speak again, or feel again or do anything again.

I looked around the room; it seemed to be full of people. Uncle John, Uncle Fred, Aunty Vera, bloody Malcolm, a policeman and a policewoman. I didn't want to be here. They were all staring at me. I felt too big standing there against the wall, my body felt as though it were swelling with all the pain that was inside it. I wanted them to stop looking at me; I wanted to be invisible. I wanted to be with my daddy.

I looked at my mum sitting there, staring into space, and I looked at Brenda, clinging onto Aunty Marge, and I felt a heaviness settle itself on my shoulders.

'Look after your sister,' Daddy had said. 'Bye-bye, sweet face,' he'd said.

He knew that he wasn't going to come back to the lagoon; he knew that he was never going to see us again. 'Look after your sister,' he'd said. 'Bye-bye, sweet face.' Had I said goodbye to him? I wasn't sure. I was angry, I had never been so angry. If I'd known he was going to bloody top himself, I would have said goodbye. In that moment I hated him. I hated him for leaving me; I hated him for not loving me enough to stay.

'Sorry for your trouble,' someone said.

I looked up. Aunty Vera was standing in front of me.

'What are you doing here?' I said, glaring at her.

'Now, Maureen,' said Aunty Marge gently.

'She's only come here to gawp. She didn't even like my daddy and I don't bloody like her, so she can bugger off home and she can take that fat lump of humanity that she managed to push out with her!'

Aunty Vera stared at me with her beady little eyes. 'You're not a nice girl, Maureen O'Connell, you never were. You and your wonderful daddy! Well, he's not so wonderful now, is he? He turned out to be the coward I always knew he was.'

Aunty Marge walked across to us. 'You've said enough, Vera Butterworth. You were a mean, spiteful child and you've turned into a mean, spiteful woman. Now do as Maureen says and bugger off!'

Aunty Vera was red in the face. 'Fred,' she shouted across the room, 'we're going home! I'm not staying where I'm not wanted.' And she flounced out of the room with Uncle Fred and Malcolm running behind her.

Aunty Marge put her arms around me. 'She's wrong about your dad, Maureen. He was never a coward, he was one of the nicest and kindest men I ever knew and he loved you and Brenda so much.'

'Why did he leave us if he loved us so much? Why did he do that, Aunty Marge?'

'Your daddy would have stayed if he could. Don't be angry with him, my love. And don't you take any notice of your Aunty

Vera, she's always been jealous of your mum, that's what that was all about.'

'I hate her, Aunty Marge. I do, I hate her.'

'She's more to be pitied than hated, my love.'

Brenda was standing in front of me, tears streaming down her face. 'I've gone and wet meself, Maureen,' she said. 'I've gone and wet meself on Jack's carpet.'

I smoothed her hair out of her eyes. 'It's OK, love.'

'It's gone into my socks and shoes, Maureen, and me knickers are soaking wet.'

I took hold of her hand, walked her across the room and knelt down beside Mum. 'Brenda needs you,' I said.

Mum didn't move.

I shook her arm. 'You have to look after Brenda, Mum. She's wet herself, you have to look after her.'

'Brenda?' said Mum, looking at me.

'Yes, Brenda. Someone has to go next door and get her some dry clothes. You have to ask someone to go next door.'

Something seemed to click in Mum. She looked at me properly, as if she was seeing me for the first time. 'Of course, yes of course, I'll ask Uncle John.' Then she took us both in her arms and held us tightly against her. She didn't smell the way she usually smelled, maybe sadness has its own smell. I wondered if I smelled of sadness as well.

'I peed on Jack's rug, Mum,' said Brenda, looking up.

Mum smiled sadly at her. 'Don't you worry about that, pet,' she said.

I could see Jack looking at me from across the room. He walked over. 'Do you want to go outside?'

I nodded and let him lead me out of the room, through the kitchen and into the dark night. Nelson followed us.

We walked to the end of the garden and sat on a bench. Jack put his arm around me and I leaned against him. It was better out here. I could pretend that nothing was wrong, that my daddy hadn't topped himself. I looked up at the sky; it was pitch-black and full of stars.

'I bet your dad's looking down on you, Maureen,' said Nelson softly. 'He'll be the brightest star up there.'

'Will he?' I said.

'I talk to my mum when the sky's full of stars.'

'Do you?'

Nelson nodded. 'We get on better now. I don't think there's any booze in Heaven.'

'I'm glad, Nelson. Won't the home be wondering where you are?' I said.

'Jack's dad let them know – I'm staying here tonight with Jack. Where are you going to stay, Maureen?'

'At home, I suppose.'

'Won't you be scared?'

'The worst thing in the world has happened, Nelson. My daddy's dead, nothing could ever be as bad as that. I'm not scared to go back home because I think that's where he is.'

Nelson put his hand on his heart. 'My mum's in here and that's where your dad will always be.'

We sat quietly together on the bench. It was comforting to sit there with my two friends beside me. I could see lights on in my house; it seemed odd that strangers were in there. I wondered if someone had cleaned the blood off the walls. I could see the shadow of my tree over the fence and I could hear Daddy saying, 'Is that two little birds up in that tree, or is it my angels?'

It's your angels, Daddy. It's your two little angels.

Chapter Twenty-Four

A light had gone out of my life and nothing would ever be the same again. I wanted to cry but I couldn't – I hadn't cried since the night Daddy died. Mum was crying all the time, so was Brenda, and I was trying to be strong for them but I didn't feel strong, I didn't feel anything. I felt so empty, there was this big hole inside me that couldn't be filled. I ached for my daddy, I wanted him back; I wanted to go back to a time when we were happy. Pushing Brenda along the seafront in the squeaky pushchair, skimming stones on the sea, running across the Downs, tumbling in the grass, feeling his arms around me. I knew that if I started to cry I would never stop, so I kept everything inside. I was finding it harder and harder to picture Daddy's lovely face. At night in bed I concentrated really hard. I remembered bits of him, like his eyes and his smile. I could smell the margarine that he smoothed on his hair but I could never find the whole of him; I could never put all the bits together. I didn't even have a photo to look at because we had never owned a camera, only rich people had cameras.

Mostly people were kind but they never knew what to say to us. They touched my arm and ruffled Brenda's hair. Some people said, 'I'm sorry for your trouble.' Of course there were the nosy old biddies on the estate that pretended to care but really just wanted me to tell them all the gory details. I told them to bugger off.

The last of the rich ladies sent Mum home because she was upsetting the children with all her crying, so that was the end of the rich ladies and Mum didn't have a job. I didn't know what to do, because there was no money to pay the rent or buy food. If something didn't happen soon, me and Brenda would end up in an orphanage, just like Nelson. Aunty Marge and Uncle John helped as much as they could but they didn't have much themselves. Aunty Vera and Uncle Fred were the only ones with the money and we hadn't seen sight nor sound of them since we chucked them out of Jack's house. Not that any of us wanted their rotten money.

Early one morning, while it was still dark, I shook Brenda awake and told her to get ready for school.

'But it's the middle of the night, Maureen,' she said sleepily.

'There's no money for the tram fare, we're going to have to walk.'

I desperately needed to get out of the house. Mom just sat around crying and staring at the walls. She didn't cook or wash our clothes. There were times when I thought that we might be better off in an orphanage because at least we'd get to eat. I was racking my brains trying to think of a way to make Mum wake up and start looking after us. Funnily enough, it was old Aquinas that made that happen.

I was called out of an English lesson and told that I was to go at once to Aquinas's office.

'What does she want?' said Monica, looking worried.

'I'm about to find out,' I said.

When I got there Brenda was already standing in front of the old bat's desk, looking terrified. I smiled reassuringly at her and held her hand.

'Right,' said Aquinas, standing up and glaring at us. 'It has come to my attention that your father is dead. Is that right?'

'Yes, Sister,' I said.

'And not only is he dead but he took his own life?'

There was not a spark of sympathy in those spiteful eyes. I could feel Brenda shaking beside me.

'So what have you got to say for yourself, Maureen O'Connell?'

'Nothing, Sister.'

'Nothing, Sister,' she mimicked in a sing-song voice.

I was confused. What the bloody hell did she expect me to say?

Aquinas was going red in the face, as if she couldn't get all that nastiness out of her mouth quick enough.

'The reason you have nothing to say, Maureen O'Connell, is because of your shame.'

I stared at her and said quietly, 'I have nothing to be ashamed of, Sister.'

'How dare you stand there, as brazen as you like, Maureen O'Connell, knowing your father has sinned against God. Your father has driven a knife into the very heart of our Divine Saviour.'

'When did he do that, Maureen?' asked Brenda, looking up at me with tears in her eyes.

'He didn't, Brenda, she's talking out of the back of her head.'

Aquinas slammed her hand down on the desk. 'Your father died in a state of mortal sin and he will burn in the fires of Hell for all eternity!' she screamed.

I could see the sweat running down her ugly fat face and disappearing into her wimple.

'No he won't!' yelled Brenda. 'My dada is with the angels in Heaven, isn't he, Maureen? Dada's with the angels?'

'Of course he is,' I said.

Aquinas reached into her drawer and took out a long ruler. 'The sins of the father will be visited on the children,' she said, advancing towards Brenda.

Before I could stop her she'd whacked Brenda across the backs of her legs. Poor Brenda squealed and tried to get away from her but Aquinas grabbed hold of her arm and went to hit her again.

'Get your hands off her!' I yelled, pulling Brenda away, then I kicked her as hard as I could in the shins, grabbed Brenda's hand and ran out of the office, down the corridor and out of the school gates. We ran and we ran until we couldn't run anymore then we sat on a garden wall to get our breath back. Brenda was crying.

'She's going to kill us, Maureen.'

'No she's not, because we're not going back.'

'What, never?'

'Never.'

'Promise?'

'I promise. Now, let me have a look at you.'

Brenda stood up so that I could see what Aquinas had done. There was an angry red mark across both her legs.

'Does it hurt?'

'Yes,' said Brenda tearfully.

'She's a mean, cruel cow,' I said.

'I don't think you should say that about a Bride of Christ, Maureen.'

'She's no Bride of Christ, Brenda,' I said, shaking my head.

'If I was God, I'd divorce her,' said Brenda.

'If I was God, I'd bloody kill her!'

I put my arm around her and we started the long walk home.

'Did you see her face when I kicked her?' I said.

'She didn't look happy, Maureen.'

'She wasn't meant to, Brenda. Vicious old witch!'

'*Maureen!*' said Brenda.

'*Brenda!*' I said. Then we both started giggling and then I stopped because I shouldn't be giggling, my daddy was dead.

When we eventually got home, Mum was nowhere to be seen, even though her coat was hanging on the hook and her old brown bag was on the back of the kitchen chair. We walked out into the garden. I was getting a pain in my tummy. *Don't tell me she's topped herself as well,* I thought. Then I looked at the shed.

I didn't want to go in there because that was where Daddy had died. He hadn't topped himself in the house at all, he'd done it in the shed. Those boys had lied about blood dripping down the walls. None of us had gone anywhere near the shed since it happened and I didn't want to go in there now.

I put Brenda behind me and slowly opened the door. I was relieved to see Mum sitting there on the floor, just sitting there. She looked up at us and smiled, as if sitting on the shed floor was the most natural thing in the world.

'What are you doing in here, Mum?' I said gently. 'You shouldn't be in here.'

She smiled at me sadly. 'Your daddy's here.'

My daddy wasn't here, only sadness was here. 'Please come into the house, Mum,' I said. 'You need to bathe Brenda's leg.'

'Brenda's leg?' she said, looking confused.

'Sister Aquinas belted Brenda across her legs.'

Mom stared at me. 'She did *what*?'

'She whacked me across the legs, Mum, because Dada had topped himself and she said he was going to burn in Hell for the rest of eternity.'

'She said *what*?' said Mum.

'That's what she said, didn't she, Maureen?'

I nodded.

'And she said that Dada had driven a knife into our Divine Saviour's heart but I don't remember him doing that.'

'Brenda, show Mum your legs.'

Brenda turned around and lifted up her skirt.

'A nun did that?' said Mum.

Brenda nodded.

'Your daddy is up in Heaven,' said Mum, 'and he's looking down on you right at this minute.'

'He's looking down on you too, Mum,' I said gently. 'And I don't think he would like to see you sitting on the shed floor.'

Mum smiled. 'You are so like your daddy, Maureen, so like your daddy.'

Me and Brenda sat down on the dirty shed floor next to Mum, she put her arms around us and held us tightly. Then we helped her to get up and the three of us walked back up the garden and into the kitchen.

'Sit down, girls,' said Mum. 'I need to talk to you.'

Me and Brenda sat down at the kitchen table and waited for Mum to speak.

'I know that I have let you down…' she began.

'No you haven't,' I said quickly.

'Hush, Maureen, let me speak.' She took a deep breath. 'Not only have I let *you* down but I've let your daddy down as well. I've been so full of my own grief that I haven't been able to help you with yours and I am so sorry. Your daddy had been ill for a very long time but he did his best and no daddy loved his family more than your daddy did. I believe that, in the end, the struggle to stay with us became too hard for him and he had to go. And so now we will keep him in our hearts and we will smile when we think of him, knowing that he is at peace and all his pain has gone away. We wouldn't want him to come back and be sad again, would we?'

I could feel Brenda's leg against mine and I held her hand under the table. 'No, Mummy,' she said, 'we wouldn't want him to be sad again.'

'So now it's just the three of us,' said Mum, 'and we are going to be OK, right?'

'Right,' said Brenda, smiling.

'What about your job, Mum?' I said.

'I shall go round to see Mrs Feldman this very minute and tell her that I am ready to come back to work.'

'Do you think she'll take you back?' I said.

'She'd be a fool not to. I'm a good worker and she knows it.'

Mum picked up her old brown handbag and smiled at us. 'Now, I want the pair of you to stop worrying because things are going to be different from now on, I promise you.'

That was the day me and Brenda got our mum back.

Chapter Twenty-Five

So that was the end of the Catholic school and, as it happened, it was also the end of the Catholic Church. A priest came round to the house and told Mum that Daddy couldn't be buried in the Catholic churchyard because he'd topped himself. It wasn't the priest's fault and I think he hated giving Mum the news. He'd even written to the Bishop, telling him what a good Catholic Daddy had been, but the Church wouldn't budge: Daddy had committed a mortal sin and couldn't be buried in consecrated ground and that was that. The little church where me and Brenda lit our candles in front of the Blessed Virgin Mary had closed its doors on us. All I knew was that if Jesus could forgive the robber man on the cross next to him, then I'm sure he could forgive my daddy, who was a good man and hadn't robbed anyone.

Aunty Marge said that she had a good mind to write to the Bishop and tell him where he could stick his consecrated ground and it wasn't at the back of the church. So even though Daddy was a good Catholic, he was buried at St Johns, the Protestant church down the road.

There was a collection on the estate so that Daddy didn't have to be buried in a pauper's grave and he could have his own piece of ground and a proper wooden box. Mum cried when a neighbour came round with the money. 'They have nothing, Maureen,' she said to me, 'yet they did this for us. In the end, people are good.'

Aunty Mary wrote to us from Ireland and said that they were all broken-hearted to hear that their little brother Pat had died. She said that they didn't have the money to pay for the boat to England but they were going to have a Mass said for him in the church where he was baptised.

On the day of the funeral people gathered at the house; even Aunty Vera and Uncle Fred were there. Mum kissed her on the cheek and thanked her for coming. I didn't even look at her – I would never be able to forgive her for what she said about my daddy.

Uncle John and Uncle Fred lifted the coffin onto Uncle Fred's barrow and together they pulled it up the street to the graveyard. The rest of us walked slowly behind it, followed by a bunch of neighbours. It was a sad little procession.

I thought my heart would break as I watched my daddy being lowered into the ground. Mum, Brenda and I stood together at the edge of the grave holding hands. The sun was shining through the trees, softening the old gravestones that stood in lines, row after row, just like Jack's soldiers. The sound of children's laughter drifted across the graveyard from the nearby school, the school that me and Brenda would be going to. Aunty Marge put a rose in each of our hands and we threw them into the hole. They landed on top of the wooden box that held my daddy. People were crying. Mum and Brenda were sobbing but I didn't shed a tear, not one bloody tear.

What was wrong with me?

That night in bed I couldn't stop thinking about my daddy, cold and alone in that dark place. I cuddled into Brenda's warm little body and I wanted to die; I wanted to be with my daddy. But I didn't die, I kept breathing and life went on. Mum got her job back and me and Brenda started at the new school. My teacher was lovely but I missed my good friend Monica.

'It's not the same without you,' she moaned. 'I'm having to sit next to Bernadette Riley and she's always trying to copy my work and she spits when she talks.'

'Wouldn't your mum let you change schools?'

'She thinks that Protestants are the Devil's spawn.'

'What's that?'

'I haven't a bloody clue, Maureen, but she's dead against me mixing with them.'

'We'll still be best friends though, won't we?'

'Of course we will, daft.'

I was grateful to have Monica as my friend and I knew that Jack and Nelson would always be there for me but nothing gave me any pleasure. I couldn't be silly any more. I would sit by the stone wall and watch the others running around the beach, splashing in the water and balancing on the old wooden groyne but it all felt pretty childish. I couldn't join in. It was as if on the day my daddy died, he took my childhood with him.

No one mentioned Daddy. Not Mum or Brenda or Aunty Marge, no one. It was as if he had never existed. I found it hard to be around people, so just like Daddy I walked and there were times when I felt Daddy walking beside me.

One day I found myself outside the big white house. I remembered that the lady had asked me to come back and see her so I opened the gate and walked up the path. She was in the front garden, digging the earth with a little spade; she was wearing a big floppy hat made of straw.

She stood up and rubbed her back. 'Maureen,' she said, smiling. 'How lovely! Now tell me, how is your father?'

I stood there staring at her. She put the spade down and walked across to where I was standing. She touched my shoulder. 'Is your daddy alright, darling?'

I couldn't tell her; I didn't know what to say, I couldn't find the words. And then I was crying – loud, noisy, wet tears, running down my face and into the collar of my blouse. Snot was coming out of my nose and dribbling into my mouth. I could taste the snot and the salt mixing together on my tongue. All the tears that I had been keeping inside me were bursting out of my body and

I couldn't control them. I was gulping for air, sucking it in but it was too thick to swallow. I couldn't catch my breath; I was dying. I had to be dying because I couldn't breathe. And then I was in her arms and the snot and the tears were soaking her dress. I clung to her as if my very life depended on it. We sank together onto the grass and she didn't let me go, not for one second did she let me go. That was the day that the lady in the posh white house saved my life. That was the day when all the pain I'd been carrying around found its way out of my body.

That night, in bed, I let myself think about Daddy and all the wonderful times we'd had together and all the love we'd shared. Even though no one mentioned his name I knew that my daddy had lived and now he would live inside my heart. That's where he would be, not in that dark hole in the ground but inside my heart. I closed my eyes and there was Daddy's face – the whole of Daddy's face, not just bits of it. I turned over and watched Brenda sleeping.

'I've found Daddy,' I whispered. 'I've found our daddy.'

Chapter Twenty-Six

Since Daddy died Jack and I spent a lot more time together, just him and me. Every evening after he'd done his homework we'd go for a walk on the Downs.

One evening we were sitting on the top of the Devil's Dyke looking out over the hills.

'There's something I've been wanting to ask you for ages,' I said.

'What's that?'

'How come your mum doesn't mind you being friends with Nelson?'

'She *does* mind but there's not much she can do about it.'

'Why not?'

'Nelson's dad and my dad were best friends. They went through the war together.'

'Nelson had a dad?'

'He might still have one for all anybody knows.'

'He's not dead, then?'

'He walked out on Nelson and his mum when Nelson was just a baby.'

'Blimey! So Nelson could still have a dad out there somewhere.'

Jack nodded his head. 'He could have.'

'If we could find him, then Nelson could leave the orphanage and have a proper home with his dad. Wouldn't that be wonderful?'

'Yes, it would,' said Jack. 'But no one's heard a word from him since the day he walked out.'

'Does Nelson *know* that he's got a dad?'

'I'm sure he knows, he must do, but I've never heard him mention him and I've never asked.'

'So that's why you're allowed to be his friend, because of your dad?'

'That's about it. My mum hated that brown jumper with a vengeance,' said Jack, grinning. 'She even knitted him a new one once but he never wore it. You know how Nelson feels about that jumper.'

'I didn't realise just how much until he asked me to look after it for him.'

Jack smiled and put his arm around my shoulder. 'I'm glad you've got Nelson's old brown jumper,' he said.

We sat quietly together looking out over the hills. It was OK not saying anything; it was like that with me and Jack. I loved being with him. I was only young but I knew that he was the only boy for me. I knew girls of my age who had kissed boys – Julie Baxter was always kissing boys. I wondered how it would feel to kiss Jack. I wondered if Jack ever thought about kissing me.

Every Saturday Jack's dad went to the orphanage and got Nelson out for the day. It was nice for all of us to be together again. Brenda had made a friend at the new school. Her name was Molly and she talked about her all the time. She didn't seem to need me so much these days but I didn't mind, I was happy that she had found a special friend.

And so the four of us spent every weekend together, just like we used to. One day we were on the Palace Pier. It was a beautiful afternoon and it had brought out the crowds. Mums and dads strolled along the old wooden planks and children ran ahead of them, clutching pink and white candyfloss on little sticks. The sea glittered in the sunshine and a soft breeze ruffled my skirt and cooled my face. A group of men were fishing off the side and Jack and Nelson were leaning on the railings watching them. Monica and I didn't like seeing the crabs desperately trying to climb out of the buckets.

'Poor little things,' she said, screwing up her face. 'I bet when they were happily swimming round this morning they didn't know they'd end up in someone's smelly bucket this afternoon.'

I thought of my dad. When I had woken up that morning, I didn't know that by the evening he would be dead.

'We never know when we're going to end up in someone's smelly bucket, Monica.'

'Very wise, Maureen,' she said solemnly.

We could hear music in the distance.

'Where's that coming from?' I said.

'Let's find out,' said Monica, catching hold of my hand.

As we neared the end of the pier the music got louder.

'It's coming from the ballroom,' said Monica excitedly. 'There must be a dance on.'

We walked towards the dance hall, through the beautiful ornate arches. There was a sign saying 'Tea Dance' on one of the railings.

'Let's have a nose,' said Monica.

We walked round the back of the building and peered through the windows.

The room was full of light and movement and colour. Dancers were gliding around the floor, circling around each other, coming together and moving apart, advancing and retreating like Jack's toy soldiers in a never-ending river of reds and yellows and greens and golds as the music urged them onward.

'Don't they look lovely?' said Monica.

I sighed. 'Don't you wish it was us?'

'Perhaps it will be one day.'

'Today, I wish it was us today.'

Monica looked me up and down. 'I don't think they'd let you in, Maureen.'

I was wearing a dress that had seen better days.

'You're probably right,' I said.

I stared back at the dancers. Jewels glittered from around the women's throats and ears, reflecting in the beautiful mirrors that adorned the walls and catching the light from the huge chandelier that shone down on them from the ceiling above. I thought they looked beautiful. I wanted to be there amongst them; I wanted to be part of the music and the lights. My feet itched to join them and my heart yearned to be one of them. I closed my eyes so that I could only hear the music and in my head I was in Jack's arms and I was wearing a beautiful dress. I could almost feel the softness of the silk brushing against my legs. That is where I wanted to be, in Jack's arms, in a beautiful dress, and I wondered if it would only ever be a dream.

'Funny sort of thing to do in the middle of the afternoon,' said Monica, breaking into my dream.

'You have no soul, Monica,' I said.

'Guilty as charged,' she said, laughing.

The boys came up behind us.

'We wondered where you were,' said Jack, smiling.

'We were looking at the dancers,' I said. 'I wish I could go to a dance.'

'Funny sort of thing to be doing on a sunny afternoon,' said Jack.

I looked at Monica and we burst out laughing.

'What?' said Jack.

Chapter Twenty-Seven

We were all growing up. I was fourteen and would soon be leaving school and I didn't have a clue where I was going to work. I'd heard horror stories about girls going into service and hating it. I didn't fancy sitting in an office all day and I didn't think I'd get a job in a shop. Mum said it would have to be a factory and I didn't fancy that much either but it was probably where I was going to end up.

One evening Monica and I were sitting on the green at the top of the road.

'What are you going to do when you leave school?' I asked.

'Mum keeps going on about that,' said Monica. 'We haven't got a lot of choice though, have we?'

'Do you know what I'd really like to do?' I said.

'What?'

'I'd like to work in a bookshop.'

'Really?'

I nodded. 'I think a bookshop would be a really nice place to work.'

'Factories pay more than shops,' said Monica.

'I know, but I don't fancy working in a factory.'

'What about that bookshop in Western Road? I can't remember what it's called but you could ask in there.'

'I might,' I said. 'If I can find some decent clothes.'

A ball came flying towards us. Monica stood up and kicked it back to the boys. When she turned round she said, 'Maureen?'

'What?'

She looked uncomfortable; she was twisting the end of her plait round and round her finger. 'Forget it.'

'Forget what?' I said.

'It's probably nothing.'

'For heaven's sake, Monica, what's probably nothing?'

Monica sat back down next to me and started pulling up handfuls of grass.

'Monica!' I yelled.

'OK, OK! You know that girl whose parents run the Jolly Sailor pub?'

'Marion Tucker?' I said.

'Yes. Look, I'm only telling you this in case someone else tells you, so don't go mad.'

I waited. I couldn't think what could be so bad that it was making Monica scared to tell me.

'Well, the other evening I had to go down to the pub to get a jug of cider for my dad and I got talking to her. I'm really sorry to tell you this, Maureen, but she said that Jack had taken her to the pictures to see *The Thirty-Nine Steps*.'

'My Jack?'

'Monica nodded. 'Your Jack. I'm really sorry.'

I felt as if someone had kicked me in the stomach.

'She's not even that pretty,' said Monica, obviously trying to make me feel better.

'You're right, Monica, she's not pretty, she's beautiful.'

'Maybe, but in a showy kind of way,' said Monica.

'But Jack's mine.'

'Maureen?'

'What?'

'Does Jack know he's yours?'

'Of course he does,' I snapped.

'Have you actually told him how you feel?'

'I don't have to tell him, we're destined to be together. You know that, Monica.'

'*I* know, Maureen, but does Jack?'

Suddenly I wasn't so sure. I shook my head. 'He must do.'

'You have to say something to him then.'

'Perhaps they just happened to meet in the cinema. Perhaps he just happened to sit next to her,' I said.

'She definitely said he'd taken her, Maureen, she didn't say they'd met in there, otherwise I wouldn't have said anything.'

I didn't know what to think. Jack had never taken me to the pictures. Why had he never done that?

'I need to go home,' I said.

'Was I wrong to tell you?'

'No, Monica, you were right to tell me.'

'I thought so.'

We hugged and I started walking home. I didn't want to go into the house in case Brenda noticed there was something wrong with me, so I went round the side and climbed the tree. Monica's questions were bothering me. Did Jack know how I felt about him? Did he feel the same? He'd never said so but that had never worried me because we didn't have to talk about it. We saw each other nearly every evening; we sat on the Downs together and held hands. I picked a bunch of leaves off the tree and, one by one, I let them fall to the ground. *He loves me, he loves me not. He loves me, he loves me not.*

I had three leaves left. *He loves me, he loves me not. He loves me.* I smiled, of course he loved me. But he'd never kissed me. I wondered if he'd held Marion Tucker's hand in the dark cinema; I wondered if he'd kissed her. I looked over the fence into Jack's garden and remembered the day we'd moved into See Saw Lane. The day that I watched him playing with the toy soldiers. The day that I fell in love with him.

'Maureen?'

I looked down and saw Nelson looking up at me.

'Hi, Nelson,' I said, climbing down. He took my hand as I jumped to the ground.

'I thought your tree-climbing days were over,' he said, grinning.

'I was thinking about the first time I met Jack… and you, of course.'

'Of course,' said Nelson.

We walked up the path and sat on the back door step.

'What's up?' he said.

'Nothing.'

'What's up?' he said again.

'Jack took Marion Tucker to the pictures.'

'Ah,' said Nelson.

'To see *The Thirty-Nine Steps*.'

'Jack likes the pictures, Maureen.'

'But he took Marion Tucker.'

Nelson put his arm around my shoulder and I leaned into him. 'And it's made you unhappy,' he said.

'Marion bloody Tucker can have anyone, why does she have to pick Jack?'

'Do you know what I think you should do?'

'What?'

'Nothing. I think you should do nothing.'

'But why?'

'Our Jack is not the sort of boy to be pinned down. Marion Tucker might be pretty but that's all she is and you wait, it won't be long before she starts telling him what to do and trust me, that won't suit Jack. He likes you a lot, Maureen, so say nothing and pretty soon you won't have to worry about Marion Bird Brain Tucker.'

'But he took her to see *The Thirty-Nine Bloody Steps*, Nelson.'

'And I bet she was bored senseless.'

'Do you think so?'

Nelson kissed the top of my head. 'It's not Marion Bloody Tucker's sort of film at all.'

'What would I do without you, Nelson?' I said, giggling.

'You'll never have to do without me, Maureen, and if you do, I will always come back.'

'Thanks, Nelson Perks.'

'You are very welcome, Maureen O'Connell.'

Chapter Twenty-Eight

The next Saturday morning I managed to cobble together some clothes that didn't look like they'd just fallen off the back of the rag and bone cart.

'You look very nice,' said Mum, smoothing down my skirt. She and Brenda gave me a hug and wished me luck and I made my way to the bookshop in the Western Road.

It was a small shop and you'd miss it if you didn't know it was there. On one side was a man selling Turkish rugs and carpets that spilt out onto the pavement. On the other side was a bakery. The smell of fresh bread wafting out of the door made my mouth water. If I worked here, I would end up as fat as a house.

I peered in the widow but it was dim inside and I couldn't see much. I opened the door and a bell jangled above my head. The musty smell that met me made my mouth water almost as much as the smell of the bread next door. I'd always loved to read but there were never any books in the house because books cost money and you couldn't eat them. It was Daddy who had given me a love of books. Every night before we went to sleep he would tell us stories about handsome heroes and beautiful heroines, pirates and desert islands and while we sat on the grassy bank in the lagoon, he taught me and Brenda our letters.

Stepping from the light into the gloom of the shop was strangely exciting. I stood still and let my eyes adjust to my surroundings. The place smelled musty and earthy. It reminded me of Uncle John's stall at the end of the day, when the fruit was on the turn. As my eyes grew accustomed to the dark, I saw the books. Shelf upon shelf of them, reaching up to the ceiling, small books sitting next to bigger books, some of them laying on their side. It looked as if they'd been thrown there. I had never seen so many books in my life. Daddy would have loved it here and I wondered why he had never taken us. Suddenly a large shape loomed out of the darkness. It took a moment to realise that it was the posh lady's horrible husband. Bloody hell, what was he doing here? I hoped he'd hurry up and buy his book and leave. He saw me and I could tell that he recognised me but instead of saying hello, he turned around and disappeared behind one of the bookcases. Well, that suited me fine because I didn't want to talk to him either.

I could hear some whispering and then a young girl appeared and walked up to me, smiling,

'Looking for a book, love?' she said.

'Not really,' I said. 'What I'm actually looking for is a job.'

'Oh, right. Worked in a shop before, have you?'

'I haven't worked anywhere before but I'm leaving school in a few weeks and I've got to get a job. I'd like to work in a bookshop.'

'You could do worse,' she said. 'Factories pay more, not that I'd wanna work in one.'

'Do you think there might be a job, then?'

'Don't get your hopes up, but you might have come in at just the right time. The boss keeps going on about retiring. Mind you, he's been doing that since I started. Bentley's has been in his family for generations. I get the feeling that he thinks it will fall apart if he's not here but lately he's started talking about getting someone in to help me.'

I stared at her with my mouth open. *Bentley's? Isn't that what the posh lady called herself?*

'Is your boss's name Peter?' I asked the girl.

'Yes, do you know him, then?'

'I know his wife.'

The girl laughed. 'That'll be the day when Peter gets a wife!'

'Does he live down on the seafront? In a big white house?'

The girl nodded. 'Yes,' she said.

'But I've been there and met his wife.'

'Peter lives with his sister-in-law. He moved in with her after his brother died. They own the bookshop between them.'

I couldn't believe what I was hearing. He was my posh lady's brother-in-law, not her husband. I was kind of glad because he was a miserable old git and she was lovely.

I often wondered what she was doing with him.

Suddenly he bumbled into the room; his face was bright red and he was sweating.

'What's wrong, Peter?' said the girl, looking alarmed.

'I have to sit down,' he said frantically, looking for a chair.

The girl fetched a chair from behind the counter and guided him into it. Then she looked at me and said, 'There's a kitchen behind that curtain, can you get a glass of water?'

I went behind an old velvet curtain into a little kitchen. I couldn't find a glass but there was a cup hanging from a row of hooks on the wall. I filled one with water and came back into the shop.

The girl was kneeling on the floor in front of him. 'Have you got a pain, Peter?' she asked.

'Not a pain, no,' he mumbled.

'Well, something's wrong with you.'

'I just can't believe it,' he said, shaking his head.

'What can't you believe, Peter?' she said.

I was beginning to feel awkward just standing there without a clue what was going on. He mopped at his forehead with a hankie. 'I was sitting out the back, having a smoke, when Hassan came round with the news.'

'What news, Peter?'

'The old king's dead, Maggie.'

'Bloody hell!' said Maggie.

'King George has died,' he said.

'I know it's a shock, Peter, but we all knew how ill he was,' said Maggie.

'But you hope, don't you?' said Peter. 'You hope.'

'Yes, you do,' said Maggie, kindly.

All of a sudden he got out of the chair, stood to attention, saluted and said, 'The King is dead. Long live the King!'

I suddenly felt as if I'd walked in on a film set and didn't know what part I was supposed to be playing. As I caught Maggie's eye I could see she was desperately trying not to burst out laughing, just like I was. We grinned at each other.

'What's your name?' she asked.

Peter sat down heavily in the chair.

'Her name's Maureen,' he said. 'What is she doing here, anyway?'

'Don't be rude, Peter. She's come for a job.'

'What, here?'

'Yes, here. And you said that you were thinking of taking someone on.'

'Did I?'

'Yes, you did.'

Peter glared at me.

'Take no notice of that face, Maureen. Sometimes Peter has trouble arranging it into anything resembling pleasant. It's a wonder he ever sells any books.'

'I sell plenty of books,' he mumbled.

'You'd sell a lot more if you didn't frighten all the customers away. Now, Maureen would like a job in this bookshop and God knows, we need someone, Peter, because the place is a mess. I think she's just what we need, so how about it?'

He glared at me again.

'Face!' said Maggie.

The grimace that Peter managed was worse than the glare but I tucked my hair behind my ears and smiled back hopefully.

'You want to work here, do you?' he said.

'Yes, please,' I said.

'We don't pay much.'

'Take no notice,' said Maggie. 'The pay's fine.'

'Is it?' said Peter, looking surprised.

Maggie smiled at him. I'd been thinking that they had a pretty unusual relationship for a boss and an employee, but it was very obvious that they liked each other.

'So are you going to offer the poor girl a job?' said Maggie.

'Do you think I should?'

'I think you should.'

'OK then.'

I wanted to jump for joy. I wanted to run around the bookshop waving my arms in the air but the whole thing had been so casual, I thought I'd better act casual too.

'Thanks very much,' I said.

Maggie winked at me. 'You can start by making us all a cup of hot, sweet tea. We drink a lot of tea here.'

I grinned at her, went back behind the curtain, put the kettle on and leaned on the sink while I waited for it to boil. What a funny old day, I thought. Ten minutes ago I'd walked in off the street and now I'd been offered a job and I was making tea. It reminded me of the crabs, not that this was a smelly bucket, but you just never knew what the day was going to bring.

Chapter Twenty-Nine

Monica started work in a factory where she had to hang bits of metal on wire frames.

'What exactly do they make there?' I asked.

'I haven't got a clue,' she said, 'but it's a good laugh.'

'Well, you must have some idea, you go there every day.'

'All I know is that a bunch of blokes in rubber aprons and welly boots dip a load of junk in a big vat of something and us girls hang them on wire frames to dry. It's a doddle. The only downside is that I've got orange fingers.'

'Yeah, I've noticed that,' I said grinning.

She grinned back. 'And they're fluorescent.'

'That doesn't sound good, Monica.'

'Sometimes I wake in the night and they scare the life out of me. They look like two little orange monsters creeping up the bed.'

'Shouldn't you talk to someone about it?'

'Well, no one else seems bothered.'

'That doesn't mean you shouldn't be.'

Monica just shrugged her shoulders.

It all sounded mind-numbingly dull to me and I was sure that Monica could do better, but she seemed happy there so I kept my mouth shut.

I didn't come home from work with orange fingers but I did come home covered in dust. I had made it my mission to sort out the hundreds of books that lined the shelves. Mum said that I was a round peg in a round hole and she was right. Me and Maggie got on like a house on fire and Peter's bark was definitely worse than his bite. It felt sort of wrong to call my boss by his first name but Maggie assured me that was what he wanted to be called.

'When I first started here I called him Mr Bentley but he said he wanted to be called Peter. He was quite definite about it, to the point where if I called him Mr Bentley by mistake he wouldn't answer. So, trust me, Peter wants to be called Peter.'

'Well, if you're sure,' I said.

'I'm sure,' said Maggie.

I actually got quite fond of Peter in a funny sort of way. He spent a lot of time with Hassan. They sat together on a bench in the yard at the back of the bookshop, smoking and putting the world to rights, while Hassan's poor wife was left to sell rugs and carpets, and Maggie and I were left to sell the books.

'It's better this way,' said Maggie. 'He tends to get in the way otherwise, bumbling about the place.'

I loved it there; I even loved the chaos of it. I loved the people who came in and rummaged through the dusty piles of books that were stacked against the walls. I loved seeing the delight on their faces when they found a rare book they'd been searching for. One day Maggie and I went down to the junk shop and dragged back a couple of overstuffed armchairs for the customers to curl up in. There was an old gramophone player in the back of the shop where Peter played his Mantovani music. As soon as he went out the back with Hassan, Maggie swapped it over for one of her Glenn Miller records. It was lovely working away to 'In the Mood' and 'Chattanooga Choo, Choo'.

Once Peter had chewed everything over with Hassan, he'd come into the shop and give us his opinion on the latest piece of news. He had a lot to say about the new king, Edward VIII, and the latest scandal involving the American, Mrs Simpson.

'That young man is going to bring down the monarchy,' he said one day. 'You mark my words.'

I was balancing on a ladder and Maggie was handing books up to me.

'But he loves her,' said Maggie.

'He's got no right to love her,' said Peter indignantly. 'He's the King! He can't just fall in love willy-nilly, he has to set an example to his people.'

'But he's still a man, he can't help who he loves,' insisted Maggie.

'He's not just a man, Maggie,' said Peter, going red in the face. 'He is King of the United Kingdom and the Dominicans of the British Empire and he is the Emperor of India. Does that sound like any man you know, Maggie?'

'I can't say it does, Peter,' said Maggie, grinning up at me.

'Queen Victoria must be turning in her grave,' he added.

I always thought that was a funny expression. It was moments like this when I wished Daddy was still alive – I could just imagine how we would have laughed about it.

'What does Hassan think about it?' said Maggie.

Peter was silent for a moment and then he said, 'It's hard to tell with Hassan, Maggie.'

I knew that I'd been lucky to have just walked in off the street and got this job. It felt good to be able to say that I worked in a bookshop and not a factory. I knew that my family were proud of me and, even more importantly, Jack was proud.

'To be surrounded by books all day is my idea of heaven,' he said.

I smiled. 'Mine too.'

One evening Jack and I were walking on the Downs. It was late January and it was cold. The Downs was a wild place in the winter; the trees were like black silhouettes against the evening sky. The grass was blowing all over the place but the dirty old sheep were quite happily snuffling about in it as if it was a summer's day.

'Do you think they feel the cold?' I said to Jack.

'Does it worry you then?' he asked.

'It does a bit,' I admitted. 'It can't be much fun living up here.'

Jack squeezed my hand. 'You're a funny old thing,' he said. 'If it makes you feel any better, I'd say they're warmer than us.'

'Good,' I said.

Jack and I held hands as we walked. I'd taken Nelson's advice and hadn't said a word about Marion Tucker and, pretty soon, she was indeed old news. Nelson was a wise boy and I would always listen to what he had to say because I knew that he cared about me and always had my best interests at heart.

I shivered.

'You're cold,' said Jack.

'A bit.'

'Do you want to go home?'

I didn't, but I was actually freezing.

'Not really,' I said.

'Let's find some shelter then,' he said.

We walked until we spotted an old barn at the bottom of the hill and quickly made our way there. Jack pushed hard against the old wooden door and it creaked as it swung open. It was much bigger inside than it had seemed from the top of the hill. The first thing that hit us was the smell: dust and must and last year's hay, mixed with the acrid, rusty smell of old, abandoned machinery. Jack pushed the door shut to keep out the wind and we were plunged into darkness. I stood still and hung onto him until my eyes got used to it. There was a line of wooden stalls that I supposed had once housed cattle. Jack led me into one of them and we sat down on the floor. It was smelly in there but it was dry. I felt a bubble of excitement in my tummy: I was alone with Jack in this dark place. I'd been alone with Jack a lot. We'd walked along the seafront, we'd sat on my back step, we'd walked on the Downs, but this felt different, as if this moment was leading to something. I looked at Jack's blue eyes in the darkness and I yearned for something, I wasn't sure what I was yearning for, only that it had to be more than we'd had.

'Warmer?' he said, putting his arm around my shoulder.

'Much,' I said, leaning into him. I breathed in his smell and counted the steady beats of his heart. I wanted Jack to hold me, *really* hold me; maybe even kiss me. I was still a child but in that moment, in that dark place, feeling the warmth of his breath against my cheek, I didn't feel like one. The feelings that were rushing around my body were unfamiliar to me and yet I knew that they were a part of me, not quite a child and not yet a woman. They were undeniably there but I didn't know yet what to do with them. I reached up and kissed his cheek but he didn't respond. Then I tried to turn his face towards mine so that we could kiss properly but he turned his head away from me.

I felt the heat rush to my face. I felt stupid, ashamed. Why had I done that? It should have been Jack wanting to kiss me, not the other way round.

Jack started to speak. 'Look, Maureen…'

I jumped up and all Nelson's advice flew out the window.

'I bet if my name was Marion Tucker, things would be different.'

Jack stood up and tried to put his arm around me but I pulled away.

'Maureen,' he began. 'It's because you're *not* Marion Tucker that things *have* to be different.'

'But—' I began.

Jack put his finger to my lips. 'We should go,' he said.

He closed the barn door and we started walking back up the hill and all the while I was thinking, *I shall never do that again. If there ever comes a day when you want me, Jack Forrest, then it's going to have to come from you.*

Chapter Thirty

Me and Monica were huddled up in one of the shelters on the seafront, eating fish and chips. The tide was out and Brenda and her friend Molly were down on the beach, collecting seaweed.

'Bloody hell, Maureen!' she said when I told her what had happened with Jack. 'I'd have died if a boy had done that to me.'

'I nearly did. I've never felt so stupid in my whole life.'

'Have you seen him since it happened?'

'I'm avoiding him, but it's making me miserable.'

Monica was shovelling pieces of hot fish into her mouth, then licking her orange fingers one by one.

'I don't think you should be doing that, Monica.'

'Doing what?'

'Licking your fingers.'

'They're greasy, anyway you lick yours all the time.'

'Yeah, but mine aren't orange.'

'You worry too much,' she said, blowing on the chips.

'Well, I just think that you should look for somewhere else to work, somewhere that doesn't turn your fingers orange.'

'There's a golf-ball factory just down the road, I suppose I could try there.'

'Well, I think you should. At least golf balls are white.'

We carried on eating our fish and chips and watching Brenda and Molly digging in the wet sand.

'Has it ever occurred to you… Now, don't get mad,' Monica added quickly.

'I won't.'

'Well, has it ever occurred to you that perhaps—'

'For heaven's sake, Monica!'

'OK, that perhaps Jack thinks of you more as a friend than a girlfriend?'

'It had crossed my mind.'

'Well, that's not a bad thing.'

'Isn't it?'

'My mum said that you have to really like someone before you can truly love them. Otherwise it's not love at all, it's lust.'

'Your mum said *that*?'

'She was drunk at the time. But the point I'm trying to make is that Jack really likes you and you really like him and maybe the kissing bit will happen when it's supposed to happen.'

'I was too forward, wasn't I?'

'You were a bit and I think that's what Mum meant about the lust bit. I think you have to be a bit more grown-up before you start lusting and you have to be sure that you like him more than you lust after him.'

I nodded. 'I think your mum is probably right, Monica, but why on earth were you and your mum having a conversation like that? I can't imagine me and my mum talking about that sort of stuff.'

'It was ages ago. My dad had come home drunk as usual and he'd locked Mum out of the house. She'd had to sleep in the shed. They made up the next day and were all lovey-dovey with each other, that's where the lust bit came in.'

'It's a good job Brenda's not listening to this, she'd be saying that word for weeks.'

'Does she still do that?'

'Yes, she collects words, she always has.'

'I remember.'

'It used to make me and Daddy laugh.'

'You still miss him, don't you?'

'Every day, Monica.'

'Do you know what I always loved about your dad?'

I shook my head.

'I loved how gentle he was with you and Brenda. I used to wish he was my dad.'

I tucked my arm through hers. 'I'm sorry, Monica,' I said.

'And do you know something else? I don't think my mum likes my dad at all.'

'You never know, Monica, your dad might mellow with time.'

'And pigs might fly,' she said.

I still couldn't face Jack, so the following Sunday I went to see Nelson at the home. They hadn't chucked him out when he was fourteen, instead they'd given him a job looking after the gardens, which I thought was really good of them and Nelson liked it.

He was fifteen now so he could come and go without an adult being present. It was too cold for the beach and the Downs, not that I wanted to go up the Downs, in fact I wasn't sure that I would ever want to go there again. So we were sitting in the rose garden, which was Nelson's favourite place.

'No Jack?' he asked.

'Long story, Nelson.'

'Have you had a falling out?'

'Something like that.'

'Not like you.'

I shrugged.

'You'll make up again.'

'I know we will.'

'Are you still enjoying the bookshop?'

'I love every minute of working there and I really feel as if I'm making a difference. It was really chaotic and now I'm getting it into some kind of order.'

'I feel like that about the garden,' said Nelson. 'I plant things and they grow, I cut dead things back and they come alive again.'

'I'm glad you're happy here, Nelson.'

'I didn't think I would be, in fact I hated it to start with. I hated the fact that strangers were deciding what to do with my life. I had no say in it, I had to go where they told me to go, and that was hard and I missed being with you lot.'

'I didn't realise that and I should have done.'

'You weren't to know how I was feeling.'

'I'm your friend, I should have known.'

'You're too hard on yourself, girl.'

'Maybe.'

'Did you follow my advice about the Marion Tucker thing?' he asked.

'I tried to but then it all went wrong.'

'Well, you tried.'

'Nelson?'

'Mmm?'

'Do you think that the King really loves Mrs Simpson or do you think he just lusts after her?'

Nelson laughed. 'Where did you get that word from?'

'It's not mine, it's Monica's. What do you think, though?'

Nelson scratched behind his ear; I'd embarrassed him.

'I've embarrassed you, haven't I?'

'A bit,' he said, laughing, 'but let me think about it.'

We sat quietly for a while then he said, 'I'm no expert when it comes to love but I think that whether it's lust or love they feel for each other, they've backed themselves into a bit of a corner. The whole world is talking about them and watching them, everyone has their own opinion on it. The monarchy is up in arms and the government are making all kinds of threats. I think the more everyone tells them they can't be together, the more they will cling to each other. They've almost got to stay together now because it must feel like it's them against the world and I should think that's a pretty powerful emotion.'

I was staring at Nelson in surprise. I hadn't expected him to come out with all that.

'Golly, Nelson,' I said. 'You might not be an expert in love but I've got the feeling you're not far off.'

Nelson smiled his shy little smile. 'Maybe,' he said.

He got up from the bench and walked over to the rose garden. 'I've got something to tell you, Maureen,' he said.

I sat there looking at his back. He'd changed so much over the last few years; he wasn't the skinny little boy I remembered any more. I wondered what he was going to say.

He turned around and faced me. 'I'm joining the army,' he said.

I was confused. 'Aren't you too young?'

'They take you when you're fifteen and a half. I'll be joining in a couple of months.'

I wanted to be happy for him but my heart was beating at a hundred miles an hour.

'Is that what you want?' I asked.

'It's what I've always wanted. My dad was in the army.'

Nelson had never talked about his dad; he'd never mentioned him at all, not ever.

I took a deep breath. I needed to say something positive to him so I said the first stupid thing that came into my head. 'Well, I suppose there's nothing much to keep you here.'

Nelson bent down and picked a rose. He walked across and handed it to me.

'You're right, Maureen,' he said sadly. 'There's nothing much to keep me here.'

We said goodbye and I started walking down the drive. I was holding the rose in my hand. The rose was yellow, its petals tinged with red. I held it up to my nose and breathed in its scent and then I was running back up the drive.

Nelson was just about to go into the house. 'Nelson!' I shouted.

He turned around and started running towards me. I put my arms around him and said, 'There's lots to keep you here. There's me and Jack and Monica and Brenda and we all love you. Lots of people love you, Nelson, and we'll all be here for you when you come home.' There were tears pouring down both our faces.

'That's all I need to know,' he said. 'That's all I need to know.'

Chapter Thirty-One

Of course me and Jack couldn't stay away from each other for long and soon him and me and Monica were spending most of our time together again. It was December and freezing cold so it was getting harder to find places to go where we wouldn't actually freeze to death.

One evening we were sitting on our back step, shivering when Mum opened the kitchen door.

'For heaven's sake,' she said. 'Haven't you lot got homes to go to?'

Three frozen faces looked up at her.

'Come on then,' she said, sighing. 'You can go up to Maureen's bedroom.'

Gratefully we all trooped into the kitchen.

'I've got some soup on the go, will that do?'

'You're an angel, Mrs O'Connell,' said Jack, giving her a cheeky grin.

'An angel, eh?' said Mum, smiling.

'Absolutely,' said Jack.

We all ran upstairs and me and Monica plonked ourselves down on the bed.

'Where's Brenda?' said Monica.

'At Molly's birthday party. Molly's dad is bringing her home later.'

Jack was standing at the bedroom window. 'So this is where you spy on me,' he said, grinning.

'I stopped spying on you a long time ago, Jack Forrest,' I said.

Monica was lying on the bed, looking thoughtful. 'Do you think that the King is going to give up the throne, Jack?' she said.

Jack nodded. 'I don't think he's got a choice.'

'Nelson says they've backed themselves into a corner,' I said.

'I think Nelson's spot-on,' said Jack.

Monica sat up. 'I don't see why he can't marry Mrs Simpson and still be King. I mean, what difference would it make?'

'It's against the constitution,' said Jack.

'That didn't seem to bother Henry VIII much, did it? If he didn't get his own way he'd just chop someone's head off.'

'I think things have moved on a bit since then, Monica.'

'OK, Jack,' said Monica. 'Forget about the constitution, what do you really think?'

'I think that a man who puts his own needs before those of his people isn't strong enough to be King.'

'He's so good-looking though, isn't he?' said Monica dreamily.

'Maybe that's the trouble,' I said. 'Maybe all his life he's been told how special he is and now that he can't have his own way he's stamping his foot.'

'I think that if the King does give up the throne, his brother might well surprise us all,' said Jack.

'He's not nearly so good-looking though, is he?' said Monica.

At which point we all burst out laughing.

On the eleventh of December we were all crammed into Jack's front room, along with a bunch of neighbours. Jack's parents were the only people in the street with a wireless and we were waiting to hear King Edward speak from Windsor Castle. Once the wireless had warmed up, Jack's dad fiddled with the dials. It eventually crackled into life and let out a series of high-pitched whistles. There was some nervous laughter from the women in the room.

'I don't trust all this modern stuff,' said Mrs Boniface from number twenty-five.

'If it was up to you we'd still be living in the Dark Ages,' said Mr Boniface, scowling at her.

There were more crackles from the wireless, then someone started to speak.

'I think we're getting somewhere,' said Jack's dad.

'This is boring,' whispered Brenda.

'Shush,' I said.

'What's he going to talk about anyway?' she said.

'He's going to talk about him and Mrs Simpson.'

'Even more boring,' said Brenda, rolling her eyes.

'This is history, Brenda.'

'Well, I hate history.'

'Cover your ears then.'

The voice that had been coming out of the wireless faded away and there was more crackling and whistling.

Jack's mum came through from the kitchen carrying a tray of drinks.

'Has it started yet?' she said, putting the tray on the table.

'Your husband's still trying to get it to work, Mrs Forrest,' said Mrs Boniface.

Jack's mum squeezed herself in between Mrs Gadd from number twelve and Mrs Hacker from twenty-four.

Suddenly the King's voice boomed into the room, startling everyone. Mrs Boniface jumped and let out a girly squeal. Mr Boniface glared at her. I always thought that, in their case, Boniface was a very unfortunate surname because they definitely weren't.

Silence descended on the room as the King started to speak.

'At long last I am able to say a few words of my own. I have never wanted to withhold anything, but until now it has not been constitutionally possible for me to speak.

'A few hours ago I discharged my last duty as King and Emperor, and now that I have been succeeded by my brother, the

Duke of York, my first words must be to declare my allegiance to him. This I do with all my heart.

'You know all the reasons which have compelled me to renounce the throne but I want you to understand that, in making up my mind, I did not forget the country or the empire which, as Prince of Wales, and lately as King, I have for twenty-five years tried to serve. But you must believe me when I tell you that I found it impossible to carry the heavy burden of responsibility and to discharge my duties as King as I would wish without the help and support of the woman I love.'

You could have heard a pin drop in the room. Mrs Gadd and Mrs Boniface were sniffing and Monica was sobbing. I put my arm around her shoulder.

'Well, that's that then,' said Jack's dad, switching the wireless off. 'It's really happened and at least he's been honest about it.'

'But it's so sad,' hiccupped Monica.

Mr Boniface took out a tin of baccy and started rolling a fag. 'I'm not sure that brother of his has got the backbone for the job,' he said.

'Well,' said Mr Gadd, 'I reckon he picked a good'n with that wife of his. That little body's got backbone and I reckon, with her behind him, he'll be alright.'

'I shouldn't think he wanted this,' said Jack's dad. 'His brother has grown up knowing that one day he would be the King, he's been prepared for it all his life but Bertie hasn't and I think he will need all the support he can get. History has been made this day, so let us all drink to the health of our new King, George VI.'

Everyone stood, picked up a glass of sherry from the tray and looked at Jack's dad.

'God bless the King,' said Jack's dad.

'God bless the King,' said everyone else.

All I could think of was Peter standing in the middle of the bookshop with tears rolling down his face. I felt like giggling but I didn't want to spoil the moment. I needn't have worried, because at that point Mrs Boniface knocked back her glass of sherry and said, 'What I can't understand is why any woman in her right mind would call a baby Wallis.'

Chapter Thirty-Two

Nelson had been sent to an army training camp in Aldershot. He wrote to me and Jack every week and we wrote back. He seemed really happy. His letters were full of war manoeuvres on the wild, windy plains with a great bunch of young men from all over the country. 'Sometimes I feel as if I'm in a John Wayne movie,' he wrote. 'Remember when we used to run around the beach shooting at each other, Jack?'

He moaned about the food and the cold barracks but you could just tell that he was loving every minute of it. 'I've made good friends with a bloke from Liverpool. His name's Albert White and everyone calls him Chalky. I can barely understand what he's saying because of his accent but we hit it off straightaway.'

I looked at Jack's face as he read the letter and wondered if he was just a little bit jealous of Nelson's new friend, but he seemed happy enough. Jack wasn't the jealous type.

Our letters were dull by comparison. I tried to make the bookshop sound more interesting than it was and the customers funnier than they actually were. I told him all about Peter and Hassan sitting in the yard, putting the world to rights. I told him about Maggie and how nice she was and the dusty bookshelves that looked like they were going to fall down at any minute.

'What can I say about college?' said Jack one evening when we were replying to one of Nelson's letters, 'that is even mildly interesting?'

'It's enough that you are there, Jack, and doing what you always wanted to do. Nelson is so proud of you. We all are,' I added.

'There must be something else we can talk about,' said Jack, 'that isn't book related.'

We both sat thinking about what we could say to Nelson that was interesting.

'I know. We could go to the pictures,' I said. 'Then we can tell him all about the films, just like we used to.'

'You are a genius, Maureen O'Connell. What are you?'

'I'm a genius, Jack Forrest.'

'I don't even mind if it's a Western,' I said. 'Nelson likes Westerns.'

'There's a film on at the Regent called *Girls Can Play* starring Rita Hayworth. We could go and see that, maybe Monica would like to come.'

I was a bit disappointed that Jack wanted Monica to come with us; I wanted him all to myself, but that was selfish because I knew Monica would love to come.

Monica had the left the orange fingers factory and was now working at the golf-ball factory. Her fingers were gradually returning to their normal colour.

We were in my bedroom when I asked her about going to the pictures with me and Jack.

'Is it OK if I bring a fella along?' she asked.

'You've got a boyfriend?'

'Well, he's a boy and he's a friend so, yes, I suppose I have.'

'You never told me.'

'I'm telling you now, aren't I?'

'Does this boyfriend have a name?'

'His name's Norman and he's a foreman at the factory.'

'Blimey!'

'Don't look so surprised, I'm not that ugly.'

'You're not ugly at all,' I said, smiling.

'Anyway, it's about time *you* got one, isn't it?'

'I'm…'

'I know, you're destined to be with Jack.'

''Fraid so,' I said, grinning.

'Has Marion Tucker been mentioned since the incident in the barn?'

Just the thought of that night made me go hot all over. I'd been trying to block it from my mind and now Monica had to go and mention it. I wished I'd never told her.

'Not a word,' I said. 'And that's how it's going to stay. I made a fool of myself and it's never going to happen again. Not ever.'

'So now you are going to wait for him to make the first move, right?'

'Absolutely.'

'I don't want to bring you down, Maureen, but I can't help thinking that you're in for a long wait. Men can be a bit slow on the uptake when it comes to romance.'

'He wasn't slow where Marion Tucker was concerned, was he?' Bloody hell, I'd said it again.

'That's because Marion Tucker wasn't important to him.'

'Where did you learn so much about love all of a sudden?'

Monica grinned. 'The golf- factory. It must have something to do with being surrounded by balls all day.'

'Monica Maltby!' I said. 'Wash your mouth out with soap and water.'

We both started giggling.

I stared at her. 'I can't believe you just said that.'

'Better get myself along to Confession,' she said, making the sign of the cross.

'I don't go any more,' I said.

'What, never?'

'Nope.'

'I wish I didn't have to go.'

'You don't.'

'My dad would kill me if I didn't go to Confession.'

'How would he find out?'

'Father Ryan is one of his drinking buddies.'

'But a priest is bound by the seal of the Confessional,' I said.

'I should think that goes straight out the window after a few beers.'

'Blimey!'

'Is it because of your dad that you don't go any more?' asked Monica.

'They wouldn't bury him in the churchyard and I find that hard to forgive. I miss the church though – you know, the actual building. I used to light a candle for two doors down's dead dog that got squashed by the milkman's horse. Me and Brenda used to pray to the statue of the Blessed Virgin Mary. I miss that.'

'Couldn't you still go there?'

'I'm not sure.'

'I shouldn't think God would mind and he's more important than the church. In fact, he owns the church.'

'So you think it'll be alright for me to go, then?'

Monica nodded.

'Maybe I will.'

'If you get struck down by lightning, we'll know it was a bad idea.'

'Thanks,' I said, making a face at her.

'So is it OK if I bring Norman?'

'What, Norman the foreman?' I said, grinning. 'Of course you can. The more the merrier.'

Norman was shorter than Monica and quite solid-looking. You got the feeling that he would probably turn into a rather round man, but he had twinkly eyes and a smiley face and I could see why Monica liked him. He was also very intelligent and said that the golf-ball factory was a stopgap: he wanted to join the RAF but his mother was widowed and he had to work. Jack liked him a lot and the four of us started going round together.

That first night we went to the pictures was the night that Jack fell in love with Rita Hayworth. In fact, I think we all fell a little in love with her. She smiled down from the silver screen as if she was smiling only at us. She was just a teenager in the film but she seemed much older. I sat next to Jack in the dark cinema and we held hands. I looked across at Norman and Monica and saw that he had his arm around her shoulder. That night I wished that I was Rita Hayworth.

The four of us went to the pictures every week after that. We saw Westerns and comedies, war films and Hollywood musicals. We laughed at Charlie Chaplin and the Marx Brothers, we fell in love with an adorable little girl called Shirley Temple and we booed James Cagney playing the part of a tough gangster. And, of course, we watched Jack's beloved Rita.

Every film we saw, we shared with Nelson. Jack was better at bringing them to life than I was and I loved reading what he had written; it was like seeing the film all over again. Nelson loved getting our letters and we loved getting his. Then we got a letter saying he was coming home.

The following Saturday, Jack and I were standing by the barrier at Brighton station, waiting for Nelson's train to arrive.

'Where's he going to stay while he's here?' I said.

'I hadn't really thought about it,' said Jack. 'He didn't mention it in his letter.'

'I wondered whether he might be staying with you.'

'Not that I know of, but if he's got nowhere else to go, then he's going to have to.'

'He could stay with us, I'm sure Mum wouldn't mind.'

We leaned on the barriers and watched the trains chugging into the station. We watched the children hanging out of the windows, waving and cheering. Doors were opening and slamming shut as the trains deposited their cargo of men, woman and children onto the platform. Mums and dads were desperately trying to keep their children in their sights as they watched them run towards the gates, clutching their buckets and spades, looking forward to a day at the seaside.

We stepped away from the barrier as crowds of people pushed and elbowed their way towards the exit. Used tickets were almost thrown at the poor ticket collector, some of them missing their target and fluttering freely across the station. I could almost see them flying down West Street, circling over the sea and the pier.

'Did he say what time he was arriving?' I asked.

'He just said around one o'clock,' said Jack.

I looked up at the big clock on the wall. 'It's ten past,' I said. 'He should be on the next train.'

It was another twenty minutes before Nelson's train chugged into the station. It stopped with a huge judder, belching white smoke over the passengers who were stepping down onto the platform. We watched impatiently as people emerged from the smoke and then we saw him. He walked towards us out of the mist, like a hero in a Western.

'Nelson!' I yelled. 'Over here.'

Nelson grinned as he spotted us. Every time I saw him he looked different to the time before. He walked confidently towards us, unfamiliar in a dark suit, more the man than the boy.

I threw my arms around him and Jack thumped him on the back. Nelson dropped his case and him and Jack proceeded to play fight as they had always done.

I looked into his eyes and we smiled at each other. And there he was, the boy in the brown jumper.

It turned out that he would be staying at the home for destitute boys and it was Mr Farley who had given him the suit.

'It's not new,' said Nelson. 'But it's better than anything I've ever owned.'

'Well, it looks new,' I said. 'And I think you look very smart.'

We took the tram back to the estate, dropped the case off at my house and headed for the seafront.

Nelson took off his jacket and laid it on the stones for me to sit on. 'I've missed this,' he said as he leaned back against the old stone wall and looked out over the sea.

'No water where you are, then?' I asked.

'Just fields,' said Nelson. 'Miles and miles of them.'

'Like the Downs?' I said.

'Nothing like the Downs. Just miles and miles of flat country-side, not a rolling hill in sight.'

I picked up a pebble. It was smooth and flat and I gave it to him. 'Take this back with you,' I said. 'Then, when you find yourself missing this place, it will remind you.'

Nelson put the stone in his pocket. 'I shall keep it forever, Maureen,' he said.

Nelson was like that, he said nice things. Sometimes he was more like a girl than a boy. I wished Jack was a bit more like it. When I thought about the life that Nelson had, I wondered where all that softness had come from.

I watched as Nelson and Jack walked down to the water's edge. I stayed sitting against the wall. I thought perhaps it would be nice for them to have some time alone. These days the two of them didn't look so very different. Nelson had filled out and he'd grown. Looking at him didn't give me that bad feeling in my tummy that I used to get; the same feeling I had when I looked at my daddy. Nelson turned back and waved while Jack threw stones across the water.

I loved Nelson but I wished it had been Jack that turned back and waved.

Nelson was only home for a short time but we made the most of that week. I was working during the day and Jack was at college so Nelson took to coming into the shop and helping out with the books. Sometimes he joined Peter and Hassan on the bench in the little yard. In the evenings we walked along the seafront or up on the Downs. I don't know if it was deliberate but both Jack and I avoided the barn. Some evenings me and Jack went to the home and sat in the rose garden. We didn't do much but we were together and that's all we wanted.

On the following Sunday we took Nelson back to the station. It was sad saying goodbye to him but he promised that he would be back on his next leave. Me and Jack saw him show his ticket at the barrier. We watched the ticket collector tear it in half and then watched as he walked down the platform and boarded the train. He hung out the window waving to us, then he held up the pebble and I blew him a kiss. We watched the train getting smaller and smaller and the smoke billowing backwards and disappearing into the clouds.

Chapter Thirty-Three

Brenda had left school that summer and was working in Wool-worths with her best friend, Molly. My little sister was growing up. Sometimes it felt like only yesterday that me and Daddy were pushing her along the seafront in the squeaky old pushchair.

With two more wages coming into the house things were getting easier at home. It was nice to see Mum looking less worried. She hadn't had an easy life; I hadn't realised just how hard it must have been for her. It was Daddy who had been the fun one, he'd been more of a playmate than a dad. It was only as I grew older that I understood why Mum had never played with us; she'd been too busy trying to pay the rent and put food on the table. She didn't have time for games. The three of us were closer now and that made me happy.

Jack got a scholarship to study medicine in London. I was proud of him. He'd worked hard for it but I knew that I would be lost when he went. There had been several Marion Tuckers since the incident in the barn; they all had different names but they were all Marion Tuckers. I'd learned my lesson and never mentioned any of them to Jack. I would lose him for a few weeks, never much longer than that, and then he would come back as if he'd popped down to the corner shop for bread. But I was afraid of the girls he would meet once he left Brighton and went to university. They would be clever, like Jack, and they'd probably be able to afford nice clothes. They wouldn't be Marion Tuckers. I was driving myself mad thinking about it. What if he fell in love with someone? I'd been waiting almost all my life for him. I'd never so much as looked at another boy. In fact, I was getting a reputation for being stuck-up. Monica thought I was barmy.

We were sitting on the lawn in front of the Royal Pavilion; this was Monica's idea. She said that we should broaden our horizons and, apparently, sitting on the lawn in front of the Royal Pavilion was going to broaden them.

'You'll get a better class of person walking past.'

'Yes, but they're walking *past*, Monica, they're not stopping to chat, are they?'

'Something might catch their eye, like my glorious mane of red hair, for instance, and Bob's your uncle, we're whiling away the afternoon with a better class of person.'

'Better than who though?'

Monica shook her head. 'Just go with it, Maureen, don't spoil my master plan.'

'I didn't know you had one.'

'Of course I've got one, the same as you have.'

'I have one?'

'Isn't your master plan to marry Jack Forrest and be a doctor's wife?'

I grinned. 'Yes.'

'You should have a back-up plan though, just in case.'

'Just in case what?'

'In case it doesn't turn out quite as you want it to.'

'I don't need a back-up plan,' I said. 'I shall marry Jack and be a doctor's wife and we'll live in a little house with roses round the door and have four beautiful children.'

'It amazes me how sure you have always been about it.'

'If I can't be with Jack, I don't want to be with anyone.'

'Well, I'm keeping my options open.'

'What about Norman of the golf balls?'

'I like him, he's fun to be with, but he's not part of the great master plan.'

'Which is?'

'To be rich.'

'What about love? Where does love come into it?'

'It doesn't. I mean, I hope I don't actually hate him but I can cope without loving him. Anyway, love doesn't last forever, does it?'

'Doesn't it?'

'Nope, and once it's gone, what are you left with? A bunch of kids you can't afford to feed and a drunken husband who can't even remember your name, let alone a time when he ever loved you.'

I realised then that she was talking about her mum and dad. 'It doesn't have to be that way for you, Monica,' I said gently.

'I can't take the chance, I just can't. I'd leave home if it wasn't for Mum and Archie.'

'I'm sorry.'

'I wish Mum would stand up to him but she never has.'

'I suppose she's scared of him. He scares *me* and I don't have to live with him.'

We got up and started walking across the lawn. I slipped my arm through hers. 'I really hope your master plan works out for you, Monica.'

'I'm going to make bloody sure it does,' she said, squeezing my arm.

I often went to visit Mrs Bentley, who said that fate had thrown us together the day Daddy asked if he could have the dolls' pram.

We were sitting in her beautiful front room. I felt more comfortable in her lovely posh house these days and I think it was because Mrs Bentley was so ordinary; she might have been rich but I knew that she never looked down on me.

'You've done wonders with the bookshop, Maureen,' she said. 'I hardly recognise it these days.'

'I've enjoyed doing it.'

'And what about my brother-in-law? Does he get in the way much?'

'He sits out in the yard with Hassan most of the time and when he's not with Hassan, he's listening to Mantovani and having a snooze,' I said, grinning.

'He dons a suit and tie every day and tells me he's going to work,' she said, smiling. 'I think he feels as if he's doing something and quite honestly, Maureen, I don't think I could stand having him here all day.'

'I used to think he was your husband,' I said.

'Good heavens, child, what made you think that?'

'Well, he lived with you, so I thought he must be your husband.'

'He decided that I needed looking after when my husband, his brother, died. As it turned out, it was Peter that needed looking after.'

I grinned. 'I think that Maggie and me look after him as well.'

'Then he's a lucky man and a very clever one, by the sound of things. He's got us all running around after him.'

'We don't mind,' I said. 'I was terrified of him to start with but I think we're friends now.'

'He speaks very highly of you, Maureen.'

'That's nice.'

'Are things alright at home now?'

'They're better. Brenda is working as well now, so things are easier for my mum.'

'I'm glad.'

'Something's been puzzling me.'

'And what's that?'

'I've never seen Peter read a book, or even look at one. Maggie says the same.'

'Haven't you realised?'

'Realised what?'

'Peter can't read, Maureen.'

I was shocked; I couldn't imagine never being able to read. Even if you are really poor or unhappy or life is getting you down, you can open a book and be transported to wonderful places and meet exciting people; you don't have to travel anywhere except inside your head. I thought that it was sad that Peter couldn't read.

'Doesn't he mind being surrounded by books every day?' I asked.

'The bookshop has been in the family for years,' said Mrs Bentley. 'It was started by Peter's great-grandfather, Herbert Bentley. Peter found school difficult, he was unhappy there, so his father would take him to the bookshop and he would spend his days amongst the books. I think that the shop became a safe place for him and, believe it or not, he loves his books. In a funny sort of way the books became his friends even though he couldn't read them.'

Listening to Mrs Bentley made me realise that you could have all the money in the world but there are some things you can't buy, like love and friendship and being able to read a book.

Chapter Thirty-Four

There was a cloud hanging over England. Some people were sure that there was going to be a war. Older men said that the First World War was the war to end all wars and that it was never going to happen.

Peter and Hassan spent hours discussing it. I'd never seen Peter look so animated. Victory marches were blasting out of the record player and strategies discussed in great detail. The little yard at the back of the shop became the centre of operations. Peter decided that, between them, they had it all worked out.

One day, Hassan's wife came into the shop, looking for him.

'He's in the yard,' said Maggie, 'plotting their next big move.'

'I wish he *would* bloody move!' said Hassan's wife. 'I'm sick of lugging these carpets around on my own while he sits and puts the world to rights. He can't even put his own shop to rights. I'm left with the buying and the selling and the cooking and the cleaning. I've had enough, girls, I've had enough. Someone should remind him that he is a seller of carpets, not a bloody politician!'

It was the longest speech we had ever heard come out of her mouth. Me and Maggie listened in astonishment.

'Would you like a cup of tea?' asked Maggie.

'How can I have a cup of tea?' she screamed, 'when I have a shop to run?'

'I'm sorry for your trouble,' said Maggie.

'Being sorry isn't going to help me lug those bloody carpets, is it?'

'Perhaps we can help?' I suggested.

'It's Chamberlain out the back that needs to be helping, not you girls.'

'We don't mind,' said Maggie.

Mrs Hassan was going red in the face. We were beginning to worry about her.

'Would you like to sit down?' I asked gently.

She ignored me and carried on complaining.

'He doesn't even call me by my name,' she went on. 'He calls me Mrs Hassan, as if I'm some sort of appendage. Mrs Hassan, where's my food? Mrs Hassan, where's my shirt? Mrs Hassan, where's my paper?' She stormed towards the back of the shop and started yelling out of the back door. 'I have a beautiful name, Hassan, it's Afshid, which means splendour of the sun. I never *see* the bloody sun, all I see are bloody carpets! I've had enough, Hassan, I've had enough. I shall go back to my homeland and you can sell the bloody carpets yourself!'

I looked at Maggie and I could see that she was struggling not to giggle; so was I.

I joined Mrs Hassan at the back door and there was her husband and Peter, chatting away as if nothing had happened. Mrs Hassan pushed past me.

'May he be eaten by a goat!' she screamed as she stormed out of the shop, slamming the door behind her.

Maggie and I doubled over with laughter.

'He didn't even look up,' she gulped, tears streaming down her face.

'Maybe he's used to it,' I said, wiping my eyes.

'Blimey, it's enough to put you off marriage!' said Maggie.

'Not me,' I said, taking some books out of a box and arranging them on the shelves.

'Tell me, tell me,' said Maggie.

I started to climb the ladder so that I could reach the upper shelves.

'I might one day,' I said, winking at her.

* * *

I worried about the war a lot; I worried about the safety of the people I loved. I suppose that is what ordinary people do, they think about those closest to them and not how a war might affect the rest of the world. I worried about Nelson because if there was a war he would be one of the first to go and I worried about Jack because although he wasn't in the army, he was young and he would have to fight, and I worried about Brenda, who would be scared and Mum, who'd already lived through one war. Every night I prayed that Chamberlain was right and there would be peace in our time.

Jack and I talked about it. We were sitting on the pebbles on our favourite beach. We'd avoided that beach for a long time because it was close to the lagoon but it held such happy memories of those times with my dad and Brenda that we started going there again. It was November but it was mild. I was happy sitting beside Jack. The sea was so calm and still, hardly making any noise as it rolled gently over the pebbles.

'On a day like today it's hard to believe there might be a war,' I said.

'Maybe there is no good time to have a war. Maybe war doesn't care where or when it strikes,' he said.

'Do you really think there will be a war, Jack?' I asked.

'Hitler has already invaded Austria and he's just marched into Czechoslovakia. Either Britain stands by and does nothing or we go to war.'

'Would Nelson have to fight?'

'I think that if we went to war Nelson would *want* to fight. He's not a coward, Maureen.'

'I'm scared, Jack.'

He put his arm around my shoulder and I leaned into him.

'I think we're all a little scared,' he said.

Hearing Jack say that he was scared worried me even more, because Jack wasn't scared of anything.

'What if you really didn't want to fight? What if you refused to fight?'

'In the First World War, men who refused to fight were called conchies. They were treated pretty badly; they were called cowards and shirkers. Some of them were imprisoned for their beliefs. I'm sure there were a few cowards amongst them but I think most of them just didn't believe in killing another human being. One of my dad's best friends was one of them and my dad said there wasn't a cowardly bone in his body.'

'What happened to him?'

'He was a stretcher bearer on the front line and he was killed in battle but he stuck by his beliefs and he never killed anyone. He refused to carry a gun, even to defend himself. My dad said he was one of the bravest men he knew.'

'Was Nelson's dad brave?'

'I think that he must have been, because I've never heard my dad say a bad word against him.'

'I'm glad about that, because I think Nelson's kindness must have come from his dad and not his mum.'

'I think you're right.'

'Does your dad know where Nelson's dad is now?'

Jack shook his head. 'Well, if he does, he's never said.'

He stood up and held out his hand. I took it and we walked down to the edge of the sea.

'This will be our best defence,' he said, looking out over the grey water.

We stood quietly together, listening to the waves trickling onto the shoreline. It was like that between me and Jack; we were comfortable in each other's company even in the silent moments.

He squeezed my hand. 'This could be our last Christmas in peacetime, Maureen.'

'Then we'll make the best of it, Jack.'

'Yes, we will, my love,' he said.

There might be a war coming but something wonderful had just happened: Jack had called me his love. I didn't say anything but my heart was bursting with happiness.

Chapter Thirty-Five

Monica and I were sitting on a bench opposite the Royal Pavilion, waiting for a better class of person to walk by. Well, *Monica* was waiting for a better class of person to walk by.

'So tell me again,' she said. 'How exactly did he say it?'

'He just said it, why?'

'Because it's important. Was the emphasis on the word *my* or the word *love*?'

I closed my eyes and thought about it. He'd said, 'Yes, we will, my love.'

'I don't think he emphasised either word, he just said it kind of softly,' I said.

'Softly is good,' said Monica. 'And you're definitely sure that he said the word "my"?'

'Definitely.'

'Because if he'd just said "love", it wouldn't have meant as much as "*my* love".'

'Wouldn't it?'

'No, you can say "love" to anyone. You can say "love" to a shopgirl or a clippie or a girl that works in a factory with you and it doesn't mean anything, it's just a friendly thing to say.'

'Bloody hell, Monica, how complicated can two words get?'

'You swore,' said Monica, looking shocked. 'You haven't sworn for ages. When you were a kid you used to swear all the time.'

'I stopped.'

'Why?'

'Two reasons. The first was that Daddy said that if I was going to be a doctor's wife I might have to stop swearing and the second was that Brenda had started to copy me.'

'Do you miss it?'

I nodded. 'Yeah, I love the word "bloody".'

'Me too,' said Monica.

'So do you think it meant something, what Jack said?'

'I think it's a start,' said Monica. 'But I don't want you to get your hopes up too much because he might not say it again any time soon. That's not to say he won't, but be prepared for a long wait.'

'I've been waiting eight years already.'

'Which means you could be waiting another eight before he gets round to proposing.'

'Thanks, Monica, that's very encouraging.'

'You're very welcome.'

Monica and I sat watching the better class of people walking by. I was beginning to think that we were wasting our time. I didn't much like it there. The Royal Pavilion was too sort of majestic and big and man-made. I preferred the sea and the Downs, the places I'd been with Daddy. Me and Daddy had never come here. We hadn't needed a better class of person to make us happy.

'I think I'd like to light a candle,' I said suddenly.

'What, now?'

'Yes. I want to ask our Blessed Virgin Mary for some help with Jack.'

'I think you might be better off going to the main altar, Maureen, and asking God for a miracle.'

I made a face at her and she grinned. 'We might as well go now,' she said, getting up from the bench. 'I think I've given up on a better class of person stopping to talk.'

'I gave up weeks ago,' I said.

I hadn't been to my old church for ages on account of the fact that I was finding it hard to forgive them for not burying Daddy. It felt lovely to be back though. I loved the stillness of the place. It was chilly inside, the only warmth coming from the rays of watery winter sun filtering through the beautiful stained-glass windows. The familiar smell of the place took me back to my childhood – I was always fascinated by the altar boys in their white robes, swinging the incense back and forth.

Me and Monica walked down the main aisle, genuflected in front of the Blessed Sacrament and headed straight for the little side altar. We knelt down in front of Our Lady's statue. I looked up at her and she smiled gently down at me; I'd missed her. We put our pennies in the old tin box and lit our candles.

'What are you going to pray for?' whispered Monica.

'I'm going to pray for two doors down's dead dog cos I haven't prayed for him for ages and he must be feeling a bit neglected. Do you think he's still squashed, Monica?'

'No, once you die you lose your body and all that's left is your spirit. I shouldn't think Anne Boleyn is wandering around the place without a head.'

'I hadn't thought of that.'

'I am a very thinking person, Maureen.'

'I never doubted it for one minute, Monica.'

'What about Jack?'

'Once I've said a prayer for the dead dog, I'm going to ask Our Lady if she can give Jack a bit of a nudge. What are you going to ask for?'

'Well, I was going to ask her if she could see her way clear to sending me a chap with loads of money.'

'I don't think you can ask for money, Monica.'

'Can't you?'

'I don't think so. Why don't you ask if she can send you someone with a good job? I mean, it stands to reason that if he's got a good job he's bound to have a bit of money.'

'Good idea, Maureen.'

I watched my candle flickering away and I felt at peace with the world. I suppose that I was still a Catholic; after all, I'd been baptised a Catholic. I just hoped that the Blessed Virgin Mary could overlook the fact that I hadn't been to Confession or Holy Communion for ages so I wasn't in a state of grace. I hoped that she would still listen to my prayers.

I left the church feeling hopeful. I was glad that we'd come. Now all I had to do was wait for the Blessed Virgin Mary to come up with the goods. I hoped we didn't have to wait too long.

Since Jack had spoken those two words I had been bursting with happiness. Maggie said it was like I'd developed some kind of awful illness and I was scaring potential customers away by walking up to them with a weird sort of grimace on my face.

'It's not a grimace, it's a smile.'

'Well, it's a very weird sort of a smile.' Maggie screwed up her face and started walking towards me looking like something from another planet. 'That's how you look,' she said. 'It's putting people off.'

I finally told her all about Jack and how he was the only boy for me, otherwise she would have thought that I was going soft in the head.

'You've been in love with him for *how* long?'

'Just the eight years.'

'Bloody hell, Maureen, please don't tell me you've never been out with another boy?'

'Never,' I said. 'My heart belongs to Jack.'

'But how can you be sure if you haven't tried another boy?'

'What do you mean, *tried* another boy? It sounds as if you're talking about a new brand of soap.'

'You know what I mean.'

'No, I don't.'

'Well, don't you want to kiss another boy?'

I made a face. 'I'd rather be boiled in oil. How many boys have you kissed then?'

'Plenty,' said Maggie, grinning. 'I love kissing boys.'

'Well, I'm saving myself for Jack.'

'But is Jack saving himself for *you*?'

I thought about it and said, 'Probably not but it doesn't matter, because he always comes back to me.'

'I don't know whether you're a complete idiot or a saint.'

'I'm a saint, Maggie. You are working with a saint.'

Maggie looked at me kindly. 'I just hope you don't get hurt, Maureen, because you deserve to be happy.'

'And I will be,' I said. 'There are some things in life, Maggie, that are worth waiting for, and Jack's one of them.'

Chapter Thirty-Six

It was almost Christmas but this year it didn't feel very Christmassy. Everyone was talking about the likelihood of a war with Germany. Everywhere you went, people were putting in their own two pennies' worth. I'd go into a shop and then I'd be kept waiting for ages while the shopkeeper held court from behind the counter. If you were desperate for a couple of sausages then you became part of a captive audience while the butcher bestowed on you his invaluable opinion on what was going to happen next. You either stared at his mouth opening and closing or the row of dead pigs hanging behind him. All in all, buying sausages wasn't going to be the highlight of your week.

Brenda and I both had Wednesday afternoons off, so we decided to do some Christmas shopping. I didn't spend so much time with my little sister these days because she was always with her best friend, Molly. They went everywhere together. Molly was a lovely girl and I was happy that Brenda had found such a good friend.

As Brenda grew up she remained the sweet funny girl that she had always been. She was scared of thunder and lightning, so on those stormy nights I would feel her crawling into bed beside me and cuddling into my back. I liked feeling her there.

We decided to have a cup of tea in Wade's department store before we started our shopping.

'Who are you going to buy for?' I asked Brenda.

'I want to get something nice for Mum,' she said. 'And Molly.'

'Why don't we buy something for Mum between us, then we will be able to get her something really special?'

'Good idea,' said Brenda.

'Well, I want to get a present for Jack, Nelson and Monica,' I said.

'What about Aunty Marge?'

'That would be nice, we can get her something between us as well.'

The waitress came across carrying a tray. She was wearing the familiar Wade's uniform of a black dress with a white apron tied around her slim waist and a little white cap on her head. She looked smart and pretty.

'Christmas shopping, are you?' she said, putting cups and saucers down on the table in front of us.

'Yes,' I said. 'But we thought we'd have a cup of tea first.'

'Well, you couldn't come to a better place than Wade's,' she said proudly. 'I find other tea emporiums very sub-standard by comparison.'

The girl was trying to speak in a posh voice but every now and then she would slip up and you just knew that she probably came from a council estate just like us but, as Jack was always saying, it didn't do any harm to try and better yourself.

'Would you like to partake of one of our scones?' she asked, smiling.

'Just the tea, thanks,' I said.

'Have a nice day then,' she said, picking up the tray and walking away.

'Tell me if I ever start talking like that,' said Brenda.

I grinned at her. 'Don't worry, I will.'

We finished our tea and headed for the shops.

'I wish we had a record player,' I said.

'I bloody wish we had a record player as well.'

'Language, Brenda,' I said.

'Sorry, but I do wish we had a record player. Molly's got one in her front room, it's lovely. It looks like a piece of furniture and her mum is always polishing it.'

'Is Molly's family rich, then?'

'I don't think they're rich but I'm pretty sure they've got more money than we have.'

'The rag and bone man's got more money than we have, Brenda.'

'I suppose so.'

'It's just that Mum loves that record by Artie Shaw called "Indian Love Call". I'd love to have bought it for her for Christmas but there's no point if there's nothing to play it on,' I said.

'Don't you just hate being poor, Maureen?'

I caught hold of her hand and squeezed it. 'We're OK.'

'Of course we are,' she said, smiling.

We made our way to Woolworths, where stuff was cheap and you could get almost anything for a few pennies. The counters were piled high with Christmas ornaments and gifts. At every counter Brenda chatted to the assistants she worked with.

'We're never going to get anywhere at this rate,' she said as we left one counter.

I laughed. 'It's the cheapest place in town so we're just going to have to do the best we can. Have you any idea what you're going to get for Molly?'

'Red lipstick,' said Brenda, grinning. 'Molly loves red lipstick.'

We walked over to the cosmetics counter and Brenda picked the brightest red lipstick she could find. It was called Hawaiian Sunset.

'I bet it's never been anywhere near Hawaii.'

'Would Monica like a lipstick?' said Brenda.

'I'm going to get Monica and Jack a book, they both love reading.'

'How much can you afford for Mum's present?' asked Brenda.

'About three shillings.'

'We'll be able to get her something great for six shillings.'

'Now, how about Aunty Marge?' I said.

'A tea strainer,' said Brenda. 'Uncle John stood on it and it's all squashed.'

'A bit like two doors down's dead dog,' I said, grinning.

We headed for the kitchen counter and chose a tea strainer that came with a little dish.

'What about Mum?' asked Brenda.

'Let's go to the bookshop first, then we'll have a good look round for Mum's present.'

We walked along, passing all the shops. Christmas lights twinkled in the windows and shone out over the grey pavements. It was still early but it was already starting to get dark. We pushed open the bookshop door and the little bell jangled above our heads. It was lovely and warm inside and the air was filled with dust and must and old books. It never failed to amaze me how much I had grown to love this old shop. The thought that I might have ended up in a factory made me shudder.

'Couldn't keep away?' said Maggie, smiling at us.

'I'll have you know we're customers and expect a bit of respect from the paid help,' I said, grinning at her.

'Get you,' she said, smiling. 'Well, you know where the books are, so carry on.'

Just then Mrs Bentley came in from the yard. 'I swear those two think they're going to win the war single-handed. Hello, girls,' she said as she noticed us. 'What brings you here on your day off?'

'They are customers,' said Maggie, making a face. 'Apparently they want some respect.'

'And so they should,' said Mrs Bentley.

'And how are you?' she asked, smiling at Brenda.

'I'm fine, thank you, Mrs Bentley. Still working at Woolworths.'

'When I think of you, Brenda,' she said, smiling, 'I always think of that sweet little girl in the squeaky pushchair.'

'And when I think of you,' said Brenda shyly, 'I always think of a very kind lady who gave us help when we needed it.'

'So we will always think of each other kindly,' said Mrs Bentley.

'Always,' said Brenda.

'Now, Maureen, who are you buying books for?'

'Jack and Monica,' I said.

'And how are they?'

'Jack is working hard at the university and Monica is working at the golf-ball factory. She used to work in a different factory but it turned her fingers orange.'

'That doesn't sound good.'

'It wasn't, that's why I persuaded her to leave.'

'So they both like to read, do they?'

'Yes.'

'And what are they interested in?'

'Jack likes anything to do with Hollywood and Monica likes anything to do with rich people,' I said, grinning.

'Well, I think you're in luck where Monica is concerned. Only this morning someone came into the shop and sold us a book about the fashion designer Coco Chanel. I imagine she was pretty rich. It's a lovely book with beautiful photos of all her designs. Do you think that she would like that?'

'I think she would love that.'

'Good. Maggie, would you mind wrapping it up for our customer? And don't forget to take off the staff discount.'

'Of course, Mrs Bentley,' said Maggie, winking at me.

I went over to the bookshelves and took out a book about Rita Hayworth. I'd been looking at it for weeks and I knew that Jack would love it. I gave it to Maggie and she wrapped it up for me.

Mrs Bentley picked up her coat that was draped across the chair. 'Where are you off to now?' she asked.

'We want to get something nice for Mum,' I said. 'Me and Brenda are putting our money together so that we can get her something special.'

'Hannington's have some lovely things,' said Mrs Bentley.

I could feel my face getting red. I didn't want to tell her that we didn't have enough money to shop in Hannington's. Maggie came to our rescue.

'The stuff in Hannington's is pretty pricey, Mrs Bentley,' she said.

'Which is why I have an account there,' said Mrs Bentley, smiling. 'If we smile very nicely at the shop assistant, we may get a small discount. I was just about to go there myself. Shall we go together?'

I looked at Brenda, who nodded.

'OK,' I said.

We said goodbye to Maggie and made our way along Western Road, then we cut through the side streets until we came to the beautiful building that was Hannington's department store. Me and Brenda gazed up at the tall structure. It was four stories high with beautiful windows; the stonework was powdery blue like the sea when the sun shone on it. I felt very small standing there – our sort shopped in Woolworths, not Hannington's. Brenda slipped her arm through mine.

Mrs Bentley was already walking through the doors. She turned back and saw us standing there like a couple of store dummies.

'Chop, chop!' she said, smiling at us.

'Come on, Brenda,' I said. 'It's only a bloody shop.'

'Language, Maureen,' she said.

Mrs Bentley strode ahead of us as if she owned the place. I'd noticed that rich people did that. It didn't matter what they looked like. They didn't have to be dripping in diamonds and pearls to get noticed, there was just something about the way they held themselves that said 'I'm rich'. Whereas poor people spent their time apologising for breathing. It wouldn't matter what you dressed me and Brenda in, you'd still know that we came from See Saw Lane and we were skint as old boots.

We hurried after her, trying not to draw attention to ourselves.

'Now,' she said as we caught up with her, 'what did you have in mind for your mother?'

'Just something nice,' squeaked Brenda.

'How about a nice woollen scarf? Do you think she'd like that?' I nodded.

'Now, do you mind if I ask what your budget is?'

Brenda looked at me blankly.

'She wants to know how much money we've got,' I whispered.

When we were sat in Wade's having our cup of tea, six shillings had sounded like a fortune but suddenly it didn't sound like very much at all. I cleared my throat. 'Six shillings,' I said.

'I think we'll find something lovely for that,' she said.

I must have looked relieved. 'Really?'

'Oh yes, the scarf counter is just over there by the lifts, you go and have a look and I'll speak to an assistant about the discount.'

We went over to the counter that was selling beautiful woollen scarves and gloves. We could tell that they were way out of our price range. There were no prices on anything. In Woolworths everything was labelled so you knew right away whether you had enough money to buy it. Suddenly Mrs Bentley was behind us.

'Aren't they lovely?' she said, picking one up. 'Feel how soft they are, girls.'

I picked up a pale lilac scarf; I'd never felt anything so soft in my life. I would have loved to get it for Mum, she deserved something as lovely as this but I knew we couldn't afford it.

'That's a good choice, Maureen,' said Mrs Bentley. 'It's a beautiful colour and it will go with almost any outfit.'

My mum didn't have outfits, she had skirts and jumpers for in the week and a blouse for best.

'And how about some gloves to match?' said Mrs Bentley.

Brenda had this frantic look on her face and I could feel sweat gathering under my armpits.

I swallowed the bile that was making its way up my throat. 'Mrs Bentley?' I whispered. 'I didn't mean that we had six shillings each, I meant we had six shillings between us.'

'You're forgetting the discount, Maureen. Now, shall we say the lilac scarf and the matching gloves?'

I nodded – I didn't know what else to do.

'Now, do you have any more gifts to buy?' said Mrs Bentley.

'Not in here,' said Brenda quickly.

Mrs Bentley laughed. 'Why don't you explore and I will see what I can do about that discount?'

Brenda and I walked away from her as fast as we could.

'Bloody hell, Maureen,' said Brenda, 'it's going to have to be one hell of a discount!'

'We should have got Mum something in Woolworths,' I said.

Mrs Bentley was walking towards us, smiling. She had a bag in her hand, which she handed to me. 'Six shillings exactly.'

I handed her the six shillings. 'We have to go.'

'Of course you do,' she said, smiling. 'Happy Christmas, Brenda.'

'Happy Christmas, Mrs Bentley.'

We left the store as fast as we could. I was clutching the bag tightly to my chest, afraid that any minute someone would yank it out of my arms. We hurried along the street, not speaking until we got to a bench outside Timpson's the shoe shop.

'What did you make of that?' I said after I'd got my breath back.

'Well, all I can say,' said Brenda, 'is that it makes no sense to give rich people money off things when it's us they should be giving discounts to.'

'I'm not convinced about the discount thing,' I said.

'What do you mean?'

'It doesn't matter. Come on, let's go home. I'm freezing.'

Chapter Thirty-Seven

Even though the threat of war was hanging over us, we had a lovely Christmas. I always missed Daddy on Christmas morning. I missed the way that he was always up first. I missed the way he couldn't wait for me and Brenda to wake up and come downstairs – I think he was more excited about Christmas Day than any of us. Me and Brenda still had the dolls' house that he had made out of Uncle John's apple box and the pieces of furniture he'd glued together from his fag packets. Christmas would never be quite the same without him.

We may have left the Catholic Church, but every Christmas since Daddy died, Brenda and I made our way there and we knelt in front of the Nativity and we lit our candles. I prayed for two doors down's dead dog, I prayed to the Baby Jesus to take care of my daddy, and I prayed for my good friend Nelson, who might have to go to war.

We walked home in the cold morning air, calling out a merry Christmas to the people we passed. As we passed Jack's house I remembered Nelson, on a Christmas morning long ago, cold and wet on the doorstep. He had looked so sad and alone that day that my heart had broken for him. I hadn't known what was going to happen to him and I was so scared. It had seemed like a terrible thing to learn that he had to go and live in the home for destitute boys but it was there that he had found kindness and his life had gradually got better. I was proud of Nelson.

Mum loved her lilac scarf and gloves. She put on the gloves, wrapped the pretty scarf around her neck and waltzed around the kitchen, laughing.

'These must have cost a fortune, girls, the label says Hannington's.'

'Ah,' said Brenda, 'you have to take into account the discount.'

'Discount?' said Mum.

'It's what they give to rich people, Mum.'

'So why did they give it you?'

'They didn't,' said Brenda, 'they gave it to Mrs Bentley. Hannington's don't give discounts to poor people.'

I winked at Mum and she didn't press Brenda any further.

'Well, they are the most beautiful Christmas presents that I have ever had and I shall forever be indebted to Hannington's and their very generous discount. I shall wear them the next time I go round to your Aunty Vera's and I shall make sure that the label is in full view,' she said, grinning mischievously.

Our house looked lovely with the sweet-smelling tree in the corner and a roaring fire in the grate. The usual decorations that were brought out year after year were strung across the ceiling and bunches of dark green and red holly decorated the mantelpiece. Daddy should have been here. There were still times when I was angry with him for leaving us; I missed him so much.

Mum had bought a big, plump chicken and Aunty Marge and Uncle John had provided the fruit and veg. Mum presented Brenda and I with a wristwatch each. We had never owned anything like it before and we were delighted. Brenda kept pestering everyone to ask her the time. I worried about how much they must have cost, but I guessed they came off the tallyman and Mum was paying for them on the never, never, along with the three-piece suite. Aunty Marge loved the tea strainer and Uncle John looked suitably shamefaced.

We pulled crackers and toasted each other with sweet red sherry. After dinner Mum, Aunty Marge and Uncle John fell asleep so Brenda went to Molly's house and I called round to see Monica. I waited on the doorstep while she got her coat because I was scared of her dad.

We walked up onto the Downs. The wind was blowing a gale but we didn't mind. There was something about the wildness of the Downs that we both loved. We only saw one family who were bravely battling the high winds; we said hello as we neared them.

'This seemed like a good idea half an hour ago,' said the man, 'but I'm not so sure now.'

'We needed to walk off the dinner,' said the woman.

I smiled and wished them a happy Christmas.

We'd only gone a short distance when the heavens opened, so I grabbed Monica's hand and headed for the only shelter I knew – the barn.

We were soaked by the time we got to the bottom of the hill. We pushed open the big wooden door and went inside.

'You look like someone's poured a bucket of water over your head,' giggled Monica.

'You don't look so great yourself,' I said, wiping the rain out of my eyes.

We sat down on the floor in one of the stalls and that's when we heard the noise. A rustling, some movement.

'There's someone else in here,' whispered Monica.

We stayed very quiet, then we heard it again, a definite rustling.

'Perhaps it's a rat,' I said.

'A rat!'

'Or a bird,' I answered quickly. 'Probably a bird.'

'Well, whatever it is, I'm getting out of here.'

'Shush!' I said. 'Wait a minute.'

'Why?'

'Listen.'

We sat there in the darkness, terrified, listening to the rain belting down on the roof of the barn.

'Perhaps it's just the rain,' said Monica hopefully.

Then we heard whispering. I stood up.

'Where are you going?' said Monica urgently.

I ignored her and walked towards the door to let in some light. The rain was coming down in torrents, blowing across the entrance of the barn and thundering down the grassy hill. It blew into my face, soaking me again.

'Maureen,' called Monica. 'What are you doing?'

I saw movement in one of the stalls, then I heard a girl let out a giggle. I recognised the voice: it was Marion bloody Tucker.

Then a deeper voice. 'Shush!' he said.

I flung open the door and started running, with Monica behind me.

'Maureen!' she was shouting. 'Wait for me.'

But I kept running. The rain was stinging my face but I kept running – I had to get away from there. Monica caught up with me and pulled at my arm. I stopped. I was struggling for breath, so was Monica.

'What the bloody hell's the matter?' she gasped.

'Didn't you hear them?' I screamed.

'Hear who?'

'That was Marion bloody Tucker in there.'

'Was it?'

'And she was with Jack.'

Monica looked at me as if I had three heads. 'How do you know it was Jack?'

'I heard his voice.'

'For God's sake, Maureen, whoever it was only said "shush!". It could have been anyone.'

I started walking away from her. 'It was Jack,' I said quietly.

Monica slipped her hand through mine. 'You're sure?'

'I'm sure.'

'There's a tea room at the top of the hill, let's go there and dry off.'

'It's Christmas Day,' I said, 'it's probably closed.'

'Let's see,' said Monica.

We were both cold and wet.

'OK.'

To our surprise it was open and a few people were sitting at the tables, including the family we'd met earlier. It was hot in there – steam was rising off the coats hanging on the backs of the chairs. Everyone looked soggy and wet and miserable.

We sat down at a table overlooking the hills; we couldn't see much because the windows were all steamed up. A waitress came across to us. She was holding a little notebook and a pencil. 'What can I get you?' she asked. She was a pleasant-looking girl with a wide, round face and eyes that looked permanently surprised.

Monica looked at me and I shrugged my shoulders. 'Have you got any cocoa?' she asked the girl.

'We're having a run on the stuff,' she said.

'How come you're open today?' asked Monica.

'I was working yesterday and I left my bag behind. I only popped in to get it but there were all these people standing out-side, soaking wet, so I opened up. I can't serve any hot food, but cocoa I can do.'

'It was good of you,' said Monica, smiling at her.

'Well, they're all asleep at home, snoring their bloody heads off. Quite honestly, I'd rather be here. Christmas can be a funny old time, can't it? Everyone determined to have a nice time with people they'd rather not be with. My aunt and uncle and three cousins are there, we only ever see them at Christmas. I never got on with them but I was forced to smile at them as they shovelled food into their mouths. No, I'd much rather be here. I'm going to volunteer next year. Listen to me going on. Two cocoas, is it?'

'Yes, please,' said Monica.

I rubbed at the window with the sleeve of my coat. It was still pouring with rain, lashing against the glass; it looked as miserable out there as I felt. Jack had been with Marion bloody Tucker. He was there with her now in the barn, when he should be at his gran's. The same barn where I'd made a fool of myself. I felt sick.

'Look, Maureen,' said Monica gently, 'you have to tell Jack how you feel because he doesn't know. As far as he's concerned, you're just friends and he isn't doing anything wrong. You have to tell him.'

I shook my head. 'I can't.'

'You have to. There might be a war and if there is, things are going to change. None of us know what's going to happen.'

'But what if he doesn't feel the same way I do?'

'Then at least you'll know. You'll be sad, but at least you'll know. You can't make someone love you, it's not enough that you love *them*. I know that Norman feels a lot for me because he's told me but that won't make me fall in love with him. Please, Maureen, tell him how you feel. When are you seeing him again?'

'This evening.'

'Then tell him. Just tell him.'

Chapter Thirty-Eight

When I got back home they had started on the leftovers and mince pies.

'Good God, girl, you're soaked!' said Aunty Marge, jumping up and peeling my wet coat from my shoulders. 'I said to your mother, "If that girl's got caught in that rain, she's going to know it."'

'We sheltered in a barn,' I said.

'Well, that barn must have a leak,' said Aunty Marge.

I knelt down in front of the fire and held out my hands towards the warm coals. I could see the steam coming off the cuffs of my cardigan.

'You should get out of those wet clothes, Maureen,' said Mum, 'before you catch your death.'

'I don't want to leave the fire,' I said.

'Go and get changed, love, then come down and have something to eat.'

'I'm not hungry, Mum.'

'Maybe later then,' she said.

I stood up and started walking towards the door.

'Was Jack with you?' said Mum, suddenly.

I turned around. 'No, why?'

'He called in earlier, I told him you were with Monica.'

'Oh.'

I left them and went upstairs. Jack's book was on the little table beside my bed, wrapped in red Christmas paper. It looked jolly, a damn sight jollier than I felt. From the moment I'd seen Jack, from my perch in the tree, I hadn't doubted for one minute that one day we would be together. I thought that I had enough love in me for the both of us. Maybe I'd been wrong all these years, maybe my love wasn't going to be enough. Maybe Jack was never going to love me. I wished Daddy was here, he would have understood. He wouldn't have thought that I was silly for feeling this way, he would have known what to say to me. I closed my eyes and tried to picture him and there he was. I could almost smell the yellow margarine on his hair. I could almost feel the stubble on his cheeks and the smell of Senior Service on his breath.

'What should I do, Daddy?'

He smiled at me and that smile seemed to say, '*You'll know what to do,*' and then he was gone. I opened my eyes. Monica was right: I had to tell Jack how I felt. I might be about to make a complete fool of myself but it was time he knew.

I pulled the curtains, took off my wet clothes and put on some dry ones, then I lay down on the bed. I must have fallen asleep because the next thing I knew, Mum was gently shaking me.

'Jack's downstairs, Maureen, shall I send him up?'

I rubbed at my eyes and sat up. 'What?'

'It's Jack,' she said, 'he's called round for you. Shall I send him up?'

'OK,' I said.

I got up, grabbed a comb and ran it through my damp hair. I looked in the mirror: the face staring back at me looked white and puffy-eyed from sleep. I'd wanted to look nice for Jack when I told him, instead I looked like something the cat dragged in.

There was a tap at the bedroom door and Jack came into the room, smiling. 'Happy Christmas, Maureen,' he said, holding a small parcel towards me.

I picked up his present and handed it to him. 'Happy Christmas, Jack.'

We sat beside each other on the bed and I started unwrapping my gift. Jack was smiling at me as I took off the paper. I folded the paper carefully and placed it on the table beside the bed.

I was holding a small black velvet box. I opened the lid and inside, laying on a bed of pink satin, was a beautiful silver cross and chain.

'I hope you like it,' said Jack. 'I know you don't go to church much these days, but I thought it was pretty.'

'It *is* pretty,' I said. 'It's lovely and I love it, thank you.'

Jack took the necklace from me. 'Let me put it on for you.'

I turned around. He gently moved my hair away from the back of my neck. Neither of us spoke as he did up the clasp. I could feel his breath, cold, on my skin and I wanted this moment to last forever.

I turned around and faced him. 'Now yours,' I said.

He grinned and tore the red wrapping paper from the parcel, then dropped the paper on the floor. 'Wow!' he said as he looked down at the picture of Rita Hayworth on the front cover of the book.

He put his arm around my shoulder and hugged me.

'Do you know what, Maureen?' he said. 'You know me better than anyone else in the world. No one but you would think of buying me this. Thank you, it's perfect.'

After that I didn't know what to say to him and it seemed by the silence in the room that Jack didn't know what to say to me either. After what seemed like forever, he broke the silence.

'I called for you earlier,' he said.

'I know you did.'

'Your mum said you were with Monica.'

'That's right. We were up on the Downs, we got caught in the rain.'

'So you sheltered in the barn,' said Jack. 'It was *you* in the barn, wasn't it?'

'And how would you know that?'

'You know how.'

'Yeah, I do. You were canoodling with Marion bloody Tucker when you told me you'd be at your gran's.'

'I *was* at my gran's, but she wasn't feeling well so we brought her back to our house. You sound angry,' he said. 'I told you, I called for you. I went up the Downs, guessing that's where you might have gone. That's when I bumped into Marion. You *are* angry, aren't you?'

'I'm not angry,' I said, getting off the bed and going over to the window. I pulled the curtain back. It was pitch-black outside and the rain was trickling down the window pane. This was the time: if I didn't tell him now, I never would. I turned round and faced him. I could tell that he was totally confused – he didn't have a clue, not one bloody clue.

'Don't you know, Jack? Don't you know?'

'Know what?'

I looked at him sitting there on the bed, the book still in his hands.

'I'm not angry, Jack, I'm jealous.'

He shook his head; he still didn't understand.

'Of Marion? You're jealous of Marion? Why would you be jealous of her?'

'Because you were with *her* in the barn when you should have been with me.'

'But you were with Monica.'

'Are you blind as well as stupid, Jack Forrest? I love you, you idiot.'

I watched the book slide off his lap. 'You love me?'

'I've always loved you. You must have known.'

He stared at me, then he pushed his hair back from his eyes and he leaned down and picked up the book. He looked worried, he looked shocked.

'But we've always been friends,' he said quietly. 'Best friends. You and me and Nelson, we've been mates. You've been great, Maureen, one of the boys.'

Then he realised what he had said and started mumbling. 'I mean, I know you're not a boy…'

'No, I'm *not*,' I spat back. 'I'm a girl, Jack. I'm as much a girl as Marion Tucker is.'

'I know, that was a stupid thing to say. I know you're a girl, of course I do, but I've never thought of you in that way. We've always been friends, such good friends. You've been like a sister to me.'

'I don't want to be your sister,' I said sadly. I could feel the tears running down my face. Jack jumped up off the bed and came across to me. 'Don't cry, Maureen. Please don't cry.'

'I'm not,' I said.

'You are, my love,' he said, gently wiping my face.

He took my hand and led me back to the bed. We sat side by side. He put his arm around my shoulder. 'I never realised how you felt, Maureen, and I'm flattered, I am, but I'm not worth your tears.'

'You are to me.'

Jack lay down on the bed and he pulled me down beside him. We lay there quietly. I'd done it, I'd told him and the world hadn't come crashing down on my head. He hadn't run from me, he was still here, beside me.

'I never realised,' he said softly. 'I just never realised. I thought maybe you and Nelson. You are both so alike, so kind, so loyal, so funny… I never realised.'

'Only you, Jack. It's only ever been you.'

He sat up and rested on his elbow. He stared down at me as if he'd never seen me before. He casually tucked a strand of hair behind my ear then he stroked my cheek, so gently, so very gently. I held my breath as his lips touched mine and then we were kissing and it was the sweetest kiss in the world. He drew away from me and shook his head. 'I've been a fool, I've been such a fool.'

I looked into his eyes that were as blue as the sea. I touched his lips that had touched mine. In that moment it felt as if the weight of the world had lifted from my shoulders. I felt like a child again, as if I'd just been born, and I wanted to laugh out loud. I wanted to dance – I wanted to dance with Jack.

He lay down again and held me close to him. My head was on his chest. I could feel his heart and mine beating in harmony. I was safe in Jack's arms, where I had always wanted to be. I had come home.

Chapter Thirty-Nine

War was raging across Europe; people were dying. Everyone was saying it was the end of the world as we knew it, but it was the beginning of mine. Everything was better – the sky was bluer, the grass greener. It was like I was living the best of every summer, every spring, every autumn and every winter that I had ever lived. I felt everything more keenly; the sun on my face and the wind in my hair. I had never felt more alive. And everyone was my friend. I even thought about calling in to see Aunty Vera, Uncle Fred and Malcolm and telling them I loved them. I felt generous in my happiness and I wanted to share it with everyone. But I didn't go and see them because they would have thought I'd lost my marbles.

I had thought that loving Jack all these years was what had made me happy, but I was wrong: to be completely happy, you need to be loved in return. I had been living a kind of dream. Wishing and hoping, making more of the little things that Jack said and then lying in bed at night and going over and over them until I had convinced myself that he loved me, when in fact he hadn't, he'd just been talking to me like one friend to another. Jack hadn't known he'd loved me, he'd never even thought of me in that way. Now he did, now he knew, and my happiness was complete. No more dreaming and longing and wanting, this time it was real: Jack loved me.

When I told my mum about me and Jack, she didn't seem a bit surprised.

'I thought you were already walking out,' she said.

'What?'

'I did, because you were always together. I just thought you hadn't got round to telling me yet.'

'Oh, Mum,' I said, smiling at her.

'As long as you're happy.'

'I *am* happy, Mum. I'm happier than I've ever been.'

'Well, the way things are going, I think this world of ours can do with as much happiness as it can find.'

'Are you scared, Mum?'

'Of the war?'

'Yes, are you scared that we are going to go to war?'

'I've lived through it before and I never thought that it would happen again so yes, I'm scared. I'd be a fool not to be.'

'It might not happen,' I said.

'You might need to go and light a few candles.'

'I've already asked the Blessed Virgin Mary to look after Nelson.'

'How is he?' said Mum.

'We haven't seen him for a while. In his last letter he said that they were confined to barracks because of the threat of war. He said the war games on Salisbury Plain didn't feel like games any more.'

'I'm almost glad your father isn't here to see what's happening. I don't think he could have coped with another one.'

'Can I ask you something, Mum?'

'Of course.'

'Why was Daddy so ill? Because I never knew.'

'I've been waiting for you to ask me that. I didn't want to say anything until you asked.'

'I didn't want to upset you, I didn't know how to ask.'

'Come and sit beside me, Maureen.'

I walked across to the couch and sat down. I tucked my legs underneath me and my mum and I held hands.

'You really want to know?' she said.

I nodded.

'During the last war your daddy was in the Navy. He didn't wait to get called up, he volunteered. His ship was heavily bombed. He saw good friends blown up in front of his eyes. He had to shovel body parts of his friends into sacks. Can you even begin to imagine that? Can you imagine having to relive those memories every single day?'

I shook my head.

'He saw things he couldn't even tell me about, so they must have been even worse than that. He came home a broken man, Maureen. He never talked about it much. I think it would have been better if he had, but he relived those nightmares at night. That dear man could get no peace. Before the war he worked on the railways and he tried to go back to it but he thought the trains were going to run over him. He came home in tears and he was never able to work again. It wasn't his fault, Maureen, but I think he was ashamed that I had to go out to work while he stayed at home. In the end, he couldn't bear the shame of it any longer and he left us.'

There were tears running down Mum's face. I put my arms around her and we cried together and then we dried our eyes and we smiled, because we had known him and we had loved him and he would never be forgotten.

'Thank you telling me, Mum. I had never understood.'

'I couldn't tell you when you were a child, it would have been too much for you, but now you know.'

'Do you think that Daddy will be pleased about Jack and me?'

'All your daddy ever wanted was your happiness, Maureen. I'd say at this very minute he's sitting on a cloud laughing his head off and wishing you all the luck in the world.'

'I miss him so much, Mum.'

'I know you do.'

We didn't do much, Jack and I, it was enough that we were to-gether. We walked on the Downs, we canoodled in the barn, we strolled along the seafront and when it was warm enough, we sat on the pebbles eating fish and chips out of the paper.

On New Year's Eve we wrapped up warm and joined a crowd of people heading towards the seafront. War seemed inevitable and there was an air of living for the moment in the crowds of mostly young people making for the beach. They were laughing and singing, kissing and dancing. We saw a young man get down on one knee and ask his girlfriend to marry him and when she said 'yes' everyone started clapping and he picked her up and swung her around. The Palace Pier was lit up, the light reflecting in the grey waters beneath. Music was coming from the ballroom at the far end. I had always wanted to dance with Jack and now maybe, just maybe, one day I would.

The sky was full of stars for as far as you could see, way, way out over the horizon. And then the bells started ringing out from all the churches across Brighton and passing ships hooted their horns. Everyone cheered and strangers kissed strangers. People jumped down onto the pebbles and those brave enough ran into the icy-cold sea. Jack took my face in his hands. 'Happy New Year, Maureen,' he said and then we kissed, cold lips touching cold lips. But I was warm inside Jack's arms and I knew that I always would be.

I put my head on his shoulder as we looked out over the inky-black water and I wondered what 1939 would bring.

Chapter Forty

Despite the threat of war, life carried on. It had been a hard winter and everyone welcomed the spring. The days were longer and the nights were warmer. It was a time of new beginnings. Everything that had been asleep came to life and turned black and white into glorious colour. Crocuses pushed their way through the earth and emerged in glorious shades of white, purple, yellow and orange. The air was fresh and the sky was blue. Bright yellow daffodils swayed in the cool breeze and sweet-smelling honeysuckle wrapped itself around hedgerows.

Jack and I spent a lot of our time walking on the Downs. The rolling green hills were dotted with white daisies and yellow dandelions and golden buttercups. Sometimes we would stand very still at the top of the Devil's Dyke and just listen. We decided that the whispering grass had a language all its own. We listened as the wind picked up the sound and carried it across the hills and out towards the sea. Nature seemed to be putting on a show just for me and Jack, or maybe it was for all young lovers. We gloried in it, we gloried in each other.

'Remember when it was snowing and we used Brenda's old pushchair as a sledge?' said Jack.

'I remember everything,' I said.

'Did you love me then?' he said, smiling.

'I always loved you.'

'And I never knew.'

'But you do now.'

'We wasted a lot of time.'

'No we didn't because even when you didn't know I loved you, we were still together. We still share the same memories. You were my friend and I was yours and anyway, Monica says you have to like someone before you can love them. I think I'm right in saying that you always liked me.'

'You were OK, I suppose… for a girl.'

'Jack Forrest!' I said, punching him playfully on the arm.

'Race you down the hill!' he said, running away from me.

I caught up with him and he pulled me down onto the grass and we lay there, looking up at the blue sky and the bright yellow sun.

We hadn't seen much of Nelson and we both missed him. It seemed ages until his next leave; this time he was staying at my house.

Jack, Monica and I met Nelson at the station. I was so happy to see him – I hadn't seen him for so long. We all hugged. The sun was shining as the three of us walked out of Brighton station. He only had a small bag with him so we headed straight to the seafront. A new cafe had opened up under the prom. It had tables and chairs outside so Monica and I sat down while the boys got cups of tea for us all.

'Nelson looks so grown-up, doesn't he?' said Monica.

'Are you warming to him then?' I said, grinning.

'Not in that way, daft.'

'Cos he's skint?'

Monica laughed. 'Not *just* that, Maureen.'

'What, then?'

'I think that you and Jack make a very good pair, because both of you are blind as bats.'

'What are you talking about?'

'Nelson's only got eyes for *you,* Maureen.'

'For me?'

'Yes, you.'

'We're just friends, Monica.'

'Isn't that what Jack said to you? He thought you were just friends?'

'I know, but...'

'But nothing. That poor boy has been mooning over you for as long as you've been mooning over Jack.'

'Jack said he thought that Nelson and I might get together.'

'Not so blind after all then.'

'What am I going to do about it?'

'There's nothing you *can* do about it. Nelson knows how you've always felt about Jack. It will be no surprise to him that you're together at last.'

'I've always talked to him about Jack. He's always known that Jack is the only boy for me but now I feel bad.'

'Don't. Nelson is a lovely chap and there's a very lucky girl out there somewhere just waiting for him to sweep her off her feet.'

'I wish he wasn't staying at my house now.'

'Maybe I shouldn't have said anything,' said Monica. 'Nothing's any different to how it's always been. He's still Nelson.'

'But if he feels like that about me, then he must be hurting and I'd hate to think that.'

'Nelson thinks enough of you to be glad for you. When you love someone you want what makes them happy. I think, in his heart, Nelson knew that there was a chance that you and Jack would end up together and he'll be glad for you.'

'Monica?'

'Yes?'

'I know that Jack cares for me and wants to be with me but...'

'But what?'

'He's never told me that he loves me. He's never said the actual words.'

'That's because he's a boy,' said Monica. 'Boys seem to find it hard to say those three words. If it's really bothering you, then

you'll have to ask him. You'll have to say, "Do you love me, Jack?"
Then you'll know for sure.'

'I'm not going to ask him, it won't mean the same.'

'Then you'll just have to be patient, and if anyone can do patient, you can.'

We couldn't say any more because just then the boys came back with the tea.

'Our Nelson's learning to drive tanks,' said Jack, putting the cups and saucers on the table.

'I don't think I'd like to be cooped up in a tank,' said Monica, blowing into her cup.

'I didn't like it myself at first,' said Nelson, sitting down. 'I felt a bit trapped. But now I feel differently about it. The alternative is hand-to-hand battle. I'd rather have a ton of steel between me and a bullet, I can tell you.'

'Do you think you *will* be going into battle?'

'I keep praying that something will happen to stop this war but the longer it goes on, the more I fear it's inevitable. We've just been told that the German flag has been raised in Prague.'

None of us spoke for a while. We just sat there sipping our tea and thinking our own thoughts.

'Bloody men! Present company excluded, but bloody men,' said Monica. 'It's not women who start wars, is it?'

'I can think of a few,' said Jack. 'Cleopatra, for a start, and then there was Boudica, Joan of Ark, Matilda of Tuscany… Shall I go on?'

'OK, clever clogs,' said Monica, grinning.

'Just saying,' said Jack.

I loved listening to Jack; I loved that he was so clever. I hoped that I would be enough for him and that he wouldn't tire of me because I didn't know all the stuff he knew. He was mixing with really intelligent girls every day at university; he must realise that I would never be like them, not in a million years. Jack was still speaking.

'So you see, Monica, it's not just bloody men that start wars, it's bloody women as well.'

She made a face. 'What else are they teaching you, Nelson?'

Nelson looked sad for a moment as he sat there looking out across the sea.

'They are teaching me how to kill people, Monica,' he said.

Chapter Forty-One

However much Jack and I wanted to shut out the rest of the world, we couldn't. We had chosen the worst of times for this great love affair of ours. I'd waited eight years for him to fall in love with me and he'd managed to do it just as the country decided to go to bloody war. I had a feeling my swearing was about to come back with a vengeance.

The government supplied gas masks for every household. They were horrible, ugly things and when you put them on, you could hardly breathe. They smelt of rubber and disinfectant. When we finally persuaded poor Brenda to try hers on, she had a panic attack. She was shaking and crying and we had to sit her down and get her a cup of hot, sweet tea.

'I won't wear it, Mum, I won't,' she sobbed.

'You might not have to, love,' said Mum. 'It's just a precaution, that's all.'

We were given cardboard boxes to carry them round in and it became a daily reminder of the dangerous times ahead of us.

Anderson shelters were delivered and erected in back gardens. The shelters could hold six people, so we shared one with Jack's family. Every evening you could hear the sounds of hammering and banging as men bolted together the six curved sheets of metal that made up the shelters. I watched Jack and his dad, with their sleeves rolled up, shovelling earth on top of it and patting it down. When it was all finished, I looked inside. It had no floor, just the damp earth that it had been built over.

'How are we all going to sit in there?' I asked Jack.

'Don't worry, love,' he said. 'Me and Dad are going to put planks down and we're going to build a couple of benches so that we all have somewhere to sit.'

We managed to get Brenda to put her head inside but she refused to go any further.

'It feels like a coffin,' she said.

'It's not a place to die, Brenda,' said Mum. 'It's a place to live.'

I had a feeling that if a bomb did fall, Brenda would be the first inside, sitting on the bench as pretty as you like.

Leaflets came through the doors advising us about blackout restrictions. Most people in the street couldn't afford to go out and buy black curtains, so we all dyed our old sheets and blankets ready to use if we needed them.

Peter and Hassan had gone up a gear. Every book about war was lifted off the shelves and taken outside to the bench. Peter had taken to wearing his father's medals pinned to his suit jacket. Afshid was going demented and forever storming into the bookshop and screaming at him out the back door.

'The stupid man says if we go to war, he will sign up. He has flat feet, lumbago and he can't see more than two feet ahead of him. If the likes of him are going to defend the country, we might as well surrender right now.'

'I'm sure he'll calm down soon,' said Maggie.

'I shall pack my bags, I shall return to my homeland and I shall leave the war to Hassan.'

We nodded our heads in sympathy. Despite all her threats we knew that she would never leave him because, in between shouting at him, she was forever supplying him with sandwiches and drinks and every morning she quite happily trotted off to buy newspapers. She would read the paper on the way back from the shop and then she'd announce the latest news to the war council. Peter and Hassan had by now acquired an old table from the junk shop down the road. The centre of operations was growing by the day. Victory marches continued to blast out of the record player, which attracted the attention of other shopkeepers. Once the baker next door had finished baking his bread and cakes he would walk through the shop and into the yard, leaving a trail of flour all over the floor. Which was preferable to the butcher marching in, in his blood-soaked apron. It was the baker who suggested they put up tarpaulin over the bench and table to protect the books and maps from the rain.

Mrs Bentley said that the only good thing to come out of this impending war was that it had given Peter a purpose in life that he hadn't had for a long time.

Jack continued to travel to London to attend university. He told us about the sand bags that were being piled up in front of the War Office and the trenches being dug in the parks; also the huge silver barrage balloons floating over the rooftops like drowsy, fat slugs. He said that sometimes in bad weather they had to be cut free and they would float around completely out of control, smashing into chimney pots and taking tiles off the roofs. It all sounded scary and I wanted him to stay at home. I feared that if bombs were going to drop anywhere, it was going to be London. I wanted him home with me, where he would be safe.

Everyone was going to be issued with identity cards and we would all be given a special number and food was to be rationed.

There were so many rumours flying about. Some people were saying that the Germans had already landed and were living amongst us. There was so much suspicion and theories around that some people almost wished the war would start, then at least everyone would know exactly who they were fighting.

On September the 1st their wish was granted, when Germany invaded Poland and Britain declared war on Germany. On September the 3rd, neighbours once again packed into Jack's front room. Mr Forrest fiddled with the knobs on the wireless and tuned in just in time to hear the voice of Neville Chamberlain.

'I am speaking to you from the cabinet room of 10 Downing Street. This morning the British Ambassador in Berlin handed the German government a final note stating that unless we heard from them by eleven o'clock that they were prepared at once to withdraw their troops from Poland, a state of war would exist between us. I have to tell you now that no such undertaking has been received and that, consequently, this country is at war with Germany.'

There was stunned silence in the room. Brenda was gripping onto my arm and tears were pouring down her face. Then a couple of women started sobbing.

Suddenly Mrs Forrest's voice broke through the silence.

'Well, at least our Jack will be alright. He's a student, you see, a medical student. He won't be called on to fight.'

Jack looked uncomfortable. 'Mum,' he said quietly. 'I don't think people want to hear about me.'

'I was just saying…' she went on.

'There's a time and a place, Moira,' said Mr Forrest, 'and this isn't it. There are women here with sons.'

I hadn't known that about medical students and part of me was relieved, but I agreed with Mr Forrest that this was not the time to announce it to the rest of the room.

Mum and Brenda went home and me and Jack walked down to the bottom of the garden and sat on the bench.

'So you won't have to fight?'

Jack looked thoughtful. 'Apparently not,' he said quietly.

'How does it make you feel?' I said.

'Less of a man, Maureen. That's how it makes me feel.'

'But at least you'll be safe.'

'We'll see,' he said.

'Promise me you won't go, Jack, promise me.'

'Look, Maureen,' he said, 'I might never need to go. The regular army will be called up first and then the volunteers. The war may be over by the time it gets to me so stop your worrying. I'm going to have enough of that to deal with, with Mum.'

But I was scared, because he hadn't said he wouldn't go. He hadn't promised anything at all.

Chapter Forty-Two

Aunty Marge and Uncle John came round to help us put up the dyed sheets. Brighton was a town in waiting; we were all holding our breaths, not knowing what was going to happen next.

It was the worst winter anyone could remember. Freezing ice and snow covered the pavements and hills but no one was dragging sledges and trays up onto the Downs and I thought that was sad.

The worst thing about the blackout was coming home from work. Not only could you not see a thing but the pavements were like ice rinks. Maggie and me would cling to each other as we made our way to the bus stop. Kerbs had been painted to help us see but we still managed to stumble all over the place. It had its funny moments though, bumping into complete strangers and grabbing hold of them to stop ourselves falling into the road. We could hear them laughing and apologising but we couldn't see their faces.

'Just imagine, Maureen,' said Maggie as the bus trundled slowly through the dark streets, 'I could have been in the arms of my future husband and I wouldn't have known it.'

'I'm not sure that this a good time to think about having a husband,' I said. 'I mean, imagine being married and having children at a time like this. I'm worried enough about Jack in London and Nelson in the army without worrying about children as well.'

We hadn't heard from Nelson in months except for the Christmas card that had arrived after the New Year. In February a letter came through the door. When I opened it, I could see that it was addressed to Jack, Monica and myself so I waited until we could read it together.

The three of us were sitting cuddled up under a blanket on my bed. I handed the letter to Jack. 'You read it,' I said.

Jack started to read.

Dear Maureen, Monica and Jack,

I hope you don't mind that I have written this letter to all three of you but I needed to get a letter out quick. We are on the move, getting ready to leave barracks. They haven't told us where we are going and I couldn't tell you even if I knew. I will be joining the Royal Tank Regiment, so hopefully all that training will have paid off.

I don't want you to worry about me cos I am a lucky fellow. I have you three as my best friends, how lucky can a guy get? You are my family and I love you all very much.

Keep safe, my friends, and take care of each other. Keep lighting those candles, Maureen.

All my love,
Nelson xxx

None of us spoke, we were lost in our own thoughts. Jack folded the letter and gave it to me. Me and Monica were struggling not to cry and I knew that Jack was too.

Jack broke the silence. 'He'll be OK,' he said.

I didn't know if he was trying to reassure me and Monica or himself.

'Of course he will,' I said, but even as I said it, I didn't know that I believed it.

We found ourselves talking about Nelson; we all had our own special memories.

'Remember the bloody awful brown jumper?' said Monica.

'I've still got it,' I said, grinning.

'Really?'

I nodded.

'I wonder why he loved it so much?' said Monica.

'His gran knitted it for him and he loved his gran,' I said.

'He didn't have it easy, did he?' said Jack.

'But he always managed to smile,' I said.

'And that's what's going to get him through,' said Jack.

'I'm banking on it,' I said.

We limped through those first few months of 1940. Brenda was a bag of nerves; every time she heard a bang she burst out crying, thinking it was a bomb.

'We'll get a warning, Brenda. There are people whose job it is to let us know when the planes come over and everyone will have time to get to a place of safety,' said Mum.

'This is a terrible time to be alive!' sobbed Brenda.

Mum held her hand. 'We'll get through it, love. We got through the first war and we'll get through this one. We all have to be brave.'

'I don't think I'm very brave at all, Mum.'

'Yes, you are,' I said. 'You were always a brave, funny little girl. It was you that kept us all going when times were hard. You have bravery inside you, Brenda, you just have to find it.'

'I'll try,' she said, giving me a watery little smile.

'That's my girl,' said Mum, hugging her.

The reality of war came home to us all when we heard that the British Army had their backs to the sea on the beaches of a place called Dunkirk. The government called for anyone with a seaworthy boat to sail to France and help in the evacuation of the men. Thirty-nine British destroyers made their way across the sea, joined by over a thousand fishing boats, pleasure crafts and lifeboats. Jack and I watched as the ferryboat called *The Brighton Belle* left the harbour to bring our men home. I had never felt so proud as I did that day.

Over three thousand soldiers were saved and the operation became known as 'The little ships of Dunkirk'. Sadly, *The Brighton Belle* was one of many ships that never made it home.

Afshid, who had become the font of all knowledge and there-fore a key member of the war committee out in the yard, in-formed me and Maggie that they were going to close the Palace Pier and take up the middle section of planks so that the enemy couldn't use it as a landing stage. The night before it was due to close, Jack and I went down to the seafront.

There were only a few people hanging around the entrance to the pier. They'd come to look at the big guns standing ready to be placed on the end of it. We stood close together, leaning on the railings and looking out across the grey water. It was as still as anything, not a ripple disturbed its flat surface. You could barely hear the gentle waves that lapped the shore.

'I wonder if Nelson is somewhere over there,' I said.

'He could be,' said Jack. 'In fact, I'm pretty sure that he is.'

It was getting dark and it seemed even darker without the light from the lamp posts that ran along the length of the prom. People had started to drift away and soon we were the only ones there.

'Come on,' said Jack, grabbing my hand.

'Where are we going?'

'You'll see,' he said, grinning.

In one leap Jack jumped over the turnstile, then helped me over.

'Are you sure we should be doing this?' I said, trying to climb over as elegantly as I could.

'There's a war on, Maureen, I shouldn't think anyone will care.'

We held hands and ran to the end of the pier. Jack stopped outside the ballroom.

'You said that you wanted to dance.'

'Yes, I did.'

Jack pushed the door and it opened. The moon was shining over the water and in through the windows.

'May I have the pleasure?' he said, bowing.

His voice echoed across the empty space.

'You may,' I said, and walked into his arms.

Jack held me close to him and started humming 'Moonlight Serenade' very softly in my ear.

I put my head on his shoulder, his face was soft and warm against my cheek. We started to dance, slowly, slowly, across the floor, our bodies fitting together just like I always knew they would.

'Happy?' said Jack, kissing me softly on the lips.

'Mmm.'

'See that woman over there?' he said.

'What are you talking about?' I said, looking around me.

'Over there,' he said. 'The brassy blonde in the red dress, you can't miss her.'

Then I realised he was joking, so I played along. I looked across the empty dance floor and said, 'Yes, I can see her.'

'Don't ever dye your hair that colour, Maureen.'

'I won't,' I said, 'I promise.'

'Because I love you just the way you are.'

'You love me, Jack?'

He nodded. 'Always and forever.'

I caught hold of his hands and spun him around. Jack was laughing.

'You mad girl,' he said.

'Jack Forrest loves Maureen O'Connell!' I shouted and my words bounced back to me across the empty floor.

Jack stopped and looked into my eyes. 'You must have known.'

'Say it again, Jack,' I said.

He took my face gently in his hands and looked into my eyes.

'I love you,' he said softly. 'I love you.'

The moon cast shadows of light across the room as we stood there wrapped in each other's arms.

Then we kissed again and we danced to the music in our heads. Round and round we went until I was dizzy with happiness and dizzy with love for a boy that I had waited to dance with for almost all my life.

Chapter Forty-Three

On 2 July the beaches were closed. Coils of barbed wire were put up all along the seafront and big concrete boulders placed on the beach to stop tanks gaining access to the town. No one was allowed on the seafront after five o'clock in the evening. It was so sad to see our beautiful beaches like this. We had spent all our childhoods here, sitting on the pebbles, paddling in the sea and balancing on the wooden groynes. We wondered if our town would ever be the same again.

Jack and I took to walking up on the Downs but even this was changing. Trenches were being carved into the beautiful hills. The whole place was crawling with big heavy tanks and soldiers. The Devil's Dyke was out of bounds. Brighton was preparing for war.

At the weekends Jack and I and sometimes Monica and Norman went to the pictures. Jack's new love was Ava Gardner but Rita Hayworth was still his favourite. Mum and I were worried about Brenda, who managed to go to Woolworths every day but refused to leave the house once she'd come home. I tried talking to her about it.

'No bombs have dropped on Brighton yet, Brenda. You should enjoy yourself while you can.'

'I know I should,' she said. 'But I hate the blackout and I'm so relieved to get home that I don't want to go out again.'

'We don't know how long this war is going to last. You can't hide yourself away, love. I don't want to scare you, I really don't, but if Brighton does get bombed, you'll be no safer in the house than you would be outside.' I held her hands in mine. 'Me and Mum are worried about you and if your dada is looking down on us, then he's going to be worried about you as well.'

Brenda's eyes were filling with tears. 'I wish he was here,' she said.

'I don't.'

'Don't you?' she said, shocked.

'It was the First World War that made him ill.'

'I didn't know that.'

'Well, it was and I don't think he could have coped with another one.'

Brenda dried her eyes.

'OK,' she said. 'I'll do my best.'

'Dada would be very proud of you.'

She cuddled into me. 'Thanks, Maureen,' she said.

Every day trains were pulling into Brighton station, carrying evacuees from London. They were a pathetic-looking bunch and I felt so sorry for them. It must have been dreadful to be torn away from everything you knew and have to say goodbye to your mum and dad. As many families as were able opened up their homes to these poor frightened children; that's how we ended up with Gertie, and it was Gertie who found the bravery in my little sister.

Mum, Brenda and I went to Brighton station. There were crowds of people, mostly women, waiting for the train to come in from London, carrying the evacuees.

Mum gave her name to an official-looking woman who was sitting behind a table. 'We'd like to take a little girl into our home,' said Mum. 'You see, there are no men in the house so we thought a girl would be best.'

'Do you mind what age she is?' asked the woman, barely looking up.

'No,' said Mum. 'We don't mind.'

Eventually the London train chugged into the station and the crowd surged forward.

'Keep back, keep back!' shouted the woman. 'It's not a cattle market.'

We watched as the train doors opened and children of all shapes and sizes climbed down onto the platform. They seemed a sorry bunch, clutching their parcels close to their chests and looking completely bewildered. My heart went out to them. They were carrying gas masks across their shoulders and they all had labels pinned to their coats.

The woman was still screaming, 'Hold hands, all of you, and line up! That's right, a nice straight line, so that the good people of Brighton can look at you.'

She had said it wasn't a cattle market but that is exactly what it was beginning to feel like. Names were called out and children were chosen.

'Look at her,' said Brenda, staring at the line of children.

'Which one?' I said.

'The one in the green coat.'

The little girl looked to be about seven or eight. She had a mass of tousled straw-coloured hair and she was grinning at Brenda, who was grinning back at her.

Brenda tugged at Mum's sleeve. 'That's the one,' she said. 'Get her quick before anyone else does.'

'I can't just walk up and grab her, Brenda.'

Luckily the woman called out Mum's name. 'Mrs Perks?' she bellowed across the station.

Mum stepped forward. The woman was just about to take the hand of a rather large child when Mum said, 'It's alright, we'd like to take that little girl,' pointing to Brenda's chosen child.

'Well, she has two brothers with her. I don't imagine you want all of them.'

'I suppose not,' said Mum sadly. She looked at Brenda and shrugged her shoulders. 'Sorry, love,' she mouthed.

'Wait a minute,' said the woman and she walked across to the little girl. When she came back, she was smiling. 'She doesn't mind being separated from her brothers and, quite honestly, it might make it easier to place the boys. Her name is Gertrude Lightfoot and she's eight years old. She must write to her family at once and let them know where she is staying.'

'Of course,' said Mum, then she walked across to the line of children and took Gertrude's hand. We ran over to them. Mum knelt down so that she was on the little girl's level. 'Hello, Gertrude,' she said, smiling.

''Allo, missus,' said the little girl in a broad cockney voice. 'You me new mum, are ya?'

Mum laughed. 'I'm not your new mum, Gertrude. I'm just going to look after you for a while.'

'Fair enough,' said the little girl. 'And me name's Gertie.'

Mum took the parcel she was carrying and we all walked out of the station.

'When we get home, Gertie, you can write to your mum and dad. They'll want to know where you are.'

'I 'aven't learned me letters yet, missus,' said Gertie.

'You can't write?' said Mum.

'Can't read neither.'

'I'll teach you if you like,' said Brenda, grinning.

'Cor, fanks,' said Gertie, smiling up at her.

During the bus ride home, Gertie never stopped talking.

'Av ya got a telly?' she asked.

'I'm afraid not,' said Mum. 'Have you got one at home, then?'

'We 'aven't even got a lavvy at home, missus,' she said, grinning. 'But me mum said I might land on me feet and go somewhere what's got a telly.'

'Well, I'm sorry to disappoint you, Gertie,' said Mum.

'I'm not disappointed, missus, I never expect much. Have ya got a dog?'

'No, Gertie,' said Mum. 'We haven't got a dog.'

'Have *you* got one?' I said.

'Yeah, 'is name's Nosebag. Mum said we should have called 'im fleabag cos he's crawlin' with the little buggers.'

Mum looked alarmed.

'Don't worry, missus, Mum got us all deloused before we came 'ere.'

'Well, that's alright then, isn't it?' said Brenda, smiling gently at her.

Gertie stared at Brenda. 'You gonna be me sister, then?'

Brenda reached for her hand. 'If you want me to,' she said.

'I'd like that,' said Gertie. 'I've got three soddin' brothers at home.'

'The woman at the station said you had two brothers,' said Mum.

'Me mum wouldn't send the baby away, she said 'e was too little.'

'Didn't you mind saying goodbye to them, Gertie?' I asked.

'No, I didn't. They're little bleeders, I was glad ta get shot of 'em.'

We all burst out laughing.

That was the day that Gertie Lightfoot came into our lives and, like her name, she brought light into those darkest of days.

Brenda and I held her hands as she skipped happily between us down See Saw Lane.

Chapter Forty-Four

The wireless, which had been at the back of the bookshop, was ceremoniously moved to the carpet shop next door. It was decided to promote Afshid to chief wireless listener to stop her screaming at Hassan every day. It was her job to report any new developments concerning the war as fast as her legs could carry her from her shop to ours. It worked and Afshid became a very important member of the war council and, as a bonus, she stopped screaming at Hassan.

One morning in July she burst through the shop door. She gave me such a fright that Maggie had to steady the ladder before I fell off it.

'What on earth's the matter?' I asked.

She was bright red in the face and it looked as if she was having trouble breathing.

'Sit down, Afshid,' said Maggie, guiding her towards the chair.

'I must tell the men, I must tell the men,' she spluttered.

'Tell them what?' I said.

'It's started, it's started! They're bombing London.'

'Oh my God, Jack!' I said. 'Maggie, Jack's in London.'

Afshid got up from the chair and ran into the yard.

Maggie helped me down from the ladder. 'And he'll be fine,' she said. 'He will, Maureen, he'll be fine.'

'But what if he's not?'

'You have to believe that he is, otherwise you'll go mad.'

Next thing the baker came running through the door, flour drifting off him like snow. He was quickly followed by the butcher in his horrible apron.

'This isn't the bloody War Office, you know!' yelled Maggie as they both disappeared into the yard.

'We might as well close up,' I said.

We turned the sign around and went outside. All the men were yelling over the top of each other. Afshid was sitting in the middle of Hassan and Peter, looking very self-important.

'I ran as quickly as I could, Hassan,' she said.

Hassan placed his arm around her shoulder. 'You did well, Mrs Hassan.' I could see her flinch at the use of the name but she didn't want to spoil her moment of glory by complaining. She had brought them the most important piece of news since war was declared and she was making the most of it.

'I shall get you all something sweet from the bakery,' she said, kissing the top of Hassan's head.

'Did they say where they dropped the bombs?' I said.

'Her Jack's in London,' Maggie reminded them.

'No, Maureen, they just said that it had been bombed,' said Afshid.

'Those planes will have been spotted coming across the Channel long before they dropped the bombs,' said the baker. 'There's a little man in Littlehampton whose only job is to spot enemy planes coming across the channel. I'm sure you have nothing to worry about.'

But I *was* worried; I was worried sick. If anything happened to Jack, I'd die.

'If our fate lies in the hands of one little man in Littlehampton then God help us,' whispered Maggie.

'Why don't you girls take a few hours off?' said Peter. 'I can manage here. You go and have a walk along the prom.'

'Thank you, Peter,' said Maggie. 'Come on, Maureen, let's go and blow the cobwebs away.'

We cut through the side streets and onto the seafront. There were rolls of barbed wire across the entrance to the pier but I was smiling, remembering my dance with Jack and the moment he told me that he loved me.

'It's suddenly becoming very real, isn't it?' said Maggie sadly.

'I'm afraid so,' I said, putting my arm through hers. 'We will just have to be very careful and keep everyone we love safe. I wish that Jack wasn't in London.'

'I know you do,' she said.

'I've never asked you, Maggie, have you got brothers and sisters?'

'I have an older sister,' she said quietly.

I looked at her and sensed that something was wrong.

'She's my older sister but she's more like my younger sister,' she added.

I didn't know what she meant.

'She's a Mongolian.'

I didn't know what she was talking about. 'She's a what?' I said.

'That's what the doctors said she was, Mongolian.'

I was confused. 'Have you got different fathers, then?'

'Why would you say that?'

'Well, you're not Mongolian, are you?'

'It's an illness, Maureen, it's not about the place.'

I felt stupid. 'I'm sorry, Maggie, I've never heard of it before.'

'That's OK, not many people have. You must meet her. She's sweet and funny and I wouldn't change her for the world. She's the best sister ever.'

'I'd love to meet her,' I said. 'Because I wouldn't change my sister either.'

We walked the whole length of the seafront, from the pier all the way to Shoreham harbour. There were some big ships in the canal. We sat on a grassy bank watching them. Some sailors waved to us and we waved back.

'Have you heard from Nelson lately?'

That's when I remembered the letter. It had come this morning, just as I was leaving for work. It was addressed to both me and Jack so I hadn't opened it. I took it out of my pocket and looked at it.

'Does it say where it's been posted?' asked Maggie.

'I shouldn't think we'd be allowed to know that.'

Maggie took the letter and looked for a clue. 'I can't make out what it says but the stamp's English. I think he must still be in England, Maureen.'

She handed the letter back to me. I looked at the stamp. 'I think you could be right. Wouldn't it be wonderful if he was?'

'Yes, wonderful,' she said.

We sat together watching the small boats coming in and out of the harbour. It was peaceful there; it was somewhere that Jack and I could come now that the beach was closed. I prayed Jack was safe. 'Please keep him safe,' I begged, to whichever saint happened to be listening. Right now I wasn't that fussed which saint granted my wish as long as one of them did.

'Feeling better?' said Maggie.

I nodded and we got up and headed back to the shop.

Peter let me leave work early so that I could meet Jack at the station. I had to know that he was alright.

I was so relieved to see him coming through the barriers, I ran into his arms.

'To what do I owe the pleasure of this?' he said, kissing my cheek.

'I heard about the bombs in London, Jack, and I was terrified.'

'They weren't near the university but they made a hell of a noise. I think everyone was shocked when the sirens went off,' he told me.

'Do you have to go there every day?' I babbled. 'Can't you stay here at home, where it's safe?'

'You're shaking,' he said.

'I've been so worried.'

He put his arm around me. 'Come on, let's go and get some tea.'

We walked across the station to the waiting room. It was pretty full but I managed to get a table in the corner. I sat down and waited for Jack to come back with the tea.

I started on at him again as soon as he put the tray on the table.

'Couldn't you study at home?' I said.

He reached across the table and held my hand.

'This is just the start of it, Maureen. Soon nowhere is going to be safe. Not here, not London, not anywhere. We have to carry on as normally as we can.'

'Why do people have to fight?'

Jack shook his head. 'I don't know, but they do. I have exams coming up and I'm not going to let anything get in my way, certainly not some stupid war. I've worked too hard for this.'

I nodded. 'I'm being selfish, aren't I?'

'Not selfish, my love. Your worries are coming from a good place, it's just that we can't give up because we are frightened. Think of poor old Nelson, he could be anywhere.'

'That's reminded me,' I said, getting the letter out of my pocket. 'A letter from Nelson, it came this morning.'

'What does it say?'

'I haven't read it, I was waiting for you. Go on, you open it,' I said.

Jack opened the letter and started to read.

Dear Jack and Maureen,

You will be surprised to learn that I am still in England. I am pretty surprised myself.

In my last letter I told you that we were on the move. Well, we only got as far as Catterick army base, which is in Yorkshire, a long way from Brighton. After being here for about a week, we were told to get ready as we would be moving out. Well, as it happened, some of us were told that we would be staying put. It turned out that I had been chosen, along with some other chaps, to help with the training of new recruits. Chalky said that I must have the luck of the Irish but I'd been ready to go and it was hard to say goodbye to my friends, especially him. I'm sure that I will soon be joining them, but for now, this is where I am. I wish you could see it. The camp is right on the edge of the Yorkshire Dales and it's breathtaking. I walk on the moors as often as I can and I always think of you. I heard that they'd started bombing London. I hope you are OK, Jack.

My love to you both and to Monica.
Keep safe.
Love,
Nelson x

Jack put the letter back in the envelope and handed it to me. 'So there you are, my love, you can stop worrying because we are all safe.'

'But for how long?' I said, sadly.

Chapter Forty-Five

In the early morning of 15 July, we were woken by the wail of an air-raid siren. At first I thought I was dreaming and then Gertie was shaking me.

'You gotta get up, Maureen, the bloody bombs are coming!' she yelled.

Brenda was screaming out on the landing. 'Gertie, where are you?'

'She's in here, Brenda!' I shouted back.

Mum was calling from downstairs. 'Grab your coats, girls, hurry now!'

We ran downstairs and put on our coats and shoes.

'I can't find me bloody shoes!' shouted Gertie.

'Don't worry, pet, I'll carry you,' said Brenda, lifting her up into her arms.

We rushed out the door and Jack met us at the gate.

'Quickly now,' he said, taking Gertie from Brenda.

We hurried through Jack's house and out into the garden. Mr Forrest was waiting at the entrance to the Anderson shelter and he guided us inside. Mrs Forrest was sitting on the bench. She had rags in her hair and was white as a sheet. I could see her legs shaking under her nightie.

We all sat down. It was dark in there and it smelt damp. I had never been so scared in my life. The only sound was Brenda's voice murmuring gently to Gertie as she held her in her arms. 'We're safe now,' she was saying. 'Those bombs can't get us in here.'

I was so proud of her because I knew how frightened she must be, but her only concern was for the little girl she was holding in her arms.

I looked across at Mum. 'Are you alright, Mum?'

She nodded but I could see how white her knuckles were as she clutched her old brown handbag on her lap.

Then we heard the drone of an aircraft and it seemed to be directly above us. Automatically we all ducked, then we heard what sounded like a whistling and screaming noise that was getting closer and closer.

Mr Forrest was just about to light a candle when the first bomb dropped. Mrs Forrest screamed and grabbed her husband, knocking the candle out of his hand. I wanted to scream as well but I looked across at Brenda, who continued to talk gently to Gertie and I stayed silent: if Brenda could be brave, then so could I. The first bomb didn't seem too close but when the second one dropped, the earth beneath our feet shook and the metal walls of the shelter rattled. A shower of dust fell from the roof, turning Mrs Forrest's white rags black. Even with Jack's arms around me I was terrified.

Suddenly Mrs Forrest stood up and started screaming, 'I've got to get out of here, Frank! I can't stand it.'

'Stay calm, love,' said Mr Forrest, gently easing her back onto the bench and putting his arms around her. 'It will soon be over.'

'Why don't we pray?' said Brenda suddenly. 'What prayers do you know, Gertie?'

'I dunno,' said Gertie.

'Have a think.'

'At home we say a prayer before we tuck into our grub.'

'We'll say that one then. Will you start us off?'

And so as the bombs continued to fall, Gertie started singing…

Thank you for the world so sweet
Thank you for the food we eat.

The rest of us joined in.

Thank you for the birds that sing
Thank you God for everything.

Gertie finished it off with a great big *amen* and we all managed to smile, even Mrs Forrest.

Brenda hugged her. 'Thank you, Gertie,' she said.

'Did I do it proper?' asked Gertie.

'You did it proper, proper,' said Brenda, smiling down at her.

After that we sat quietly, until we heard the welcoming sound of the all-clear.

We later discovered that the second bomb had indeed been very close to See Saw Lane. A row of houses not far away had been destroyed. Four people died that morning and many others were injured. The war in Brighton had begun.

Peter and Hassan erected an Anderson shelter in the yard, which doubled as a place of operations when it rained. The baker was sent down to the junk shop to pick up another table for more books and maps. Peter informed us that the German plane that had dropped the bombs was a Do 17. As far as the war was concerned, we were the most well-informed bookshop in Brighton and Peter and Hassan were the two generals in charge of operations.

If you can get used to bombs dropping out of the skies, then I suppose that most of us got used to them. As soon as we heard the wail of the sirens, we ran for cover, either in the yard or in Jack's garden. If we were on our way home from work, we ran to the closest shelter we could find. If we happened to be on the bus, the driver would stop and lead us to safety.

September the seventh saw the start of the Blitz on London; hundreds of people lost their homes and their lives. Most of the bombs fell on the East End, near the docks, and I was grateful that Jack's university was on the other side of the city but I lived in daily fear for his safety.

Afshid was like a woman possessed as she rushed in and out of the bookshop, carrying news that we would rather not hear.

'Entire streets have vanished!' she yelled, rushing through the shop. 'Men, women and children are buried beneath the rubble.'

'I wish she'd stick to selling bloody carpets,' said Maggie. 'I could live without hearing about the blood and gore. I'm scared enough as it is.'

Bombs were dropping daily and Gertie's school had closed. She couldn't be left on her own, so between us we looked after her. Sometimes Mum took her to work with her and sometimes she helped Aunty Marge and Uncle John on the fruit stall, but mostly, she spent her days with me in the bookshop. Brenda was teaching her to read and she loved being amongst all the books. She looked so happy curled up in the big comfy chair with a book in her hand.

She happily made cups of tea for the War Council. 'I used to make tea at home,' she said proudly, 'so I knows 'ow to do it.'

'You're a clever girl, Gertie,' I said.

'I know I am,' she said, giving me a cheeky grin.

The generals loved her; everyone loved her.

'You make the best tea in Brighton, Gertie,' said the butcher.

'Fanks, mate,' she said, grinning.

'In fact,' said Peter. 'We have decided to promote you to lieutenant.'

'Bugger me!' said Gertie, grinning.

With the beaches mined and the piers closed, people flocked to the town's cinemas. We were lucky in Brighton; the town had loads of picture houses. There was the Regent, the Odeon, the Savoy, The Duke of York and that was just a few of them. I think the picture houses served as a place of refuge from the grim re-

ality that we were all living through. Gertie loved going to the
pictures and she loved spending time with Jack. We laughed at
Old Mother Riley and Arthur Askey. We rode the plains with
John Wayne and we cried with Celia Johnson and Trevor Howard
in *Brief Encounter*. For those few hours we could forget about the
war and the bombs. Very often, air-raid sirens went off halfway
through the film. At first people ran for shelter but as time went
on we grew more gung-ho and stayed in our seats, much to the
anguish of the manager.

One Saturday afternoon, Maggie and I were sitting on the
bench in the yard while Peter rummaged for more war books. It
was late September and we were making the most of the warm
day. All of a sudden, we heard Afshid screaming.

'Ignore her,' said Maggie, lifting her face up to the sun. 'I can
live without any more bad news.'

Then I heard her saying something about a cinema. I ran into
the shop.

'What's happened?' I said.

'Oh dear God!' she said, running her hands through her hair.

'Tell me, Afshid,' I said urgently.

'They've bombed the cinema.'

I could feel my blood run cold.

'Which cinema, Afshid? Which cinema has been bombed?'

'And it's full of children,' she moaned.

'Which cinema?' I screamed.

Peter came across. 'What's wrong, Maureen?' he said.

'Brenda has taken Gertie to the matinee at the Odeon.'

Peter knelt down in front of Afshid and said gently, 'Is it the
Odeon that's been bombed?'

'Yes, the Odeon, a bomb has dropped on the Odeon.'

I was shaking; I didn't think my legs would hold me up. I had
to get there but I couldn't move.

Maggie came in from the yard. She took one look at me and said, 'What's happened, Maureen, you're as white as a sheet?'

'They've bombed the Odeon cinema, Maggie,' said Peter. 'And Brenda and Gertie are in there.'

'Oh my God, Maureen!'

'I've got to get there.'

'I'll come with you,' said Maggie.

'You stay here,' said Peter. 'I'll take her in the car, it'll be quicker.'

As we raced through Brighton, all I could think was: 'Not them, please not them.' This was only the second time that I had been in Peter's car and I'd been praying that time as well. 'Please, dear God, let it be different this time.'

Chapter Forty-Six

As we drove along the Western Road, ambulances and fire engines were racing past us, sirens screaming.

'Hurry, Peter. Hurry!'

'Nearly there, we're nearly there.'

As we turned into West Street we could see people running down the middle of the road, towards the cinema. Smoke was billowing up the street and the sky above us was pitch-black.

'We'll have to leave the car,' said Peter. 'I can't get any closer.'

He pulled up and I jumped out and started running. The air blowing up from the sea was full of ash and bits of rubbish and the smoke was burning my eyes. A young couple staggered past me, clinging to each other.

As I got closer to the cinema, I heard the screaming. Then I froze; I wanted to turn around and run back to the shop. But Peter had caught up with me.

'Come on, dear, let's find them and bring them home.'

Yes, that's what I had to do: I had to find them. I started running again. As I reached the Odeon, I was faced with the full horror of what had happened. The cinema was wrecked, most of the roof was blown away and there was a gaping hole in the side of the building. It was a scene of utter chaos. People were stumbling around, dazed and injured, covered in dust and blood. Terrified children were wandering around, crying. The street was blocked with ambulances and fire engines. People were being carried out of the cinema on stretchers and loaded into ambulances and cars. There were people everywhere.

'I can't see them,' I said frantically. 'Can you see them, Peter?'

'We'll find them,' he said, taking my hand. 'We'll find them. Let's split up.'

As I made my way through the crowds I stepped over people sitting on the ground, dazed and confused. I watched as mothers were reunited with their children and I searched for the two precious faces that I loved but I couldn't see them anywhere.

I ran towards the front of the cinema but I was stopped by a policeman, who put his hand on my arm.

'You can't go in there, miss, the building's not safe,' he said.

'But my sister might be in there. I have to look for her.'

'We've brought everyone out, there's no one left in there.'

'Have people been killed?'

'Look, miss, if you can't find your sister, you should check the hospital,' he said gently. 'That's where they've taken the injured.'

'Which hospital?'

'The Royal Sussex County.'

'Thank you.'

'You're welcome and I hope you find your sister.'

Peter walked across to me.

'Any sign of them?' I said.

He shook his head. 'I think we should check the hospitals, Maureen.'

'That policeman said they've taken the injured to the Royal Sussex County.'

'Let's go then.'

So we started running back up the road to where Peter had parked the car. We were just about to drive away when a woman banged on the window. She looked frantic.

'Are you going to the hospital?' she said.

'Yes, do you want a lift?' said Peter.

'Oh yes, please,' said the woman. 'My children were in the cinema but I can't find them. I can't find my babies.' She was white-faced and tears were running down her cheeks.

'I'm trying to find my sister,' I said, 'and our little evacuee. Come with us.'

We stopped a couple of streets away from the hospital. It was just as chaotic there as it had been at the cinema. Ambulances were queued up outside, trying to get in. Doctors and nurses were running between them, giving aid to the injured. Stretchers were rushed through the hospital doors. Patients were being treated on the ground.

'Oh dear God!' said the woman. 'Where are my children?'

I held her hand as we ran into the building.

'What are your children's names?' asked Peter urgently.

'Tony and Carol,' she said tearfully. 'Patton.'

There was a desk but there were so many people crowding around it, all shouting at once, that it was impossible to get anywhere near it.

'Come on,' said Peter, taking control. 'Let's find some help.'

We followed him through some swing doors and started to hurry down the corridor. Nobody stopped us, so we kept going. It was awful: people were screaming, there was blood smeared on the floor and everywhere was the smell of burning that people had carried with them from the bombed cinema.

There was a young nurse sitting on the floor outside one of the rooms. Tears were pouring down her face. I knelt down beside her and held her hand. She looked at me and shook her head.

'I don't think I can do this,' she said.

'You can, you know,' I said softly. 'I think that you can.'

'But I'm not helping. Mothers and fathers have lost their children and they need me to be strong but all I'm doing is crying with them. What help is that?'

'I think you're allowed to cry,' I said. 'We're all crying inside, you're just letting yours show. It means you care about what they are going through and they'll remember you for that. They'll remember the kind young nurse who wasn't afraid to share their grief.'

She dried her eyes and together we stood up.

'Thank you,' she said. 'I needed to hear that. I think I'll be alright now. Yes, I think I will.'

We started to walk away when she called us back. 'Do you need my help?'

I turned around and nodded. 'I'm looking for my sister and a little girl and this lady is trying to find her children.'

She stopped another nurse that was running past.

'Jenny, can you help this lady?' she said, indicating the woman who had come with us. 'She's looking for her children.'

'Of course,' she said. 'I've just got to deliver these bandages to cubicle eight.'

The woman turned back and smiled at us. 'Thank you for your kindness,' she said.

'You are very welcome,' said Peter.

'I hope you find them,' I said. 'And I hope that they are alright.'

We watched as they hurried down the corridor.

The nurse turned back to us. 'Now, let's find your sister and the little girl.'

We started walking down the corridor, looking into rooms as we went.

'They have to be here,' I said. 'They weren't at the cinema.'

'If they're here, we'll find them,' said the nurse.

We turned a corner and there, leaning against the wall, was Brenda. We fell into each other's arms.

'I knew you'd come,' she said.

'Where's Gertie?'

'She got hit by some shrapnel. They have to operate on her leg.'

'But she's going to be alright?' I said.

'Yes, she's going to be alright. She's such a brave little girl, Maureen.'

Brenda was covered in the same white dust that we'd seen at the cinema.

'Are you OK' said Peter.

'We were lucky, we got there late so we had to sit near the back. It was the first few rows that got the worst of it. It was awful, Maureen. I will never forget the screams of the children.'

I put my arms around her.

'You're safe now, my love, you're safe.'

And together we cried, for each other, for the injured, for the people who had died, and for those poor innocent little children who had just gone to watch a film. We waited until Gertie came out of surgery and then we sat by her bed and watched her sleep.

'Mum will be worried once she hears about the bombing but I don't want to leave.'

'I'll phone Mrs Bentley and get her to call on your mother and put her mind at rest,' said Peter.

'Thank you,' I said.

Peter had really surprised me that day with the way he took control and how he kept me calm when I thought that I was going to go mad with worry. He was usually such a bumbling kind of chap who couldn't even make a cup of tea but that day he had been wonderful. It just went to show that people have bravery inside them that they don't know is there until someone needs them. That day I needed him and he hadn't let me down.

A little while later our nurse came into the room with a tray of tea. 'They've put me on tea duty,' she said. 'I think they realised that I wasn't coping very well.'

I stood up and took the tray from her. 'There are times when tea is just what people need,' I said.

'I hope so,' she said, smiling.

Eventually, Gertie woke up. The first thing she said was, 'I never got to see the end of the soddin' film.'

'You're a tonic, Gertie Lightfoot,' I said. 'Now, how are you feeling?'

'I've got a ringing in me ears and I can't hear very well.'

'I expect that will soon get better,' I said. 'The main thing is that you are still with us.'

Just then a doctor came into the room.

'Will she be alright?' said Brenda.

'They make 'em tough in London and this is one tough little girl,' he said, smiling down at her.

He walked across to the bed. 'I thought you might like this, Gertie,' he said, handing her something wrapped in a bandage. 'It's the shrapnel we took out of your leg.'

Gertie took it from him. 'Fanks, mate,' she said. 'I'll give it to the generals.'

Then she yawned and went back to sleep with the sweetest little smile on her lips.

Chapter Forty-Seven

We learned from Afshid that seven bombs had dropped on Brighton that terrible day. A German bomber was being chased by a Spitfire across the town and in his hurry to get away, he released all his bombs. There were three hundred people in the cinema for the matinee performance of *The Ghost Comes Home* and people said it was a miracle that more hadn't died. Altogether, fifty-two people lost their lives and many more were injured. The town was in mourning.

Bombs were now dropping almost daily and all schools remained closed. Nowhere was safe but people carried on with their lives: they went to work, they took care of their children and the women made meals out of what little food they could get hold of. People were kinder to each other. Our estate was poor but people shared what little they had, even more than they might have done before the war. Women happily took in children so that their mothers could go out to work. I heard stories of warring neighbours having to share an Anderson shelter and becoming friends as bombs rained down over their heads.

Gertie seemed happy to come to work with me. Everyone loved her. The baker gave her little iced cakes and the butcher saved two sausages for her every day. She sat on the bench with the generals and pretended to pore over the maps and books just like they did.

One day she came in from the yard, plonked herself down in the chair and said, 'Bloody hard work, this bleedin' war.' Gertie made us all laugh – that was why the next lot of bad news left us all devastated.

One Sunday morning someone knocked on the door. I opened it to find an official-looking woman on the doorstep.

'Is your mother in, dear?' she said.

'Mum,' I called. 'Someone to see you.'

Mum came through from the kitchen, wiping her hands on a towel. The woman shook her hand and said, 'Am I right in thinking that Gertrude Lightfoot lives here?'

At first we didn't know who she was talking about.

'Oh, you mean Gertie,' said Mum. 'Yes, she lives here. Are they opening the schools again then?'

'Perhaps we could speak inside?' said the woman.

'Of course,' said Mum, ushering her into our front room.

'Maureen, get Brenda,' said Mum, looking worried. 'She's in the garden with Gertie.'

I opened the back door and called her. 'Come in, Brenda! You stay out here, Gertie.'

'What's wrong?' asked Brenda, coming into the kitchen.

'I don't know but there's a woman in the front room wanting to know if Gertie lives here.'

'Why does she want to know that?'

'I think we're about to find out,' I said, going into the front room.

'Ah, Brenda,' said Mum. 'Sit down, love.'

Brenda and I sat on the couch and stared at the woman.

She was perched rather than sat on the chair, as if she was about to run off at any minute. Her head was too small for her body; it looked as if she'd been made out of leftover bits, nothing about her matched. She was wearing a two-piece costume that was too big on the shoulders but too tight round her middle. Her legs were encased in thick Lyle stockings. The three of us stared at her, waiting to see what she had to say. We didn't have a clue who she was or why she was sitting in our front room. She cleared her throat and pushed her glasses down her nose. Then she peered at us over the top of them and started to speak: 'Due to the increased bombing in Brighton, the government want all evacuees to be moved to safer areas,' she said.

'But Gertie's happy here with us,' said Brenda.

'I'm very glad to hear that, because I'm afraid not all of our children have had a happy time of it. Some have been so unhappy that they've made their way back to London.'

'But we make sure she's safe,' said Brenda.

'I'm sure you do and I can see that you have become very fond of her.'

'We love her,' said Brenda passionately.

'Then she's been a very lucky little girl,' said the woman. 'But you want her to be safe, don't you?'

'Of course,' said Brenda softly.

'I'm afraid that this is an order from the government, so it's out of my hands. Please have her ready to leave on Tuesday. All the children will be assembling at the station at eleven o'clock in the morning.'

'But where is she going?' asked Brenda.

'I don't exactly know but I think the evacuees will be spread across the villages and towns in the countryside.'

'You make them sound like slabs of butter,' said Brenda, angrily.

The woman stood up. 'I can see that you're upset,' she said, 'but we have to do what's best for the child and right now, the best thing for Gertrude is to move her to a safer place.'

Mum saw her to the door. I looked at Brenda and I could see that she was near to tears.

'Oh, Brenda,' I said.

She shrugged her shoulders. 'I suppose I always knew that she would have to leave sometime, but…' She couldn't finish the sentence.

'We'll all miss her, Bren, but I don't think there's anything we can do.'

Mum came into the room. 'I wasn't expecting that,' she said, sitting down. 'But I suppose she's right. Maybe Gertie *will* be better off in a safer place but, oh dear, we're going to miss that little girl.'

'We'll have to tell her,' I said.

Brenda stood up. 'Is it OK if I tell her?'

'Of course,' said Mum. 'And I'm so sorry, love, I know how fond you've become of her.'

Brenda nodded and left the room.

The evening before Gertie was due to leave us, we all gathered in the bookshop. Gertie's eyes were like saucers as we came through the door. Peter had managed to get hold of a Christmas tree and some lights that sparkled away in the corner of the shop. Underneath the tree was a pile of presents. Maggie turned off the light and the baker came in, carrying a beautiful cake, complete with eight candles flickering in the darkness.

'Blow them out, Gertie,' said Brenda.

'And don't forget to make the wish,' said Afshid.

'I don't fink it's me birfday,' said Gertie. 'And I don't fink it's Christmas.'

Brenda knelt down in front of her. 'This is for every birthday and Christmas that you spend away from us, my darling.'

Then Peter, Hassan, the baker and the butcher walked solemnly towards Gertie.

Peter cleared his throat.

'We, the generals of the war council, are honoured to present to Gertie Lightfoot the medal for bravery beyond the call of duty on the field of battle.'

Then he took off one of his medals and pinned it on Gertie's cardigan. They stood to attention. All four men had tears in their eyes as Peter said, 'We salute you, Lieutenant Lightfoot.'

'Bloody Nora!' said Gertie and burst out crying.

The rest of us were trying hard to hold back our tears until, that is, Afshid put 'We'll Meet Again' on the record player. Then we were blubbing like babies. We would all miss this special little girl and I think each of us was wondering if we would ever see her again.

Chapter Forty-Eight

Bombs continued to rain down on Brighton and, although we all missed Gertie terribly, we were thankful that she was safely in the country. We were delighted to receive our first letter from her: she was living on a farm and was happy. The letter was mostly little drawings of pigs and chickens and sheep and a dog called Albert:

I love Albert. And I love you.
From Lieutenant Gertie xxx
PS: The missus helped me write this letter but I wrote Gertie all on my own. X

We continued to go to work but we never knew where the bombs would drop next and we worried about each other every day. Sometimes the raids went on all night and we had to sleep as best we could in the shelter next door. Houses and shops were being destroyed and many people lost their lives.

On Friday, 29 November the Savoy cinema had a direct hit and Hannington's store was bombed. I thought of that lovely shop and the day that Mrs Bentley took me and Brenda in there to buy the beautiful lilac scarf and gloves for Mum and it made me sad. Everything about this awful war made me sad. But amidst all of this I had Jack. Our feelings were getting stronger every day, heightened perhaps by the fear that at any moment we could lose each other.

Monica hadn't met her better class of person yet and she was still going out with Norman.

One evening me and Monica were up on the green. It was freezing cold and the bench we were sitting on was damp. We could see the shadowy outlines of kids kicking a football around. There were houses all around the edge of the green. Some of them had damage to the roofs and some were boarded up. So far, our street had been lucky but I knew the next bomb could very likely have See Saw Lane written on it. I pulled the sleeves of my coat over my hands and shivered.

'Have you and Jack, you know…?' said Monica.

I knew what she meant. 'No, but it's getting harder every time we see each other.'

'Why don't you just do it, then?'

'Where would you suggest we do it, Monica, in a field?'

'Why not?'

'I want the first time to be special. That's why not.'

'There's always the barn.'

'I've got bad memories of the barn.'

'Would you do it if you could though?'

I could feel my face going red but luckily it was too dark for Monica to see.

'Part of me is scared at the thought but sometimes when I'm with Jack, I'm not scared at all and I want to do it so badly I get this pain in my stomach.'

'That's because you're denying your body what it needs,' said Monica, as if she knew everything there was to know about doing it. 'So you get a belly ache. You have to listen to your body, Maureen.'

'Have you done it with Norman, then?'

Monica laughed. 'Plenty of times,' she said.

I was surprised to find that I was shocked. 'But you don't love him,' I said.

'So?'

'So how can you do it with him?'

'You don't have to be in love with someone to do it.'

I was confused. 'But—'

'But what?' asked Monica.

'Well, isn't being in love what it's all about?'

'People make love for all kinds of reasons, Maureen. When they're lonely or sad or scared. Sometimes, especially now, people just need the comfort of another person's body beside them, because we don't know from one day to the next if we're going to survive this war. I for one don't intend to wait for Mr Right to come along.'

'I never thought about it like that,' I said.

'Don't get me wrong,' said Monica, 'I couldn't do it with someone that I didn't like, but I like Norman, he's a nice chap and I know that he would never hurt me. But love? I am never, ever going to fall in love.'

But she did. Passionately, deeply, and with all her heart. The man in question was Flight Lieutenant Chester McQuaid from Santa Monica, California. She bumped into him on her way home from work during the blackout; she literally fell at his feet. Poor Norman!

We were in my bedroom talking about it.

'Don't you think it was just meant to be?' she said. 'I mean, he comes from Santa Monica, of all places. I'm going to be Mrs Monica McQuaid from Santa Monica! How brilliant is that?'

'You're going to *marry* him?'

'Of course I am.'

'But you've only just met him.'

'But I think I've known him all my life.'

'Well, Monica Maltby, I think you might have blown the "I'm never going to fall in love bit".'

'Guilty as charged, but at least now I can understand how you feel about Jack.'

'Lovely, isn't it?' I said, smiling at her.

'It's divine,' she said, flopping back on the bed and cuddling my pillow. 'Now you'll have to do it with Jack, because if you feel about Jack the way I feel about Chester and I know you do, then you'll end up being ill if you don't do it immediately.'

'OK, I'll inform Jack tonight and the two of us can go in search of a field that hasn't got any thistles in it.'

Monica pulled me down beside her. 'You're daft, do you know that?'

'That's why you love me so much.'

'Right now I love everyone… well, everyone except my dad. I shan't miss him when I go to America.'

I was feeling a bit worried. I mean, what did she know about this Chester bloke? He could be married with ten kids for all she knew. What if she got pregnant and then he disappeared back to Santa Monica, California? What then?

'I know what you're thinking, Maureen O'Connell.'

'Do you?'

'You think he might leave me.'

'Something like that.'

'He won't, but even if he did, I will know what love is and nothing else will do. Not money or a big house or a flashy car or tea at the Savoy. I've learned that nothing else matters. I don't care if we have to live in a mud hut as long as we're together.'

'Brave words, my friend,' I said, grinning. 'But somehow I can't imagine you in a mud hut.'

'Well, luckily I won't have to be because Chester McQuaid III just happens to be fabulously, deliciously, disgustingly rich.'

I burst out laughing. 'Trust you to fall on your feet or in this case at *his* feet!'

'I know! I brought him home, I thought he'd better see the dump I live in before he commits. Mum fell in love with him and so did Archie. Even my rotten excuse for a father took to him. Of course the nylons, chocolates and tobacco might have helped,' she said, giggling.

'I'm happy for you, Monica,' I said. 'I really am.'

'I know you are and I'll really miss you when I go to America.'

It was still amazing to me that she was so sure about everything. She didn't seem to have a doubt in her mind. She was going to marry Chester McQuaid III and live in America and that was that.

'Now about you and Jack,' she said.

'What about me and Jack?'

'You have got to do it.'

'Oh. That.'

'How would you feel if you woke up dead one morning and you'd never done it?'

'Well, obviously I wouldn't feel anything, would I?'

'Considering all those candles you've lit to the Blessed Virgin Mary, you're bound to get into Heaven – you've even got a squashed dog rooting for you. So there you will be, sitting on a cloud, bored out of your skull, watching your Jack doing it with Marion Tucker.'

'*Don't!*' I said, giggling and digging her in the ribs.

'Well, I'm only saying,' said the future Mrs Monica McQuaid III, from Santa Monica. Looking as innocent as you like.

Chapter Forty-Nine

We were all hoping that Nelson would be coming home for Christmas. We hadn't seen him for so long and we missed him. We still wrote to him and told him all the news but we didn't hear back very often. Then we got a letter.

Dear Maureen and Jack,

It sounds as if you've been having it tough in Brighton but I am thankful that you continue to be safe. You must have been worried sick about Brenda and Gertie when the Odeon was bombed. I am so glad that they came out of it alive. Please give Brenda my love. I wish I could have met Gertie.

Well, the time has come for me to join my friends. Our job here is done and we are on the move. We haven't been told where we are going, but as I said before, I wouldn't be allowed to tell you even if I knew. In a way, it's a relief. I want to do my bit and so do the other chaps.

Think of me, as I am always thinking of you.

Keep safe.

Love always,

Nelson xxx

Jack folded the letter and handed it to me.

'Let's go for a walk,' he said.

We took the bus into town and got off at the clock tower. Everyone knew the clock tower – it was as much a part of Brighton as the two piers. Now it looked sad, standing there all smashed up, with the hands of the clock dangling down its face like tears.

'Poor old clock tower,' I said.

Jack held my hand and we continued down West Street and onto the seafront. It was still a shock to see the ugly coils of barbed wire all along the prom and the warnings telling us that the beach was mined.

'Let's go to Shoreham Harbour,' I said. 'It's nice there and there's no barbed wire.'

There was a cold wind blowing off the sea as we walked along but it didn't bother us, we needed to walk.

We passed the new King Alfred building. Everyone had been excited when the building went up because it was going to be a public swimming baths but then the war broke out and now it was being used as the Royal Navy training base.

When we got to the lagoon we could see that there were sandbags all along the front of it and two armed soldiers were standing guard at the gate. They nodded as we passed. I still found it hard to be near the lagoon; I still remembered waiting for Daddy that day, the day he didn't come. Eventually we came to the bank where Monica and I had sat watching the ships.

Jack and I hadn't really spoken much on the way there. I imagined that his thoughts, like mine, were full of Nelson.

There were more big ships in the harbour than when Monica and I had gone there.

'It looks like a couple of the ships have seen action,' said Jack, pointing to the largest one in the harbour that seemed to have damage to its side.

I watched the water lapping the shingle and I thought about Nelson.

'Do you think he's scared?' I said.

He nodded. 'He'd be daft not to be but I think he's probably a bit relieved too. I mean, he always knew that he would have to fight, he just never knew when and the waiting must have been hard.'

Jack seemed quiet and withdrawn. In fact, now I came to think about it he hadn't really been himself for ages. I tried to pinpoint when he had started to change but I couldn't.

'There's something troubling you, isn't there?' I said gently.

'Nothing for you to worry about.'

'I want to worry about it, Jack. I want you to be able to talk to me if something's on your mind, so tell me.'

He rubbed the bridge of his nose and stared out across the water. 'I'm getting funny looks, Maureen, because I'm not in uniform. Well, it started with funny looks and now it's progressed to name-calling. It's getting pretty nasty.'

'Oh, Jack.'

'And the thing is, I don't blame them. All they see is a young chap who looks fit enough to fight for his country and they're right, I should be fighting.'

'You're studying to be a doctor, Jack, that's just as important.'

'We're at war, Maureen, I'm being judged and I hate it. What good would it do for me to say, "I'm going to be a doctor, I don't have to fight, I'm exempt" when they're calling me yellow belly and coward? They're not going to say, "Oh sorry, mate, we didn't realise". No they're not, they're more likely to laugh in my face.'

'I didn't know this was happening.'

Jack sighed and put his arm around my shoulder. 'Sometimes I feel like a coward. Sometimes I wonder if I *am* hiding behind this exemption thing and feeling justified in staying behind, while other young men of my age are out there fighting.'

'Students are exempt for a good reason,' I told him. 'This war isn't going to last forever and when it's over we're going to need doctors and engineers and architects.'

'Are you saying my life is more important than theirs?'

'Well, it's more important to me, but no, that's not what I'm saying. I'm saying you are just as important to this country as the men that are fighting with guns and bombs.'

Jack looked at me and smiled. He brushed the hair away from my face and said, 'What you're saying makes sense, but right now,

I'm thinking with my heart and not my head, and my heart is telling me to join up.'

'Your mother will have a nervous breakdown if you go to war.'

'I know she will. Sometimes I wish I had brothers and sisters then she wouldn't concentrate on me so much.'

I wondered if I was being selfish too. Was I being like his mum, who didn't care about other mothers, only about her own son? And did I blame her? Wouldn't I be the same if I had a child? Wouldn't I be relieved my son didn't have to fight? I thought that I would.

I watched the birds splashing about at the edge of the shore without a care in the world. They didn't know there was a war on and even if they did, they could fly away. I wished that me and Jack could fly away.

I took a deep breath. 'I don't want you to go, Jack, you know that, but if that is what you need to do, then I promise I won't fight you on this.'

'Have I told you how much I love you, Maureen O'Connell?'

'Not in the last couple of hours,' I said.

Jack took my face in his hands. 'I love you, Maureen O'Connell,' he said.

'And I love you, Jack Forrest. I have always loved you and I always will.'

We lay back on the grass and kissed.

Chapter Fifty

In the early hours of Wednesday, 11 December, there was a banging on the front door. It was my day off so I was still in bed. I heard Mum answer the door, then talk to someone. After a while she called up to me, 'Maureen, I think you should come down!'

I threw some clothes on and ran downstairs. Mr Forrest was standing in the hallway.

'I thought you'd want to know that several bombs have dropped on Western Road. By all accounts they didn't explode but I think they have caused quite a bit of damage. That's where your bookshop is, isn't it?'

'Yes, it is. Oh God, I hope it's OK!'

'I've got the car outside, would you like a lift so that you can see for yourself?'

'Oh yes please, Mr Forrest.'

'Come next door when you're ready,' he said.

'It's a long road, Maureen,' said Mum, following me upstairs. 'There's a good chance that the bookshop is fine. Try not to worry.'

But the bookshop wasn't fine. I knew as soon as we got close that it was far from fine. Pages from the books were flying all down the road. Some were caught up in the trees; they clung to the branches, fluttering away like hundreds of white butterflies.

Mr Forrest parked as close to the shop as he could. I hurried down the road. As I got closer, there were more pages flying about. They were blowing everywhere. They covered the pavements and the road. They were under my feet and I was treading on them.

There were police and soldiers and wardens everywhere. I couldn't get near to the shop but I could see Peter running around, gathering up the torn pages of his books.

'I have to get to the bookshop,' I said to one of the wardens.

'No chance, miss,' he said, looking for all the world as if he was in charge of the whole thing. 'There's an unexploded bomb in there.'

Then Mr Forrest was at my side. 'This young lady,' he said to the warden, 'works in that shop and that gentleman is her friend and he looks as if he needs her help, so be a good chap and let her through, eh?'

The warden scratched his head and looked at Mr Forrest, who was wearing his work suit and looked important.

'Oh well,' he said. 'Perhaps I can see my way clear to letting her through but don't come running to me if the building falls down on her head.'

We thanked him and I walked towards Peter. I touched his arm.

'It's not safe here, Peter,' I said.

He looked dazed and bewildered. 'My books,' he said.

'We can replace the books, Peter, but we can't replace you.'

A soldier was shouting at us, 'Get out of the bloody way!'

'Come on, old chap,' said Mr Forrest gently. 'Let's get you home, eh?'

Peter stood for a moment, staring at his beloved books, broken and ruined on the ground, flying up into the sky and over the tall buildings. 'My books,' he said again. He was holding the torn pages to his chest as if they were his children and yet he had never been able to read them.

'Let's go,' said Mr Forrest and slowly, Peter allowed himself to be led away.

The bomb had dropped straight through the roof and landed at the back of the shop. A bomb disposal team would come in and make it safe. If it had gone off, there would have been no shop left so we'd had a lucky escape. Four bombs had fallen that morning on shops and houses in Ship Street, Western Road and Upper North Street and, for some reason, none of them had gone off. People started calling it Brighton's luckiest air raid.

As soon as we could, Maggie and I got to work cleaning the place up and saving what books we could. We moved the undamaged ones to the front of the shop and we put some in boxes on the pavements so that we could still trade. The war council, out in the yard, had been demolished and so had the record player and all Peter's records.

Volunteers were in the street, clearing rubble from the road. The women from the WRVS were supplying them with hot drinks and food. Everyone was pulling together and, despite the damage that the bombs had caused and maybe because there had been no loss of life, it felt like a big street party.

Peter hadn't been back to the shop since, but Mrs Bentley had come in to help us get the place in order.

'I'm worried about him,' she said. 'He's gone into himself, he won't talk about what has happened. I think he just can't face it. Those books were part of a happy time in his life, when he spent his days here in the shop with his father. In a strange way I think he feels that he's let him down.'

'But it wasn't his fault,' I said.

'Peter is a simple man, Maureen. He promised his father that he would take care of the books and in his head he hasn't fulfilled that promise.'

'Is there anything we can do?' I asked.

Mrs Bentley shook her head. 'I really don't know.'

'Will you keep the shop open?' said Maggie.

'We'll need to get someone in to assess the damage. I've been told that the building itself is sound, so it's safe for you to be here. I can get the place repaired but I'm not sure how easy it will be to repair Peter,' she said sadly.

And so Maggie and I continued to go to the shop every day. The roof was repaired and we'd cleaned the place up. Yes, some books were lost but we had so many that it was barely noticeable. In fact, it looked a lot tidier now that the shelves weren't stacked so full.

Hassan and the baker next door had some damage to their roofs but it was the bookshop that had got the worst of it. Maggie and I told them about Peter and how sad he was and so, along with the butcher, they said they would try and think of a way to make it better for him.

We left them to it. Every day there was hammering and banging out in the yard and every so often one of them would come in and rummage through the shelves. Mrs Bentley had given them the keys to the shop so that they could work in the evenings. We had a fair idea what was going on but we were under strict instructions not to look.

On the evening of the grand reveal Mrs Bentley managed to persuade Peter to visit the shop. Me and Maggie were shocked at his appearance: his clothes were hanging off him, his face was thinner; he looked like a broken man.

Mum and Brenda were there and so were Aunty Marge and Uncle John. Gradually other people started drifting in. That's when we heard the music. We couldn't understand where it was coming from.

Then Hassan came in from the yard. 'Hello, general,' he said to Peter.

Peter just nodded.

Hassan winked at us and we led Peter outside. We couldn't believe what we were looking at: where the bench had been was a large shed that took up most of the yard and over the door was a sign that simply said 'PETER'S PLACE'.

We all watched as Peter opened the shed door and went inside and then we heard the sobbing. I wanted to go to him but Mrs Bentley said, 'Leave him, Maureen.' Eventually he came out, he shook his head and said, 'Thank you, my friends.' We all clapped.

It seemed that everyone had donated something. The man from the junk shop provided another table, someone had wired the place for electricity and Mrs Bentley had brought a new record player and some records. There were books on the table and maps on the wall. It was indeed Peter's place. Afshid turned up the volume on the record player and we all sang along to Vera Lynn singing 'The White Cliffs of Dover'.

'Gertie would have loved this,' said Brenda.

'She would, wouldn't she?' I said.

The next morning Peter arrived at the shop in his suit and tie. He smiled at us and went straight out to his shed. Later on, he was joined by Hassan, the baker and the butcher: the war council had resumed operations. The kindness of these people had brought Peter back to life.

Chapter Fifty-One

On Christmas Eve, Mrs Bentley invited Mum, Brenda, me, Maggie and the war council to her house for a celebration and to thank everyone for Peter's shed. The house looked lovely, like something you might see in a magazine. The rooms were filled with the scent of fresh flowers that were displayed in beautiful vases placed on shiny glass tables. There was a lovely tree in the hallway, ablaze with lights, which reflected in the gilt mirrors that hung from the walls. Mum had never been there and I could see by her face how overwhelmed she was by it all.

'No fag packets on that tree,' whispered Mum.

'I rather liked the fag packets,' whispered Brenda, grinning.

The food was delicious and we ate it in the cream and pale blue dining room. Crystal glasses gleamed on the long table and crisp white napkins were folded beside our plates. Peter stood up and thanked me and Maggie for taking care of the shop and he thanked Hassan, the butcher and the baker for building his shed.

'To friends,' he said, lifting his glass.

'To friends,' we echoed.

Then Mrs Bentley stood up. 'To peace,' she said.

Together we all raised our glasses again. 'To peace,' we said in unison.

After we'd finished eating, Mrs Bentley sat down at the grand piano and played for us. We sang hymns and carols at the tops of our voices. Peter sang 'Silent Night' on his own. His voice rang out pure and clear into the hushed room. Then Afshid sang a song from her homeland. By the end of the evening there wasn't a dry eye in the house.

At the end of the night we thanked Mrs Bentley and started the long walk home. The sky was inky-black, twinkling with a thousand stars, and as we walked along the prom we could hear the soft sound of the sea as it washed over the shore. I loved this town and I loved being here, in this place, on this night, with my family and friends.

Christmas Day was perfect: there were no air raids and we could just relax and have a nice time. Mum and Aunty Marge had put their ration books together and we had a feast. We had chicken and roast potatoes, carrots, cabbage and beans all covered in a rich, tasty chicken gravy. For pudding, Mum came in with an apple pie.

'I'll have you know that the pastry is made with real butter.'

'How did you manage that?' said Aunty Marge, amazed.

'I winked at the grocer,' said Mum, grinning.

'Pity you didn't do a bit more,' said Aunty Marge. 'We might have had a bit of custard to go with it.'

'Cheeky bugger!' said Mum, laughing.

It was fun seeing Mum so happy, she deserved to be.

In the evening Jack came round and we played charades and gin rummy.

We all wished that Nelson had been there to share this day with us. We wrote regularly but, so far, we hadn't heard back from him. We could only hope and pray no news was good news; Jack and I worried about him constantly. Jack gave me a silver compact and I gave his some cufflinks with the letter 'J' engraved on them. He had said no more about joining up and part of me was hoping he had decided not to.

We saw in 1941 with Monica and Chester. He was lovely, a gentle giant of a man, who very obviously adored Monica. I was so happy for my friend who had found her better class of person. He talked about his family and his home in Santa Monica with such love and pride. He and Jack spoke of the war. Chester didn't judge him for not fighting, instead he asked him about his studies and his dream of one day becoming a doctor. The two of them got on great.

The four of us walked along the seafront to Shoreham Harbour and sat huddled up on the grassy bank, looking out over the canal. The big ships were black silhouettes on the far side of the canal and at twelve o'clock their horns went off. The sailors gave a loud rendition of 'Auld Lang Syne' and they shouted 'Happy New Year' across the dark water. Monica whispered in my ear, 'There's no thistles on this bank, Maureen.'

Off in the distance we heard the bells from all the churches in Brighton ringing in the New Year. A year that we hoped would bring peace.

But it was not to be. Bombs were dropping almost every day, air-raid sirens were screaming us awake and we would then spend hours squashed into the damp Anderson shelter.

Churches were holding funerals almost daily and my heart broke when I saw tiny coffins on the backs of carts, being pulled along by weeping families. I wondered if this war would ever end.

Brenda and I were constantly down at the church lighting candles.

'Do you really think that anyone's listening to our prayers, Maureen?' she said one day.

'I'm not sure. Maybe they're all a bit busy at the moment, what with the war and all.'

'Why can't God stop the war if he's all-powerful?'

'Not sure about that one, Bren.'

'I mean, he can bring people back from the dead and he can cure lepers and turn water into wine, so why can't he stop this bloody war?'

'Well, Aquinas used to say that you can't blame God for everything because he gave us all a free will.'

'But don't you think that's a bit of a cop-out?'

'Yep.'

'So why do we bother with the candles?'

'Because there's always the chance that we're wrong and there is someone up there listening. We're going to look like right idiots if we find ourselves at the Pearly Gates and it's swarming with saints and angels being all saintly and angelic and St Peter says we can't go in because we didn't have faith.'

'So we're hedging our bets, right?'

'Spot-on.'

'Fair enough.'

Spring came early that year, bursting out of the ground in a glorious display of colour as if it knew that it was needed. It gave us hope in these darkest of times. Jack and I walked on the Downs, trying to ignore the tanks and the soldiers. The Devil's Dyke was still out of bounds so we walked across the hills towards the cliffs that looked down over the sea.

Jack lay down with his hands behind his head. I sat beside him hugging my knees and gazing out over the water. It was one of those days that made you feel glad to be alive; you could almost forget there was a war on and even harder to believe that on this beautiful day people were dying in their thousands. The water was so calm, hardly moving at all, and it sparkled like a million diamonds under the bright sun.

I lay down beside Jack, he put his arm around me and I rested my head against his chest. I didn't know what the future was going to bring and where it would take us but right now, on this lovely spring day, being held by the boy I loved, I was happy. And then he spoke.

'I'm joining up, Maureen.'

I didn't move, I didn't speak. I just concentrated on the beating of his heart, trying to match the hammering of mine to the steady beat of his.

He leaned up on one elbow and looked down at me. 'I have to go, Maureen, I can't hide behind this student thing any longer. I've tried to, but I can't.'

'I know you have.' I looked into his beautiful blue eyes. He wanted my approval, he wanted me to say that it was the right thing to do and, after all, it's what I'd promised him.

I got up and walked a few steps away from him. The sun had gone behind a cloud. I looked out over the sea. It looked grey without the sun; it needed the sun to turn it blue, it couldn't sparkle without it. I knew that I would be the same when Jack went away; my blues would turn to greys without him by my side. I took a deep breath and turned to face him. 'You have to do what's right for you, Jack,' I said. 'And I will be here waiting for you when this is all over.'

Jack got up and stood beside me. He kissed the back of my neck so softly, so tenderly.

'That's all I needed to know,' he said.

We stood together, looking out over the sea. Each with our own thoughts and hopes and fears for what lay ahead of us.

Chapter Fifty-Two

Those spring days were short-lived as wind and rain battered the coast. And then there was this awful war: blackouts, stumbling around in the dark, rationing and daily air raids. So when a letter came from Nelson, we couldn't have been happier.

I met Jack at the station and we walked down to the cafe on the seafront. We ordered a pot of tea and some sandwiches because Jack said that he was starving. It was too cold to sit outside so we found a table that looked out over the sea. The window was all steamed up, so Jack took a hankie out of his pocket and wiped it so that we could see out. The sea looked angry and grey, bashing and splashing against the sea wall. The barbed wire all along the beach looked horrible. But inside the little cafe it was warm and cosy and, even better, we had a letter from Nelson. I opened it and we started reading.

Dear Maureen and Jack,

The first thing I want to say is that I'm OK, so you don't need to worry. I've been injured, not badly, just enough to get me sent back to England for a while. Yes, I'm in good old Blighty with a shrapnel wound to my leg. You may be wondering where my sturdy tank was in all this. Well, I was walking at the time. A bunch of us were sent to check out a town when we were attacked. Some of the others got it worse than me but, thank God, we all made it back to camp alive. They are operating tomorrow to remove the shrapnel and then they are sending me to a convalescent home on the seafront in Hastings! Can you believe it? I'll be just along the road from you and I will be available for visitors.

I hope that you are both well.
Can't wait to see you, my friends.
Love,
Nelson x

Jack and I were grinning from ear to ear.

'I can't believe it, can you?' I said.

Jack shook his head. 'I don't suppose we should be this happy to hear that he's been injured, but it's not serious and we get to see him.'

We held hands across the table; we were both grinning. We were going to see our friend.

We waited until we received the letter from Nelson letting us know that he had arrived in Hastings and that he couldn't wait to see us.

The following Sunday, we got up early and made our way down to the Brighton bus depot at Pool Valley. I'd never been to Hastings, in fact I'd hardly been out of Brighton, except to see Daddy at Haywards Heath, so I was really excited as the bus made its way along the coast road. As we approached the town we could see that Hastings had had its fair share of the bombing.

We got off the bus and started walking back along the seafront. I took Nelson's letter out of my bag. 'We're looking for Valerie House,' I said. 'Nelson says it overlooks the beach.'

We passed beautiful houses that had been badly damaged or were completely gone, just a pile of rubble where they once stood. One house had the side of it completely blown away. You could see the wallpaper, an intricate pattern of pink roses and green trailing leaves, and a perfectly intact bed standing against one of the remaining walls.

'I bet when they chose that wallpaper they didn't think that the whole world would end up looking at it.'

'I bet they didn't,' said Jack.

'I expect that when they bought it they were wondering whether it would go with the bedspread.'

'Or the curtains,' said Jack, laughing.

'Sad really, isn't it? It's like ending up in the bottom of a smelly bucket.'

'A smelly bucket?'

'I'll explain another time,' I said.

'I wonder why it's called Valerie House?' I said, looking at Nelson's letter.

'It was rumoured that an architect who designed a street or an avenue used to name the roads after his relatives,' said Jack. 'Maybe Valerie was his wife.'

Valerie House was a beautiful building on four floors. It was painted white, stained yellow in parts from the salty wind coming in from the sea. We walked up the front steps and rang the doorbell.

It was opened by a young chap on crutches and he grinned at us.

'Visiting the poor, heroic wounded, are you?'

'Nelson Perks?' I said, smiling at him.

'Ah, Nelson! He said he was expecting his friends. He's in the garden, breathing in the sea air. I'll take you to him.'

We followed the man as he expertly swung along on the crutches with surprising speed. He led us along a hallway to the back of the house and opened a door that led outside.

'You'll find him out there,' he said, pointing down the garden.

Nelson was sitting in a wheelchair. One of his legs was extended out in front of him and he had a red and grey checked blanket draped across his knees. I called his name and his face split into the biggest smile. I ran over to him and put my arms around him. Then I stepped back and took in how pale he was and how thin but it was Nelson and, for now, at least he was safe and he was home.

'Oh, Nelson, it's so good to see you,' I said.

Jack walked up behind me and knelt down by the wheelchair. 'Sorry about your leg, old chap. Are you in any pain?'

'A bit,' said Nelson. 'But I'm alive, so I can put up with a bit of pain.'

'Are they looking after you well?' I asked.

'We're all getting spoilt rotten by a bevvy of pretty nurses, how much better can it get?'

It became clear that Nelson didn't want to talk about the war, so we told him all the news, even stuff we'd already told him in our letters. Like the cinema being bombed and the bomb that fell on the bookshop that never went off. I told him about how it had affected Peter.

'Poor chap,' said Nelson. 'But it sounds as if he was a hero the day the cinema was bombed.'

'Oh he was,' I said. 'He really was.'

'It takes some people like that,' said Nelson. 'Raw young recruits too thin for their uniforms arrive on base and you don't think they'll last a week but they surprise you and end up becoming unlikely heroes.'

'They say there's a hero in all of us,' said Jack. 'I'm yet to find mine.'

'Your day will come, Jack,' said Nelson. 'You don't have to blow a man's brains out to become a hero. You are going to become the biggest hero of us all, because you will be saving lives, not destroying them.'

'Actually, Nelson, I've joined up,' said Jack.

'I had a feeling you might.'

'Didn't have a choice really.'

'What regiment are you joining?'

'I'm going as a combat medic, that's all I know at the moment.'

'Well, let's hope that by the time you finish the training it will all be over.'

'That would be good,' said Jack. 'For everyone.'

We stayed for about an hour and then one of the pretty young nurses walked down the garden. 'Enough excitement for one day, I think,' she said, stepping on the brake and turning the chair around.

'You'll come again, won't you?' Nelson called as he was wheeled away up the garden.

'Next Sunday,' called Jack.

'Give my love to the others,' shouted Nelson.

On the way home I stared out of the bus window and I thought about Nelson. I was glad that he was being looked after so well by the pretty nurses but it had made me feel not exactly bad inside but strange, maybe even a bit unhappy. Now, what the bloody hell was all that about?

Chapter Fifty-Three

We visited Nelson every Sunday. Sometimes we spent the entire visit in the shelter under the house but we didn't mind. We got to know the other patients at Valerie House and those times became quite jolly. I found myself making memories of those days we spent together.

Some days we were allowed to wheel him along the seafront. We'd get ice creams or fish and chips. The beach at Hastings was out of bounds, just like our beach in Brighton.

'Won't it be great when we can walk on the pebbles again?' said Nelson.

'And paddle in the sea,' I said, smiling.

'And play cowboys and Indians,' said Jack, laughing.

'I'm sure that day will come and I pray we'll all be together when it does,' said Nelson.

'I'll second that,' said Jack.

'And I third it,' I said.

We all laughed but there was a sadness in the laughter. Would we all be together at the end? I hoped with all my heart that we would.

One evening Jack and I were sitting at the end of my garden. It was still warm. We could hear children playing in the street and one of the neighbours mowing his lawn. We could smell all the cooking smells wafting out of all the open windows on the estate. Everything was so normal, a spring evening when children played and mothers cooked and men mowed the lawn. You could almost forget that we were at war.

I treasured every moment I spent with Jack, taking pictures in my mind, tucking them away so that I could take them out and look at them again when he had gone.

His Mum had taken the news as badly, as we both knew she would.

'She just can't, or won't, understand why I have to go.'

'She'll get used to it, Jack. Once she's got over the shock.'

But he shook his head. 'I'm not sure that she will,' he said. 'I've tried to explain how I feel but she won't listen.'

'And your dad?'

'He understands, but I knew he would. I think he's a bit proud of me, but of course, he can't say that. Not in front of Mum, anyway.'

'What does being a medic mean? Will you have to fight?' I said.

'I'll know more when I start my training.'

'And when will that be, Jack? When will you have to go?'

'I'm waiting to get my orders but I think it will be soon.'

'I'm scared,' I said, leaning into him.

'So am I, my love,' he said, holding me tightly.

'I'll light a candle for you,' I said.

'Me and the dead dog?'

'You and the dead dog.'

'Don't you think you've lit enough candles for him?' he asked, grinning.

'I think that sometimes, but then when I kneel down, I feel I have to. You know, like I'd feel bad if I didn't.'

'You're an old softy, do you know that?'

Suddenly we heard the sound of Jack's mum. 'Are you over there, Jack?' she shouted.

Jack put a finger to his lips. 'Shush,' he whispered.

'Shouldn't you go?' I whispered back.

'No, I'm where I should be.'

OK, she was his mum, I accepted that, but I needed him too and he needed me. I knew she didn't approve of my relationship with Jack. Nothing was ever said but I just knew and I knew that she resented the time he spent with me.

Jack's orders came through at the beginning of May. His mother was in a terrible state. Mr Forrest came round and asked Mum if she would go next door and sit with her.

'I didn't know whether to put my arms around her or slap her,' said Mum when she came back home. 'I know how scared she is and I know how disappointed she is that Jack has gone against her wishes. I wanted to tell her to be proud of her son and to respect his decision but she's making it all about her, about how she's going to feel, about how he's her only child and his place is with her. Honestly, Maureen, I felt like shaking her. Her husband looks like he's at his wits' end, poor man.'

Everything that Jack's mum was feeling I was feeling as well, so I did feel sorry for her, but I didn't let Jack see how worried I was. I wanted to make the most of the time we had together; I didn't want to waste it on regrets. I had to believe that he would come through the war safely and I wanted Jack to believe that as well.

I wanted us to do the things we normally did; I didn't want things to be any different. And so we went to the pictures and sometimes Monica and Chester joined us. We avoided sad films and films about the war. Instead we laughed at George Formby and giggled at Old Mother Riley. They were silly films but that's what we needed and, judging by the laughter in the cinema, it was what everyone needed.

We sat in bus shelters in the blackout, eating fish and chips out of the paper and we kissed in doorways and we held onto each other as tightly as we could. We knew that in time Chester would also be shipped out and there was a kind of desperation to these outings.

'Have you done it yet, Maureen?' asked Monica one day when we were on our own.

'No, we haven't,' I said.

'You should, you really should,' she said.

'Have you and Chester?'

'Of course we have, daft!'

'Where did you do it though?' I said.

'You'd be surprised how inventive you can be when you have to.'

We were sitting on the green at the top of the road.

'We've done it here actually,' she said, giggling.

'Here?' I said. 'On the green?'

'More than once.'

'More than once?'

'For heaven's sake, Maureen, they're going to war! They need comfort and so do we. It gives them something to remember and to come home to.'

'I *want* to do it,' I said.

'Do it then. He's going to be gone in a week. It's no good wishing you'd done it when you're waving him off on the train. It'll be too bloody late then.'

'I don't fancy doing it on the green.'

Monica raised her eyes. 'I'll tell you what, why don't we talk to Brenda and get her to take your mum to the pictures one evening? Then you can do it in the comfort of your own bed. Would that be more to your taste, madam?'

Monica was a tonic and I hoped that she would never change. She made me brave.

'Aren't you scared?' asked Brenda when I told her the plan.

'A bit,' I said.

'I'd be terrified,' she said, making a face.

'That's because you haven't met the right boy. When you meet the right boy, I don't think you'll be so terrified.'

'But how will you know you're doing it right?'

'It can't be that difficult. Think of all the millions of women who've done it, even Aunty Vera's done it.'

'Yeah, and look what she ended up with!'

I giggled. 'Imagine doing it with Uncle Fred.'

'I can't even go there.'

'Nor me.'

'Do you know what really bothers me, Maureen?'

'What?'

'I'd be worried that Dada was watching.'

'Thanks for that, Brenda, I really need that image in my head.'

'Sorry, but doesn't that bother you?'

'Well, it didn't till you mentioned it.'

'I shouldn't think he'd mind though, do you?'

I thought of Daddy and how much he loved me and how he had always known how much I loved Jack. 'I don't think he'd mind at all,' I said, smiling at her.

'How long does it take to do it?'

'For God's sake, Brenda, you don't half ask some odd questions! How do I know how long it takes? I've never done it before.'

'It's just that I need to know how long to keep Mum out for.'

'Like I said, I don't know how long it takes and I've never spoken to anyone who's timed it, but I reckon not much more than half an hour. Happy now?'

Brenda nodded. 'You'd better get started as soon as we leave the house, just in case you have to practise first.'

'Bloody hell, Brenda! It's nice to know that romance is still alive and well in See Saw Lane.'

'And I'll want to know all about it.'

'Well, you'll just have to want it, Brenda O'Connell.'

We had decided that Thursday evening was when Mum and Brenda would go to the pictures. All day long at work my tummy was in knots.

'What the hell's wrong with you today?' said Maggie after I'd dropped the third pile of books.

'Nothing,' I said.

'Yes there is. I can read you like one of those books, Maureen O'Connell, so spill the beans. I can tell you want to.'

I picked up the books that were scattered on the floor. 'Mum and Brenda are going to the pictures tonight.'

'So?'

'So me and Jack will be alone in the house.'

I could see Maggie's brain ticking over. 'You and Jack will be alone in the house?' she said. Then it dawned on her. 'Oh right, you and Jack will be *alone* in the house.'

'Correct,' I said, grinning.

'And I presume by the way you've been acting all day that this will be the first time?'

I nodded.

'Put the kettle on and I'll talk you through it,' she said seriously.

'Must you?' I said, screwing up my face.

'Best be prepared,' she said, going to the door and turning the sign around.

'How do I get prepared?'

'You know, in your head.'

'Won't it just happen naturally?'

'It might, but be prepared for a bit of fumbling.'

'Fumbling?'

'Yeah, you know.'

'No, I don't know, Maggie, and I don't think I want to.'

'I'm only trying to help.'

'I know you are but I had no idea that it could be that difficult.'

'It depends.'

'On what?'

'No, you're probably right. You might get lucky and it'll just happen naturally, like you said.'

'I'm beginning to wonder if it's all worth it if it's going to be that complicated.'

'Oh, it's definitely worth it, Maureen.'

'Well, thank God for that,' I said, grinning at her.

'You love each other, don't you?'

'Very much.'

'Then it'll be OK.'

When I got home that evening I couldn't eat my tea – my stomach felt like it was full of frogs. Just as Mum and Brenda were going out the door, Mum turned round.

'Are you sure you won't come with us?' she said.

'I'm seeing Jack, Mum.'

'Well, you have a lovely time with him.'

'Don't do anything I wouldn't do,' said Brenda, winking at me.

If I'd had anything to throw at her I would have done, instead I made a face.

Once they were gone, I went upstairs. The house suddenly seemed so quiet. I couldn't remember a time when I had been alone there and it felt strange. I walked across to the window and looked out over the garden. I thought of the child peering through the branches and seeing Jack for the first time: the child had gone and she was about to become a woman.

I sat on the bed and waited for Jack.

Chapter Fifty-Four

Jack and I said goodbye up on the Downs. We lay on the grass wrapped in each other's arms. Something had changed between us since we'd made love. I'd always loved him but now I was a part of him in a way that I'd never been before. I knew that Jack felt the same, there was something in his eyes when he looked at me. I'm not sure what it was, but we were different, as if we'd made a commitment to each other to be together forever, in a sort of 'Till death us do part' kind of a way. Yes, that was it, I felt that we were married. As married as if we'd stood in front of Father O'Malley and been given his blessing. But I didn't need all that. I didn't need a piece of paper to tell me that we belonged to each other, I already knew. I'd always known.

I looked across at Jack; his eyes were closed. Jack was beautiful, in a way that many boys aren't. There was something almost girlish about him. His lashes lay dark against his cheeks hiding for a moment his eyes that were as blue as the sea. I leaned across and gently brushed the hair away from his forehead. His hair reminded me of a fairy tale that Daddy once told me, about a princess who spun straw into gold. That was what Jack's hair looked like, it looked like spun gold. Yes, Jack was beautiful.

I lay there looking up at the sky and I remembered our special night. I suppose I should have been scared after all the advice I'd been given but something told me that I had nothing to be scared about. There were no surprises, no fumbling. I knew Jack's body like I knew my own. I'd watched him grow from the boy into the man. I knew the soft places and the hard places, the curve of his spine, the pale downy hair on his arms and legs that caught the sun as he ran along the beach. The sharp bones jutting from his hips that dug into me as we tumbled together on the snowy hills. I'd felt the softness of his belly and seen the hollow at the base of his throat, glistening with sweat. I wasn't lost, I needed no signs to follow; I knew where I was going. I had always known where I was going. I welcomed the heaviness of him and when the pain came, it was a pain like no other pain I had ever felt. It filled every part of me with joy and it made me grateful to be alive on that night, in that place with the boy that I had always loved.

Jack opened his eyes and smiled and I cuddled into him. I lay my head on his chest and listened to the soft beat of his heart. Jack and I were as close as it was possible to be, our bodies touching from our shoulders down to our toes, but soon one of us would move and there would be a gap between us, just like the gap between the tree and his back garden. We would walk home holding hands, our skin still touching, and then the gap would widen; other people would get in the way. Like the dancers at the end of the pier, coming together and moving apart, circling each other and smiling across a crowded room until the music faded away. The music always faded away.

'Let's walk,' said Jack, getting up.

We walked across the hills towards the cliffs. We held hands as we always did, our steps perfectly matched as they always were. I had never been so aware of his hand in mine; I wanted to hold onto him forever. How was I going to find the strength to let him go?

We stood at the edge of the cliff and looked out over the sea.

Jack turned my face towards him. 'Promise me something,' he said.

I didn't know what he wanted and I didn't know if I could promise him anything.

'Promise me.'

'I'll try.'

'I might not come back.'

I pulled away from him. 'Don't say that,' I sobbed.

He caught hold of me and pulled me back.

'I might not come back,' he said again.

I shook my head. 'I don't want to hear that, Jack. How can you say that? Are you trying to break my heart?'

'I wouldn't hurt you for the world, Maureen.'

'Then don't say it, don't say that you might not come back, because you have to. If you don't come back, I'll die. I will, Jack, I'll die.'

Jack tried to put his arms around me but I didn't want him to touch me. I walked away from him, tears streaming down my cheeks. How could he say that? How *could* he? And then he was behind me, his arms holding me tightly, his soft lips gently kissing the back of my neck.

'I know it's not what you want to hear, my love,' he said softly, 'but we can't pretend that I'm going on some kind of holiday. People are dying and I might be one of the unlucky ones. I will try and stay safe, I promise you that, because we have a life together, you and I. I want nothing more than to marry you, Maureen, and have children and grow old with you, but if that can't happen I want to know that you will be alright. I want you to remember what we have had and how lucky we have been. Not many people have had what we've had. We've grown up together, Maureen, we didn't have to search the world to find each other. You were there up in the tree and I was just over the fence. I can hardly remember a time without you. Even if I don't make it back, we have already spent almost a lifetime together and all those memories will be there in your heart. I will be there in your heart and I will stay there until the day comes when you don't need me any more.'

I listened to him and I knew that what he was saying was right. He didn't want to hurt me but he did have to prepare me. He was saying these things because he loved me.

I turned in his arms and looked into his eyes.

'A lifetime would never be long enough for you and me,' I said. 'And there will never be a time when I won't need you any more.'

'I want you to be happy, Maureen…'

I put my finger on his lips. 'Just come back, Jack, that's all I want. Just come back.'

Jack's mum looked as if she'd been crying all night and his dad looked serious as he helped her into the car, so I had smiled as if I was waving him off to university and not off to war. I waved as the car pulled away from the kerb and I watched as it turned the bend in the road and was out of sight. As I stood there on the pavement I had never felt more alone.

Chapter Fifty-Five

Those first few days after he'd gone were awful. Jack said that he would write as soon as he was able to and I longed for his first letter.

Me and Monica were lying on my bed. I was miserable.

'Bloody war,' she said, plumping up her pillow.

'Any idea when Chester will be leaving?'

'Not a clue, he doesn't know either.'

'Has he ever said that he might get killed?'

'Bloody hell, Maureen! Why would he say that?'

'To prepare you, if the worst happens and he doesn't come back.'

Monica leaned up on one elbow and stared down at me.

'Has Jack said that to you then?'

I nodded. 'Do you think he's had a premonition?'

'No, I don't and I don't know why he would say something like that. We all think it, but we don't say it out loud. Chester makes a joke about it and maybe that's not right either, but you have to believe that they will come home safe and, even more importantly, *they* have to believe they'll come home safe.'

'Jack's different. I think he's different, Monica.'

'It's all that education, it's messing with his head.'

'Do you think so?'

'Why else would he come out with stuff like that?'

'He wanted me to promise him that I'd be alright if he died.'

'How can you promise him something like that? How do you know what you'll be like?'

'Oh, I know what I'd be like.'

'He'll come home, Maureen, you'll see.'

'He has to, Monica. He has to.'

Suddenly we heard a hammering on the front door and then Mum was running up the stairs. She burst into the room.

'Monica, it's your Archie. He says the Yanks are moving out! You'd better get up to the camp quick.'

'I'll come with you,' I said.

We ran downstairs. Archie was standing in the hallway, trying to catch his breath.

'I run all the way, Monica. There's loads of trucks up there and all the soldiers are getting into them.'

'Did you see Chester?'

'No, I just thought I'd better get you.'

'You did the right thing, Archie. You're a good boy.'

Then Archie burst into tears. 'I don't want the Yanks to go, Monica. They're really nice, I like 'em.'

'I know you do, love, but they have to fight now, that's what they have to do.'

The three of us ran up the road and up onto the Downs. Trucks full of soldiers were passing us as we ran. We were scanning their faces, trying to find Chester.

'Can you see him, Maureen?'

I shook my head. 'There's so many of them.'

When we got to the camp trucks were still coming through the gates. There were loads of girls outside the fence, screaming and crying. As a truck passed us Monica called out to one of the soldiers, 'Chester McQuaid, have you seen him?'

The soldier shook his head. 'Sorry, ma'am, it's chaos here. We were given fifteen minutes' notice that we were leaving. Try the station.'

'The station?' said Monica.

'That's where the trucks are heading, you might find him there.'

Tears were rolling down Monica's face. 'We'll never get there in time.'

'Move along, lads!' shouted the soldier. 'We've got company.'

'Go home, Archie!' yelled Monica as strong arms lifted us up onto the truck.

'Keep your heads down, ladies, I'm breaking the rules here.'

'Thank you,' said Monica. 'Thank you so much.'

'You're very welcome, miss, Chester is one of the best. I'm happy to help.'

As the trucks rattled through the streets people were coming out of their houses, waving them off. 'Good luck, lads!' they were shouting.

Loads of kids were running after the trucks and the soldiers were throwing chocolate and chewing gum to them.

'I think there will be a few broken hearts in Brighton this day,' I said.

'There'll be one more if I don't find Chester,' said Monica.

'We'll find him,' I said, holding her hand.

It was as chaotic at the station as it had been at the camp. As soon as we were lifted down from the truck, we started running into the station. It was full of noise and soldiers and doors slamming and women crying.

'We'll never find him, Maureen.'

'We bloody well will!'

There was a truck next to us, still unloading soldiers.

'OK, Monica, we need to stand on the bonnet.'

'What?'

'We need to stand on the bonnet of this truck so that we can see over the crowd.'

'I'll ruin me nylons.'

'This is no time to be thinking about your nylons, Monica.'

'No, you're right.'

'Give us a leg up,' I said to a young soldier.

'You wanna get up on the truck, miss?'

'Yes,' I said. 'On the bonnet.'

'No problem,' he said, saluting us and grinning.

Once we were safely balanced on the bonnet I said, 'Now, shout as loud as you can, Monica.'

Monica took a deep breath and shouted, 'Chester McQuaid!' as loud as she could over the top of the crowd. Then I added my voice to hers.

'It's no good,' said Monica.

'Try again,' I said.

'Want some help?' said the young soldier.

'Yes, please,' said Monica.

He turned to a group of lads that were loading kit bags onto a trolley.

'These young ladies are looking for Chester. I want you to climb up on the roof and yell as loud as you can.'

So with a group of soldiers on the roof of the truck and me and Monica on the bonnet, we all shouted across the station. 'Chester McQuaid!'

And suddenly there he was, running towards us, weaving in and out of the crowd, grinning all over his face. 'Monica!' he was shouting. He lifted her down from the truck and swung her round and then they were in each other's arms and they were kissing and laughing and holding each other.

I sat down on the bonnet with my legs dangling over the side and I watched them. Monica had got to say goodbye to Chester and, for a moment, I had forgotten about Jack.

It was easier at the bookshop; joking with Maggie and taking tea out to the war council in the shed. The roof was mended and we had a new little kitchen at the back of the shop. Bombs continued to fall. Four days after Jack left, three German planes came in low over the sea and dropped bombs on the viaduct over London Road and the railway station, putting two lines out of action. Luckily, no one was killed.

Being in love made me selfish. We were in the middle of this awful war, men, woman and children were dying every day and yet all I could think about was Jack. When would I see him? When would I be in his arms again? When would I get a letter? I barely listened to Afshid's news as she raced through the shop and into the shed. If it wasn't about Jack then I wasn't interested. Yes, love had made me selfish.

After work I went straight to the church and lit a candle. I put my penny in the box and knelt down. 'Please take care of him, Mary,' I said. 'And please forgive me for thinking only of him and not all the other poor people that are dying. I don't mean to be selfish, I do care really, but right now all I can think about is Jack.' I looked up at the statue of the Blessed Virgin Mary smiling down at me and said, 'Have you ever been in love, Mary? I know that you were married to Joseph, but did you love him? Did you love him like I love Jack? If you did then you'll know how I feel so please, please keep him safe.'

I got up and started walking back up the aisle, then I went back and lit a candle for two doors down's dog and Nelson's leg.

I could hear the noise as soon I turned into See Saw Lane. For an instant I couldn't tell where it was coming from. Then I saw her: Jack's mum, kneeling in the middle of the road, screaming Jack's name. I noticed she had a letter in her hand.

I couldn't move, I couldn't take in what was happening; it wasn't making any sense to me. Then I saw my mum running out of our house. I watched her kneel down beside Jack's mum. I watched her cradle Jack's mum in her arms. I listened as the screaming turned to wailing that seemed to come from the very depths of her soul. Other women were coming out of their houses. One of them was holding a blanket and she put it around Mrs Forrest's shoulders. They crowded around her, sheltering her, protecting her. She was one of them, she was a mother. They could afford to be kind, because for now, today, their sons and husbands were safe. Maybe God would look kindly on them if they gave comfort to this woman.

I didn't go to her; I didn't want these women to see me, I didn't want their comfort. I didn't want any kind of comfort, no one could comfort me.

Then Mum saw me. Her eyes were full of pity as she walked towards me.

'Oh, my love,' she said. 'Come on home.'

I shook my head. 'I can't,' I said and I started running.

Chapter Fifty-Six

It was Jack's dad and Uncle John that found me. I had been gone all night and Mum, Brenda and Aunty Marge were frantic with worry. They found me the next morning in the old barn. I couldn't remember how I got there; I couldn't remember anything. I could only remember running and running and running. They wrapped me in a blanket and, between them, they carried me down the hills and home.

I couldn't speak and I couldn't cry. Mum and Brenda did their best; they washed me, they fed me, they sat on my bed and talked to me, they never left me. Even during an air raid they never left me. I was loved but I was lost. What was I supposed to do with all this love that was inside me? It didn't die with Jack; it was still there. What was I supposed to do with it? No one tells you that bit, do they? I've heard people say that death leaves them with an empty feeling. I *longed* to feel empty but I didn't, I felt full of love for a boy that was never coming back. Time meant nothing, life meant nothing. I wanted to be with Jack; I wanted to die. I stayed like that for weeks. During that time they buried him. Mum and Brenda gently urged me to go to the funeral but I couldn't. I couldn't watch them put him into the ground. I was drowning and no could save me.

Nelson came every day. They brought him by car in the morning and they collected him in the evening, but I wouldn't see him. I wouldn't see anyone except Mum and Brenda. I was scared to leave my room; I was scared to face a world that didn't have Jack in it.

One day Mum came into the bedroom. She sat on my bed and took hold of my hand.

'You are not the only one that is grieving, Maureen. Nelson has lost his best friend and he needs you. He has come every day; he is sitting downstairs now. I think you should see him.'

I looked at her and shook my head and I said the first words that I'd said since Jack died. 'I can't, Mum.'

'Well, I think you can, and I think that you should. Nelson needs you, love, and we want you back. You can't run away from life, however much you might want to. It's there outside this room and so are all the people that care about you. Greta Garbo might get away with it, but I don't think Maureen O'Connell can. It's time, my precious girl.'

After she left I thought about what she'd said. She was right: this pain wasn't just my pain, this loss wasn't just mine. I remembered when Daddy died and how sad Mum was, but she didn't allow herself to grieve for long because she knew we needed her. I walked across to the window. It was raining; water was running down the glass like tears.

I pressed my forehead against it. Then I looked down the garden and I stared at the tree and started to cry. Gut-wrenching wailing, just like Mrs Forrest, which brought my mum rushing back into the room and into my arms. I cried like a baby and all the while Mum held me and soothed me and rocked me, until there were no more tears left.

Slowly, slowly, I learned to live without Jack. It was painful and it was hard and I didn't always succeed. Some days were too hard to face, but those days became fewer and fewer. I still hadn't gone back to the bookshop but I knew that I would when I was ready. Maggie came to see me, bringing flowers and chocolates from Mrs Bentley.

'It's bloody boring without you, Maureen! Mrs Doom and Gloom next door is driving me mad and Peter says I don't make his tea the way you make it. I need you back.'

'Soon,' I said.

'I'm really sorry, Maureen.'

'I know.'

'But I don't know what to say.'

'You don't have to say anything, Maggie. It's enough that you're here.'

'Good,' she said, putting her arms around me.

It was nice to see Nelson again, I'd forgotten how much I liked being with him. We couldn't go anywhere much because of his leg, so we sat in the house or in the garden. One day we were sitting on the bench, talking about Jack. It was nice to sit beside Nelson and to feel the sun on my face.

'It's so strange, Jack, not being next door.'

'There's no one next door,' I said.

'What do you mean?'

'They've gone.'

'They've moved?'

I nodded. 'Mr Forrest came round to tell Mum that his wife couldn't stay there any more, too many memories, so they had to move away.'

'I can kind of understand that,' said Nelson.

'So can I,' I said. 'But I need those memories, it makes me feel closer to him.'

'Have they gone far?'

'Scotland. Mrs Forrest has a sister living there.'

'They were good to me. I know I wasn't the kind of kid that Jack's mum would have chosen to be his friend but she looked out for me, she fed me, she even knitted me a jumper once – she hated that brown one.'

'I know,' I said, smiling.

'Have you still got it?'

'Of course I have,' I said.

'Maybe it's time I got rid of it.'

'Why?'

Nelson shrugged his shoulders. 'Seems like a daft thing to do, to keep it.'

'I think that we all do the best we can. We hide away in bedrooms, we run away to Scotland or we hang onto old brown jumpers. I don't think that you should get rid of your old brown jumper just because you think it's daft to keep it. One day you might not need it any more so, if I was you, I'd wait for that day and get rid of it then. Or keep it forever.'

'You're a wise girl,' he said.

'Sometimes,' I replied.

Nelson ran his hands through his hair. He reached across and held my hand. 'I'll always be here for you, Maureen. You know that, don't you?'

'I'm banking on it, Nelson.'

What was wonderful about our friendship was that I could talk about Jack without upsetting him. People found my grief hard to handle. I saw neighbours cross the road to avoid talking to me. It wasn't that they didn't care, I knew that, they just didn't know how to deal with it. Some people liked grief to be neatly packaged and put away, not raw and exposed for all the world to see.

I guess you could say that Nelson and I worked through our sadness together. When one of us was down, the other was there to pull them back up. We could laugh together remembering the good times and we could cry together remembering the good times and that's what got us through. Our love for Jack is what got us through.

I hadn't asked how Jack had died. What difference would it have made if I'd known? He was gone and he wasn't coming back, that's all I knew. That was all I needed to know. But as I got better, his death started to bother me. How could he have died so soon after he went away? it didn't make sense. Suddenly I wanted answers. I asked my mum.

She sat me down. 'You didn't ask, Maureen, so I didn't tell you. He was on a train, love, going up north. The train was bombed and Jack was killed. I don't know any more than that. I don't know why he was on the train.'

'I'd like to see his grave, Mum.'

'You're sure?'

I nodded. 'Yes,' I said.

'Do you want me to go with you?' she asked.

'Yes, but I'd like to spend some time on my own with him. Would that be OK?'

'Of course.'

Jack was buried in the graveyard of St Nicholas church. It was a beautiful building with long stained-glass windows and a tower. Part of the tower was damaged; I suppose it had been bombed. A plaque over the door told us that it was the oldest church in Brighton. The graveyard itself was full of ancient gravestones, covered in ivy and moss. Some of them were toppling over and some of them already lying on the ground. I followed Mum as she made her way to Jack's grave. We'd brought some flowers with us. She picked up a glass jam jar and went looking for a tap, leaving me alone.

I knelt down and stared at the ground. How could I even start to imagine that Jack was underneath this soil? I gently touched the mound of earth.

'I'm here, Jack,' I said. 'I'm sorry it took me so long.'

I looked around me. Everywhere was so quiet and still. There was a cool breeze but it felt as though nothing was moving, as if everything had frozen in time. There was something that I had to tell him, something I'd been keeping to myself for weeks. I gently touched my stomach.

'We're going to have a baby, Jack,' I whispered. 'We're going to have a baby.'

Chapter Fifty-Seven

I was on the bus going to Hastings; I needed to tell Nelson. Strangely enough, I didn't know how he was going to take it. I was pretty sure how most people would react, but not Nelson. My family had been amazing.

'You're not ashamed of me, Mum, are you?'

'I could never be ashamed of you, Maureen,' she'd said. 'You loved Jack and he loved you, and I'm sure that you would have got married after the war.'

'He never asked me, you know. I thought he would, but he never.'

'The war takes boys in different ways. Some want to get married as soon as they get their call-up papers. They want to know that their girlfriends are going to stay true to them while they're away fighting. Others, like Jack, fear that they might not come home and they don't want the girl they love to end up a widow. I can understand Jack not asking you and I know that it wouldn't have been because he didn't want to.'

'Don't you mind that people are going to talk?' I'd asked.

'People will always talk. They talked when your dad died. Let them gossip if it makes them feel better about themselves. Hold your head up high, my girl, you've done nothing wrong.'

'Thanks, Mum. I'm going to have to tell Mrs Bentley and Peter and they might not want me working in the bookshop.'

'They don't seem like judgemental people to me.'

'They're not, but the customers might be.'

Then Mum had taken my face in her hands. 'This child will be a blessing, Maureen, and this child will be loved because it was born out of love. If people want to think otherwise, that's up to them.'

My family were amazing.

* * *

It was strange going to see Nelson without Jack; it made me feel lonely inside. The seat next to me was empty so I put my bag on it. I missed him, I missed him so much.

I got off at the bus station and started walking back along the seafront. I passed the house with the missing wall. The flowery wallpaper was still hanging off in strips but the bed was gone. Jack would have had something funny to say about why the bed was gone. I couldn't believe that I would never hear his voice again.

It was a warm day and the front door to Valerie House was wide open. I stepped into the cool hallway and waited for someone to come. There was music coming from behind a closed door to my left and I could hear the muffled sound of people talking and laughing. As I opened the door, I saw Nelson right away. He was standing beside a piano, turning the pages of the music for the young boy who was playing.

'Nelson?' I called.

He turned around and his face split into a huge grin when he saw me. 'Maureen, I didn't know you were coming,' he said.

'Sorry, mate,' he said to the boy and walked over to me.

I smiled at him.

He immediately looked concerned. 'Are you OK?'

I nodded but Nelson knew me, he knew me like Jack knew me.

'You're not, are you?'

'Can we talk?' I said.

'Of course. We'll go into the garden, we'll have a bit more privacy out there.'

We walked to the far end of the lawn.

'You're walking better,' I said.

'It's getting easier,' he told me, sitting down on a bench. 'Now, come here and tell me what's wrong. Because I know that something is.'

'There's nothing wrong,' I said, sitting down next to him. 'At least, I hope you won't think that it's wrong.'

Nelson reached across and held my hand. 'Whatever it is, you know you can tell me.'

'I'm going to have a baby, Nelson. I'm going to have Jack's baby.'

I held my breath. Nelson's opinion seemed suddenly very important to me. It felt like ages before a huge smile spread slowly across his face and I could feel myself relax. 'I didn't know how you'd feel about it,' I said.

'You didn't?'

'I wanted you to be happy.'

'How could I not be happy? This baby will be a part of Jack, I can't think of anything more wonderful than that.'

I smiled. 'Neither can I.'

'A baby, eh?'

I nodded. 'Should I tell Jack's parents?'

'Do you want to?'

I looked down at the ground. 'I don't think so.'

'Then don't.'

'But if they find out then they'll know it's Jack's.'

Nelson went quiet and stared out across the garden, then he looked at me.

'Not if you're married, they won't,' he said.

'What do you mean, if I'm married? Who's going to want to marry me now?'

'Me?' he said softly.

I didn't know what to say. What the hell was he on about? I actually found myself laughing. 'We can't get married, Nelson, you're like my brother.'

'I had a feeling you'd say that, but what if I told you that I wouldn't expect anything from you?'

'Then why marry me?'

'I could take care of you, you and the baby. I could give the baby my name. I'd be proud to do that, Maureen. Perhaps I'm being selfish, I hope not. But I could give you the protection of a marriage, people wouldn't talk. I know it sounds mad, but will you think about it?'

I shook my head. What was he thinking? I couldn't marry Nelson – he was my friend, he was Jack's friend. It was a stupid idea. I loved Jack, I hadn't stopped loving him because he'd died. I couldn't just suddenly marry Nelson, could I? Could I?

I stood up and walked away from him; he didn't follow. I passed young men in wheelchairs, some of them had lost legs. I saw a man being guided around by two nurses, his eyes were bandaged. None of us knew what was going to happen, none of us knew the moment we'd end up in the bottom of a smelly bucket, we just joined in the dance until the music stopped. I leaned against a tree and looked out across the lawns. I listened to the sound of the gulls and breathed in the salty air and I thought about Nelson: he would look after me, he would look after the baby. He would never hurt me, he would never let me down – but was that a good enough reason to marry someone? Especially someone you didn't love? I think I had always known that Nelson cared for me, so would it be fair to expect him to put up with half a marriage when there was probably a girl out there who would love him the way he deserved to be loved? Wouldn't I be taking advantage of his feelings for me?

I was tempted. I shouldn't have been, but I was. Nelson was offering me marriage and respectability; my child wouldn't be looked down on. But if I accepted his offer, then I had to do something for him. I thought about Nelson and the rotten childhood he'd had. He'd never had a loving home and I could give him that. I could take care of him and I could give him a home. It might work, it just might work.

Chapter Fifty-Eight

Nelson and I were married at Brighton town hall. I had always dreamed of getting married in a church but the Church had let me down. They wouldn't bury my daddy and the Blessed Virgin Mary didn't look after Jack, even though I'd lit enough candles over the years to deserve a sainthood.

Once I was able to I went down to the church. I went straight to the side altar and stood in front of the statue of Mary.

'You're just a statue, aren't you? You're just a stupid statue made of plaster. I've been lighting candles to a lump of bloody plaster!' I was shouting now. 'I hate you, I hate you and I'm never coming back here. Do you hear me? Of course you don't, cos you've got no bloody ears. You've never listened to me or to Brenda. You've never taken care of Jack or Nelson or the dead dog. You never cared that Nelson was getting beaten up or that Jack's train got bombed.' Tears were streaming down my face. 'And you let my daddy die!' I yelled. 'You let my daddy die!'

Father O'Malley came rushing out of the presbytery. 'What on earth's the matter?' he demanded, running over to me. 'Oh it's you, Maureen. What's wrong, child?'

'*That's* what's wrong!' I said, pointing to the statue.

'Now what has the Blessed Virgin Mary done to you, Maureen?' he said gently.

'She's not the Blessed Virgin Mary, she's just a lump of stone. I've spent half my life praying to a lump of stone.'

'Let's sit down,' he said, leading me towards a pew.

'I hate her, Father.'

'No you don't, Maureen, you hate what's happened and you want someone to blame and why not God and his sweet mother? Yes, this is just a lump of stone, as you put it, but it's somewhere for people to come, it gives comfort. Do you think that your Jack or your father are underneath the ground, Maureen?'

I shook my head.

'Of course you don't, because you know that their souls are with Almighty God. But their graves are somewhere for you to visit, to sit and remember, to talk with them. It's the same with the statues in this church. We know they are not real but they allow us to sit for a while and light a candle and pray and find some peace. No, Maureen, the statue can't hear your prayers but God can and so can the Blessed Virgin.'

I thanked him and left the church. On the way home I thought about what the priest had said. It didn't change anything; it still meant that no one had listened. I felt like asking for a refund on the bloody candles.

When I'd told my mum that I was going to marry Nelson she was, of course, a bit concerned – in fact she was worried about the same things that I was worried about. The main thing being, was this fair on Nelson?

'He's always cared for you, you know,' she said.

'I know he has and that's what worries me. Am I stopping him from marrying someone who could love him properly?'

'You know you are, but it seems that Nelson would rather be married to you on any terms than be married to anyone else.'

'So should I have turned him down?'

'Do you know what I think, Maureen?'

'What?'

'I think the pair of you will be fine. Being in love doesn't always guarantee a perfect marriage. Some of the best marriages are arranged between families. I'm not saying they all work out, but I think a lot of them do and believe it or not, love doesn't conquer all. What you and Nelson have is a deep friendship and that's about as close to love as you can get.'

'Thanks, Mum,' I said.

Monica, on the other hand, was definitely against it.

'Marry Nelson!' she screamed. 'You can't, Maureen, you just *can't*!'

'Why not?'

'Bloody hell, where do you want me to start? You don't even love him. Isn't love kind of important in a marriage?'

'I think friendship is just as important, Monica,' I said. I didn't know whether I was trying to convince her or myself.

'Look, Maureen, maybe you're right. My mum and dad reckon they're in love and look at the state of them. I'm not going to tell you what you can or can't do. Nelson loves you and he'll look after you and if that's enough for the both of you, then I wish you all the happiness in the world.'

'Thanks, Monica. Fancy being my bridesmaid?'

'I thought you'd never ask,' she said.

'Well, it was a toss-up between you and Marion Tucker, but…'

'Oh, *you*,' she said, grinning.

Our wedding day was actually lovely. All the people we cared about were there. Mrs Bentley loaned me a grey silk dress and a little pale pink hat – I had never worn such lovely clothes. Nelson looked very handsome in his suit and Monica looked pretty in a pale green dress that set her red hair off beautifully. Mr Farley from the orphanage was Nelson's best man and Uncle John gave me away.

We had our reception at Mrs Bentley's house. She had always been so good to me. From the day Daddy had asked for the old dolls' pram, she had been like a second mum. It was a beautiful day and we were able to sit in the garden. Peter brought out chairs and spread blankets on the grass.

When I was a child my world was small, just Mum, Daddy and my little sister. Aunty Marge and Uncle John, of course, but mostly it had been just the four of us. Now, as I looked around the garden, it made me happy inside to see all these people who were a part of my world. Good people, like Maggie, the butcher and his wife, the baker and his wife, Hassan and Afshid, Monica, Mrs Bentley and Peter. These people had helped me in so many ways. They had all been there, nudging me along, accepting my grief, allowing me to mourn and gently guiding me from that dark place back into the sun; they made losing Jack easier than it would have been. And then I looked across at Nelson, dearest Nelson. He wasn't Jack, he would never be Jack but I would do my best to make him happy. I watched him laugh at something Chester had said and suddenly I felt proud of him: Nelson deserved all the happiness he could get and I was going to make sure he got it.

The day after our wedding Nelson and I went to visit Jack's grave. We knelt on the ground.

'I hope you'll be happy for us, my friend,' said Nelson. 'I promise you that I will take care of Maureen and your baby. It should be you, Jack, and I hope you don't mind that it's me. A poor second best, I know but—'

'Don't say that, Nelson, it's not true,' I said.

'I think it is but I'm not complaining, Maureen, not for one second. I've always loved you and I want nothing more than to take care of you. I just hope that Jack can understand.'

We had brought some flowers with us. I stood up and handed the jam jar to Nelson.

'Would you fill this with water?'

He nodded and walked across the cemetery to the tap.

I knelt down again. 'I hope I've done the right thing, Jack. I was scared, you see. Scared of bringing up this baby on my own without you. I care for Nelson, I trust him to look after us and I will do my best to make him happy. So look down on us, Jack, and help us to make this work, that's all I'm asking.'

Nelson came back carrying the jam jar full of water. I arranged the flowers and we stood them on the grave.

I miss you with all my heart and I will love you until the day I die, I thought.

'Rest in peace, Jack,' said Nelson.

Chapter Fifty-Nine

Rita Perks came into the world on 23 February 1942, during one of the longest air raids that anyone could remember. She weighed eight pounds and two ounces. She was also two weeks overdue and I was the size of a barrage balloon. I gave birth to her in the hospital and Nelson wasn't allowed into the labour room but I knew that he was sitting outside in the corridor the whole time. I thought that I was going to die with the pain and I was told afterwards that I had screamed out Jack's name, which totally confused the nurses, as they knew that the man sitting outside the room was my husband and his name was Nelson.

When I looked into Rita's eyes it was like looking into Jack's. They were as blue as the sea and her hair, what there was of it, was nearly white. She was Jack's child alright and as I held her soft little body against mine it was love at first sight, just as it had been the first time I'd seen Jack from up in the tree. I closed my eyes and fell into a deep sleep.

When I woke up, Nelson was sitting beside my bed.

'Are you alright, love?' he asked.

'How did you get in here?' I said.

'I know one of the porters,' he said, grinning.

'Have you seen the baby?'

'She's beautiful, Maureen,' he said. 'And she—'

'Looks like Jack?'

He nodded.

I winced as I shifted myself up the bed. 'She may look like Jack but she's your daughter, Nelson. You're her father now.'

'I want to be.'

'Well, you are and you're going to be a great dad.'

He smiled and reached for my hand. 'Thank you,' he said.

'No one has to thank anyone for anything here, Nelson. We're a family now and we're going to be the very best family that we can be.'

Mum came to visit me and I shall never forget the look on her face as she looked into the cot.

'Can I hold her?'

'Of course you can.'

She gently lifted Rita into her arms and kissed her little cheek. 'She's beautiful, Maureen, she's perfect.'

'And she looks like Jack,' I said.

'She does indeed, but she's got a look of you too.'

'Has she?'

'You had a round little face like that.'

I didn't answer her.

'What's wrong, love?' she asked.

'I've got something on my mind, Mum.'

She lay the baby back down in her cot and waited for me to speak.

'Should I tell Jack's parents that they have a grandchild?'

'I've thought about that myself, Maureen, and for the life of me I don't know what's the right thing to do. They've lost their only son and my heart goes out to them. To know that they have a grandchild would be a wonderful thing.'

'I know, but I want Rita growing up believing that Nelson is her father and I want that for Nelson too. If I let Jack's parents into her life then she'll know she's not his. She'll know that Nelson is not her real dad.'

'What's your head telling you to do?'

'Tell them.'

'And your heart?'

'Say nothing.'

'I can't tell you what to do, love, but I *can* tell you that family comes first and you, Nelson and Rita are family now, so you must do what's best for all three of you.'

'Thanks, Mum.'

'So you're going to keep quiet?'

I nodded. 'That's what's going to be best for my family.'

'Then you've made the right decision.'

Everyone adored Rita. Mum was besotted by her first grandchild and Brenda couldn't wait to get home from work every evening to see her and pick her up and spoil her. But, apart from me, no one could have loved her more than Nelson did – he couldn't have loved her more if she *had* been his. This little baby was truly the apple of his eye. We had decided on her name together: Rita, after Jack's favourite film star, Rita Hayworth.

When Rita was a tiny baby I was still able to go to the bookshop. When the weather was fine, I would put her pram out in the yard and everyone would keep an eye on her.

Afshid would swap the victory marches for Glen Miller and Rita would fall asleep to the gentle strains of 'Moonlight Serenade'. But as she got bigger it became more difficult and so I had to give up my wonderful job where I had been so happy. I hated saying goodbye to everyone but I knew that I had to. It wasn't fair on Rita, I had to be a proper mummy to her.

'You will pop in sometimes, won't you?' pleaded Maggie.

I felt like crying. 'Of course I will,' I said.

'You bloody better!' she said, hugging me.

* * *

Nelson was discharged from the nursing home in Hastings and he moved into See Saw Lane. At first it seemed strange to have a man in the house but as Mum and Brenda had known him almost all his life, it wasn't like they were having to share the house with a stranger. We had become a family. OK, it wasn't your usual kind of family but it was ours and that was all that mattered. I had thought that the only thing I could give Nelson was a home but I had given him so much more than that. I had given him Jack's child and no child could have been more loved and no child could have had a better father. He looked so proud as he wheeled Rita along the seafront.

Sometimes I looked at him and wondered if he was truly happy. We were loving towards each other – we held hands, we cuddled – but that was as far as it went. I knew that wasn't enough, of course it wasn't, but I never asked, because I didn't want to know.

Of course Monica had an opinion. We were down the lagoon and Rita had fallen asleep in her pushchair.

'It must be killing him,' she said.

'Well, he looks happy enough.'

'He might look happy but it can't be easy for him. He's a man and a man has his needs.'

'Well, he'll just have to have his needs, won't he? There's nothing I can do about it.'

'I'm only saying,' said Monica.

'I know you are and I'm sorry I snapped, it's just that I feel so guilty I can't bear to think about it.'

'He knew what he was letting himself in for, Maureen.'

'I know, but I still feel guilty.'

'You couldn't, you know—'

'No ,I flippin' couldn't!'

'Just a thought.'

'Could you make love to your Archie?'

'Don't be stupid,' said Monica, looking shocked.

'Well, that's how I feel about Nelson. It would be like making love to my brother.'

That shut her up.

When Rita was eight months old, we got a letter telling us that Nelson must report for duty. I guess we both knew that it was going to happen but had always hoped that the war would have ended by the time his leg had healed.

I didn't want him to go; I felt safe with him around. And I knew Nelson was dreading going back. He had never talked about how it had been out there but I knew it must have been awful. This time it was going to be harder for him to go because he was leaving behind his family and that included Mum and Brenda.

The bombings in Brighton were getting worse. There was more damage and more people were losing their lives.

On the 12 October four planes came in low over the sea and dropped bombs on St Dunstan's, the home for blind ex-servicemen. In the same raid, bombs fell on St Anne's home for disabled and invalid children. Nelson was worried about us.

'I want to know that you will both be safe while I'm away,' he said.

'We've survived so far,' I said.

'But you have a child now, Maureen, and Brighton's not a good place to be.'

'But where would I go?'

'Further into the country, I suppose.'

'Amongst strangers?'

'It won't be forever and I'll feel better knowing you're away from the bombs.'

I told Mum about what Nelson had said.

'I have to agree with him, Maureen. You have a baby to think of now and it's not safe here.'

'But what about you and Brenda?'

'Don't worry about us, it's you and the baby that need to get away.'

'But I'll be with people that I don't know.'

'I think I might have an idea,' she said.

Chapter Sixty

The day after Nelson left, Peter drove me up to London and saw Rita and I safely on board the train that would take us to Wales, where we would board the boat to Ireland. It had been hard saying goodbye to Nelson and even harder leaving my family. Aunty Marge and Uncle John had turned up with a bag of food for the journey.

There wasn't a dry eye as we waited by the gate for Peter to turn up in the car. As the car approached the house, Mum had kissed Rita and handed her to me.

'Stay safe,' she'd said.

Brenda put her arms around me, her eyes full of tears.

'I wish you were coming with me,' I said, hugging her. We'd never been apart and I was going to miss her.

'Me and Molly will soon be called on to do war work and we'd like to do it together. You don't mind, do you?' she said.

'Of course I don't, I just want you to be safe.'

'I'll write,' she'd said. 'You will write back, won't you?'

'Of course I will,' I'd answered.

'I wish I could have persuaded Mum to come with me,' I said.

'Mum will never leave her house, too many memories of Dada.'

'I know.'

'Take care, Maureen.'

'I will.'

Uncle John helped me into the car and Peter started the engine. I waved to my family until they were out of sight.

Peter parked the car and walked me across to the platform where the train was waiting. He helped us into the carriage and lifted my case onto the rack above my head.

'Take care of yourself, Maureen,' he said, handing me an en-velope.

'What's this?'

'Mrs Bentley says it's for emergencies.'

I put the envelope in my pocket. 'You are the kindest people I know,' I said, hugging him.

'Just be sure to come back to us,' he said. 'We'll all miss you.'

'I'll miss you too,' I said, hugging him.

I watched him walk across the station and out of sight. Suddenly everything seemed very real. I was going to another country, leaving behind everyone I loved. I wanted to run after Peter, call him back, tell him I'd changed my mind and to please take me home, but I didn't. I settled down in a seat by the window, holding Rita on my lap.

Luckily she was a good baby. She slept most of the way and when she needed feeding or changing, I took her into the toilet. There was a young sailor in the carriage who kept an eye on my case. Because of the blackout there was only a very dim light on the train, which made changing Rita's nappy difficult. It took eight hours to get there and it was midnight when we pulled into a place called Fishguard on the coast of Wales.

Everyone started pulling cases down from the racks above our heads and piling out into the narrow corridor.

'Best to wait until last,' said the sailor. 'Don't worry, the ship won't leave without us.'

He lifted my case down. 'I'll carry this,' he said in a strong Irish accent. 'You just look after the little one.'

'You're very kind,' I said.

'Me mammy would never forgive me if I didn't lend a hand to a pretty young girl like yourself.'

I smiled – I guess this was what they called the Irish blarney.

Once everyone had got down from the train, we left the carriage and made our way along the platform. It was pitch-black and the wind coming off the sea cut right through me. I pulled the blanket closer around Rita.

We were soon being carried along by a crowd of people all making their way to the boat. There seemed to be hundreds of them, men and woman dragging cases and clutching the hands of children as they made their way down a long tunnel towards the quayside.

'It's always the same,' said the sailor. 'Like a bloody cattle market.'

I don't know what I would have done without his help. Rita was like a dead weight in my arms so I could never have managed the case as well.

'I have to stop for a minute,' I said, leaning against the wall of the tunnel.

'Here, give her to me, I can manage both,' said the sailor.

I gratefully handed Rita to him. I was exhausted and suddenly wished that I had stayed at home. I was mad to have started on this journey with a small baby, what was I thinking of?

The tunnel emptied out into a huge shed. There were lines and lines of tables and people were piling cases onto them.

The sailor led me over to a bench that was set against the wall.

'You sit there,' he said. 'And I'll go through Customs.'

I looked up at him, he had been so kind to me. 'What's your name?' I asked.

'Jack,' he said, smiling.

So my guardian angel was called Jack.

'Thank you, Jack,' I said.

Rita started to stir in my arms. 'The sailor's name is Jack,' I said, kissing her cold little cheek. 'The same as your daddy's.'

There were so many people on the gangplank and so little light that I thought we would all fall into the sea. Terrified, I held tight to Rita. I looked behind me to make sure that Jack was still there.

Once on board the ship things were no better. It was crowded, there were people everywhere. All the seats in the lounges were taken and people were sitting on cases in the corridors. I had to find somewhere for me and Rita to rest.

'Stay here,' said Jack. 'I won't be long.'

I sank down onto the floor and waited for him to come back. Rita started to whimper; she needed changing and feeding and I felt like crying. The smell of oil and the swell of the waves were making me feel sick. I wanted my mum, I wanted Nelson. I wanted to go home.

Just then Jack came back. He held his hand out and helped me up.

'I need to feed the baby,' I said.

'I've sorted something,' he said. 'Come with me.'

I followed him down some steep stairs and along a corridor that had doors leading off it. He stopped outside one of them. Then he opened the door and we were in a small cabin with a single bed against the wall.

'You can stay here,' he said.

'Really?' I asked.

'The chap whose cabin this is, is on the night watch. He said you are very welcome to it.'

I sat down on the bed and lay Rita down beside me. 'I'll never be able to thank you enough,' I said.

'Just get a good night's sleep,' he told me and he was gone.

I changed Rita, then lifted her onto my breast. Her little mouth closed around me and her chubby hand pressed into my skin as she sucked. Then we lay down together and slept. I knew nothing else until I was woken by a soft tapping. Jack put his head around the cabin door.

'Come with me,' he whispered.

I looked down at Rita; she was fast asleep.

I put my coat on and followed Jack up onto the deck. It was blowing a gale and my hair was flying around my face. I was glad that I'd left Rita tucked up warm in the little cabin.

'Ireland,' he said, pointing into the distance.

At first I couldn't see anything and then, as the mist started to lift, I saw the outline of land.

'Welcome home,' said Jack, putting his arm around my shoulder.

As I stared through the mist I felt like crying, not sad tears but tears of joy. I felt as if I was indeed coming home.

I went back down to the cabin. Rita was awake, she grinned at me. I changed her nappy and fed her. I loved these times when she latched onto my breast and looked up at me with her beautiful blue eyes. She was such a lovely baby; I wish Jack could have seen her, he would have been so proud. After I'd fed her I wrapped her up warm in her blanket and went back up on deck.

As the big ship sailed up the River Lee into the heart of Cork city, I grew more and more excited. People waved to us from the banks. Passengers were leaning over the railings, waving back. It felt as if the ship and everyone on it was being welcomed home.

'This is Ireland,' I whispered to Rita. 'Where your granddaddy came from.'

There was a great crowd of people waiting on the quayside for the boat to dock. They were waving and calling out. I knew that I was being met by my Cousin Sean, but had no idea what he looked like. I searched the faces in the crowd, looking for someone who might look vaguely familiar to me.

Our guardian angel Jack carried my case down the gangplank while I held onto Rita.

'We'll sit on that bench over there,' he said, 'until the crowd clears a bit, then we'll see who's left.'

We didn't have to wait long.

'Maureen O'Connell?' said a voice.

I looked up into the most handsome face I had ever seen in my life. 'Sean?' I said, standing up.

He shook my hand and said, 'Welcome home, Maureen.'

'This is Jack,' I said. 'He has taken care of us. I don't know what I would have done without him.'

Sean shook Jack's hand. 'Thank you for looking after them,' he said, smiling. 'I'm grateful.'

'I'll say goodbye then,' said Jack. 'And I wish you and the little one lots of luck.'

I handed Rita to Sean and threw my arms around Jack's neck. 'I'll never forget you,' I said.

'Nor me, you,' he said. 'Now, go and have a great life.'

I watched him walk away. He had indeed been our guardian angel. The journey would have been so much more difficult without him. He had been a stranger to me, but I'd trusted him to look after us. I guess it had helped that his name was Jack.

'Let's go home,' said Sean. 'Half the town are waiting for you.'

We boarded a bus that would take us to Youghal.

I sat by the window and looked out at the passing villages and fields. I was amazed at how green everything was.

'Now I know why they call it the Emerald Isle,' I said.

'It's the rain,' said Sean. 'It never bloody stops.'

I smiled at him. 'It's beautiful,' I said.

'It surely is,' he said.

Rita started to grizzle, she was hungry. 'She needs feeding, Sean,' I said.

Sean took off his coat and draped it across me so that I could breastfeed my little girl.

'Thank you,' I said.

My cousin was a lovely boy.

The bus took us along a coastal road. A watery sun was pushing through the clouds making the sea sparkle, reminding me of home. Rita fell asleep in my arms.

'She's a good baby,' said Sean.

I smiled at him, 'Yes, she is.'

'We're here,' he said, picking up my case.

I looked out the window as we drove into the old town.

'Not far now,' said Sean, helping me down from the bus. 'The cottage is at the other end of the town, can you manage?'

I felt dizzy with tiredness and I could still feel the motion of the boat under my feet. Rita was asleep and heavy in my arms.

'Give her here,' said Sean and he took the sleeping baby from me.

We walked through the main street, under the arch of a tall clock tower. To my left were a series of narrow steep hills rising up from the main street, lined with cottages, and, on my right I could see glimpses of a river between the houses.

'The Blackwater,' said Sean.

My daddy's river, I thought.

As we neared a row of low white cottages, people were running towards us and I was enveloped in the arms of strangers. They were crying and hugging me. Someone took Rita from Sean's arms.

'This is your family,' he said, laughing. 'And this,' he said, putting his arms round a small woman wearing a black shawl, 'is your Aunty Mary.'

Tears were rolling down her face as she took me into her arms.

I was almost carried into the house as more and more people poured into the tiny room, all of them wanting to meet the girl from England. Aunty Mary eased me down into a chair by the fire. She took my face in her hands. 'You look like your daddy,' she said, her eyes full of tears. 'You look like Pat.'

'She's the image of him, Mary,' said a voice from across the room.

I looked around for Rita. Someone had put her in a basket next to the fire.

'She'll be grand there,' said Aunty Mary. 'Let the child sleep.'

It was warm in the little room and my eyes were heavy with tiredness. I was desperate for sleep.

'Let's get you upstairs,' Aunty Mary said. 'We can talk later.'

'Rita?'

'I'll take care of her.'

I said goodbye to everyone and followed Aunty Mary up the steep little staircase.

The room was tiny; the bed took up almost all the space. There was a picture of the Sacred Heart of Jesus on the wall.

'Now, you get some sleep,' she said, kissing my forehead. 'Welcome home, Maureen, welcome home.'

I lay on the bed and looked out of the little window, over the old slate rooftops and chimneys. I had never felt more at peace, or more welcomed. We were safe, we were being taken care of. We had crossed an ocean to the land of my father, to the town he loved and a hill that looked down on a river. I closed my eyes and slept.

Chapter Sixty-One

I explored every inch of that little town. One of my many cousins turned up at Aunty Mary's door with a pushchair, so I was able to push Rita up the steep streets, past the little cottages and the children sailing paper boats along the gutters that flowed down the hill. It reminded me of pushing Brenda along in the squeaky old pushchair.

I trod the unfamiliar places and I walked for miles along the wood road towards the old bridge that spanned the Blackwater River. Then out of the town and along the strand. I sat on the rocks beside the lighthouse. I let Rita play in the sand and I looked across the sea and thought of home. Here in Ireland you could almost forget that there were bombs dropping and that people were dying. There was no war here, no bombed buildings, no air-raid sirens, only peace. I wished that Mum and Brenda could have come here as well but I had to accept that Mum wouldn't leave the house and Brenda wanted to stay with Molly.

'We'll all be together again when this awful war is over,' Mum had said.

I hoped with all my heart that this would be true and that my family would stay safe until I returned.

Aunty Mary was poor, all my Irish family were poor. Not like we were poor in England, but dirt poor. There was no water in the little cottage in Tallow Street, which meant that there was no toilet. We fetched the water from a pump and the end of the road and we did our business in a bucket behind a curtain. To begin with I was too shy to use the bucket and I ended up with a terrible tummy ache, but like everything else in this new life of mine, I got used to it. I realised that things didn't matter, only the people mattered, and these people were wonderful.

'We have very little, Maureen,' said Aunty Mary one day. 'But what we have is yours, yours and the baby's. We manage and when we can't, our neighbours and our families help us. That's the way it is in this town, we all help each other.'

The envelope that Peter had given me contained five pounds. Five pounds was a fortune and I knew what I was going to do with it. I gave it to my Aunty Mary, who cried all week and wouldn't stop. My Aunty Agnes who lived across the passageway said, 'Leave her be, Maureen. The woman's in shock, she's never seen that amount of money in all her born days. You should have given it to her in bits, then the shock wouldn't have been so great.'

'I feel terrible, Aunty Agnes,' I said.

'Sure, don't you be worrying about that. Once she realises that she's a woman of wealth she'll soon get over it. Take her down to the church and she can have a word with Himself.'

'Who's Himself?' I said.

'The Lord.'

And so I took my weeping aunty down to the church. Somehow people had heard about her windfall and took no notice of her tears as we walked through the town.

The church was huge. It towered over the humble cottages that nestled in the shadow of its tower. I had a bad feeling about it. Why was the church so rich when its congregation were so terribly poor? I didn't say anything though, because I had a feeling it wouldn't go down well.

We dipped our fingers in the holy water font that was just inside the door, then we walked down the centre aisle and knelt in front of the altar. Aunty Mary was still crying her eyes out, I wondered if she would ever stop. Her wailing brought the priest out of the vestry.

'Ah, Mary,' he said, walking across. 'I heard about your bit of good luck. Have you come to give a donation to the Lord?'

Before I could stop myself I said, 'No, she hasn't, Father. She's come to thank Him.'

'What you must remember, Mary,' he said, completely ignoring me, 'is that the money came from God.'

'No, it didn't,' I said. 'It came from Mrs Bentley.'

'And wasn't it the Lord Himself that gave it to her?'

'I shouldn't think so,' I said. 'She doesn't believe in God.'

'It makes me very sad to hear that. I will pray for her.'

'Thank you, Father,' said Aunty Mary.

'Bloody cheek!' I said after he'd walked away.

Suddenly I noticed Aunty had stopped crying and she was actually giggling.

'God forgive me, Maureen, but his face was a picture,' she said.

'He didn't look happy,' I said.

'He's bound to read my name out at Mass on Sunday.'

'What do you mean?'

'If someone upsets Father Paul, he reads their name out at Mass. He had a bad stomach and he swore it was the bit of beef he'd got from the butcher. He demanded that people not buy their meat there. The poor butcher nearly went out of business.'

'That's awful. Why do people listen to him?'

'Because he's God's voice on earth. He is the vessel through which Our Blessed Lord speaks.'

I was dying to tell Aunty Mary what I thought of that but I had to respect that this was her town and her religion, so I said nothing but I bloody thought plenty. We put our pennies in the box and lit our candles. Aunty Mary prayed for all the souls in Purgatory and I lit my candles for my family and Jack and Nelson and two doors down's dead dog. I thought he'd be pleased that I'd remembered him even though I was in another country.

* * *

One morning I wrapped Rita up in her blanket and I carried her up the hill behind the town, to the place that Daddy loved so much. I sat on top of the hill with Rita in my arms and looked down over the river. I could almost imagine Daddy as a little boy standing here, thinking himself the King of the Castle.

I kissed the top of Rita's head and breathed in her baby smell. 'This is where your granddad used to come,' I said. 'This was his favourite place. He would have loved you, Rita, and you would have loved him, but I know that he is looking down on us and I know that he will be so proud.'

I looked down at the beautiful river flowing beneath me. 'I'm here, Daddy,' I said. 'I'm here.'

Chapter Sixty-Two

I wrote to Nelson every week. I never knew how many of my letters got through to him but still I wrote. I wanted him to know that he wasn't alone, that there were people who cared about him, who worried about him. I had a few letters back; he said he was OK but I think he was just telling me that so I wouldn't worry. In one of the letters was a photo. A blurry picture of Nelson and a group of soldiers, they were smiling into the camera as if they were on holiday but if you looked closer you could see that behind the smiles they looked tired and Nelson looked thinner. I kept that photo under my pillow.

I found myself questioning my feelings for Nelson. When I thought about him I felt confused, I always had. It was all mixed up with feeling sorry for him, for wanting to care for him, for wanting his world to be a better world. Sometimes when I thought about that old brown jumper I felt like crying. And then there was another feeling that would catch me unawares, like when Nelson told me about the pretty nurses looking after him in the nursing home. The boy who walked in the shadow of Jack was now my husband. I cared about what was happening to him. I suppose it was a kind of love, maybe just not the right kind.

As well as writing to Nelson, I wrote to Mum and Brenda and Monica. I also wrote to Mrs Bentley, thanking her for the money and letting her know the huge difference it was going to make to my family. I related the episode with the priest; I thought she would find it funny.

One morning when I came downstairs there was a letter from Brenda propped up on the mantelpiece. I sat down beside the fire and started to read:

Dear Maureen,

Molly and me are going to join the Land Army. We both hate the thought of working in a munitions factory and that's where we will end up if we don't volunteer now. We are going to Somerset in the West Country and we will be working on a dairy farm. It feels like a kind of adventure and we can't wait.

Some bad news. Aunty Marge and Uncle John have been bombed out of their flat. Luckily it happened during the day when they were working on the stall, so neither of them were hurt. They are moving into See Saw Lane until they can find somewhere else. One good thing about it is that Mum won't be on her own. With both of us gone that was worrying me.

I hope you are well and happy, we miss you and Rita so much.

Love from your Sister Brenda xxx

Brenda and Molly remained as close as they had when they were children and I was glad that they were going to be working together. I knew Brenda was frightened of the bombs and the air raids and now, at least, she would be in the country with her best friend.

One evening, Aunty Mary and I were sitting in front of the fire in the only downstairs room of the cottage. Rita was asleep upstairs.

Aunty Mary got up and went across to an old dresser that stood in the corner, under a picture of Saint Anthony. 'I thought you would like to see this,' she said, handing me a photograph. It was yellow with age and it had a crease across the middle of it as if it had been folded at one time. It showed a family, all of them unsmiling, staring into the camera. She pointed to a woman in the centre of the photo.

'That was your grandmother, Maureen. Your daddy's mother.'

'And the children?' I said.

'That was the rest of us.'

She pointed to each child. 'That's Connor, the eldest, and next to him is Breda, then Kathleen, Thomas and Teddy. That's me and your Aunty Agnes standing behind Mammy and that's the baby Billy on Mammy's lap. Kathleen died when she was nine and Billy when he was three.' Then she pointed to a boy who was leaning against his mother's knee. 'And that's Pat,' she said. 'Your daddy.'

I could feel the tears welling up in my eyes. 'That's my daddy?'

Aunty Mary nodded. 'He was his Mammy's favourite, we all loved him.'

I gently traced his face with my finger, trying to see the man I had loved in the serious little boy staring out at me. I looked up at my aunty. 'That's really my daddy?'

'Isn't he handsome?'

'He's lovely,' I said. 'But why do you all look so solemn?'

'It was like that back in the day. Having your picture taken was a rare occurrence and had to be taken seriously. It's the only picture that was ever taken of us and I treasure it.'

'Where did you all live?'

She looked around the room. 'Here,' she said.

'You all lived here? All of you?'

'We did.'

'But there's only two rooms upstairs.'

'It was all we knew. It was home. Things were even harder in those days. I don't know how my mother managed but she did.'

'There's no man in the picture.'

'My father would have been at sea. Your grandfather was in the Irish Navy.'

'I wish I'd known them,' I said.

'You would have loved your grandmother.'

'And not my grandfather?'

'He was a desperate drinker, Maureen, so were all his brothers. Mammy used to have to go down to the quay and wait for his boat coming in, so that she could beg him for some money before he drank it all away in the pub. She wasn't the only woman waiting on the quayside. That's the way it was. The women had hard lives back then.'

'I can't imagine how it must have been for her, with so many mouths to feed and so little money.'

'Your daddy helped as much as he could. Even from a young age he was out running errands to put a few pennies on the table. It broke his heart when she died, he was only eleven.'

'What did she die of?'

'She pricked her finger on a rose thorn. There was no money for a doctor, she died of blood poisoning. We were left with a drunkard for a father. One by one, they all left. Connor and Breda to America, Thomas ended up in Canada and Teddy in Scotland. Agnes and I stayed and we looked after Daddy until he died.'

'And my daddy?'

'He joined the army and fought in the war.'

'It was the war that made him ill,' I said.

'He was always a sensitive child. The war was no place for him but he couldn't stay at home, Daddy picked on him something terrible.'

I looked down at the photo. 'It's the only picture I have ever seen of him as a boy.'

I went to hand it back to her but she shook her head. 'You keep it, Maureen,' she said, smiling.

'I can't, it's precious to you. I can't take it.'

'I've had the pleasure of it for years. Now take it, it's yours.'

I stood up and put my arms around her. 'Thank you so much,' I said.

I could hear Rita stirring upstairs. 'I'll go up now,' I said. 'Goodnight, Aunty Mary.'

'God bless,' she said.

I changed Rita and put her to my breast. She stared up at me as she fed. People told me that her eyes would change colour as she got older but they hadn't. They were still as blue as Jack's. As I held my baby in my arms I looked towards the little window. The sky was black and it twinkled with a million stars. I liked to think that maybe Daddy and Jack were amongst them, looking down on us. Wouldn't that be wonderful?

I lay Rita back down in her basket; she was already asleep. Then I put the photo of Daddy under my pillow along with Nelson's. I liked to think of them both together.

'Take care of him, Daddy,' I said.

Chapter Sixty-Three

Rita was getting bigger. She was walking now, hanging onto chair legs as she staggered round this little room that had become her world. She was beginning to babble away in her own little language. I wondered if, when she did talk, she would have an Irish accent.

I loved everything about Ireland and this little town; I felt as if I could stay here forever and be happy. I missed my mum and I missed Brenda but this beautiful place was beginning to feel as much like home as Brighton. I wished that I could gather up everyone I loved and bring them here to this lovely place, where they would be safe.

It's funny how quickly you get used to things. I got used to the bombs dropping and the daily air raids at home but, just as quickly, I got used to the gentle pace of life here in Ireland.

Every morning Aunty Mary would get up at the crack of dawn and walk out to the strand, where she cleaned for the nuns at the convent. I did all I could to help her. I pushed Rita down the wood road in her pushchair and gathered sticks for the fire. I carried water from the pump to the cottage. I cleaned the rooms and I washed the clothes. I wished I could have done more but I didn't know what else I could do. The answer came in the form of my handsome cousin Sean, who worked in the bakery across the lane.

'Do you think that you could sell bread?' he said one afternoon.

'Bread?'

'Yes, bread. Mrs Flanagan has sold bread and cakes in the shop since she was old enough to reach the counter, but her son has come home from America and he's bringing her back to live with him, so we need someone and I thought you might be interested.'

'That would be perfect, Sean. It would mean that I could help Aunty Mary out.'

'That's what I thought. Will you come over and meet the boss then?'

'When?'

'Now if you like.'

'OK.'

I asked Aunty Mary if she'd keep an eye on Rita, then I ran upstairs and brushed my hair.

The baker's name was Mr Hurley. Everything about him was big; he towered above me but smiled as I opened the door. I was immediately hit by warmth and the smell of fresh bread and sweet cakes, which made my mouth water.

'Ah, so you're the little English girl, are you?' asked the baker.

I nodded.

'Sean has told me all about you and your little girl and how you're staying with your Aunty Mary.'

'That's why I'd like a job,' I said. 'I'd like to pay my way.'

'I heard about the fortune you gave her. That was good of you, child.'

'She's given me and my baby a home, Mr Hurley, I just want to pay her back.'

'Your aunt's a good, kind, God-fearing woman and she was a beauty in her day. I would have married her myself but she chose to look after that eejit of a father of hers. If there's any justice in this world he'll be burning in the everlasting fires of Hell as we speak.'

I grinned.

'Have you had a job before?'

'I worked in a bookshop, so I'm used to selling to the public.'

'What hours can you do?'

'I'll have to ask Aunty Mary if she'll look after Rita and, if she can, then it would be afternoons when she finishes work. Would that be alright?'

'That would work out fine because Mrs Hurley works in the mornings.'

And so I worked in the bakery and not only did I get paid for it, I was able to take home the bread and cakes that hadn't sold during the day. Being there day after day I was getting to know the people of the town and, as it turned out, I was actually related to most of them.

'That's what it's like here,' said Sean. 'I used to have trouble finding a girl to walk out with who wasn't me cousin.'

'And did you find someone, Sean?'

'I did. Her name's Orla, she's from Waterford. She has a cousin in town and I met her at a dance at the town hall when she was here for a visit.'

'I'm glad you have someone special.'

'Oh, she's special alright and she's beautiful. Do you believe in love at first sight, Maureen?'

I thought of the first time I saw Jack, playing with the tin soldiers. 'Oh yes, Sean, I believe in love at first sight.'

'Well, that's how it was when I clapped eyes on Orla. I had to make my move fast because all the lads were after her but she chose me, thank God.'

'Then she's wise as well as beautiful.'

'That's what I keep telling her.'

I liked Sean a lot. His hair was as black as coal and his eyes were a piercing blue. No one ever talked about his father but word had it that he was a tinker passing through the town and Aunty Agnes had got carried away with his roguish looks and winning ways. It made Sean seem more mysterious in a way.

People were getting to know me; they said hello as I walked through the town. I stopped being the little English girl and became Mary's girl. I was happy and began to imagine living here forever, finding a little cottage of my own and raising Rita in this town that my daddy had loved so much.

'I'd love you to live here, Maureen, but you have a family who loves you and once this war is over, they will want you home,' said Aunty Mary.

Sometimes I wondered if the war would ever end. Rita and I had been here for almost a year and there was no sign of it ending. Aunty Mary didn't have a wireless so I had no idea what was happening. There was no Afshid to bring the latest news.

Mum and Brenda continued to write to me. Brenda loved being a Land Girl and had met a boy in the village that she liked.

'His name's Ernie Pratt,' she wrote. 'He's nice, I really like him, Maureen, and I think he likes me.'

I was happy for my little sister and I was glad that she had found someone special.

One day a letter came from Monica.

Dear Maureen,

I really miss you and I hope that you and Rita are well and happy in Ireland. I have some news that will surprise you. I am going to America, to Chester's family. We are going to be married as soon as this war is over and he wants me to be there when he comes home. I'm a bit scared but I really want to meet his family and see where he grew up. If you were here we could talk about it. Am I doing the right thing, Maureen? I hope I am. I really love him and I want to spend the rest of my life with him but will I ever see you again?

We never know where life will lead us, do we? But of one thing I'm certain it won't be in the bottom of a smelly bucket. Not for either of us.

Wish me well.

Love always,

Monica
PS Have you heard from Nelson?

Well, the answer to Monica's question was no, I hadn't heard from Nelson, not for months, and I was terribly worried about him. I continued to write every week. I told him about the town and my job in the bakery and I told him about Rita and how much she had grown. I told him about Aunty Mary and Aunty Agnes but I had no reply. I needed to know that he was safe and that he would be coming home to us.

I missed him. I missed Nelson; I missed my husband.

Chapter Sixty-Four

It was almost Christmas and it was cold and wet. Sean had been right about the rain, it never seemed to stop. The funny thing was that no one seemed to mind very much. If it poured with rain, they said it was good for the crops and if it was misty, they called it a soft day. The Irish seemed to carry within them a cheerfulness and optimism that was missing at home and I envied them.

One morning I put Rita in her pushchair and Sean and I went down the wood road to gather holly for the cottage. Rita toddled around while Sean cut the holly from the trees and I piled it into the chair. She had started to talk and, for some reason, her first word was Dada; she said it over and over again. That was what Brenda used to call Daddy. I loved hearing it coming from her little mouth.

I must tell Brenda the next time I write to her, I thought.

'I don't know where she got that word from,' I said to Sean. 'Apart from you, there aren't any men in her life at all.'

'She's a clever little girl, maybe she can sense her granddaddy here in his hometown.'

I looked across at her. She was picking up little sticks and throwing them into the air and laughing her head off.

'Time to go home,' I said. 'I don't want Rita getting cold.'

Sean lifted Rita onto his shoulders and I wheeled the push-chair through the woods and back to the cottage, laden with the bright green and red holly. Inside the cottage it was warm and cosy and we draped the holly around the mantlepiece and round the holy picture of Saint Anthony.

'Aunty Mary will love it,' I said, smiling.

* * *

One afternoon Mr Hurley said that I could leave work early to buy some Christmas presents for Rita. I walked around the shops looking in all the windows. Merrick's was the biggest store in town and I spent some time in there. At the end of the town was Bridie Quirke's shop and in the window was a pale lemon baby cardigan. I thought that Rita would look lovely in it so I went in.

'Could I look at the little cardigan in the window, Mrs Quirke?'

'Oh, Maureen,' she said. 'I'm glad you came in. You must go home right away. Your Aunty Mary has been scouring the town for you.'

'But why?' I said.

Bridie looked down at the counter and started rubbing at it with the sleeve of her cardigan. 'There's been a letter,' she said.

'It's not my mother, is it, Bridie?'

She looked up. 'Not your mother, no.'

I was beginning to feel sick. 'My sister?'

I could almost have felt sorry for her if I hadn't been so frantic. I felt like pulling the poor woman over the counter by her throat and demanding she tell me, because it was obvious that she knew. In fact, I wouldn't have been surprised to learn that the whole bloody town knew.

'Just go home, Maureen,' she said gently.

I pulled open the shop door and hurried out into the street.

'I'm sorry for your trouble,' she called after me.

I ran through the town. Several people called after me as I raced past them. 'Your auntie's looking for you, Maureen.'

The cottage was full of people, just like the day I arrived. Aunty Mary was sitting by the fire, tears running down her face. Auntie

Agnes was standing behind her. She had an open letter in her hand. Several of the women were also dabbing at their eyes.

'Oh, Maureen,' she said as I came into the room.

'Is the letter for me?' I demanded, wondering why she'd opened it.

'Sit down, love.'

The crowd parted like the Red Sea as I was guided to the chair. I was the star of the show, they had all been waiting for me to come home. The show couldn't start without its star. That's how it felt anyway.

'It's from your mother, Maureen,' she said sadly.

'Your mother sent it to Mary,' said Auntie Agnes.

'To lessen the blow,' said another voice.

I stared into the fire. Everyone in the room knew what was in that letter except me and I didn't want to know; I wasn't ready to know.

Just then Sean came in. 'Show's over, ladies,' he said. 'Come on now, or we'll have your husbands down here demanding their dinner.'

I smiled gratefully at him as the woman reluctantly started leaving the cottage. They all dipped their hands into the holy water font as they left the room.

'Do you want to go for a walk?' he said.

'Yes, please,' I said, taking the letter from Aunty Mary and putting it in my pocket.

'Thank you, Sean,' said Aunty Mary.

We climbed the hill in silence and stood on the top. Sean reached over and held my hand. 'It's Nelson, isn't it?' I said.

He nodded.

'Is he dead?'

'Missing,' said Sean.

'Presumed dead?'

'Your mother didn't say, she just said he was missing. Do you want me to read the letter to you?'

'Yes, please.'

We sat side by side on the grass and Sean began to read.

Dear Mary,

I'm writing to you and not Maureen as I don't want her to be alone when she hears the news. A telegram came to say that Nelson is missing. I don't know anything else only that he is missing. I'm sorry to burden you with the task of telling her, Mary, but I thought this way was best. Please take care of my girl and help her at this sad time. We are all devastated, we all love Nelson. Give her my love and tell her how sorry I am. I don't know what she will want to do now but I think she needs to come home. Whatever she wants to do, Mary, is alright by me.

Love,

Kate x

Sean folded the letter and handed it to me.

'Everyone knows, don't they?'

He nodded. 'That's the way it is here. Births, deaths and marriages… the good times and the bad. You are never left alone, even if you want to be. Our lives are played out for all the world to see, it's the way it's always been. I imagine it's different in England?'

I thought back to when Daddy died, how people crossed the street when they saw me coming. 'Yes, it's different,' I said.

'What will you do?'

'What do you mean?'

'Will you go home?'

I stood up and walked to the brow of the hill. I looked down on the river flowing past the town and out to the sea.

There was nothing left for me at home, only memories of people I had loved who were gone: Daddy, Jack, Nelson, even Monica. The places were still there; the places would be there long after I'd gone. The sea didn't mourn the dead, neither did the fields and the hills. The old barn would welcome in other lovers. The sea would continue to tumble the pebbles on the shore. They didn't need me.

'I think that maybe this is my home now, Sean,' I said.

Chapter Sixty-Five

How many times can your heart break? Once? Twice? A million times? And how many times can you fall in love? I had always believed that you could only fall in love once. That's what I'd told Monica. 'Jack is the love of my life,' I'd said. 'I will love him until the day I die.' As it happened, I loved him until the day *he* died. So losing Nelson shouldn't have hurt this much, should it? If you only love once, it should be easier the second time. I was wrong, the pain that I was feeling now was every bit as bad as when I lost Jack. Why hadn't I realised? What was wrong with me? I'd let Nelson go to war without knowing how much he meant to me, how precious he was to me and, most important of all, how much I loved him, how much I had always loved him. Standing in the shadow of Jack, I hadn't always seen him for who he was. A sweet, kind boy who never complained about his lot in life, who was always there for me, who allowed me to love Jack and still remained at my side.

Aunty Mary said that I must have hope, the letter didn't say that he was dead.

'When someone is lost, you have to find them,' she said.

I shook my head. 'And how am I supposed to do that? He could be anywhere, he could be lying injured in some foreign land, he might already be under the ground. Where do I look for him?'

'In here,' she said, placing her hand over her heart. 'Look for him in here. We don't know if he's dead, so you must keep hope in your heart until we do know.'

'I never told him that I loved him.'

'God is good, Maureen, and with his divine help he may bring Nelson back to you. Then you can tell him. You can tell him how much you love him.'

'I don't have faith like you,' I said. 'Sometimes I wish that I did.'

'Go down to the church, Maureen, and light a candle to Saint Anthony. He's the saint of all things that are lost.'

'I think it's me that's lost, Aunty Mary.'

'Then ask Saint Anthony to find you.'

But I didn't go down to the church – the Church had a habit of letting me down. Instead, I tried to carry on. I couldn't stop the world and get off, even if I'd wanted to. I had a baby who depended on me and I was so thankful that I did. She made me smile when I thought that I would never smile again. This poor little girl hadn't been in the world long and yet she'd already lost two daddies. But she had me and I would always be there for her. I would make it up to her; I would make her world as wonderful as I could. Love had to go somewhere, didn't it? And all mine would go to Rita.

I wrote to my mum and told her that I wasn't ready to come home, that I would stay in Ireland, that I was happy there. I hoped that she would understand. Then I went back to work in the bakery. Every day people came into the shop and told me how sorry they were; they took me into their arms as if I was one of their own. These wonderful people who had nothing gave me everything. I was not alone in my grief – it was shared with a whole town.

I had been dreading Christmas but I was determined to put my sadness aside and make it as magical as I could for Rita. Sean, Orla and I decorated the little room with paper lanterns and coloured chains. There was a roaring fire in the grate, filling the cottage with the sweet smell of peat, and the holly around the mantlepiece looked lovely.

Neighbours came in and out all day, bringing little gifts for Rita; she was the centre of attention and she loved it. Aunty Agnes had knitted her a little doll and Aunty Mary had crocheted a set of clothes. Bridie Quirke presented me with the lemon cardigan I'd seen in her window on that awful day.

Sean went next door and came back with an accordion.

'I didn't know you were musical,' I said.

'All the Irish are musical,' said Orla, smiling.

Sean was right about Orla; she was indeed beautiful and it was clear that she adored him. She had beautiful red hair just like Monica and I hoped that we could be friends.

Sean played the songs of his homeland. 'Danny Boy' and 'The Rose of Tralee'. Soon everyone was singing along. I looked around the little cottage at the faces of these dear people and I felt truly blessed.

Towards the end of the day people started to drift away. An exhausted Rita was asleep before her head hit the pillow.

'Fancy a bit of a walk?' said Sean.

I looked at Aunty Mary, I didn't want to leave her alone on this Christmas night.

'You go along,' she said. 'The fresh air will do you good.'

I went upstairs and got my coat. We said goodbye and went out into the street.

It was frosty outside but the night was clear.

'Shall we walk to the strand?' said Sean.

'Would you like that, Maureen? asked Orla.

I nodded.

Our feet crunched on the icy pavement as we made our way through the town. People called out to us. 'Happy Christmas, Sean, Happy Christmas, Orla, Happy Christmas, Maureen.' I couldn't have felt more at home if I'd lived here all my life.

We walked under the arch of the clock tower and out towards the strand. The wind coming off the sea was biting cold. It reminded me of the night I caught the boat that brought me to Ireland. That night seemed like a lifetime ago. I shivered.

'Let's run, girls,' said Sean, catching hold of both our hands. 'Let's just run.'

'Are you completely mad, Sean O'Connell?' said Orla, laughing.

'We're young, we're alive and it's Christmas,' he said, swinging her around. 'So let's run.'

And that's what we did. We ran until we were out of breath and we could run no further. We stopped and leaned over the railings. Sean had his arm around Orla. I looked out over the dark sea. The lighthouse in the distance shone its beacon of light across the dark water, guiding home those who had lost their way.

Was there a light somewhere in the world that would guide Nelson home? I hoped there would be.

I tried to think of him alive but I couldn't and I didn't want to think of him dead. And then, suddenly, on that most silent of nights I found him. Not the man but the boy. Playing marbles in the gutter, sliding down the hill in the old pushchair, racing across the beach…

Come home to me, my love. Come home.

Chapter Sixty-Six

On the afternoon of 7 May, Aunty Mary burst into the bakery with Rita running behind her. She was laughing and crying, she couldn't speak. She plonked herself down on a sack of flour. I came around the counter and knelt down in front of her. Seeing her aunty in such a state, Rita started wailing. It brought Mr Hurley and Sean out of the bakehouse.

'Holy Mother of God, Mary O'Connell, what the devil has happened to you?' cried Mr Hurley.

Aunty Mary touched my cheek. 'The war is over, Maureen. The war is over.'

I took Rita in my arms. 'Hush now,' I said.

Mr Hurley handed Rita a cream cake and she immediately stopped crying.

I was happy and sad all at once. Happy for my loved ones that had survived and sad for those that I'd lost.

'I'm glad for you, Maureen,' said Sean.

Tears began rolling down my cheeks but then I looked at Rita who was sitting happily in the sawdust, her face plastered with cream and laughing her head off.

Thank God for Rita.

That night we had a party in the little cottage in Tallow Street. Neighbours crammed themselves into the tiny room. Orla and I sat together on the stairs. Sean played his accordion and he was joined by Mr Hurley on the fiddle and his son on the Bodhran, which was the Irish drum. Aunty Mary and Aunty Agnes did some step-dancing and Rita tried to copy them, which had us all roaring with laughter. At the end of the night Aunty Mary lit a candle in front of the statue of Saint Anthony and we all made a silent prayer of thanks that the world was once more at peace.

I couldn't believe that it was all over; I was beginning to think that it would go on forever. I wondered how Maggie and the war council were feeling – I bet that Peter would be playing his victory marches at full volume in the shed. I wished that I could be there with them; I suddenly missed them.

Soon, the beaches would be open, children could run into the sea once more and dig in the wet sand. Soon, the lovers would dance again at the end of the pier.

A week later, I received a letter from Mum.

Dear Maureen,

You have missed a celebration to end all celebrations. I'd say that half of the people in Brighton are still nursing hangovers. There was a great party in See Saw Lane, with tables running down the middle of the road full of sandwiches and jelly for the children. Someone dragged a piano into the street and we had a fantastic knees-up. Uncle John got so drunk that we had to carry him to his bed. Aunty Marge is still giving him earache a week later. Brenda and I wanted so much for you to be with us at this happiest of times and I so wanted my own little grand-daughter to be amongst those children.

Every day trains are arriving at the station bringing home the soldiers. The platforms are full of women – wives, mothers and girlfriends, all waiting to see that one person step from the train. It is all terribly emotional. I hope you don't mind, Maureen, but Brenda and I take it in turns to join them. You see, we still have hope that Nelson will be amongst them. If he does come home, then we want to make sure that one of us is there to meet him – we don't want him to be alone.

Please come home, my darling girl, I need to hold you and
the baby.
  Love always,
  Mum xxx

I sat on my bed and cried. It should be me waiting on that platform. Mum and Brenda still had hope when I seemed to have lost mine. I felt ashamed of myself.

I dried my eyes and went downstairs. Aunty Mary was struggling through the door with a bucket of water and I took it from her.

'I told you I'd get the water in.' I said.

'I'll have to get used to getting it myself again when you go home, Maureen.'

I put the bucket down on the floor and took her in my arms. Her hair felt rough against my cheek.

'For you are going home, aren't you?' she asked gently.

I nodded.

It was the hardest thing saying goodbye to everyone. I had become so close to them all and to this town. I had never expected to find such love when I'd set out on my journey to Ireland. But I didn't regret coming and I would never forget them, or this place.

On the day before I was due to travel back to England I left Rita with Aunty Mary and I climbed my daddy's hill. As I looked down over the old town I knew that I would forever carry a piece of this place in my heart. I looked down at the river as it made its way out to sea and I wondered if that sea would one day bring me back to this hillside.

Chapter Sixty-Seven

Sean travelled up to Cork with us and saw us safely onto the boat. I held Rita in my arms as the boat pulled away from the dock, tears running down my cheeks as I watched Sean getting smaller and smaller as the boat sailed up the River Lee and out towards the sea.

I was leaving Ireland behind me and it felt as though I was leaving home all over again. This beautiful land had taken me into its arms, it had made me feel safe. It had made me feel loved. I would miss this place, I would miss its people and I would miss my daddy's hillside. I thought about the little town, I thought about Sean and Auntie Mary and the little cottage in Tallow Street and then I thought about Nelson. I had found love in places I never expected to find it and whatever happened now, I would forever be grateful for that.

The journey felt different this time as it was a day crossing and Rita wasn't a baby any more so I didn't have to carry her all the time. We stayed on deck watching the land of my father disappearing into the mist. 'I'll come back one day,' I whispered softly.

It was a calm crossing and we were able to find a seat in the lounge. With the gentle swell of the sea Rita fell asleep in my arms and pretty soon, I had joined her.

The train journey from Fishguard to London seemed endless. I wanted to see Mum and Brenda, I wanted to sleep in my own bed; I wanted to look out of my window at my tree. I wanted to be home. I suddenly just wanted to be home.

The train pulled into Paddington station with a hiss of steam and a shudder. A kind man lifted my case down from the rack and carried it out onto the platform.

The thought of negotiating the Underground with Rita and my case made me want to sit down and give up. But I knew it was just because I was tired, I knew I'd be OK – I'd come this far, I'd crossed an ocean. I wasn't going to let the bloody London Underground defeat me. So I took a deep breath, held onto Rita's hand and started to walk across the station to the escalators. That's when I heard someone calling my name and saw Peter running towards me. I had never been so pleased to see anyone in my life.

I put down the case, flung my arms around him and burst out crying. 'Oh, Peter,' I said. 'You don't know how happy I am to see you.'

'There now, there now,' he said, smiling. 'I thought I was going to miss you. Bad accident on the way here, no, not me but it held everyone up.'

'Well, I'm glad you're here. Thank you so much, Peter.'

He was smiling down at Rita. 'Is this really that little baby I remember?'

I nodded.

'Well now, you must both be tired after your long journey, shall we go home?'

'Yes, please.'

This was only the fourth time that I had been in Peter's car. The first time was the day my daddy died and the second time was when the cinema was bombed with Brenda and Gertie inside. Then at the beginning of my long journey to Ireland. All of those times I had been worried, but this time was different; this time I could enjoy the lovely car with the comfortable leather seats. With Rita on my lap I looked out of the window and watched the fields and villages rushing past. I wasn't tired any more, I was full of excitement: I couldn't wait to see my family, I couldn't wait to be home.

As the car turned into See Saw Lane my stomach clenched with pleasure. It felt as if I'd been gone a lifetime.

And, suddenly, the door opened and my family were running down the path. Mum, Brenda, Aunty Marge and Uncle John. Mum threw her arms around me and kissed my face. Everyone was laughing and crying. Then she picked up Rita, Uncle John took the case and Brenda and I walked into the house behind them with our arms around each other.

'Welcome home, Sis,' she said.

'It's good to be home,' I said.

Mum had Rita on her lap and she was gently taking off the baby's coat and undoing the ribbons on her bonnet.

'She hasn't changed a bit, Maureen. She has the same face that I remember.'

'Well, I should hope so,' I said, laughing.

'Marge, would you get us all a nice cup of tea?'

'Of course I will,' said Aunty Marge, heading for the kitchen.

'The good tea set, Marge, and plenty of sugar. We have our girls home.'

'Will you stay for some tea, Peter?' I asked.

'No, no, I'll leave you all to it.'

'Thank you for collecting me.'

'You are very welcome,' he said. 'Now, be sure to bring the baby for a visit, my sister is dying to see you both.'

'Of course I will, Peter, and thank you again.'

'I'll see myself out,' he said.

'Did you know that Peter was going to collect me?' I asked Brenda.

'I let him know when you were coming home. I didn't even have to ask him to meet you, he offered.'

'Thanks, Bren, I've never been so glad to see anyone in my life.'

It was lovely sitting beside the fire drinking tea with my family. The house seemed so much bigger than I remembered it but I suppose that was because Aunty Mary's cottage was so small.

'Now,' said Mum, 'I suggest you take a nice bath and then go for a little walk.'

'A *walk*?' I said, horrified. 'I just want to sleep.'

'If you go to bed now,' said Aunty Marge, 'you'll never sleep tonight. A nice stroll on the Downs is what you need. Blow all those cobwebs away.'

'I'll come with you,' said Brenda.

'OK, if I don't fall asleep in the bath.'

I lay down in the warm water. The bath was a good idea; I felt dirty after the journey and maybe a walk wouldn't be so bad.

Brenda and I left Mum and Aunty Marge cooing over Rita and started walking towards the Downs.

'Now, what about this boyfriend of yours?'

'I love him, Maureen, and he loves me.'

'I'm glad for you, Bren.'

'And the Land Army?'

'Hard work but an absolute hoot! I never want to see another pig or chicken as long as I live. And Molly has vowed never to meat again, although I'm not sure how long that's going to last.'

As we neared the top of the Devil's Dyke Brenda suddenly stopped walking.

'I'm sorry, Maureen, but I've left something behind. I'm going to have to run back to the house.'

'Left what behind?'

But she was running back down the hill.

'Just something!' she yelled into the wind.

I couldn't think what she could possibly have left behind that she would have to go all the way home for. I mean, what did she need up here on the Downs that was so important?

I stood where I was, the wind blowing my hair all over my face. I didn't see him at first and then I was running and laughing and crying. And then I was in his arms, touching his face, kissing him. He was here, he was alive, he'd come home! I couldn't get enough of him; I didn't want to let him go.

He held me away from him and looked into my eyes.

'Maureen?' he said softly.

I nodded and then he took hold of my hands and twirled me around and around until I was dizzy with love and happiness and wonder.

'She loves me!' Nelson shouted across the hillside. 'You do, don't you?'

'I think maybe I always have.'

'Oh, my love!' he said, holding my cold face in his hands.

We lay down on the cold, damp grass and kissed each other. I was in the arms of the man I loved and I knew in that moment that I had truly come home.

EPILOGUE

Nelson and I settled into See Saw Lane and became a family. First we had a little girl who we named Dottie, after Dorothy Gale in *The Wizard of Oz*, and, two years later, we had Clark. So that was our family: Rita Hayworth, Dorothy Gale and Clark Gable.

Dottie looked like Nelson and Clark was a mixture of the two of us. Rita ruled the roost, she was beautiful and she was clever. Clark was the comedian with a dry wit and a love of life. And then there was Dottie, sweet little Dottie, without Rita's beauty or Clark's confidence. My little girl who asked Father Christmas to bring her a best friend and a rocking horse. We couldn't afford a rocking horse but I would have given anything to have found her a best friend.

Brenda married her Ernie and they had a little girl. They called her Carol Gertrude in remembrance of little Gertie. We never heard from Gertie after she left us but we often talked about her and hoped that she had made it through the war.

Every now and then Nelson and I visited Jack's grave. One day I told him that I would like to go alone.

I walked through the cemetery gates and made my way between the old tombstones. It was a beautiful spring day. The grass was dotted with purple and yellow crocuses. It was the sort of day on which Jack and I would have walked on the Downs or over the hills to the cliffs that looked out to sea. He and I would never walk that way again.

I knelt beside his grave. Then I took a deep breath. 'I have to let you go now, my beautiful boy,' I said softly. 'But I know you will understand. Nelson deserves all of my heart, he has to know that he's not second best and he's not, not any more. If things had been different, I know that we two would have been happy for the rest of our lives but we never had a chance, did we? Whoever is in charge up there had other plans for us. You would be so proud of your daughter, Jack. She's smart and beautiful. I see you every time I look into her eyes. Nelson is a good father to her and a good husband to me. Be happy for me, Jack. I will never forget you or the night that we danced at the end of the pier.'

I kissed my fingers and placed my hand on the grave. 'Sleep tight, my love,' I said and I walked away.

When I got home Nelson was digging in the garden.

'Cup of tea?' I asked, kissing his cheek.

'Lovely,' he said.

I had just put the kettle on the stove when Dottie burst into the kitchen. She was out of breath and her cheeks were red as if she'd been running. She was smiling.

'You look happy, Dottie,' I said, smiling back at her.

'I am, Mum, I am!'

I waited for her to speak.

'I've got a best friend, Mum. I've got a real best friend. She's coming to call for me in a minute,' she said, taking the stairs two at a time.

'What's her name?' I called after her.

'Mary Pickles!' she shouted. 'Her name's Mary Pickles.'

A LETTER FROM SANDY

Thank you for choosing to read *When We Danced at the End of the Pier,* the final book in the Brighton Girls trilogy.

These books have been a joy to write and your comments and reviews have been a pleasure to read.

If you have enjoyed my little story I would be very grateful if you could take a moment to post a short review. These reviews are very helpful to new writers like me.

To keep up to date with the latest news on my new releases, just click on the link below to sign up for a newsletter. I promise to only contact you when I have a new book out and I'll never share your email with anyone else.

www.bookouture.com/sandy-taylor

Thank you for all your support and encouragement. I think that I have the best readers and I really appreciate you all.

Sandy x

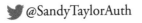 @SandyTaylorAuth

SandyTaylorAuthor

ACKNOWLEDGMENTS

There are so many people to thank for walking beside me on this journey as a writer. First my wonderful children and grandchildren who give me so much joy and love, you mean the world to me. As do my brothers and sisters, nieces and nephews, and all my family, here and in Ireland.

I had a present recently from one of my close friends it was a plaque that read, 'I get by with a little help from my friends' this is so true. I have been very lucky in my life to have been blessed with so many amazing friends. Angela, Lynda, Linda and Lis. To my dear friend Val in Canada. To dearest Louie who has always been here for me through the good times and the bad. To my special friend Wenny, love always.

To my lovely talented friend, fellow writer and chip lover, Lesley.

To the wonderful award-winning team at Bookouture: Oliver Rhodes, the amazing Kim Nash and my lovely editor Claire Bord for always believing in my little stories. Thanks to Lauren Finger, and my copyeditor Nicky Lovick and proofreader Jane Donovan for doing such a sensitive job on my book.

To my lovely supportive readers for enjoying my books and sharing your thoughts with me, you truly are the best.

I would like to mention my childhood friend Eileen Burke, where it all began.

And last but never least, my amazing agent and friend Kate Hordern. Thank you for everything you have done for me. We got there in the end, didn't we.

Lightning Source UK Ltd.
Milton Keynes UK
UKHW02f2239170718
325863UK00017B/505/P